A Shattering Vision
of Betrayal

How dare they! How dare they!

There was no light in the dressing room, but from under the door to the bedroom there was a beam showing.

As her hand gently sought the handle of the door, Nancy Ann heard her husband's voice, then the woman's tone, soft and laughter-filled . . .

She did not thrust open the door but turned the handle gently; then she stepped into the room that was lit by the two pink glass shaded lamps, and there on the high bed lay her husband and the woman. For a moment the sight seemed to blind her.

There was a moment of utter silence: then Dennison was sitting bolt upright, crying, *'Nancy Ann! My God! No . . . !'*

Books by Catherine Cookson

The Bannaman Legacy
The Black Velvet Gown
The Moth
The Parson's Daughter
The Whip

Published by POCKET BOOKS

CATHERINE COOKSON
THE PARSON'S DAUGHTER

POCKET BOOKS

New York   London   Toronto   Sydney   Tokyo

POCKET BOOKS, a division of Simon & Schuster, Inc.
1230 Avenue of the Americas, New York, N.Y. 10020

Copyright © 1987 by Catherine Cookson
Cover artwork copyright © 1988 Bob McGinnis

Published by arrangement with Summit Books,
a division of Simon and Schuster, Inc.
Library of Congress Catalog Card Number: 86-30122

Published in Great Britain by William Heinemann, Ltd.

ISBN: 0-671-64854-3

First Pocket Books printing April 1988

10 9 8 7 6 5 4 3 2 1

POCKET and colophon are trademarks of
Simon & Schuster, Inc.

Printed in the U.S.A.

❧ CONTENTS ❧

PART ONE

Sundays

☙ 1 ❧

"To think unkindly is a sin, but to give voice to your thoughts and allow them to direct your actions is a greater sin. Who are we to condemn? Did not Christ say, 'He that is without sin among you, let him first cast a stone'?"

Oh dear me! some people were moving restlessly in their seats. Nancy Ann looked towards the pulpit where her father seemed about to topple out of it, so far was he leaning over. He always looked too tall for the pulpit, but when he became agitated about righteousness, as he was now, he appeared about to do a somersault right into the front pew, where sat Mrs. McKeowan the churchwarden's wife, and her two daughters Jancy and Eva; and next to them were Mr. and Mrs. Taylor from the village who had the grocery store that sold everything, and behind them were Mr. and Mrs. Pollock who kept the hardware and oddments shop. Then between them and Mrs. Norton was an empty space reserved for Mr. Norton the baker, but likely he had got drunk again last night and couldn't get up. It was known he often got drunk on a Saturday, because he hadn't to work on a Sunday, not till after midnight when he made his first batch of dough for the Monday morning bread. Yet, he sometimes appeared in that seat. These were the times when he tried to go "on the wagon" as her grandmama said; but she also said that the wheels would come off before the next Sunday, and she was usually

3

right. Her father, though, said Mr. Norton had to be given credit for trying. In her father's opinion everybody had to be given credit for trying. She loved her father.

There was nobody seated in the front seats of the gentry gallery. Hardly anybody sat there these days even when Mr. Harpcore was in residence. He himself never came to church, but more servants would attend than usually did. But this morning she could count only seven: three men, three women, and a boy. Two of the women looked elderly; the other was the pretty young woman who came to church every other Sunday and sat in between them.

Her father was going on and on this morning and she knew why, although she wasn't supposed to; she had heard Peggy talking to Jane: it was about the Winter family who had left the village to go into Gateshead and work in a factory. Of course, as Cook had said, If Jed Winter hadn't got one excuse for leaving the village he would have found another because he had known he was going to be stood off on the farm and would lose his cottage, for things were bad all round and the corn wasn't selling. It was them Americans, Cook said, who were sending the cheap stuff over here and taking the bread out of decent people's mouths. But Peggy said the real reason the Winter family had left was because Nellie had got a baby and her husband who went to sea had been gone these twelve months. But what that had to do with it, she didn't know; people had babies when their husbands were away. Her grandmama had said her father had been born when her grandpapa was at the war. Anyway, Mr. Winter couldn't stand the disgrace of his daughter having a baby.

There was something she couldn't get straight here, because why bring Farmer Carter into it.

Her father had liked Mr. Winter. He always said he was a God-fearing man, and his wife too. Nellie was their only surviving daughter. One way and another they had lost four children. Nellie had been God-fearing too: she had come to church every Sunday, at least she had until some months ago when she had stopped all of a sudden. It was about this time her father had become agitated about Nellie.

A small clearing of the throat and a slight dig in her ribs caused her to glance to the side and at her brother James. He made a funny little twitching movement with his nose that always made her laugh, even when it came as a warning: she must have been fidgeting and not aware of it.

She was looking up towards the pulpit again from where her father was at last drawing to a close amid a rustle and coughing among the congregation not unmixed with sighs, when she felt a heel pressed on to her toecap. And this caused her to emit a stifled groan and to turn sharply, an indignant look on her face, to see her other brother Peter staring solemnly towards the altar, a look of pious intent on his handsome face. She, too, stared back at the altar; then, lifting her foot, she brought her heel sharply into the narrow-trousered shin to the side of her, and when she felt her brother jerk and cough deep in his throat, and saw her mama who was sitting to the right of him cast an enquiring glance towards him, she said to herself: I warned him. I told him what I'd do if he did it again. Now I'll have skinned toes before I get home and unblock the cap.

Why had she to wear such shoes anyway? Other girls didn't. Her mama said it was because she kicked the toes too quickly out of ordinary shoes; and only yesterday she said that such tomboyish behaviour was excusable up to eight years old but not when one was on thirteen. Her mama, she noticed, never blamed her brothers for inciting her. But of course, they weren't boys any longer and couldn't be chastised; they were young men, university men. A feeling of sadness took the place of her indignation now as she realized that tomorrow they would both return to that university and life would become dull once more.

Although Peter was seven years older than her and James eight, they had always been like playmates, and the only time she could say that she was really happy was when they were vat home. It had always been like that.

She understood they had been at boarding school when she was born, and when they first saw her they had fought as to who would hold her. Everything she knew and which she felt was worthwhile, they had taught her: how to climb a tree; how to stand in a loop of rope attached to a sturdy branch and swing out across the river; how to bowl at cricket and how to strike out with the bat; how to run the hills without losing your puff; how to fish, and even wrestle a bit, and fence; although they would never let her fence with anything but sticks.

She loved them, next to her father that is and equally as she loved her grandmama. Why didn't people love her grandmama? Likely it was because of her voice; and she was rude at times and didn't care what she said and how she offended people. And she offended her mama most of all. She knew that her mama considered Grandmama a trial, but she also was aware that her mama had to put up with Grandmama, because it was she who had, for years, paid for the boys' education and was now to pay for her own.

Oh my! She didn't want to go to another school. She liked the village school; at least she liked most of the children there, although, as her mama said, they were all of common folk. She didn't mind that at all, because they were all nice to her, all except the McLoughlins. Oh, they were common all right, the McLoughlins.

James and Peter used to laugh about the McLoughlins. There were thirteen of them and they lived in a little three-roomed hovel cottage, and they were all hard and healthy, and their father drank and their mother smoked a clay pipe, and they never came to church. But then of course, they wouldn't, not this one, because they were Catholics. Catholics were queer, funny, and very common.

. . . "In the name of the Father, and of the Son, and of the Holy Ghost, Amen." And now her father had stepped down from the pulpit, and they were standing up and singing the last hymn: "Rock of Ages."

There were Jancy McKeowan vying with Mr. Taylor. But Jancy couldn't beat her own father, nor could Mr. Taylor, for the churchwarden's voice rose above everyone else's, and when the hymn should have finished his voice still trailed on, as her grandmama said, giving God the benefit of his very own amen.

Her grandmama wasn't at church this morning; she had a late summer cold. It had come on very suddenly because she had been all right last night. She often took quick colds, some in the spring, some in the summer, and a number in the winter.

The church was emptying now, and her father was shaking hands with each member of the congregation. Some hands he always shook more warmly than others; some people he had a word with, others he couldn't let pass him quickly enough, his handshake seeming to help them down the four steps to the gravel drive.

She was walking down the drive between her brothers. The hard cap of her right shoe was pressing on her toes. Looking straight ahead she said, "You're horrible, Peter Hazel. Yes, you are." And he, also looking straight ahead, answered, "And you're a vicious little madam, Nancy Ann Hazel. Yes, you are, and you'll never grow up into a refined young lady."

"And whose fault will that be?"

Peter now looked across her to James and said, "Don't blame me; she was born like that."

"Oh, you!" She now took her doubled fist and dug Peter in the thigh, and as Peter said with an exaggerated groan, "See what I mean?" James put in, "Stop it, you two. Look who's out there."

From beyond the lych-gate a tall young woman smiled at them, saying first, "Good morning, Mr. James," then "Good morning, Mr. Peter."

"Good morning, Miss McKeowan." They both inclined their heads towards the thin fair girl.

"I hear you are to return to the university tomorrow." Her voice was soft, her words precise.

"Yes. Yes." Peter nodded at her. "We go up tomorrow."

"Oh, I do envy you." The well-shaped lips pursed themselves; the fair eyelids blinked; the white cotton-gloved hands joined and gently lifted the tightly laced breasts upwards. "It must be like going into another world, a world where minds are allowed to expand, where ideas count." She was now looking directly at James, and he, his long thinnish face a replica of his father's and red to the brim of his hat now, said stiffly, "The minds are much the same as they are in this village, Miss McKeowan: narrow and nasty in the main. Good day."

The light went from the young woman's eyes. She looked from Peter to Nancy Ann and they both said, "Good morn-

7

ing, Miss McKeowan,'' and, turning, hurried to catch up
with James.

"That was a bit stiff.'' Peter's voice was cold.

"What did you expect me to say? A world where minds
count? . . . Huh! you know something? she frightens me, she
does. She was walking in the lane last night just on dark. I
had gone to get my coat that I'd left on the garden seat and
there she was strolling past the gate, up and down, up and
down."

"Well," Peter said on a laugh now, "if you were so afraid
of her why didn't you go in and fetch Grandmama? She would
have settled her hash for her."

"You could say you are engaged to be married. That would
stop her chasing you."

Both young men paused and looked down on their thin
ungainly sister; then glancing at one another, they burst out
laughing and simultaneously put their arms about her; and
she, giggling, hung on to them for a moment as James said,
"You haven't only got a big head, sister Nancy Ann, you've
got something in it too. Yes, of course: I'm going to become
engaged to a young lady in Oxford. Spread it around, will
you?"

"Yes, all right, I'll spread it around . . . for a price."

They were again looking down on her, their faces stretched.
Then, Peter, nodding towards his brother, said, "This is a
new one."

"Yes, yes, indeed. And what is the price, sister?"

"That we have a game of cricket this afternoon."

"Oh . . . ah!'' "Oh . . . ah!'' They made their usual re-
joinder together. "Now you know that's impossible," James
said. " 'Tis Sunday, 'tis banned. 'Tis banned for you on other
days too—you know what Mama said—but on a Sunday . . .
oh, impossible."

"No cricket, no engagement in Oxford."

"You imp of Satan!'' Peter went to catch hold of her hand,
but she ran from them, whirling around like a top. At this
James called to her quietly but firmly, "Now stop acting like
a child. If Mama were to see you, you know what would
happen. You had all this out the other day. You've got to grow
up. And you promised her. . . ."

"Oh, shut up, will you. And anyway, I didn't promise Mama; I kept my mouth shut and never said a word."

"She's right." The brothers were walking on either side of her again, and it was now Peter, who had in the past encouraged her into many of her tomboy ways, who said, "And James is right too; and Mama is right too, Nancy Ann. We've all had fun together, but now . . . well, we want to see you turn into a pretty young lady, and . . . and go to balls, and have all the young men fighting to dance with you, and then you'll meet. . . ."

She stopped dead in the road and stared up at her best beloved brother, but she did not utter a word; and Peter, looking down on her, thought, What am I talking about? Pretty young lady. Stooping now, he said, "Let me have your shoe." And she lifted her foot for him to unlace her shoe, and pulling it off, he thrust his thumb inside and pushed the stiff cap upwards; then he put it back on her foot and laced it up again. And when he straightened his back, they smiled at each other.

Turning now, they passed through a gateway and silently made their way across the field which led to the vicarage and to the cold midday meal that had been prepared last night by Peggy Knowles the cook and Jane Bradshaw her assistant, because no menial work must be done on a Sunday, only the washing of the dishes after the housemaid Hilda Fenwick had cleared the table. Such was a Sunday.

So how would anyone dare to play cricket? It had been a silly idea of hers, and she knew it.

❧ 2 ❧

THE VICARAGE WAS A VERY COLD HOUSE. IT HAD FOURTEEN rooms, and all were large, high-ceilinged and provided with ample windows that were so weathered and warped the pine needles blew in between the sashes in wild weather.

Although there was a mine only two miles away, coal was still expensive—except for the miners who brought it from the earth. And because the vicarage garden only ran to an acre and a half, there weren't many trees, not enough to cut down for firewood. But even if there had been an ample supply, the vicar would not have countenanced the felling of one tree even though it be half dead.

Even in summer there were very chilly days so that for most of the time the house was like an ice-box everywhere except the kitchen, and Madam Hazel's bedroom, for, summer and winter alike, Jessica Hazel had a fire in her bedroom, and no matter how hot and uncomfortable the other members of the household might find it in attending her, she herself said, she never sweated.

Jessica was a tall woman. Her only son took after her. She had a bony frame, and it was easy to imagine she must have looked like Nancy Ann when a girl, although paintings of her in middle life showed her to be a handsome woman. She had lived with her son for the past twelve years. She had a deep affection for him, even though at times she considered he was like the man in the story who tilted at windmills. And by what the boys had told her with regard to the essence of his sermon this morning he had certainly tilted at one today.

Here he was forty-seven years old and still hadn't grown used to the ways of the world. Of course, people threw stones—there were no Christs to stop them—what did he expect from his rantings? This child sitting here, this beloved child who was very like herself both inside and out, she had more sense in her little finger than her father had in his whole body, or ever would have. She would never tilt at windmills.

And what would she herself do when, as was now being discussed downstairs, they took her away from the village school and planted her in that Dame school in Durham to be shaped, into what? A young lady? She shook her head. She couldn't see it happening; moreover, she didn't want it to happen. Not that she didn't want the child to become attractive and marry well, but what she didn't want was to be bereft of her company for most of the year. What would she do during such a period? Sit in the sitting-room at night punching her embroidery frame while her daughter-in-law cut up old clothes to make garments for the children at the orphanage, and which she never herself sewed. No, she passed over the sewing as a pastime pleasure to Peggy and Jane and Hilda in the kitchen, to be done when the evening meal was over and the evening prayers said, and the tables cleared and the dishes washed up. They could then enjoy making unwieldy trousers and coats for lesser brethren, little lesser brethren.

Why had her son become a parson? There were no such in her own family, and it went back for many generations; nor in her husband's—he and his ancestors were all fighting men. And why had he to marry a woman more pious than himself?

"Grandmama."

"Yes, dear?"

"The boys have gone to the Manor to see Mr. Mercer. Why don't they ever take me with them?"

"Well"—Jessica cleared her throat—"they are young men. They . . . they grew up together so to speak, although Graham is a little older. I . . . I suppose they just want to talk men's talk, and that would be no place for you."

"I . . . I don't think that's right, Grandmama."

"That they want to talk men's talk?"

"No. I . . . I think it's because Mr. Mercer doesn't like women, females . . . girls."

"Who told you that?" Her voice was sharp.

"I heard Hilda and Jane talking."

"And what did Hilda and Jane say?"

"Well, as far as I could gather"—she paused and nodded her head while looking into the fire that was burning her shins and making her sweat—"it's because he was crossed in love, right at the altar . . . well, nearly, and now he doesn't go anywhere and doesn't see anybody, only . . . I suppose men, like Peter and James. Hilda said. . . ."

"I don't want to hear what Hilda said, and you shouldn't go eavesdropping."

"I don't go eavesdropping, Grandmama. They were in the kitchen and they were saying he was a good man wasted, and they laughed and said they would see what they could do."

"They want their ears boxed, and I'll see to it."

"Oh, Grandmama." Nancy Ann leant forward and patted the rug that covered her grandmother's knees, saying, "They were being funny. It sounded very funny. It made them all splutter. I like to see them laugh. I like to listen to them. They're happy. That's what Peggy once said to me, they were happy here; it was a good house to work in in spite of there not being plenty of everything, which I took her to mean that Mama watches the bills. And"—she giggled now before she went on—"Peggy said that her stomach took over every morning and evening when she's praying in the dining-room. In the morning it says: How are you going to spin things out the day? And at evening prayer it says, I'll make dumplings again. What doesn't fatten will fill up."

She now watched her grandmother throw her head back and give vent to a hearty laugh that denied the croak that up till now would issue from her throat whenever anyone entered the room. And she joined in.

"Grandmama." She had sat back in her seat and rubbed the laughter tears from her eyes with the side of her finger, and when Jessica Hazel once again said, "Yes, my dear?" she said, "How long does it take for a baby to be born?"

"What!" Jessica's face was stretched now. "What do you mean, how long does it take?"

"Well, what I said, how long does it take? I . . . I. . . ."

"Why do you ask?"

"Just because I'd like to know."

The old lady now gently shook her head before she said, "It all depends how long the labour is, you see; that is, how long the baby takes in deciding . . . well, to . . . to come into the world."

"No, I don't mean that kind of long. I mean. . . ."

"What do you mean?"

"Well, I'm puzzled, Grandmama, as to why they should send Nellie away when she's going to have a baby and her husband at sea?"

Oh God above. Jessica looked towards the far window and her head moved in small jerks before she looked back at her grandchild and asked, abruptly now, "Hasn't your mother talked to you?"

"About what?"

"About the question you're asking, girl."

"No, and I wouldn't ask Mama. I . . . I couldn't. Mama doesn't talk about things like that."

"No, she doesn't." The head was jerking again. "But she should, and to you. Anyway, you're only twelve years old, coming thirteen I know, and you shouldn't be asking questions about that kind of thing for . . . well, years ahead."

"Why?"

"Don't keep asking why, either."

"Nellie sinned, and all I want to know is how has she sinned if . . ."

Jessica sighed twice before she leant forward and, taking her granddaughter's hand, she shook it gently, saying, "A baby takes nine months to be born. Now, if its father is not at home for those nine months then the child doesn't belong to the father. . . . You understand me?"

Nancy Ann stared into the misted blue eyes. Her mind was working fast but she remained silent for almost two minutes, and then she said, "Yes, Grandmama, I understand."

"Well"—Jessica straightened up, sighed again deeply, then

said—"now that's finished. We'll talk about it no more, and you won't discuss it again with anyone, will you?"

"Oh, no!" The words were said with deep emphasis. Talk about something like that? Never! Nellie had sinned. 'Twas surprising, and she a regular churchgoer, but she had sinned. She looked towards the fire; she felt she couldn't bear the heat anymore. She stood up, saying, "I don't like Sundays, Grandmama."

"Neither do I, my dear. Neither do I. Never have."

"You can't do anything on Sundays, not even fish."

"No, I suppose not. But you could take a walk, or you could go to Sunday school."

"I don't want to go to Sunday school; I'll have to go to evening service."

"Your mama would expect you to go to Sunday school."

"Yes, I know, but I'm not going today because I don't want to get into trouble."

"What do you mean?"

"Well, you know I nearly always come back messed up on a Sunday and Mama gets angry, but it's the McLoughlins; they wait for me, and I can fight them at school and on any other day, but not on a Sunday, and they always have the advantage."

Jessica quickly turned her gaze from her granddaughter and looked towards the fire to prevent herself from now being seen to laugh, and she said, "Go for a walk. Yes, go for a walk."

Once outside the bedroom door, Nancy Ann ran across the landing to the top of the stairs, and there, stretching her arms out wide, she gripped the substantial rails on either side of her and, head down, she skipped two stairs at a time. But on looking up as she neared the foot of the stairs she saw her mother standing in the middle of the hall and as usual she was shaking her head from side to side.

Rebecca Hazel looked sadly at her daughter, who in no way resembled herself, either in appearance or character. She herself was of medium height, very fair, and slim; her eyes were bright blue, her skin was cream coloured, and her mouth, if not entirely rosebud shaped, was small and full-lipped. Her voice had a pained sound as she said, "Nancy Ann, that was no way to prepare yourself for Sunday school."

"I have a headache, Mama, and . . . and I feel slight nausea."

"Headache? You didn't appear to be in much pain as you came bounding down those stairs, child."

"I . . . I was wanting to get into the air, Mama. I . . . I have been with Grandmama; the room was very hot."

"Oh, yes, yes." Now her mother nodded her head in agreement as she said, "Indeed, yes, enough to roast an ox. And on a day like this, too. Well, I would suggest that you go and rest for a while."

"I would rather have fresh air, Mama."

Rebecca stared at her daughter while asking herself if there was something behind this. She was well acquainted with her daughter's ruses for getting out of Sunday school; and yet she never baulked at attending morning or evening service. She was a strange child. She troubled her. She pursed her lips, then said, "Well, go and ask Papa to give you a suitable reading, and then you may sit in the garden quietly."

"Thank you, Mama." Nancy Ann had no need to ask where her father was. She turned slowly about and crossed the hall, went down a narrow passage and knocked at a stout oak door, and when she was bidden to enter she did so slowly. Closing the door behind her, she looked at the tall figure seated at his desk. But he hadn't been writing because there was no paper in front of him; nor apparently had he been reading because the space in front of him was clear. She felt a deep sense of guilt as she went slowly towards him. Somehow she didn't mind deceiving her mother, but she never liked using deception of any kind on her father.

He held out a hand towards her, saying, "What is it, my dear? You look peaky."

"Grandmama's room was very hot."

He now poked his long face towards her, and there was a twisted smile on it as he said, "Is it ever anything else? You know, my dear, if my mother was not such a very good woman I would imagine at times that the devil himself was preparing her for the nether regions."

She let out a high laugh, then clapped her hand tightly over her mouth. Her father, this man of God, as her grandmama sometimes referred to him, could say such funny things. Oh, she loved him. She went to his side now and leant her head against his shoulder, and his frankness, as it always did, encouraged her own and she said, "I don't like Sunday school, Papa."

"I know you don't, my dear. But it is necessary, and it shows a good example."

Still with her head pressed close to him, she murmured, "I can't stand Miss Jancy or Miss Eva McKeowan. They yammer."

A slight shudder under her cheek found an answering gurgle in herself and it was a few seconds before her father replied, "They mean well. They are good women."

"The younger one, Eva, makes eyes at James."

"Oh, now." He pressed her from him, and pulled his chin into the high collar on his thin neck, and, his voice reproving, he said, "Now you mustn't say things like that."

" 'Tis true, Papa. And James is scared of her."

"Oh, that is nonsense: James is scared of nothing and no one." There was a proud note in his voice now as he went on, "James is a very strong character. In a way, he takes after your grandmama." And his tone altered as he ended, "I'm afraid I know somebody else who does, too."

"You think I'm like Grandmama, Papa?"

"You are showing many of her characteristics."

"What ones?"

"Which ones? Oh, we won't go into that. Anyway, I must get down to work. You know I go to Durham tomorrow to meet the Bishop and the Dean, and I've got to think about that."

"Mama said, would you give me a suitable reading, Papa."

"Suitable reading." His eyes travelled over the bookshelves lining the wall in front of him, and he got to his feet, saying, "Ah. . . . Ah. Suitable reading for a Sunday." And looking down on her, he said, "You have your books upstairs."

"Yes, I know, but Mama told me to ask you."

"Dear, dear. Suitable reading." He was walking along by the bookshelves now and touching one book after another, murmuring as he did so, "Not suitable, not suitable." Then picking one from the shelf, he scanned through it before replacing it, saying, "Too old. Too old." Then turning about, he went to another row of shelves to the right of his desk, and she watched him take out one book after another and read a line here and there. And a smile passed over his face before he returned the last book to the shelf, saying regretfully, "Not Sunday reading. Adventures."

"I could take Gyp for a walk, Papa."

He nodded at her, seeming to consider for a moment, then sighed and said, "Yes, yes, you could." But now, once again bending his long length towards her, he added, "But I'd go out this way." He pointed to the half-open window. "It's closer to the kennel."

They looked knowingly at each other, and when he pushed the sashed window further up she bent to step through it; then quickly straightening, she reached up and put her arms around his neck and planted a quick kiss on the side of his bony chin before scrambling through the opening, then along by the side of the house, and to the dog's kennel.

At the sight of her the young labrador pranced wildly and gave a howling bark, and she shushed him by gripping his mouth tightly between her hands and looking into his eyes, saying, "Quiet, Gyp, else we'll both get wrong." Then unlinking the chain attached to his collar, she threw the offending deterrent against the wall where the other end was fastened to an iron loop. And once again she told herself that when she was older and had more to say, she would see that Gyp wasn't attached to that thing. Animals shouldn't be tied up.

"Come on," she whispered to him now, and wagged a warning finger at him; and seemingly taking her cue, he walked quietly beside her. But as soon as they left the vicarage grounds and entered the field that ran down to the river she grabbed up the skirt of her Sunday dress until it came just below her knees, then raced down the field, the dog bounding at her heels. And they didn't stop until they reached the bank of the river where, dropping down on to the grass, she put her arms about him, and when his lolling tongue travelled the complete length of her face, she fell back onto the ground laughing.

She looked up into the sky. It was high and clear blue. She blinked her eyes against the glare of the sun, then brought her gaze down on to the river, but it too made her blink, for there were a myriad stars dancing on the water. It was running fast here and would continue to do so all the way until it reached Durham.

It was a beautiful river; she loved walking beside it. The only thing was that such walking was checked by the Rossburn estate on her left, for just round the corner about a quarter of a mile away the boundary railings, all barbed wired, went down into the river. She always felt slightly resentful when she came up to them, telling herself it wouldn't have hurt him to let people walk along the towpath. No damage would ever have been done because it was only afternoon strollers and fishers who used the bank, at this end anyway; the children from the village had access to the river right on their doorstep.

She always thought of the owner of Rossburn House as "He." She had only once glimpsed him, and that seemed a long time ago. He was rarely at home as he had other houses he stayed at, so she understood. At times, Peggy and Hilda talked about the goings-on at The House, but their voices always sank to undertones and she could never follow the gist of their words: their sentences were always short and often remained unfinished. They named names. One in particular she had heard more than once, and she connected it with one of the women, the pretty one, who came to church every other Sunday.

But The House and its doings were of no interest to her, other than that the man who owned the place had made it impossible for her to continue her walk along the river bank.

Last year there had been a kind of rumour going around that it was questionable if the owner of The House had a right to bar the public from the towpath; it concerned ancient rights or something. But she had heard no talk of it lately; and so, as Mr. McLoughlin had shouted when he had come to the school drunk that day, she presumed, there was one law for the rich and one for the poor.

Mr. McLoughlin had been angry because Mr. Bolton had lathered Mike good and hard with the strap. That was after

Mick McLoughlin had lit a candle in a jar and pushed it under the desk at Katie Thompson's feet and the bottom of her frilly pinny had caught alight, and she had screamed, and all the children had screamed with her. And Miss Pringle had run in from the other room with a wooden bucket of water that always stood at the door, and she had thrown it over Katie, and Katie had screamed worse. And there had been a terrible to-do. She herself had rather enjoyed it all, and later she had made her grandmama laugh describing how Mr. McLoughlin had challenged the head teacher to a fight. And Mr. Bolton had let the children out of school early and had locked himself in with Miss Pringle until the constables came and took Mr. McLoughlin away.

She leant forward and hugged her knees. She'd miss the school. She had been happy there, and she liked Miss Pringle because Miss Pringle let her read aloud to the class; and she picked her for monitor too. What would it be like at this Dame school? She hated the sound of it. Would Sundays be the same there as here? Perhaps worse. Yes, perhaps worse.

She rose to her feet now and walked slowly along the bank. Ahead of her was the fence going down into the water. Again she felt frustration. She'd often thought if it hadn't been for the barbed wire on the top she would have climbed the fence and sneaked along the bank.

Gyp was sniffing in the long grass to the side of the path and she called him, "Here! Here, Gyp. Stay. Stay with me."

For once, Gyp took no notice of his young mistress's voice but went on sniffing through the long grass until it gave place to a green sward, and at the far side of it, sitting near the fence, were two rabbits. One second they were there, the next they were scrambling under the fence with Gyp in hot pursuit. But being unable to follow them through the small opening at the bottom of the wire, the dog ran madly backwards and forwards; and then, of a sudden, he disappeared.

It had all happened so quickly that Nancy Ann hadn't even found her breath to shout out. But she raced to where the dog had disappeared and recognized that he had got easily through a badger walk. In a moment she was on her hands and knees with the intent of trying to scramble after him; but realizing that this was impossible, she began to call, "Gyp! Gyp! Come here. Gyp! Gyp!"

But there was no sound from Gyp, not even a bark.

She stood with her hands tightly across her mouth. There were traps. Gentlemen laid traps all over their estates to catch foxes. It was illegal, so she understood, but they still did it. *He* might be one of them who defied the law. Oh, dear me! Dear me! She was now running up and down by the fence.

Suddenly she stopped and looked to where it went down into the water. In a second she had her shoes off, and she tied the laces together and slung the shoes from her neck, but she left her stockings on, telling herself that they would easily dry in the sun. Then, pulling her skirt above her knees, she stepped down into the water which immediately swirled round her calfs. Gripping the staves of the railings, she made towards the end one, and she shivered visibly as the water gradually came above her knees and soaked the bottom of her dress at the back. But she was round the end railings and now scurrying towards the bank, and having climbed up it, she knelt for a moment, gasping; then again began calling softly, "Gyp! Gyp!"

She now pulled her shoes on to her sodden feet and grimaced as she did so; then she was running along the towpath, again crying, "Gyp! Gyp!" Once she stopped and looked to the side and into where the thick brushwood between the tall trees cleared a little, but with the thought of traps in her mind she was afraid to venture near them.

Once more she was running along the bank. Then quite suddenly she stopped dead. The trees had opened out, and there before her was a grassy sward and a kind of sandy-pebbled beach leading in to the water, and sitting on a flat slab of rock was a small boy, and by his side was Gyp. On the sight of her, the boy didn't move, but the dog turned and whined.

She approached them slowly and, looking down at the dog, she said, "You are a naughty boy, Gyp;" then staring at the child, she said, "You . . . you caught him?"

"What?"

"You . . . you caught my dog?"

"No. He . . . he came and sat down." The voice was

hesitant but the words were rounded: he spoke like some of the younger children in the school who were learning their letters.

"Nice dog." The boy put out his hand and patted Gyp's head.

She stared at him. He was an odd-looking child, at least part of him was. His face was round and he had two large brown eyes, but it was his hair that gave him the odd appearance; there was something wrong with it. It was wet and there was a brown stain running from it down one side of his face.

He now surprised her by saying, "Hello," as if he hadn't previously spoken, and she answered, "Hello." Then she added, "My name is Nancy Ann. What is yours?"

"I'm David."

She now looked about her. He was a little boy. What was he doing here on his own? Was he from The House? Well, that was the only place he could come from. But she didn't know that *He* had a family. Somehow she had imagined *He* wasn't married, because *He* was very old. But this child could belong to one of the servants. She said, "Where is your mother?"

"In . . . in the kitchen . . . sometimes." He had added the last word as an afterthought.

"What is your other name?" She watched him consider. Then when Gyp suddenly turned on to his back, the boy put out his hand and gently rubbed the dog's stomach, and he continued doing so for some time before he answered, "My mother is called Jennie."

"Does . . . does she know you are here?"

He looked up at her and blinked his eyelids and said, "No, but . . . but I like to walk. It is hot up in the roof. I came down the back stairs. No one saw me."

He spoke so clearly for such a small child, and she shook her head in bewilderment, then said, "Your hair's wet."

He put his hand up and ran his fingers from the crown downwards, and the sun, glinting on it, brought out the different shades. It looked almost white in parts, then brown, and white again, but the ends were all brown. She screwed up her face in enquiry when he said, "It's the tea." And she repeated, "The tea?"

"Yes. Jennie washes it in tea. I don't like the tea, it's sticky."

"And . . . and you try to wash it off?"

"Yes." For the first time he smiled, a small tentative smile, then said, "Do you wash your hair in tea?"

"No." She shook her head and put her hand up towards her hair and instinctively thought: Oh, dear me. She had been walking outside without a hat and that was almost unforgivable, and on a Sunday too. She should have gone to the summerhouse and got a straw bonnet.

"I would like a dog." He continued to stroke Gyp's tummy; then thumbing over his shoulder, he said, "There are dogs over there but they are all big and they bite. Jennie says they bite and I mustn't touch them."

They both started now as a voice came from the wood beyond the little bay, calling in a sort of hiss, "David! David!"

The child rose to his feet. He was dressed in a frock that reached to his ankles. And now he started to run from her; but stopping, he said, "Will you bring the dog again?"

She did not speak but nodded her head; then, grabbing Gyp by the collar, she dragged him back along the little bay and up into the shelter of the trees. She did not see the meeting between the child and the owner of the voice, but she heard a strong reprimand in the tone as it said, "You mustn't. You mustn't. Oh! just look at you. I've told you now, I've told you." Then the voice faded away.

She had to keep her body bent while holding tightly on to the dog's collar as she made her way back to the railings. And there she was confronted by an obstacle. If she let go of the dog he would likely make back, not for the rabbits now, but for the child, and she couldn't go through the tangle that was to the right of her and find the place to push him through. There was nothing for it, she saw, but to take him into the water with her. And she wouldn't be able to take her shoes off while holding on to him; they would just have to get wet, as the rest of her would likely be before she got round the barrier.

Gyp was nine months old and as yet had had no acquaintance with the water, but once he had been dragged into it he paddled for dear life, and his effort was much easier than Nancy Ann's, because now, with one hand holding him and the other grabbing at the railings for support, her long skirt became wet almost up to her thighs. And when eventually she dragged herself and the animal out on to the bank she let go of him and lay face downwards, gasping. When the dog shook himself vigorously all over her, she made no protest.

After a few minutes she got to her feet and looked down at herself. She knew her skirt was ruined, as were her shoes because they would dry hard and she wouldn't be able to wear them because her toes were tender and skinned easily.

As she walked along the path, the dog quietly at her heels again and steam rising from both of them, she continually asked herself what she was going to do, how she was going to explain what had happened without telling lies.

It wasn't until she had crept stealthily along by the back of the buildings and tied up Gyp again, which surprisingly he didn't seem to resent this time, but went into his kennel and laid down on the sacking almost immediately, that she decided the only avenue likely to offer any help was the kitchen. She now ran back along the way she had come earlier, then entered the courtyard and in a scampering dash made for the kitchen door, and her bursting into the room caused a gasp from the three women sitting at the table. Two of them rose simultaneously to their feet, but Cook, Mrs. Peggy Knowles, just looked at Nancy Ann and shook her head, and it was she who said, "Child! What's this latest?"

"I . . . I fell into the river . . . slipped."

"Slipped? You?" She now rose and walked between her two companions and, putting out a hand, she felt the top of Nancy Ann's dress. Then looking at Jane, her assistant and maid of all work, she said, "She fell in the river, slipped, and dry as a bone up top. Eeh! Miss, what next! Your mother'll go mad."

"She needn't know. We can dry her out."

Cook looked at the housemaid, Hilda Fenwick, and said, "How much time have we got?" and glancing at the clock she answered herself, "Not an hour afore tea." Then grabbing hold of Nancy Ann's shoulder, she commanded, "Let's get them off. And you, Jane, put the irons on the stove; her things'll want pressin'."

Three pairs of hands now almost tore the clothes from her, but when they came to her shoes, they looked at each other and it was Hilda who said, "Well, nothing can be done with these. Anyway, they won't show the wet. She'll just have to put them on as they are, although it won't be much use dryin' her stockin's."

"Here, put this round you." Cook was bundling her into a large shawl, and as she did so she looked at Hilda, saying, "Could you sneak a pair of bloomers and a couple of petticoats downstairs? We'll never get all these dried and ironed in that short time. Where's the mistress, do you know?"

"In the little sitting-room; the master's still in his study. At least that's where they were five minutes or so gone."

"Well, go and see what you can do and be sharp about it."

During all the fuss Nancy Ann hadn't opened her mouth, and it wasn't until Hilda had returned with a pair of bloomers, a pair of stockings, a waist petticoat, and a bodice petticoat that she looked from one to the other and said, "Thank you. Thank you very much."

"You're an awful child, you know." Hilda was leaning towards her, a broad grin on her face; then she added, "But life would be very dull without you. I hate the idea of you goin' to that school. You don't like it very much yourself, do you?"

"No, Hilda, I don't. . . . Hilda, why should anyone wash a child's hair in tea?"

"Wash hair in tea?"

The three women now looked from one to the other and smiled, and it was Jane who said, "To dye it likely. My Aunt Sal used to do that. Her hair should have been white but it was a queer brown. What makes you ask that?"

"Well, truthfully"—and she nodded her head from one to the other now—"I took Gyp out and he got under the fence into the estate . . . Rossburn's. He was chasing rabbits and I couldn't get through and I had to go into the water and round the fence, and . . . and when I found him he was with a little boy, and the little boy had been washing his hair, trying to get the tea out of it. He said somebody called Jennie washed his hair in tea."

"You . . . you went into the estate"—Hilda's voice was full of awe—"and saw a little boy?"

The women were looking at each other again, and it was Cook who said, "What was he like, miss?"

"He . . . he would have been pretty, but his hair was all streaked. It was light in parts, almost . . . well, fair, and then had patches of brown. The ends were all dark though, and it was long right onto his shoulders."

The women once more exchanged glances, and it was Jane who now said almost in a whisper, "Eeh, my! I thought he never got out only when she walked him; she had to keep him in the attic."

"He spoke about the attic . . . or the roof." Nancy Ann nodded at them again. "He said it was very hot up there. I think that's why he wanted to come out. He was a nice child. Who does he belong to?"

No one answered her question for a moment; then Hilda said, "One of the staff, miss, and if I was you, miss, I wouldn't mention to the master or the mistress that you saw the boy."

"She's not stupid." Jane's voice broke in curtly. "She's not gonna let on that she was where she shouldn't be an' on a Sunday afternoon at that." She turned now and looked down on Nancy Ann and added, "She's got a head on her shoulders, haven't you, miss?"

Nancy Ann didn't give an answer to this compliment; but when she shivered Jane said, "Look at that now. I'll bet she's in for a cold. What about a hot drink for her, Cook, eh?"

"Yes, yes, the very thing."

Now began a scurrying around the kitchen: a pad being put on the end of the table, and an old sheet thrown over it, and the flat iron stand placed on the corner of it; then the kettle was pressed into the heart of the fire and a jar marked ginger taken down from the cupboard shelf. And all the while they talked to each other in an undertone, and the gist that Nancy Ann could catch here and there conveyed to her that Cook had been talking to the assistant cook from The House, who had told her that the master of the house was due home next week and that they had been ordered to get ready for a shooting party coming. Apparently at the moment he was in London.

When suddenly she sneezed, Cook exclaimed, "There you are then! This is the beginnin'. Is the kettle boilin'?"

"Yes, Cook."

"And have you squeezed that lemon, Hilda?"

" 'Tis all ready, an' I've mixed half a teaspoonful of ginger with it."

"Oh, that's too much; it'll burn her bowels up."

"Well, I've done it now."

"Put more water in it then, an' thin it down."

"Oh dear, dear."

"There you are, miss, sip that."

"Thank you. Thank you, Cook."

At the first gulp of the hot liquid Nancy Ann coughed and almost choked. But Cook insisted she keep on sipping, and when the glass was half empty and she could take no more she gasped and pushed it from her, and at that moment the kitchen door opened and, to the consternation of all, her mother entered.

Rebecca Hazel came to an abrupt stop in the middle of the room and she looked from one to another of her small staff; lastly, her eyes rested on her daughter huddled in the shawl and now sneezing, and slowly she said, "What is this?"

None of her maids answered but stood silent, eyes cast down. And then she was standing in front of Nancy Ann who, sniffing loudly, said, "I'm sorry, Mama, I fell in the river."

"You what?"

"I . . . I fell in the river."

Rebecca Hazel was about to ask, How on earth did you do that, child? but she couldn't at the moment bear to hear the explanation true or false as it might be.

"Come along. . . . Come!" she said, holding out her hand towards her daughter. Nancy Ann sidled from the wooden settle and when she stepped off the clippy mat that fronted the open fireplace on to the stone floor she sneezed again.

Rebecca, tugging her up the kitchen now, murmured under her breath, "Your papa will be greatly distressed about this, greatly distressed. And on a Sunday, too. Whatever next will you get up to, child!''

Her father was sitting by the side of the bed and holding her hand, and he said, ''I am to blame. I should have insisted that you attend Sunday school. Your mother is right, quite right. I am to blame.''

''No, Papa. No, Papa.''

''Oh, yes, yes. This is what happens when we do things to please ourselves and those we love without taking into consideration there are rules to be obeyed in all things and if we break them we must stand the consequences. In this case, poor child, it is you who are suffering from the consequences. But how on earth did you manage to fall in the river? You're so surefooted; you run like a deer without tripping.''

''I . . . I went after Gyp, Papa.''

''And . . . and he swam into the river?''

She waited for a moment, her mind racing around to find an outlet that wouldn't be a lie. Then she saw herself hanging on to the dog as he paddled furiously and in a small voice she said, ''Yes, Papa, he . . . he swam in the river.''

''Well, if he swam, my dear, he wouldn't have drowned. You shouldn't have gone in after him.''

''He had never been in the river before, Papa.''

She wasn't lying.

''No, you're right; he's still little more than a puppy. How old is he now?'' As he considered, she said, ''Nine months, Papa.''

''Yes, yes, of course''—he smiled at her—''nine months.'' He rose from the chair, and saying, ''Be a good girl. And don't worry, I'll take the blame,'' he stepped back from the bed smiling, and her throat was so full she could make no comment. Dear, dear Papa. She was overcome by guilt. . . .

A short while later, when her brothers came in, she felt no such emotion. ''Well, well!'' Peter laughed down at her, and James said, ''Leave you for five minutes and this is what you get up to.'' He bent above her. ''What really happened? Come on now, that pup is terrified of water. I tried to get him in myself.''

Forgetting for a moment how her head and throat ached,

she said, tartly, "If you had taken me with you it wouldn't have happened."

"What wouldn't have happened?" Peter demanded, sitting down on the side of the bed now. "You had a fight or something . . . the McLoughlins?"

"No, no, I didn't have a fight or something. I . . . I had an adventure."

"Oh! Oh!" The brothers exchanged glances and pulled long faces, and James said, "She had an adventure."

"Oh, I love adventures." Peter wriggled on the bed, and joined his hands under his chin; then, his voice changing, he said, "Come on, spill it out."

She looked from one to the other before she asked the same question of them as she had of the maids, but put in a slightly different way. "Why should you wash your hair in tea?" she said.

"What!" they both said together. "Wash our hair in tea? What do you mean?" James added.

"Just that. Why should anybody wash a small boy's hair in tea?"

Now James pulled a chair up to the side of the bed and, his face straight, he said, "Let's have it from the beginning."

And so between much coughing and clearing of her throat she told them what had happened; and when she had finished she was surprised at their remaining silent, and she watched them exchange glances again, then look down at the bed quilt.

It was Peter who, getting to his feet and letting out a long drawn breath, said, "Well, the only explanation I can give you is that the child's mother didn't like the colour of its hair. People do dye their hair with tea, you know."

"They do?"

"Yes."

"But it looked funny; it was all streaky and he didn't like it. Sticky, he said it was. And he had been trying to wash it off."

"Oh, well. Mothers can do what they like with their own children. Now go on to sleep, trouble." Peter bent and kissed her on the brow; then James did likewise; and when they reached the door they turned and waved to her, and she said, "I wish you weren't going tomorrow."

"So do we," said James. Then bending forward he hissed, "Don't forget about my engagement."

"No, no, I won't." She smiled and nodded at them, and when the door closed she snuggled down into the pillow and waited for her grandmama's visit. . . .

But her grandmama was delaying her visit; she was sitting in her room looking at her two grandsons who were seated as far away from the fire as they could get, which wasn't all that far for the room was crowded with furniture and the backs of their chairs were tight pressed against the foot of her bed.

Peter was now saying, "Do you think he's been kept up in the attic all these years? He must be four now."

"All maids sleep in the attics. She's likely had to keep him up there in one room. You two were up in the nursery until you were five. What's the difference?"

"A great deal, I should say," said James. "Nancy Ann said she heard a person scolding the child for being outside."

"Well, of course, she would have to, because what would happen if he was running wild and Mr. Bighead Dennison Harpcore came across him. That was the agreement, so I understand, that he was kept out of the way."

"I never knew exactly what did happen," Peter said. "I knew there was a mighty fuss after the brother was drowned; but what took place before exactly?"

"Well, you were both at school at the time and such things were of little interest to you. You know the outline of the story: Jennie Mather was put into service there when she was ten. She came half-day to school here. She was a pretty child. She had no parents but an uncle, Tom Bristow. He drove Gibbons's cart. He was a youngish fellow, well set up. Anyway, Jennie eventually became chambermaid and when she was sixteen she came under the notice of Timothy. He was eighteen. A nice pleasant young fellow, as I remember him, very fair, but not a very strong and brewster character like his brother. Anyway, Harpcore was five years older and already making a name for himself, and not just academically. So, as I said to myself at the time, what right had he to act like an outraged father when his brother came into the open. And yet, on the other hand, it must have been like a gun at his head when Timothy, at nineteen, told him not only that he had got one of the maids into trouble but also that he wanted to marry her. The young fellow was very much in earnest. Jennie had grown into a very beautiful young girl and she had a bit of a brain to go with it apparently. She had been bright at school and had kept up her reading, and as Peggy down below would say, she didn't act common. But nevertheless, she was a chambermaid, and when people of her class give way to their masters' whims, they should know what to expect.

"Well, the story goes that Harpcore, naturally, was for sending her packing, but that young Timothy threatened to go with her. It must be said for Harpcore that he loved his brother. You see, the mother had died when Timothy was seven and Dennison had, in a way, you could say, brought him up because they had been inseparable until Dennison was packed off to school. And he felt all the more responsible for his younger brother when their father died when Timothy was twelve. And so here was Timothy telling his brother, who was now master of the estate, that he intended to bring a working-class girl, a maid, into this old well-connected family. It just wouldn't be even discussed. I understand that he tried to make the boy see that his feelings were just a flash in the pan. He even consented to providing for the girl as long as Timothy had nothing more to do with her. But apparently Timothy wouldn't see it this way. Anyway—" She paused here and said, "Hand me that glass of lemon water off the table, James. I'm thirsty; I've never talked so much at once for years."

James handed her the glass, and after draining it she wiped her mouth and said, "Where was I? Oh yes. You remember the big flood? It started just as a spring tide, but then it rained for a solid week, and the wind blew and trees came down. Well, you won't recall it because you were at school, but, you know, the river along the stretch where that little monkey went today is always hazardous; even when the water's running calm, there's eddies there. Well, what possessed the young fellow to take a boat out in that weather God alone knows; but you know the rest, they found the boat a mile down the river. But they didn't find the body until four days later. They said that Dennison nearly went insane. One thing he did do was order the girl to be sent from the house. And now this is where her uncle comes in. He was a strong-minded fellow, Tom Bristow: he agitated for unions and the like for every kind of work; he spoke on platforms; he was that kind of man. Anyway, what does he do but storm into the house, after levelling the footman, and come face to face with the half-demented Dennison. As far as I can gather and again it was hearsay, but he said as much that the child that was to be born was of that house and of his blood, and if Dennison turned the girl out there was no place except the workhouse for her because he himself was about to emigrate to Australia, but that he wouldn't go until he saw justice done. And his justice demanded that she remain in her post and the child remain there.

"Apparently, at this, Dennison yelled to his servants to throw the man out to prevent himself from laying his hands on him. But when the butler and the second footman came into the room the fellow took up such a stance that they were awed by him, or, as the tale goes, by the ornaments he scooped up from the table in order to throw at them.

"Well, he is supposed to have given Dennison an ultimatum: either he let the girl stay in her job, or he provide her with a house and income, or he himself would give the story to the newspaper together with the information that his brother had wanted to marry the girl. And how would Dennison stand up to that scandal, he is said to have demanded.

"But Dennison couldn't have said much because nothing seems to have been passed on. I think though he must have considered that setting up the girl in a house would have been taken as acceptance of the responsibility for his brother's child; or, on the other hand, that should he turn her out it would create a scandal that the newspapers would spread countrywide, whereas if he let the girl stay and ignored her existence, the affair would not reach beyond local bounds. And . . . well, that's what he has done: Jennie was allowed to stay, but she was relegated to the kitchen; and it was understood through the household that when the child was born the master mustn't set eyes on it; and too, that if they wanted to remain in his employ they didn't speak about the matter outside the house.''

She nodded from one to the other, then said, ''And now about the tea business. Young Timothy was very fair, as fair as Dennison is dark. His hair was almost golden, and I've heard that when the child was born it had hair on its head the colour of silver. And over the years the child seems to be growing into a replica of its father. Again, so I am told. So now you can understand the tea business, for had the child's hair been left alone and Dennison had come across him, he would have recognized him immediately. But a brown-haired child might pass unnoticed, or be taken as belonging to one of the outside staff. That's if he takes notice of any menial the short time he's home.''

''But what's going to happen when the child grows up? Will he make a claim on him do you think? I mean on Mr. Harpcore.''

''Perhaps. I don't know, that's in the future. The present is that your little sister has the knack already of creating chaos wherever she goes.'' She smiled now, then added, ''I was for trying to persuade your mother—with an iron hand in the velvet glove, you know''—and she smiled—''to forget about this Dame school business, because I shall miss the little monkey, but after this, I think a little discipline and the company of other than the village children might help to shape her future.''

''What a hope!'' James rose to his feet. ''I can't see her changing. Anyway, Grandmama, you wouldn't want her to really, because she's too much like yourself, isn't she?''

''Well, is that a bad thing?'' The voice was curt.

James shrugged his shoulders as if, were he to reply, it would be positively. But there was a smile on his face, and she cried at him, ''Go on, get yourself away. I'll have to go into her now and listen to the story for myself; and knowing the teller, it will undoubtedly be embroidered for my benefit, being an old lady who has to be entertained.''

As they both made grunting sounds, the bell ringing in the distance turned them towards the door and Jessica, a tight smile on her face, said, ''There's your appetizer before your meal. I've always disliked Sundays because you're expected to pray more on a Sunday, and for less food. Enjoy your cold repast. I'm so glad I'm ill and can have warm gruel.'' She laughed wickedly, and the boys laughed with her.

When they muttered something as they opened the door, she said, "What's that you say?" And Peter, poking his head towards her, said in an undertone, "You heard. You're a wicked woman.''

She still continued to laugh after the door had closed; then getting up smartly, she walked across the room, unlocked the drawer of her writing desk, took out a flat tin box, lifted up the lid, and extracted from the box a small meat pie and a fruit tart. Then, spreading a clean handkerchief on the small table to the side of her fireside chair, she laid the pastries on it. But before sitting down again she went to the door and pushed in the bolt. It was known in the household that she always bolted the door when she was relieving herself. Returning to her seat, she made herself comfortable, stretched her feet out and rested them on the rim of the scalloped brass fender; then picking up the pie, she bit into it and munched happily.

❧ 3 ❧

IF THE RULING MEMBERS OF THE HOUSEHOLD HADN'T ALready agreed that if Nancy Ann was ever to take on the refinement of a young lady she must be sent away to the Dame school, they would certainly have come to this decision through two incidents that occurred during the following three weeks.

Nancy Ann was in bed for three days and housebound for another three days, but on the following Sunday she was considered well enough to attend the morning service and Sunday school in the afternoon.

Miss Eva McKeowan was winding up the proceedings of the Sunday school with, "Now we shall sing your hymn, children, 'Let Me Like An Angel Be.' " Thus saying, she went to the harmonium in the corner of the room, and, turning her head to face the class, she called, "After three . . . one, two, three."

> Let me like an angel be,
> Let me always trust in Thee.

The voices squeaked and rose in disharmony:

> Ever present at Thy knee
> Let me like an angel be.

It was a silly hymn: Ever present at Thy knee. Nancy Ann did not raise her voice because she knew she couldn't get the tune right.

The hymn ended with Amen being sung in several different keys. Then Miss McKeowan stood up and said, "Now you will depart quietly."

Why did she always say, "depart"?

Nancy Ann herself was about to depart hastily when Miss McKeowan's voice stopped her, saying, "Nancy Ann, stay for a moment, will you?"

Slowly and reluctantly she walked back to where Miss McKeowan stood near her reading desk, and she waited to know what was required of her. But Miss McKeowan didn't speak until the last of the children had gone. And then smiling, she looked down on Nancy Ann, saying, "I'm glad to know you are so much better, Nancy Ann."

"Thank you."

"I have a little present for you." She lifted the lid of the reading desk and took out a small box, and when she opened it, it revealed what looked like a gold chain with a heart-shaped locket on the end. She now dangled it from her finger, saying, "I . . . I would like you to have this, Nancy Ann, as a keepsake, seeing this is almost your last visit to Sunday school. A week tomorrow, I understand, you go away to school, and perhaps you will be so busy next Sunday you may not attend. So I thought I would give you this today. It's a very pretty locket, isn't it?"

She now swung the chain backwards and forwards like a pendulum while Nancy Ann thought, Oh, dear, dear. She wasn't fond of trinkets and she couldn't accept this one because she knew why it was being given to her: it wasn't that Miss McKeowan liked her, it was a way of finding favour in James's eyes.

Of a sudden she felt sorry for Miss McKeowan and realized, as Peter said, that she was blinded by love; and she must be, or else she would have understood James's attitude towards her, which had become rude of late. At one time he would stand and talk to her, and sometimes she had seen him laugh with her, but afterwards he would always relate what had passed between them to Peter, and they would both laugh.

"Take it. Put it on. It will show up against your blue dress."

"I'm . . . I'm sorry, Miss Eva, but . . . but I must first ask Mama, because it looks, well, an expensive gift, like . . . I mean, it's very like the one James . . . James bought."

She knew what she was saying was dreadful, yet it would be wrong to accept this gift, because this poor young woman—and now she thought of her almost in her grandmama's words as a poor young woman—would gain nothing by its giving.

"Mr. James has purchased one like it?" Miss McKeowan's voice was high, her words running up the scale as if she were going to burst into song; and there was a smile in her eyes and hovering around her mouth as she brought her head down towards Nancy Ann and said again, "Your . . . your brother has bought one like this?"

Nancy Ann stepped slightly back from the bright hopeful look and she swallowed deeply and coughed before she brought out in a rush, "It . . . it is a present for his fi . . . financée." She had pronounced the word wrongly but that didn't matter; what mattered was the changed expression on the face that had now stretched itself upright and away from her. The finger no longer swung the chain holding the heart-shaped pendant, but the whole was crushed in her hand and this was held tightly against the buckle of the broad belt that spanned her narrow waist and helped to flounce her print skirt.

Now she was speaking again, her words coming through lips which didn't seem to move: "What did you say? He has a . . . a fiancée? When? Where? Whe . . . when? Who?"

Nancy Ann took three steps backwards until the back of her knee pressed against the harmonium seat, and she stared at the agitated young woman. What she wanted to do was to go to her, take her hand away from her belt and pat it and say, " 'Tis all right, 'tis all right. I was only . . . only saying that. It isn't true." But if she were to do this she could see Miss McKeowan becoming enraged and even slapping her. She had slapped Mary Jane Norton once because she had caught her mimicking the way she walked and how she announced the hymn "Let Me Like An Angel Be." And she couldn't risk being slapped: having always endeavoured to join with her brothers' games, her reaction to either their teasing or roughness had been to retaliate and this had become almost a natural reaction and had been of great help to her whenever she came up against the McLoughlins.

"*Go away!*" yelled Miss McKeowan.

But she remained standing, the desire still on her to take the awful look off the young woman's face: she looked as though she were about to cry, yet was too angry to do so.

"*Get out!*"

She got out, at a run now, and when she was outside she continued running until she reached the back gate, where she bumped into Johnny.

Johnny Pratt was the vicarage handyman. He had been handy, he would tell you, for fifty years. He was now sixty-two. He drove the trap, tended the horse, saw to the kitchen garden, neglected the flower garden—he had no use for frivolities, he said. He believed in, and obeyed, the parson; not so his wife, for he considered her like the parsons' wives before her, aiming for a front seat in heaven. The old 'un, he respected, even if she had a tongue like a newly stropped razor. The lads he liked: they were fine young chaps, always civil. But this one here—he looked at Nancy Ann—he could say he more than liked her. She was a chip off the old block. He was sorry they were packing her off to a fancy school. Well, he supposed he could see their point; she was a bit of a rough 'un for a lass.

"What's wrong?" he said.

"Nothing, Johnny."

"You're lyin', an' on a Sunday an' all. You know where you'll go for doin' that? And you've been runnin' an' all, and you know what your ma thinks about runnin' an' on a Sunday . . . among other things," he added.

"Where are they?" she asked, in a whisper now.

"Well—" he pulled out a large round watch from his waistcoat pocket. It was in a case from which any supposed silver had long since disappeared, leaving the metal the colour of dull brass, and after studying it for a moment he said, "Well, if things go according to Sunday plans, and I can't see them altering here, they should be in the sitting-room having their cups of tea and''—he bent down to her, a grin on his be-whiskered face, adding now—''and no cake, 'cos it's Sun-day.'' At this he nodded at her, then walked on; and she, too, walking now, went down the yard, round the side of the house and in by the garden door.

In the hall she took off her hat and coat, examined her hands to see if they were clean enough, decided they were as she hadn't been dealing with chalk, then tapping on the sit-ting-room door, she opened it and went in and stopped what she recognized immediately was a tirade from her grand-mama which had been directed towards her mama. ''There you are.'' Rebecca turned a thankful glance on her daughter. ''Did you enjoy the lesson?''

''It . . . it was as usual, Mama.''

''It would be with that one taking it . . . the Eva one I suppose.''

She looked at her grandmother. ''Yes, Grandmama.''

''You would like a cup of tea?'' Her mother was looking at her.

''Yes, please, Mama.''

She sat down behind the round table on which the tea-tray was set and as she did so her father smiled at her. She re-turned the smile, then let out a long sigh and relaxed against the back of the chair. She didn't know now what she had been frightened about. She had done James a service and Miss Eva wouldn't be silly any more, at least towards him.

She was startled out of her reverie by her grandmother's voice crying, ''Disraeli! That old woman! Instead of running round the Queen's skirts . . . Empress of India, indeed!'' She sniffed—''it would suit him better if he attended to those Turks.'' And she rounded on her daughter-in-law: ''And don't tell me, Rebecca, that this is not Sunday talk; massacring Christians is a talk for any day in the week to my mind. Those Bazouks, or whatever you call them, killed thousands.''

''Oh, Mother-in-law, that is an exaggeration.''

''No exaggeration whatever, woman. You don't read your newspapers. Isn't that so, John Howard?'' She addressed her son, as she always did, with his full Christian name. ''Wasn't there twelve thousand of them polished off?'' And before he could answer, she again rounded on her daughter-in-law, crying, "And it could happen here. It all started there because of a bad harvest, and it could happen here, I'm telling you."

"Mother . . . Mother, please don't become so excited. Yes, you are right, there were Christians massacred by the Bashi—Bazouks, but it's all so far away, and. . . ."

"Oh, my Lord!" Nancy Ann watched her grandmama put her cup down on the side table with such a bang that the remaining tea in the cup splashed over on to the saucer, then on to the table. She watched her mother look towards the table in dismay and yet make no move to go and wipe it. And her grandmama went on, "So far away, you say. Don't forget, what happened yesterday in France could happen here tomorrow, and in that Germany too. And there's that stupid little man standing firm, as he calls it, on his support of Turkey while other countries are aghast at the atrocities in Bulgaria. John Howard"—she looked sternly at her son—"did you not read the pamphlet that James brought home, that Mr. Gladstone got published, showing up the Bulgarian horrors? No, I'm sure you didn't. Well, it's in the library; at least it was a week ago, if it hasn't been tidied up." She now cast an accusing glance towards her daughter-in-law before going on. "James, Peter, and I discussed this situation. James has a head on his shoulders; looks beyond these shores. He could do well in Parliament."

"Oh, Mother." John closed his eyes and, his voice weary, he went on. "You know as well as I do that James won't think seriously along such lines. He knows . . . well"—he lowered his head—"it's only because of your generosity that he has managed to remain at his studies so far. Please, Mother, I beg of you not to encourage him in such costly. . . ."

"Encourage him! He's got a mind of his own. And don't worry, I could no more support either of them in such a career than I could fly; I couldn't even now buy us a new tr . . . ap." Her voice trailed away, and she grabbed at her cup and gulped at the now cold tea that remained in it. And when she replaced the cup and the saucer this time, it was done quietly, and she raised her eyes and looked at her son and daughter-in-law. They were staring at her, and John, in a small quiet voice, said, "Oh, Mother."

"Oh, don't 'Mother' me in that tone of voice. I've been only too pleased to do it. I thought they might as well have it now as wait till I was dead. And there's enough left to see madam there through her schooling. And then that's that, except for my quarterly pension. Now, if you don't mind, I'll away to my room before I stiffen and die here, because that fire"—she turned her head towards the small amount of glowing coals in the large grate and, a twisted smile on her face, she ended—"they may have stopped the human sacrifices by that king on the Gold Coast, but if they lived in this part of the world I'm sure the poor beggars would prefer the stewpot."

And so saying and chuckling to herself, she walked smartly from the room, leaving, as she usually did, consternation behind her.

Nancy Ann watched her mother go quickly over to her father and, putting a hand on his arm, say in an undertone, "Do . . . do you think it's right, John, she has spent her all on . . . on the boys and . . . ?"

"If she says so, my dear, it is right. I . . . I never guessed. I . . . I didn't know what Father left her. I thought it must be a very substantial sum because she's been so generous." He looked into his wife's face. "She is generous, Rebecca. Underneath all her brusqueness she is generous and warm of heart."

Rebecca's head drooped, and in a low voice she said, "Yes, yes I know, John; and I also know that she considers me a very stupid being."

"No, no, my dear; it is only her manner."

"But I am a very stupid being, John."

"Oh, my lo . . ."

It seemed that for the first time they both became aware that their daughter was still present, and now they looked towards her and John said, "Would you leave us, Nancy Ann, please?"

Gulping in her throat, because now for some reason or other she wanted to cry, she had the urge to run to them and put her arms around them both, and hold them tightly to her; instead, she rose from the chair, saying quietly, "Yes, Papa," and hurried from the room.

It had been an afternoon threaded with emotion, emotion that had to be sorted out. She hurried now to her room and there, sitting on the end of the bed, she put her arms on the brass rail and leant her head against it. And in the quiet moments that followed she realized that she had never understood her mother and never loved her as much as she did at this moment. She would try, in future, to be good and always do what she was told, and never upset her.

It was four hours later, and her mother was still very upset, as was her father, and even her grandmama was asking, ''Why . . . why say such a thing?''

Nancy Ann was in the drawing-room again, and there they were, her mother and father and grandmama, as they had been in the afternoon, but the atmosphere was entirely different.

It should happen that in the vestry after conducting evening service, John had noticed that his churchwarden, Harry Mc-Keowan, was unusually silent. After a service it was Harry's custom to give a running commentary on who had been present and who absent and the reason for the latter, and how little or much had been put on to the offertory plate. But, this evening, he had not spoken, not even to comment on the main colour of the coins on the plate, for there were very few silver pieces shining amongst them. Feeling that his warden might be in some personal trouble and needing help, he said, ''Aren't you feeling well, Harry?''

''I'm as usual, Vicar.''

''Oh, I'm glad to hear that. But is there anything else wrong?''

''No, nothing wrong as you could say.'' The churchwarden had stroked his graying hair back from his temples, using the thumb pads of his plump hands. And having done this two or three times, he said, ''I've known your sons for a long time, Vicar.''

''Yes; yes, you have, all of twelve years since we came here from Gateshead.''

''And I happened to see them last Monday afore they left for the train, and wished them God-speed and a safe journey.''

"Yes, yes, you did, Harry; I was there. Now go on, tell me, what have they done that seems to have upset you?"

"Well." The man moved his stout body as if about to rock it; then his tone changing, he said, "Well, if not them, I would have thought you, Vicar, could have told me about Mr. James's coming wedding."

"What? What did you say?"

"I said . . . well, I think you heard what I said. It took the young miss to break the news to Eva. And I . . . well, I must be truthful, Vicar, it came as a bit of a shock, not only to her. Well, no, not only to her, but to us all. It's all right, it's all right, Vicar, don't trouble yourself like that." John had moved towards the table and, gripping the edge, had leaned over it. "I know what women are: 'tis likely your good lady wants to surprise the village with an engagement party or some such, and so persuaded Mr. James to keep quiet about it. Anyway, that's how I see it, and that's how I explained it to Eva, but nevertheless, it was a bit of a shock. Well, I'll go and finish my duties. Is there anything more you require of me, Vicar?"

It had taken an effort for John to say, "No. No thank you, Harry."

And now here he was confronting his daughter and asking for an explanation, and when in a tearful voice she gave it, she left him and the others quite dumbfounded. Then her father was speaking to her slowly and quietly, and as she looked at him she saw him in the pulpit again, for he was saying, "You know what you have done? You have lied deliberately in order to hurt someone. I am sure James never meant you to say such a thing, and you, in your heart, as young as you are, must have realized this. Why? What possessed you to such wickedness?"

The lump in her throat was almost choking her. She moved her head from side to side before muttering brokenly, "I . . . I didn't mean to hurt her. It . . . it was as I said, it . . . it was just to stop her thinking of James, and . . . and she was giving me the necklace as a sort of"—she gulped and sniffed and wiped the tears from each cheek with her fingers before she finished—"a sort of bribe, to get him to like her."

"You're almost thirteen years old, Nancy Ann; you should

know right from wrong by now. I'm disappointed in you. Go to your room.''

She was crying audibly now as she left the room.

When the door had closed on her they looked at each other. Then Jessica's body began to shake, and when her laughter became audible John remonstrated with her severely, saying, ''Mother!''

''Yes, yes, I know, she's put you in a fix, but it's funny when you think about it. And''—the laughter going from her voice, she ended—''as for that silly, flighty man-crazy girl, it's the best thing that could have happened. Because whether you've noticed it or not, John Howard, she's cow-eyed James every Sunday as far back as I can remember. And as for the older one, Jancy, if all tales are true, Farmer Boyle almost took a gun to her, because she was after his eldest and the lad was already promised and had been for three years. Now, John Howard, you take my advice and let things be as they are. If it gets round, which it will, that James is engaged, well and good. You write to him and, after laying into him, tell him to look round and put some truth into the rumour, but see that she's got a bit of money behind her. And—'' She looked at her daughter-in-law now, and a softer tone creeping into her voice, she said, ''And, Rebecca, remember, she is but a child still. But I'll say now, which I haven't up till this time, I agree with you that she needs direction of another kind from that given by her doting parents and her stupid grandmother.'' She nodded her head at herself. ''Your idea of school was a good one, and there is enough to see her through until she is sixteen or seventeen. Now, go on up to her. Be firm, but not too firm: you'll only have her another week, and then life will change for all of us.''

Almost on the point of tears now, Rebecca muttered, ''Thank you, Mother-in-law,'' before turning away and hurriedly leaving the room.

Jessica looked at her son. ''Why in the name of God!'' she said, ''did you ever want to become a parson, because your children are always going to disappoint you, for not one of them will ever become a saint.'' And all John could answer was simply, ''Oh, Mother.''

* * *

A week had passed. She had been kept in her room for the first two days with the strict order that she must not divulge to the maids why she was being punished; she was just to say she had told a lie. But today was her last Sunday at home. Yesterday, she had said goodbye to her friends in the village: Mrs. Taylor, from the grocers, had given her a box of candy; Mrs. Norton had given her a blue hair ribbon, and Mr. Norton, who had been sober, had said he would miss her face; Mary Jane Norton gave her an embroidered needle case; Miss Linda Waters, the dressmaker, had given her a velvet band for her hair; in fact, everybody had been so kind and seemed sorry that she was going away.

There had been no mention of her attending Sunday school, or the evening service. She had attended morning service and her father had preached a sermon on lying and the different forms it could take, such as deviousness. She had never heard that word before, but somehow she knew that it applied to her and what she had said to Miss Eva McKeowan.

With a little surprise she had noted that the gentry stalls had been almost full, at least that there were lots of servants in them, but no real gentry sitting in the high front pew, even though she knew that the master of Rossburn House was home and had a lot of friends with him. Later, she had asked her mama if she could go for a walk along by the river bank for the last time, and after some hesitation Rebecca had said, "Yes, but put your shower coat on because I think it could rain, and if it does, come straight home. You will, won't you?" It was put in the form of a request and she had answered, "Yes, Mama."

And so, here she was walking by the river bank. The water was grey and choppy; the sky was low and grey; the whole world was grey. She hadn't brought Gyp with her. Although he had whined when she had passed through the back gate, she had resisted the temptation to go to him and let him have one last run with her, because she didn't want anything more to happen that would upset her mother and father.

She had gone some distance when she decided to leave the river bank and go through the copse and so call in and say goodbye to Granny Burgess.

Granny Burgess was a very old lady, but she still looked

after herself: did her own housework and garden, and even made treacle toffee. She liked Granny Burgess. She was the only old person in the village and round about who, Peggy said, didn't expect you to go trudging through the snow, carrying soup to her in the winter, because she would always have her own broth pan on the hob and a ladleful for anyone who was passing.

She had no sooner reached the road than she heard the McLoughlins. She couldn't as yet see them but she recognized their raucous voices; and there was one thing she knew for certain, she mustn't meet up with them today. Apart from wearing her Sunday dress, she had on her shower coat and her second-best hat; her best, a brown straw, was being kept for the journey tomorrow.

But the McLoughlins were all fast runners and before she could retrace her steps again to the gate that led down to the river bank, they had come round the corner and espied her. And now they were whooping towards her and she knew that if she turned and ran down the river bank they would come after her, and the encounter could be fraught with more danger on the river bank. So she took a deep breath and held it for a moment as she walked slowly forward.

They had stopped now and were waiting for her, shoulder to shoulder across the road. This was their usual form of mustering for an attack.

She came to a stop in front of the eldest one who was just as tall as herself but twice as broad. The other children were small made, but all were wiry. Her mind was telling her that whatever she did, or whatever they did to her, she must not retaliate: it was her last day at home and she mustn't upset her mama and papa. Oh no. So, slightly to her disgust, she heard herself saying in a placating one, "Will you please let me pass?"

"Will ya please let me pass?" The eldest boy was mimicking her in a broad Irish accent. "Pass, she said, she wants ta pass." And he looked at his two brothers and two sisters lined up either side of him. The smallest girl standing at the end of the row could have been about seven years old and she was the only one who wasn't laughing.

Nancy Ann's lips began to tremble. She said a hasty little

prayer as the boy stepped closer to her. He was now within an outstretched arm from her and, putting his head on one side, he said, '' 'Tis true then what I'm hearin' that they're packin' ya off to a fancy school to make a lady out of ya?''

When she didn't answer, he turned his head towards the others, saying, ''She's lost her tongue. She didn't last time though, did she now? She was brave last time, wasn't she now? 'cos she was at the end of the village near the blacksmith's shop. An' what did she call us then?'' He nodded towards one brother, and the boy shouted, ''Scruffs.'' And the other one added, ''Dirty scruffs. That's what she called us, dirty scruffs.''

He was facing her again. ''Are we dirty scruffs, Miss Vicarage? Miss Parson's Prig? 'Cos that's what you are.'' His voice lost its banter now and his arm shot out and he pushed her as he added, ''A prig. A stuck up little nowt. A Protestant prig!''

''Don't do that!'' All placation had gone from her voice now: her face was tight, her whole body quivering.

''Who d'you think you are tellin' me what to do?'' His arm came out again and now pushed her so hard that she stumbled backwards and almost fell.

It wasn't to be borne. In a flash her doubled fist caught the boy on the side of the mouth; and the impact brought his lip sharply against his teeth and a trickle of blood ran down his chin.

In amazed silence the brothers and sisters stared at her for a moment; then came a loud chorus of, ''Get her, Mick! Let her have it, Mick!'' And as quick as her own fist had contacted his chin, so he was now pummelling her, or at least trying to, for only some of his random punches were finding a target, she was warding most off with her forearms.

This tactic seemed to infuriate the lad further, because he had his own method of fighting, a few punches, then get his arms around his opponent, bring his knee up and they were on their back. But the next moment he couldn't believe what was happening to him. Encouraged by the jeers and cries of his brothers and sisters, he had been about to clutch her when he felt a searing pain in his face and he imagined that his eye had been knocked out. But that was nothing to what he ex-

perienced when her knee caught him in the stomach and his
feet left the ground and the back of his head came in contact
with the stony road.

The children were all screaming now, the two girls kneeling by their brother, one of them crying, "Mick! Mick! Are
you all right, Mick?" And when Mick merely groaned, she
screamed, "Killed him, she has!" Then looking towards her
other two brothers, she commanded, "Get her!"

Nancy Ann wasn't prepared for the next move. The boys
weren't as big as their brother, but their impact and flailing
fists bore her to the ground.

So intent had they all been on the fight that they hadn't
noticed or heard the two horsemen galloping across the field
beyond the ditch at the other side of the road.

When the horses jumped the ditch there was something
akin to pandemonium in the road for the two boys scrambled
off their victim and ran to where their sisters were dragging
their brother to his feet.

"What is this, eh? What is this?" One of the riders had
dismounted, but no one answered him. He looked towards
the boy with the bleeding lip who was holding one hand to
his stomach and the other to an eye, and the eldest girl cried,
"She hit him. That one from the vicarage, she knocked him
out."

The rider now turned sharply when a small voice from
behind him said, "Mick hit her first."

"He did, did he?" He stared down on the child and her
large blue eyes looked up at him fearlessly as she said, "Aye,
Mister, he did. But she belted him right, left, an' centre, she
did at that, Mister."

"Shut that squawkin' mouth o' yours, Marie McLoughlin." Her bigger sister was now making for her, and the small
girl, rounding on her, shouted, "You lay a finger on me, our
Cathy, an' I'll tell me da."

While this was going on the other rider had dismounted
and raised Nancy Ann into a sitting position, and when he
asked, "Are you hurt?" she answered weakly, "I'm all right,
sir."

She wasn't all right, she was feeling battered all over.
Dazedly, she looked at one of her hands. It was tightly

clenched, and when slowly she opened it, it was to disclose a strand of brown hair. Quickly she flicked it from her, and the man who was holding her smiled and said, "Spoils of war. You should have kept it as a souvenir. Come on." And he assisted her to her feet, but finding that she was unable to stand, he put his arm around her shoulder and she leant against him. She felt dizzy. Her mind was muzzy. Then, her eyes were brought open by a raucous shout coming from somewhere behind her and the resulting consternation among the group standing a few yards in front of her.

" 'Tis our da comin' up from the river."

"Oh God Almighty!"

"He'll belt the daylights outta you, our Mick."

"He's had the daylights belted outta him."

"You shut up, our Marie, else when I get you on the quiet, I'll skin you."

"You and who else?"

This exchange among the McLoughlins was carried on in loud voices while they waited for their father to approach. And now here he was, doffing his cap to the two gentlemen and crying, "What have I here, sirs? What have I here? You've knocked them down?"

"No, McLoughlin." It was the man holding Nancy Ann who spoke. "We haven't knocked them down. More's the pity. It was this young girl here whom your son attacked, and in defending herself, she floored him. . . . Look at him."

"In the name o' God! Tell me me eyes are not seein'. You . . . you big lout!" The man was striding towards his son now who was still holding a hand to his eye. "Don't tell me. Aw, please God, don't tell me that you let the little chit from the vicarage knock you out. Oh, you gormless idiot, you!"

"She kneed me, Da." The words came as a mutter.

"She kneed you? Begod! I've heard it all. She kneed you, that bit lass? Then if she did, I'd like to shake her hand, an' after that I'm gonna kick your arse from here to the Crown and Anchor. . . . Get!"

They got, the older girl helping her brother, the younger boys walking behind, rubbing different parts of their anatomies as they went. Only the little girl stayed. Her face unsmiling, she looked to where the gentleman was leading the vicarage girl towards his horse and talking to her da as he did so. His voice was almost as loud as her da's, and he was saying, "I've warned you, McLoughlin, haven't I? And now for the last time. . . ."

"I'll belt him, sir, I will. I'll take it out of. . . ."

"Don't change the subject, McLoughlin; you know what I'm referring to. Birds, McLoughlin, birds. I hear they've thinned out."

"Never, sir. Never me, sir, your worship, your lordship."

"Shut up! Shut your mouth!" The man now turned to his friend saying, "Here, hold her a minute till I get up." And when he was mounted, he turned a hard glance down on the Irishman, saying, "One more time, McLoughlin, and you go along the line. Now that's my last word, understand?"

The man remained quiet for a moment. Then touching his cap, he said, "Good enough, sir. Good enough."

"Give her here." The rider bent over and caught Nancy Ann under the arms as his friend hoisted her up towards him.

There was a buzzing in Nancy Ann's ears and a strange aroma in her nose, a mixture of sweat, tobacco fumes, and leather mixed with a distinctive smell of horseflesh. Her body was being rocked and she found it soothing. She could go to sleep like this. . . .

Hilda Fenwick had just changed into a clean white apron preparatory to going downstairs to serve the afternoon tea when she happened to look out of the attic window. The window was in the back of the house which was only separated from the road by the kitchen garden, and was bordered by a low drystone wall. Behind this wall she could see the tops of two horsemen riding but there was something peculiar about one, yet something familiar. Quickly she pushed up the lower sash of the window and poked her head out. The road curved as it made its way to the front gate of the vicarage; then she exclaimed aloud, "Eeh! dear Lord!" The next minute she was flying from the room, down the attic stairs, along a passage and on to the main landing, then down the main staircase, and as she reached the hall she shouted, "Mistress! Mistress! Ma'am! Ma'am!" And at this she burst into the sitting-room and there startled its only occupant as she gabbled at her.

Rebecca had been sitting quietly reading but now she was on her feet, crying, "What did you say?"

" 'Tis true, ma'am, two horsemen and . . . and Miss Nancy Ann lying across the front of one of them."

Rebecca stared at her maid, wondering if the girl's mind had become deranged. Then she looked towards her husband standing by the door; and Hilda turned to him now, saying, " 'Tis right. They should be comin' up the drive now. She was half lyin' across the saddle."

Almost as soon as John reached the front door Rebecca was at his side, and they stood close together at the top of the steps open-mouthed watching the two riders come slowly towards them. And there was their daughter lying limp in the saddle being supported by none other than Mr. Dennison Harpcore.

Rebecca told herself, she wouldn't believe it, she wouldn't, she wouldn't: the child's things were all packed, the arrangements were made; the appointment at the school was for eleven o'clock tomorrow morning.

Nancy Ann was lifted carefully into the house and placed on the sitting-room couch. She wasn't unconscious, she hadn't fainted, but she wasn't fully aware of what was going on.

Dennison Harpcore had given an explanation of what he had seen to happen and he ended, "She may be slightly concussed. I would get the doctor to her to be on the safe side."

Rebecca forced herself to thank him for his services, and when he said, "Please don't thank me; it brought a little sauce to a very unappetizing Sunday. Although I would wish that she hadn't suffered in the process. Yet I can assure you she did not suffer half as much as her opponent. She must have put up a fight to floor that boy; he's a lout of a boy, a chip off the old block." He now turned and, glancing down on Nancy Ann, he commented, "She looks delicate, rather fragile, yet I understand she succeeded in delivering a black eye and a belly"—he coughed—"a stomach punch, with her knee. Of course"—he nodded now—"your two boys, or young men as they must be, they most likely have been her tutors. Where are they now?''

It was John who answered him, saying, ''They are both at Oxford.''

''Oxford! Oh, good, good. What are they taking?''

''My eldest is reading mathematics, the younger one, natural science.''

''Indeed! Indeed!''

John did not like the note of surprise in this visitor's tone; there was even a touch of condescension in his manner. He looked at the man. He hadn't seen him for two or three years. How old was he now? Nearing thirty, he imagined. He looked much older, the result of the life of dissipation that he led no doubt. He also noticed that Harpcore's friend hadn't spoken a word since he came in. He was much older than Harpcore, and both his silent manner and his look were supercilious.

Mr. Harpcore was bidding farewell to Rebecca, saying that he hoped the doctor would find nothing serious wrong with her daughter, other than perhaps a few bruises and, as he had suggested, slight concussion.

John accompanied the two men to the door where, he thanked Mr. Harpcore formally before making his way back across the hall to the sitting-room. But he was stopped halfway by the sight of his mother descending the stairs and asking loudly, ''What's all the narration about? There's horses on the drive; who's here?''

Without a word he waited for her to reach the bottom of the stairs; then taking her arm, he led her into the sitting-room and, still silent, he pointed towards the couch.

After she had been given the explanation why the horses were on the drive and her granddaughter lying with eyes closed on the couch, Jessica said, ''Well, she can't go tomorrow.''

''No.'' Rebecca rose from her chair and, looking at Jessica, she said, ''No, not tomorrow, Mother-in-law, but she must go.'' And Jessica said, ''Yes, I agree with you entirely: blacking eyes and kneeing people in the belly, no matter who they are, has got to be stopped. Oh, yes''—she inclined her head towards her daughter-in-law—''I agree with you.''

Yet, a few minutes later, sitting by the side of her granddaughter, both her son and daughter-in-law having left the room, he to send Johnny for the doctor, she to get Hilda to prepare the bed with a hot oven shelf, Jessica took the limp hand in hers and she muttered to herself, ''But Sundays will never be the same again.''

PART TWO

The Blossoming

❧ 1 ❧

"YOU ARE NOT SORRY YOU HAVEN'T GONE?"

"No, Grandmama."

"You sure?"

"Yes, Grandmama, very sure."

"You . . . you didn't like her very much, did you?"

"No, Grandmama, truthfully, I didn't. Did you?"

Jessica leant her grey head to one side and replied, "No, Nancy Ann, Truthfully, I didn't." Then they both smiled.

"But you would have made a very pretty bridesmaid."

"You think so, Grandmama?"

"Oh yes, yes."

"I'm gawky, Peggy says."

"Peggy!" Jessica almost spat. "What does she know about it? You're but fourteen yet and you're developing fast. Give you another couple of years or so and you'll be like I was at your age. And let me tell you—" She now leant forward, a mischievous grin on her face as she whispered, "I was something to look at in those days. You know I could have married a title."

"You could? Then why didn't you?"

"Oh"—Jessica leant back—"I was in love; I loved your grandfather then."

"Didn't you love him after?"

"Don't be cheeky, miss. Yes, of course I did. I loved him

55

till the day he died. I wonder if Miss Nicolette Hobson will be able to say the same of James.''

Nancy Ann made no reply, but if she had, her reply would have been, ''I doubt it, Grandmama.''

James had left university last year with a first class Honours Degree, and almost immediately had been offered a position to teach in a school in Bath. While at university he had made friends with a John Hobson, and for the past two years had spent weeks of his summer vacation at his home, which happened to be part of a large private school of which his father was headmaster. John Hobson had a sister. She was of the same age as James, and apparently their courtship had started immediately. He had returned home in the Easter vacation of '78 to say that he was going to propose marriage to Miss Nicolette Hobson. At that time Nancy Ann recalled she had greeted this news with pleasure, for it seemed to prove that her lying had not been a lie after all. But from her first meeting with Miss Nicolette Hobson she had asked herself how James could possibly love her: she wasn't pretty, she wasn't even smart, but what she proved to them all to be, and within a very short time of entering the vicarage, was that she was a highly intelligent and knowledgeable young woman who knew her own mind and what she wanted; and it was apparent she wanted James. As her grandmama had said after their first meeting, ''She talked at him as if they were already married, and the fool of a boy seemed to like it.''

James was being married today and her mother and father had made the journey to Somerset, reluctantly, it would seem, on her mother's part, for Nancy Ann knew her mama was vexed that her daughter had not been asked to act as a bridesmaid, an honour being enjoyed by two of Nicolette's younger sisters and two cousins.

Peter was acting as James's best man, and he had said to her yesterday morning, before he left, that his heart wasn't in it, and it was a shame she wasn't coming. But she had assured him that she didn't mind in the least. And this was true. Also that somebody had to stay at home to see to Grandmama.

She now looked at the clock on the sitting-room mantelpiece. It had just struck three and Jessica, following her gaze, said, "Yes, it will be over by now. We have lost James. Oh, yes, yes." She nodded her head vigorously towards Nancy Ann. "Don't let us delude ourselves. That young madam will do her best to sever the ties with this end of the country, let me tell you." She wagged her finger at Nancy Ann, saying, "I know women. Oh, I know women." Then, her voice changing and her expression softening, she said, "I only hope, my dear, I'll live to see your wedding day, and from this house. Oh yes, I pray the good God will spare me till then."

"Oh! Grandmama, my wedding day? Me getting married? I shall never marry. I'm not . . . well, not that type."

"Oh! When did you come to this conclusion?"

"Well, Belle . . . you know, Belle Tollington, my friend at school, she says there are types that marry and types that don't."

"Stuff and nonsense! And I suppose she says you're not the type?"

"Well . . . well, I feel, Grandmama. . . ."

"Oh, shut up! And that Belle wants a strap to her backside, that's what she wants. How old is she?"

"She's nearly fifteen, like me."

"Well, my dear, the quicker you get a new friend the better. You will marry and you'll marry early if you're wise. Now some two years ago, I might have agreed with that Miss Belle." She laughed now. "Remember the day you had your fight with the McLoughlins? Well, I nearly gave you up myself on that particular Sunday. Eeh! my! The parson's daughter giving the McLoughlin hooligan a black eye and kneeing him in the stomach. Oh, you can laugh. It's funny now. And oh"—she flapped her hand—"I remember when I related it to the boys Peter actually rolled on the floor. Apparently it was he who had shown you how to use your knee. Wasn't it?"

"Yes, it was, like the wrestlers do." Nancy Ann laughed. "But it was James who showed me how to use a straight left."

"Anyway, you've grown out of all that. Praise be. That school has worked a small miracle on you. In the curriculum it said they turned out young ladies, and it's no lie."

"Oh, Grandmama, huh!"

Nancy Ann's derisive "huh!" caused Jessica to say, "What do you mean, huh!? Well, they do, don't they?"

"You should see some of them in the dormitory tearing each other's hair out, rolling about. My affray with Mick McLoughlin was child's play."

"You don't mean that. It's another one of your tales."

"I do, Grandmama, it's true. It nearly always happens towards the end of term. It's frustration; it builds up over the weeks. It's mostly with the girls who can't go home at all. Well, say, with one that can't go home. Her parents are abroad, or some such, and she's always talking about her home life. I've often wanted to bring Eileen Talbot home. But . . . but then I thought Mama has enough to do, and she hasn't been well."

"No, no, you're right there. I'm worried at times about your mama. She hasn't been well, as you say, but when you ask her how she's feeling, she always says she's quite all right. But the flesh is dropping off her. I'm going to have a word with Doctor McCann shortly about her. Well now, look, the day's still bright, go out and get some air, make the best of it. Take Gyp with you; he doesn't get much exercise these days, he's getting fat; only don't go down by the river with him on your own."

"Why not, Grandmama?" She was standing by her grandmother's chair now, and Jessica, lifting her hand, slapped at the thin arm, saying, "Why not, Grandmama? in that innocent tone of voice! Remember what happened one Sunday afternoon when you took him along there?"

"Oh, that!" She smiled now. "I'd forgotten about that, it's so long ago."

"Yes," Jessica mimicked, "oh, so long ago, all of two years in fact, a lifetime. Go on with you now, only keep to the road. And I mean that, because if anything happened I couldn't cope. . . ."

"Oh! Grandmama. Really, you make me feel awful, you know; it is as if you imagine I go out looking for trouble."

"I'm sorry, my dear, I am sorry, for you've been so good of late. Your mama and papa are really proud of you. And they are delighted with your school reports. At least they are now." She pulled a face. "Those they received during that first year. . . . Oh dear! Do you remember? When you didn't settle in and had to be kept down. But what I mean, my dear, is I feel I'm responsible for all that happens in the house until they come back. You understand?"

"Yes, yes, of course, Grandmama. Don't worry, put your mind at ease. I'll just go towards the old toll gate; I'll not even go in the direction of the village and certainly not"—she now moved her head from side to side—"anywhere near the McLoughlins." Then laughing again, she added, "It's funny about the McLoughlins, isn't it? I can pass them on the road now and nothing happens; in fact they give me a wide berth. Remember last Christmas when Mr. McLoughlin gave me a rabbit? He had a sackful of them and he pulled one out of the top like a conjurer might out of a hat, and said, 'There, missie, that's for you. You're a grand lass. You are that.' "

She had dropped into the stance and accent of the Irishman and caused her grandmother to let out a bellow of a laugh, and as she dried her eyes she said, "You know, you have a gift there, keep practising it. One day you could entertain with it."

"I'll do that, ma'am, I will, I will. 'Tis yourself I will pleasure. I will, I'll practice it, honest to God!" Almost before the last words were out of her mouth she put her hand tightly over it; then turned and hurried from the room, closing the door behind her. But in the hall she could still hear her grandmama laughing, and as she took her coat out of the hall wardrobe she thought, Yes, I'll do what Grandmama says. I will . . . I will practice at it. It's the only accomplishment I seem to have.

She pulled on her coat, then went to take her straw hat from the shelf above, but her hand stayed on it: Why should she wear it; she hated hats. She loved the wind through her hair and there was quite a breeze blowing today. Her mother and father weren't here, there was no one to chastise her for going outside with her head uncovered, and anyway, she was just going along the road.

She went out through the side door and ran to Gyp where he was tethered as usual to the wall, and she endeavoured to silence his hysterical barking as she undid him. Then she was running through the gate and into the paddock, the dog bounding round her. In the middle of the field she stopped, slightly out of breath, and as she stood gasping while looking up into the sky there swept through her a feeling such as she had never before experienced. It came like lightning flashing, only it whirled upwards from the pit of her stomach and seemed to corkscrew out of the top of her head, lifting her from the ground. And now she was running again. Or was she dancing? The dog was barking its loudest as it raced away from her and raced back again. She came to a stop near the railings that bordered the field and as she leant over them the feeling seeped down through her and seemed to drain away through her legs.

She turned her back to the railing and became limp for a moment. She was breathing deep and slowly. She had never before felt like that: it was, she thought, as if she had only in those moments become alive. Was this what they called joy? It had come and gone so quickly, yet her mind retained the essence of it, and she told herself she would never forget this moment, this thing that had made her feel beautiful for a flashing space in the middle of the meadow.

Her hair ribbon had come loose and was dangling from the bottom of her four curls. Always when she was at home she put her hair into roller rags at night, but at school she had to plait her hair. It was long, thick and wavy and reached down below her shoulder blades; its colour was chestnut brown, and she knew it was nice. She considered it the only thing she possessed in the way of attraction, although Belle said, when she would later have to put it up she would have trouble with it because it was too coarse to fall into shape.

Gyp was foraging in the grass and she called him to her, saying now, "Behave yourself. We're going to walk along the road. And don't forget you are now being attended by a young lady. Do you hear me?" She laughed at herself and resisted the desire to run once more, for the road was now in sight.

At the end of the field railings there was only a shallow ditch to be jumped, and then she was walking along the road, the dog trotting sedately by her side as if he really had taken his cue from her.

She was nearing a part of the road where it narrowed and turned sharply towards the old turnpike gate long since demolished, and with the keeper's cottage in ruins to the side. This often provided habitation for tramps who had stripped most of the wood away from the building to make fires. But she had promised her grandmother she didn't intend to go as far as that today, and so she was on the point of turning about when, above the noise of the wind that was swaying the trees along the edge of the wood to the left side of her, she heard the sound of a horse's hoofs. She had actually turned round in the direction of home when she swung back again to see coming towards her, and at a terrifying rate from around the corner, a high dogcart driven by a woman. The horse was almost on top of her when with a scream and one swooping action she grabbed at the dog and took him with her headlong into the ditch.

There had been rain during the night and although there was no water lying, the grass and silt at the bottom was soggy, and as she lay gasping on top of the dog she knew she wasn't hurt, nor it, but she also knew she was angry, in fact, consumed with anger, blazing with it. It was as strong as the wonderful feeling that she had experienced in the field only minutes earlier.

Clawing her way out of the ditch, she stood in the roadway and looked to where the woman had pulled the horse to a standstill and when the voice, in a high-falutin tone, came to her, saying, "Are you all right?" she screamed at her, "Yes, of course I'm all right. You have just about run me down. You are an idiot. That's what you are." She had moved forward and was standing now glaring up into the face that hung above hers. It was a soft-skinned, plump face, topped by a high red velvet bonnet to match the velvet suit that had a white ruffle at the neck, and the neck of the wearer was fat.

"You don't know how to drive a cart; you shouldn't be allowed on the road."

"How dare you speak to me like that."

"I dare, and if I'd been dead, somebody would have said to you: how dare you drive like a madwoman! And look at your poor horse." She stepped to the side and pointed to the animal. It was in a lather. "There should be a law forbidding people like you being in charge of an animal. And look at me!'' She pointed to the streaks of mud on her light alpaca coat, and to the shoes covered with mud.

''You should not have been meandering in the middle of a road. It is a public road.''

''Yes, that's what it is, a public road for all peoples, not for maniacs.''

''Who are you?''

''Never mind who I am, who are you? Because I intend to make a complaint against you.'' Dear, dear. She closed her eyes for a moment and put out her hand and grasped the wheel of the cart. She felt dizzy. Was it going to be a repeat of the McLoughlins' business?

At this point another dogcart came round the bend and when it was brought to a stop, the man driving it called, ''You must have gone hell for leather and come over the field. That's cheating, Rene.''

Nancy Ann's dizziness ebbed, and it was she who answered the newcomer, shouting, ''Yes, she went hell for leather, and nearly killed me and the dog. You want to give her lessons in driving. Come on, Gyp!'' She called to the dog, and now began to walk past the dogcart, but when she came to the horse's head she stopped and pointed to it and, looking back at the infuriated face of the lady, she said, ''Look! Poor thing, it's foaming at the mouth.'' Then squaring her shoulders, she walked away, attempting to keep to a beeline although her legs were trembling so much that she wanted to drop down on to the grass verge and rest a while.

The man drove his cart closer to the young woman's side now, saying, ''What was all that about?'' And she, her deep blue eyes blazing, replied, ''She fell into the ditch as I came round the corner. Insolent little slut! Who is she? Do you know?''

''How should I know! you are here more often than me.''

''She's the parson's daughter.'' The voice came from the bank bordering the wood, and there jumped down into the road a tall man carrying a gun. And the woman addressed him, saying, ''Parson's daughter? How do you know, Larry?''

Before the man could answer the man in the other dogcart put in, "Oh, Larry knows everything and everyone."

"Yes, yes, you could say that." There was a coolness in the tone and it had an ominous ring. And this for the man in the other dogcart seemed to close the matter for he turned his horse about and trotted it off. But the woman continued to look at the man with the gun who was now standing close to her, and she said, "The same one I suppose that you tell me the tale about being a miniature Amazon?"

"The very same one, although she's grown somewhat and looks promising from what view I had of her."

"Well, parson's daughter or no, she's an uncouth little slut and wants putting in her place. I'll see Dennison as soon as I get back. He should do something, and I'll see that he does."

The man smiled into the round furious blue eyes now and, his voice still cool, he said, "Yes, I would do that, Mrs. Poulter Myers. Yes, I would do that."

"Oh, you!" She flounced round in the seat, jerked sharply at the reins, crying, "Get up! there," then turned the horse and dogcart in the narrow road, almost backing into the ditch as she did so; following which, she wielded the whip and once again sent the animal into a gallop. And the man standing in the road pursed his lips, raised his eyebrows, nodded to himself, then jumped the ditch and re-entered the wood.

"Oh, Grandmama, I'm sorry, not for what I said to her, but that somehow . . . well, I've seemed to slip back. I actually used a swear word: it was as if I'd never learnt anything at school; I . . . I could have been one of the McLoughlins. I know I was rude but . . . but I was furious. And you know, Grandmama, I . . . I could have killed Gyp, because in holding him so I fell on him."

"You could have also broken your neck, child."

"Yes, yes, perhaps."

"What swear word did you use?"

"I said, hell for leather! Like Pratt says it."

"My! My! 'Tis well your mama isn't here." Jessica pressed her lips together and closed her eyes. Then she added, "How are you feeling now?"

"Better, since Peggy gave me the cordial."

"Oh, yes, her cordial, you would feel better. I'll have to have a word with Peggy about her cordial. Did she give you much of it?"

"Oh, just a drop in the bottom of the glass, and then she filled it up with hot tea."

"Well, now, sit yourself down there quietly and be thankful you're in one piece. I wish your parents were back. You are a responsibility. Do you know that, Nancy Ann?"

"No, I'm not really, Grandmama. What I mean is, who was to know that was going to happen? There was I, walking quietly along the road, about to turn for home, when she comes round that corner. And oh, that poor horse! *That poor horse!*"

"Never mind that poor horse. It would have been poor you if you hadn't been able to jump quick enough, by the sound of it. That horse could have trampled you."

She did not answer but she thought, Yes, yes, it could. I could have been dead or badly crippled. So, no, I'm not going to be sorry for what I said. Grandmama's right, I could have been dead. For a moment she wished she was back at school; it was much safer there. Anyway, you were protected from madwomen who didn't know how to drive. . . . And she was fat, wasn't she? So fat for a young woman! . . .

They'd had a lovely dinner. Jessica didn't ask from where the pheasants came: she knew that Peggy, although not even a distant relation of the McLoughlin man, considered him in kinship, because, as she said, and often, they had both come from the old country and that made them kin under the skin. Moreover, both their feet were dry and they had no intention of paddling back across . . . the water. In other words, as translated by Hilda, they both knew where they were well off.

The meal had begun with soup; then the pheasant, with potatoes, and cabbage, and buttered parsnips, followed by apple pie and cream, and, of all things at a dinner, homemade biscuits, and cheese. When that was finished, what did Hilda say? "Shall I serve your coffee in the sitting-room, ma'am?" And Jessica had answered, "Thank you, Hilda, that would be very nice."

They were now sitting one at each side of the fire in the

sitting-room drinking their coffee. And they smiled at each other, slightly wicked smiles because they both knew that such a repast would never have come their way in the everyday course of events: on Christmas Day perhaps, but on no other.

It was towards eight o'clock that Jessica noticed her granddaughter's head was leaning against the side of the winged chair and that her eyes were closed, and she sat studying her as she thought: She'll be somebody someday, that's if she can control her temper. And now she smiled to herself, then said softly, "Nancy Ann."

"Oh, yes, Grandmama?"

"I should go to bed if I were you."

"Yes, yes, I will, I'm feeling a little tired and"—she patted her stomach—"packed full. It was a lovely meal, wasn't it?"

"Yes, it was indeed, a lovely meal. We had our own wedding party. Tomorrow morning you must go to the kitchen and thank the girls."

"Oh, I will. Yes, I will."

Jessica did not need to suggest that she should keep her mouth shut when her parents returned; that would have been an insult to this child.

"Are you coming up too, Grandmama?"

"No, my dear, not yet. I would like to sit here and read for a while, because for once we've got a decent fire on." She pulled a face which Nancy Ann copied.

"Turn up the lamp wick for me." She motioned to the table near the end of the couch, then added, "Come, kiss me, then off you go."

Nancy Ann not only kissed her grandmama, but put her arms tightly around her neck and hugged her for a moment, before she hurried from the room.

Left alone, Jessica stared into the fire, and her voice just a mutter, she said, "Dear God! Let me live to see her settled. And don't lay on her the fate of so many only daughters who sacrifice themselves to their aging parents, particularly vicarage ones."

She did not read, but continued to sit quietly, and the pictures in the fire led her back down her life. But she told herself she would not have a day altered, except for one thing, and that concerned her son. Until the day she drew her last breath, she would never understand what had made him choose the ministry.

When the door opened suddenly and Hilda hurried up the room, she thought, She's wanting to get cleared away. Doesn't she remember that they won't be back until tomorrow night?

"Ma'am."

"Yes, Hilda?"

"There's a gentleman called."

"A gentleman?" Jessica pulled herself up straight in the chair. "A gentleman, at this hour? Who?"

Hilda swallowed deeply, then bent down and whispered, " 'Tis Mr. Harpcore himself. He . . . he wants to speak to you."

Jessica allowed some seconds to pass before she said, "Well. Well, show him in."

As she watched Hilda scurrying from the room, she thought, I didn't hear the knocker; I must have dozed off. She stroked down her hair, adjusted the lace cap that she wore on special occasions, quickly picked up a book from the table and put it on her lap, then waited.

The door opened again and Hilda announced in an overloud voice, "Mr. Harpcore, ma'am."

As the man entered the room, he glanced about him for a moment, then came swiftly towards her and, extending his hand, he said, "I'm sorry to disturb you at this late hour, Mrs. Hazel, but just a short while ago I heard that one of my guests had been the cause of your granddaughter's having to . . . well, jump into a ditch to save herself from being run down. I . . . I do hope she is none the worse."

"Take a seat, Mr. Harpcore." She pointed to the one that Nancy Ann had vacated earlier. And she watched him flick back the tails of his long coat, pull each side of his trouser leg slightly up above the knee, and seat himself halfway into the chair. Then they were looking at each other.

It was Jessica who spoke first, saying. "This is your second visit to the vicarage, Mr. Harpcore, and both on account of my granddaughter's escapades, although I don't think she can be blamed for what happened today. Yet I understand, even from herself, that she was . . . well, to put it mildly, some-what rude.''

He now answered her smile with his own as he said, ''I . . . I wouldn't call it rudeness, more like retaliation justly deserved, which I understand left my guest at a loss for words.''

''Yes, it would do.'' Jessica nodded her head now. ''I'm afraid that is her one failing, in my eyes, anyway, her very quick temper. Fortunately, it subsides as quickly as it rises, but it is something to be encountered when at its height. . . . You know she has been away to school for some time past?''

''No, no, I wasn't aware of that.''

''Oh, yes, yes.'' Jessica nodded proudly now, and went on. ''She is a boarder at the Dame school in Durham, and I would have said until three o'clock this afternoon that they had done a very good job on her, filing down her rough edges. Yet, when she came in mud-bespattered, I realized it was all wishful thinking on my part.''

''Oh, no, I wouldn't say that. She was provoked. And I understand, too, from one of the grooms, that the horse the lady was driving home is in a pretty rough state and will need rest for a day or two. So, I think your granddaughter was justified in anything she said, and I just wanted you to know that I'm sorry it happened, but relieved that there is no real damage done.''

''Thank you. It was most kind of you to come. I'm sorry my son and wife are not here to greet you. You see, my eldest grandson is being married today down in Somerset.''

''Oh, really? Really? I remember the boy. He was. . . .'' He paused, and she put in, ''James.''

''Yes, yes, James. How old is he now?''

''Twenty-three.''

''I understood he and his brother were at Oxford. But he must be down by now.''

''Yes, yes, last year. He passed . . . with honours?'' She wasn't quite sure if that was the term.

''Really? What class? A first?''

That was it. She nodded now, ''Yes, he got a first, and Peter too is doing well. And if—'' she brought her head slowly forward now and repeated, ''And if there were such careers for women, I'm sure that Nancy Ann would equal her brothers because she is very bright.''

"Yes, yes, I am sure she is.''

She watched him now rise slightly then settle back into the chair. For a moment she had thought he was about to take his leave. She stared at him. How old was he now? Oh—she did a quick reckoning in her head—over thirty. Oh, yes. But not all that much, perhaps thirty-two. He wasn't all that tall, about the same height as Peter. And what was Peter? Five foot seven or eight? But he was well built, rather thickish; his hair was dark brown, yet his eyes looked light, which was a strange contrast; they were greyish, she supposed. He had a full-lipped mouth, and strong-looking teeth. His complexion wasn't very good: it was likely the life he led with women and drink. And then there was his gambling. He was noted for that. He spent a lot of his time in London, it was said, just gambling. And also, she had heard a little while back through Peggy, who was in touch with the assistant cook up there, another one of the Irish breed, that he had a mistress and she was a married woman who didn't live twenty miles away in Northumberland. Yet, looking at him, who would guess he was such a roué? He was so polite and his manner was kindly . . . warm. She could see where his attraction lay. There was something about him that stirred even her cold blood. But why, if he needed women so badly, didn't he get himself a wife? She said now, ''Are you intending to stay long, I mean in your home?''

"Just another week or so, then I'm going to Scotland for the shoot. I . . . I have a little place up there.''

Yes, she had heard about the little place he had in Scotland, almost as big as his house here, it was said. Her feeling became bitter for a moment as she thought of the fortune it must take to run those two places, not forgetting his house in London, and here was her John Howard barely able to feed them on the pittance that he received from the church. If it hadn't been for her own money these past few years they would have had short commons, and the boys, clever as they were, would never have made Oxford. As for the staff, there would have been one little runaround. Yet, here was this man keeping three houses going and a mighty staff in each just for himself and his pleasures.

Her embittered thinking was interrupted by the door bursting open and there, running up the room, came the subject of their conversation. And as Jessica uttered her name in surprise, the tone holding a reprimand, Dennison Harpcore rose swiftly from his chair and looked at the girl who was now gaping open-mouthed at him.

He was seeing a slim figure in a long white nightgown partly covered by a knee-length dressing-gown of an indistinguishable colour, except to call it a muddy grey, and from her head down each side of her cheeks and on to the dressing gown there hung three long corkscrew ringlets, and what made them noticeable was that from below her ears they were entwined with strips of rag. The cream coloured skin on the oval shaped face looked stretched, as indeed it was, because the eyes were wide and the jaw dropped.

Jessica had also risen to her feet and she said, "This is Mr. Harpcore. He . . . he has called about the incident this afternoon. He wondered if you were all right." She hesitated whether to say, "Go back to your bed, child," or "Come here, child," because there she was attired in her nightie and looking at this moment less than her age. And when, having told herself that this man was old enough to be her father, she managed to say, "Come here, child," Nancy Ann did not obey the order, but, hugging her dressing-gown around her, said, "I only came down to tell you—" She did not finish what she had to relate, but looking from her grandmother to the visitor, she said, "I'm all right, sir. And . . . and I'm sorry I was rude to your guest."

He took a step to the side but not towards her as he said, "You have no need to apologise. My guest was at fault, and through her thoughtlessness you could have been badly hurt." Smiling now, he added, "We seem to meet only on occasions of disaster."

"Yes, sir." Within the circle of the lamplight he looked to her to be very big, very broad, very dark . . . very . . . there was something else she couldn't put a name to. It wasn't frightening, yet it wasn't pleasant. Of a sudden she said, "Good night, sir," then forgetting all she had learnt at school about decorum, how a young lady should enter and leave a room, especially if there was company in it, she ran out of it.

Jessica looked towards the man. He was staring towards the door and smiling. Then he turned to her and said, "She has grown considerably since we last met. She seemed such a little child then."

"She is still a child"—there was a stiffness in Jessica's tone—"she is but fourteen." She did not say "coming up fifteen," as Nancy Ann herself would have said.

"Is that all? I . . . I would have thought she was older."

"No, that is all, she is but fourteen, and has another three years at school, by which time"—her tone altered—"I hope she will have learned to control her temper."

"That would be a pity, I think, if she became typed. Don't you agree?"

She thought for a moment, then said, "She is of a turn of character that I doubt will ever conform to type."

"Well, I hope so. So many young ladies today are turned out to pattern; you can't tell one from the other. But I must not keep you, and I must add another apology for calling upon you so late in the evening."

He held out his hand and she took it, saying, "I've been very pleased to meet you." Then she added on a laugh, "Formally. I remember when I first came to live here with my son I saw you in church one Sunday morning, but only once." She now pulled a slight face, and he lowered his eyelids, and bent his head and there was a light touch of mockery in his voice as he said, "I'm afraid I am a great sinner." But when she answered, "I'm sure you are speaking the truth there," he lifted his head sharply and laughed aloud; then bending towards her, he said softly, "I am sure you and I would get along very nicely were we to meet frequently." And at this she surprised him again by saying, "I don't know about that."

His laughter was louder now as he said, "That last statement proves that I am right." His manner changing suddenly, he looked at her for a moment without speaking, then said, "So few people speak the truth while looking into your face. Your friends never; even your enemies do it behind your back."

She watched him now bow towards her, then step back from her before turning away and walking slowly from the room.

She stood where she was until she heard Hilda say, "Good night, sir," and the front door close.

When she resumed her seat by the fire, she looked into the flames and asked herself why bad men were always so attractive.

⚮ 2 ⚮

NANCY ANN DID NOT STAY AT SCHOOL FOR ANOTHER THREE years; she left when she was sixteen. She refused absolutely to stay on for another year, knowing that her mother was ill.

Six months previously Rebecca had collapsed. She had been coughing quite a lot of late, in fact, she'd had what she referred to as a ticklish cough for some years, but she had refused to find out the cause. Even when Doctor McCann, on John's request, had offered to give her, what he called a run-over, she had indignantly refused. And then came the day when she collapsed and Doctor McCann did examine her. For some time he'd had his suspicions that she was suffering from tuberculosis, and this was confirmed. But it wasn't the main cause of her collapse. His examination showed her heart to be in a very bad state, and he ordered immediate rest. If she did not obey his orders, he said, there would be nothing for it but to put her into a sanatorium, which brought a reaction from her of more firmness than he had imagined she possessed: Never! Never would she go into a sanatorium. Anyway, she was needed at home.

And at home she stayed: at first protesting, albeit inwardly, then gradually becoming resigned to the fact that the time she had left to her was limited.

The breakfast-room had been turned into a bedroom. It was the most pleasant room on the ground floor, as it had a

French window leading out into a small conservatory, this in turn showing a stretch of lawn bordered by the low stone wall beyond which was the road.

A single bed was placed at one side of the room, but fronting the entrance to the conservatory was a couch, and it was on this that Rebecca spent most of her days. And when the weather was fine the outer door of the conservatory was opened so she could see people passing along the road, and perhaps the occasional carriage or rider. A number of villagers, especially when on their way to church on a Sunday, would pause at the wall and wave to her, and she would wave back even if she couldn't make out who they were.

Nancy Ann had her sixteenth birthday on the ninth of January, eighteen eighty; she left school at the end of the Easter term. Now it was September and she had been acting as part nurse and housekeeper for the past six months, and but for the reason of her new role she would have said she was happy to be at home. This is what she repeatedly told herself, for up to the beginning of the year she'd had the idea of following her brother's footsteps—not, of course, going to Oxford, but going to one of the new training colleges that fitted young ladies to become teachers. Miss Craster, head of the Dame school, had encouraged her ideas along this line. But apparently it wasn't to be.

Her disappointment was somewhat modified when she had a talk with James who, on hearing of his mother's illness, had paid a quick visit to see her. He had not been accompanied by his wife and, of course, this was natural as she was now carrying his second child. But what he said to her about teaching was, "I shouldn't worry about missing such a career, for it isn't all milk and roses; it is very nerve-racking at times. Likely, I shall get used to it. I'm new to it, I admit, but. . . ."

He had stopped there. She had been troubled about James. She didn't think he was as happy as he should be, and this seemed to be borne out when, on the point of leaving, he looked around the hall and said, "I never realized how happy I was here, Nancy Ann. All my young days it seemed to be a cold house without much comfort; I didn't take into account the love that was in it. We all helped each other, didn't we?

And we had fun." Then he had smiled and said, "Who would have thought, in those days, when you were a fighting, punching little termagent that you would blossom into . . . well, now look at you, a beautiful young lady."

"Oh, James." She had flapped her hand at him, saying, "Don't tease. Beautiful young lady indeed!"

"All right, you are not a beautiful young lady." He had put his arms around her, and they had hugged each other. And she had been on the point of tears when she said, "I love you. We all love you. Be happy, James."

Only this morning they had heard that James had another son, and here they were talking about the event. She was arranging some late roses in a vase on a side table to the head of her mother's couch. Her grandmama sat at the foot plying her needle on a small embroidery frame. She had just said, "Well, they are coming thick and fast; they are wasting no time." And when her mother had replied, "I think it's better to have them when you are young," she thought how strange it was that they could talk so in front of her. Her mother's illness had seemed to change everyone in the house. Her grandmama had suddenly become quite agile, and she nearing seventy. She didn't have her fire lit in her room until the evening now, and spent most of her time in this room, and even insisted on taking her turn at the nursing. And strangely, she seemed to have got her hearing permanently back for there had been times in the past when she would apparently endure periods of deafness. She smiled at herself at the thought. Then there was the changed relationship between the two women: the antagonism that had lain under the surface for years had vanished; they had become close, they talked or sat silent together. She had come into the room one day last week and was surprised to see her grandmama patting her mother's hand. They had been talking, but the conversation stopped abruptly as she entered the room, and she guessed that their topic had been herself.

Only yesterday her mother had asked her a question that had left her absolutely tongue-tied for a moment. She had said, "Nancy Ann, do you ever think of marriage?"

When she had got over her surprise, she had said, "Marriage, Mama? Me? No, I don't honestly think I do. Well," she confessed now, "once or twice I have. When I saw Elsie Ridley married last month, I suppose I wondered then if I would ever get married, but I doubt I ever will; in fact, I'm sure I never shall."

"What makes you so sure?"

"Well whom do I know, Mama? Who would want to marry me? There are Farmer Reynolds' two sons, but one's married to the sheep and the other to the cows; and they are old, well over twenty."

She was so pleased when she saw her mother laugh. She liked to make her laugh. And when she had added, "Of course, there's always Mick McLoughlin. Now I know he has his eye on me," her mother had put her hand to her chest and had started to cough, spluttering, "Oh, Nancy Ann. Nancy Ann."

When her coughing bout was over and she had got her breath back enough to speak, she said, " 'Tis very funny about that boy McLoughlin. He was the one you fought with, wasn't he, on what was to be your last Sunday at home before you went to school, remember? And there he is, your papa says he has turned out quite smart. Of course, it is since Mr. Mercer took him into his service. Your father says he looks very presentable in his livery. In a way it just shows you, there's no one so lowly that cannot be risen up if given the chance."

It was her grandmama's voice that startled her now, saying, "Would you like to go to a ball, Nancy Ann?"

"A ball?" She put the last flower in the vase, then turned and looked at her grandmama, repeating, *"A ball?"*

"That's what I said, a ball; Peter is thinking of going to one in Newcastle. You can dance, can't you?"

"Oh, yes, I can dance. I have proof of that because our singing mistress once remarked to me that what music I had was in my feet. . . . But would I like to go to a ball?" She considered for a moment. "Yes and no. I've never been to a ball. Farmer Ridley's barn dance, yes, and I got my shins kicked." Quickly now she went into a mime and, assuming the posture of a stout man, she pulled an imaginary waistcoat down, then the cuffs of her coat, squared her shoulders, and, walking over to face her grandmama and with her toes turned outwards, she bent towards her and said in a deep country burr, "How would you like to take the floor with me, missie, eh?" And as her grandmama, laughing aloud, pushed her away, she went into an imaginary dance with the farmer: one, two, three, hop; one, two, three, hop. She danced into the conservatory. Her right hand held high on the imaginary shoulder, she hopped and stumbled until her grandmama's voice came at her sharply, crying, "No more! No more!" and she stopped abruptly and ran back to her mother who was gasping for breath, her hand pressed to her side.

"Oh, Mama, I'm sorry."

After a moment, Rebecca relaxed into her pillow, saying, "Don't be sorry . . . child . . . because—" She now turned her face to look at her mother-in-law, adding as she pulled at the air, "I don't think I've laughed so much in my life as I have done these past few months." Then patting her daughter's hand, she said, "You have a gift, dear. You have a gift."

"My only one, sadly," Nancy Ann now said in a low voice.

"Nonsense!" It was her grandmama's strident tones, and she turned to her and said, "Yes, yes, of course, Grandmama, it's nonsense: I can sing like a corncrake, play the pianoforte like Beethoven, talk rapidly in French, and sparkle in company; in fact, I'm so sought-after for parties and soirées that I now have to rush and see to my staff before my maid gets to work on me for my dinner tonight at the Manor."

"Well, you could sparkle in company, miss, if you so wished. Why, with a tongue like yours, you don't let it rattle on such occasions I'll never know."

"Nor shall I, Grandmama. Nor shall I. Oh." She turned and looked towards the conservatory window, crying now, "There's The House carriage again. I wonder what he's sending you this time? Can't be strawberries, they're over, and the girls have made enough conserve to last for years. Peaches are over too, and the apples are not quite ripe. I hope it's something this time we can get our teeth into, say, half a sheep, or a sirloin of beef; I'd even accept a brace of pheasants."

"Oh! Nancy Ann, how can you? He has been so kind."

"Yes, he has." She pulled a face at her mother.

And he had. He was likable in a way and she could talk to him quite ordinarily, that is when he was on his own, but should he be accompanied by his friend, she found herself tongue-tied, as apparently did his friend: the older man hardly ever spoke, just stared at her. She knew she didn't like him.

When she reached the kitchen it was to see Peggy at the back door taking a hamper from a liveried coachman, saying, "Thank you, Mr. Appleby. Thank you indeed." And she heard the coachman now ask, "How is Mrs. Hazel? The master would like to know."

"Oh, about the same, no better no worse. Between you and me she could linger on for a time, or go out like the snuff of a candle."

Nancy Ann closed her eyes and bit down on her lip. She knew that her mother was very ill and could linger on for a time, but she never thought of her going out like the snuff of a candle. Hilda, standing near the table, saw the effect Cook's words were having on her, and so, going to the door, she said, in a loud voice, "Here's Miss Nancy Ann, Cook."

At this, Peggy stepped back with the hamper and Nancy Ann, going to the door, looked at the coachman and said in a quiet, polite, formal tone, "Would you please convey to your master my thanks and those of my mother and father for his kindness?"

"I shall, miss. I shall." The man touched his cap, then moved away, and she closed the door, then turned towards the table where Peggy was already lifting the food from the hamper, exclaiming as she did so, "My! My! Now this is better than your fruit. Two brace of pheasants. And look at that! a bottle of wine, and another. What kind will they be, miss?" She handed the bottle to Nancy Ann, and Nancy Ann, looking at the label, said, "It is Burgundy."

"And what's in this box, miss?"

"Oh, that's cheese."

"In a box?" Hilda put in now, and Nancy Ann answered, "It's a French cheese."

"My! My! I wonder what it'll taste like."

"Well, you'll never know because all you'll get is a snip," said Hilda.

"And here's another box, two of them. I know what's in

that one, sweetmeats. Eeh! My! He's not as black as he's painted, is he?''

"Shut your mouth, Jane Bradshaw." Hilda pushed her big, ungainly companion.

"Well, I'm only sayin' what. . . ."

"Get over to that sink and finish those dishes." It was Peggy who was now going for her assistant. Then she turned to Nancy Ann, saying, "We'll put them on a couple of trays and we'll take them in to your mama to see, eh? to cheer her up. She always appreciates people's kindness, does the mistress. And them bottles'll put colour into her cheeks again, eh, miss?''

"Yes, Peggy, I'm sure they will. I'll leave you to see to it.''

"Do that, miss. Do that."

When, a few minutes later she had finished giving her mother a list of things in the hamper, it was her grandmother who said, "He's good at bottom. You've got to say it, he's good at bottom.''

He's not as black as he's painted, and he's good at bottom. Why did everyone insinuate that he was a bad man? Well, if not bad, not quite nice. They never spoke like that about Mr. Mercer. Of course they couldn't, could they, because *he was* nice. And he wasn't what you would call a recluse any more; he was getting about, in fact he had visited her mother twice and sat talking to her about the boys. He was quite old in years, three or so older than James, but he still looked young; not handsome, yet not plain, and he was kindly in a stiff kind of way. Oh yes, he was very proper; yet he had joked with her grandmama over something Peter did when he went out in a boat one day. It was when they were very young and Peter was learning to row.

He had also sent her mother flowers and fruit, but not in such lavish quantities as came from The House. Her papa liked him, he liked him very much, but what his opinion was of Mr. Harpcore she didn't know because it was his rule never to judge.

And what happened the following Sunday bore out how right her papa was.

Attendance at the Sunday services over the past months had

been arranged in such a way that there was always someone left at home besides Jessica, in case of need. So on alternate Sundays Nancy Ann attended either morning service, or evening service, and this applied to Peggy, Jane, and Hilda too.

On this particular Sunday morning it was Jane's turn to attend the service which began at half-past ten. What time it ended depended on how long John decided to preach. When he was feeling strongly about anything it could be an hour. But his sermon must have been short this morning, for Jane came almost at a run up the drive and into the kitchen, which caused Nancy Ann, who was leaving by the far door, to stop as she heard her cry, "He was there! He was there!"

"Who was there?" Peggy was in the act of cutting a shoulder of lamb into thin slices, and she repeated, "Who was there?"

"Himself, from up above . . . The House. He was there, sitting in the front row of the specials. And there was a lady with him, and she kept fidgeting."

"What kind of lady?"

"A lady. She was an old 'un. She had a bonnet on and a very fancy cape with big blue silk bows at the neck. She wasn't used to church, you could see that. And there were more staff there. Oh aye. Must have been twelve or more. Couldn't see them all from where I was sittin', and I didn't get a chance to count them 'cos when I came out they were all packed into the brakes, their noses in the air as usual. But he and the lady were in the coach. Eeh! There was quite a stir among the folks. Hat liftin', cap touchin', knee bendin', an' things. You would think it was a visitation from the Lord himself."

"Don't be blasphemous, Jane Bradshaw. . . . But how was he got up?"

"Oh, smart like, plain, but smart like. He's handsome in a way, you know. I wonder what brought him to church this mornin'? Turned over a new leaf likely."

"Shut up! Shut your mouth! There's dishes waitin' for you there in the sink. So get your things off."

Peggy now turned to where Nancy Ann was still standing, and she called, "D'you hear that, miss? Good news isn't it, himself at the service?"

"Yes, Peggy, yes." She went through the door, then closed it and walked slowly across the hall, thinking as she did so of how pleased her father would be. Oh, yes, and so would her mother. She now quickened her step into the breakfast-room. Her mother was in bed this morning: she felt a little tired, she'd said, and wouldn't rise until later in the day.

"Mama."

"Yes, my dear?"

"Guess what?"

"Well, I don't know what I have to guess at."

"Mr. Harpcore was at church this morning."

Her mother didn't answer for a moment, and then she said, "He was?"

"Yes. Jane came bursting with it. He must have caused a stir." She laughed now and, turning to her grandmama who had been sitting near the window reading but now had her full attention, she said, "Jane seemed more surprised at the sight of him that she would have been if she had seen the devil kneeling in his pew. Why does everyone think him a wicked man?"

"He is not a wicked man." Jessica now slapped the open pages of her book. "He is merely a man of his time. He's only doing what other so-called pious individuals in the village get up to, but he does it in a bigger way, and. . . ."

"Mother-in-law!" The voice came quiet, and Jessica now swivelled round in her seat and looked out into the conservatory as she said, "I'm sorry. I'm sorry, Rebecca. But you know yourself the poison that drips from tongues soon makes a pool."

"Yes, yes, indeed I do, Mother-in-law." And now Rebecca put her hand out and drew her daughter towards her, saying, "My dear, Mr. Harpcore is not a bad man in that sense. He . . . well, he has led a gay life. As . . . as your grandmama has just said, he's a man of his time: he lives in a society that acts differently from ours. Yet"—the smile on her pale face widened—"'tis amazing news that you have brought. If he has started to come to church, then it shows that he is settling down. They generally do about his age. How old would he be?" She moved her head to the side and looked towards Jessica. And the old woman, turning now and facing her again, pursed her lips and said, "Oh, thirty-three to middle thirties I should say. And as you rightly comment, Rebecca, 'tis the age for settling down, among his kind anyway." Then looking towards Nancy Ann, she said, "I'll just trot into the kitchen and inspect the contents of that hamper that came earlier and see there's nothing halved or quartered before it reaches us."

As the door closed on her, Rebecca moved her head slowly on the pillow, saying, "Your grandmama would suspect the Archangel Gabriel himself."

"She's right though, you know." Nancy Ann now pulled a face at her mother. "She knows people and all their funny little ways."

"Yes, yes, she does indeed, my dear. And she was right about Mr. Harpcore. There is good in everyone. Always remember that, my dear. And there's a great deal of good in him. He has shown it with his kindness; even when he was absent from the house, his gifts still came. And they've been most welcome, haven't they?"

"Oh, yes, Mama, most welcome. I . . . I've never eaten so well for ages. . . ." She paused now and hung her head, and Rebecca, taking her hand, said lightly, "You know you are very like your grandmama, you think a lot of your stomach."

"Well, I have four years of workhouse diet to make up for, Mama; the food at school was really awful. I'm amazed that I didn't grow fat. A number of the other girls did."

"You have grown just nice." Rebecca gazed at her daughter, from her hips up to the top of her shining hair, and her thoughts were a prayer as she said, Dear Lord, let me see her safely settled before I go into Your Kingdom. Guide me to know what is right. Show me that the thoughts I am harbouring, or by wishful thinking, have substance. Show me by some sign that I am not mistaken. . . .

Rebecca's prayer was answered again and again during the following months. And during this time her condition remained stable; in fact, there seemed to be a slight improvement: she coughed less, there was no trace of blood in her sputum, and the condition of her heart remained stable.

PART THREE

The Leopard's Spots

☙ 1 ☙

"So that's what it's been working up to. I imagined your visits to be in the way of finding a little amusement. Perverseness on your part as usual, going from the devil to his opponent. . . . You can't mean it, Denny? She's just a chit of a girl; you could quite well be her father."

"I'm aware of that, Larry, well aware that I am old enough to be her father. But as for her being a chit of a girl, you're wrong there. She'll be seventeen, as I understand it, in January, but she appears older; and she is a beautiful and intelligent young person."

The two men studied each other for a moment before Laurence Freeman said, "Have you thought of how she'll fit in here? How will she manage to run this place? Don't forget I've seen the girl. I've met her. Can you visualise her giving orders to Conway who is something of a tyrant, and in age she'll be on a par with your maids in the kitchen and. . . ."

"Say no more, Larry. She'll never be on a par in any way with the maids in the kitchen. She is the daughter of a clergyman, a highly intelligent man, whose own father was a colonel in the army. Her mother is from good stock, the Bennets of Northumberland. They were poorer than their proverbial church mice, but they were of the class."

"My! My! We have gone into their heredity, haven't we?"

"Yes, you could say that, Larry. And it might prove to you

now that my future action in this matter doesn't stem from a flash in the pan; I've thought deeply on it.''

''And she . . . what does she say?''

Dennison turned away and walked down the length of the long library, and he stood looking out over the lawn to where the barrier of topiary birds cut off the view; then slowly but firmly he said, ''I have yet to find that out.''

''What if she doesn't accept you?''

There was a long pause before the answer came: ''Then I am back to where I am standing now.''

Again there was a pause before Larry Freeman asked, ''Have you considered the effect on one temperamental wench of all this?''

''Yes, I have; and I hope Rene will understand. . . .''

''God Almighty! I never thought to hear you utter words denoting utter stupidity. Understand? Rene Myers? God! you are besotted. Others have come and gone, but she's been firmly within your horizon for a long time. Do you think she's just going to slip away and say, 'I understand, Denny, dear boy. You want to take a sweet little girl into your bed, so I shall return quietly to the arms of my husband.' ''

''Stop it! Shut up! It isn't only Rene you're thinking about. And I must say this, Larry: I can't see you liking the changed situation when I do marry. So, if you wish to find new quarters I shall understand.''

They were facing each other now over a distance and the older man's countenance had darkened. His thin lips were drawn in tight against his teeth; his eyes unblinking held a look of anger. The whole of his tall, stiff body expressed anger. And when he spoke his words came sieved through his teeth: ''Marching orders then.''

''No, not marching orders, Larry. It's up to you. We can be friends as always, but either way I'll ever be grateful for your companionship over the years.''

''I cannot believe it.''

''What can you not believe?''

''That I'm getting my marching orders.''

''If you wish to take it like that, Larry, then that is up to you. You'll always be welcome here, but there comes a time in one's life when a stocktaking is necessary, and I have reached that stage. I have no heir and no close relative except Beatrice. And the thought of dying and the estate passing to her keeps me awake at night. Imagine a house filled with dolls. She brought twenty-five with her on her last visit.''

"Her claim could be challenged. Have you ever thought of that?"

''*No*, and I don't intend to, because there's not the slightest possibility of that happening.''

"I wouldn't be too sure.''

"You would enjoy such proceedings, wouldn't you, Larry?''

"I would find it interesting, seeing you being forced to open your eyes to the fact that for the last eight years or so he's been under your nose.''

Dennison stared at the older man. He had always seen him as a cold imperturbable individual, and he had admired this part of his character since, as a young man escaping sorrow, he had, in a way, been taken under his worldly-wise wing. It was he who introduced him to his first mistress even though he himself had been inclined to shun any such intimacy. He hadn't probed into his new friend's life, he only knew he had been cashiered from the army abroad, supposedly for an affair he'd had with a superior officer's wife. Yet he had somehow felt that wasn't the whole story. He had always found him an amusing companion because he had a cunning wit. But in latter years he had detected a possessiveness that irked at times. He had never allowed himself to admit that he was an expensive companion: friend Larry, like himself, loved to gamble, and he wasn't always lucky, and with the passage of time whatever debts he incurred had come to be automatically settled with his own.

Now, and not for the first time, doubt about the true value of this friendship was entering his mind. But he had never seen his friend look as he was now: the calm, suave poise had gone, there was on his countenance an expression that could only be termed hate.

But no, no, he wouldn't go that far. Larry could never hate him. For one thing, he owed him too much. For the past ten years he had provided him with a home and all the advantages that went with it. No, he was wrong, the expression must be one of hurt and disappointment and, in a way, he could understand that. But then he was startled by his friend's next words, deep-throated and full of bitterness: "If you take her you lose me . . . entirely."

Dennison found himself stretching upwards and he knew that his face had become scarlet as it always did when it evinced temper. Indignantly he cried, "An ultimatum? My God! you're giving me an ultimatum? Well, Larry, let me tell you this, you have the answer and I don't need to voice it, do I?"

The man glared at him, then muttered thickly, "No, you don't. And yet I can't believe it." He drew in a deep breath and let it slowly out before he added, "So this is the end of an episode. Well, I'm going to say one more thing, I wish you luck with your little vicarage piece, and my God, you're going to need it, because Rene will tear you both to shreds. It's a pity she's abroad because I would like to be present when the battle begins, and begin it will." He now brought his thin lips tightly together, and sucked them inwards before swinging around and making for the door. But there he stopped and, looking back, he demanded, "The coach, I suppose I can order it to take me to the station?"

When Dennison made no reply to this he went out, and the sturdy panelling in the room shuddered as the door clashed to.

Dennison now sat on the window seat, but he did not look out for his eyes were closed and his hand was covering them. He leant his back against the deep stone bay and his breath escaped in a long slow sigh. It was over. It had to come one way or another. Perhaps this was as good as any, perhaps better than indicating to him that he couldn't afford his companionship any longer. He had been finding it difficult enough to pay his own gaming debts, but that last five hundred had been a bit too much. And all taken for granted.

That had been the odd thing about Larry's friendship, he had never discussed money but from the start whatever he bought, or owed, had been put down to his name. It was as if he himself could draw from a spring that would never run dry, but the spring had dwindled to a mere trickle of late, aided by both his and Rene's call on his purse.

The name brought him up from his seat and he thumped one fist into the palm of his other hand; Larry had been right about Rene's reactions. There'd be hell to pay in that quarter. For some long time now, he had to confess, he had become weary of her too. He also felt that Poulter Myers was tired of being made a cuckold of. It was known that he had his own leisure occupation, set up in a house in Newcastle, but then he was discreet about it; unlike his wife who flaunted her pastimes, and he himself had been openly declared as one of them for some time now. Of course, he must own to having enjoyed the game, for that's what it was. And she had proved to be a lively companion, often acting like a bawdy eighteenth-century wench in that she lacked subtlety of any kind. Yes, what Larry had said was true, there would be hell to pay in that quarter. But he had some respite, for she was with her husband on his diplomatic business across the channel: it could be a month, perhaps two before she returned; she hated the English winters especially in these northern climes, and undoubtedly she would spend most of her time in the South of France. It would be the longest separation between them in the last three years, and from now on it would be extended. Oh, yes—he walked up the room now, shaking his head—if he could make that charming child his wife then the disassociation with Rene would have to be extended indefinitely.

Even so, doubtless he would have to explain away, in the lightest manner of course, his past connection with Mrs. Rene Poulter Myers. The parson, at a stretch, might accept that he was a man of the world, now determined to settle down, but the man's wife was another matter altogether, as was his mother. Oh, yes, as was his mother.

He sighed deeply as he gnawed at his lower lip for a moment. Tomorrow he would start his offensive by paying the vicarage a visit and inviting Miss Nancy Ann Hazel and her brother Peter, whom he understood was coming home for the Christmas holidays, to the ball, which had been a yearly event used as a means of bringing his friends together for a romp. But now there must be no more such romps, and he would have to think, and think carefully, about whom he should invite.

✴ 2 ✴

Dennison sat on the straight-backed chair towards the foot of Rebecca's couch. The vicar was sitting on a straight-backed chair close to the head of the couch. The couch today was placed with its back to the bed and facing the fire. The doors leading into the conservatory were tightly closed to keep out the wind that whirled through the slack panes of glass of which there were many devoid of putty, much of it having being picked out by the hungry jackdaws in the winter.

As usual, Jessica sat nearest the fire, while furthest away from it, slightly behind her father but facing the visitor, sat Nancy Ann, trying her hardest to comply with the Dame school's training of how one should act in company: not to fidget or show too much excitement, not to laugh loudly or speak out of turn. And she had managed very well till now, when, on a high note, she exclaimed, "Yes! Yes, I'd love to come to your ball. Thank you."

"Nancy Ann, please!" Her mother's soft voice held a deep reprimand, and she brought Nancy Ann to stillness by saying, "It is for your father to decide."

"Of course. I'm sorry." She bowed her head, knowing that the guest was smiling to himself, and also, from the stiffness of her father's profile, that he didn't approve of the invitation. And she had been silly, oh, so silly to make such an outburst.

Now she had placed him in a position that would make it difficult for him to refuse Mr. Harpcore's request. Yet, the invitation had been for Peter too. Peter would have enjoyed a ball, she knew that. He had wanted to take her to one in Newcastle, but her mother had had a turn, and so the treat had been deferred.

"I'm sorry if my proposal has caused some embarrassment." Dennison had risen to his feet and was looking directly at the parson, who had slowly risen from his chair too, and he went on, "As it was the festive season I thought that perhaps your son and daughter might like to come up to the house. I used the word ball, but I think I should have explained myself better by saying there will be a select gathering of my friends. We always meet the day following Boxing Day and have a little dinner and a dance. But if it doesn't meet with your approval I'll understand. May I take my leave of you, Mrs. Hazel?" He bowed towards Rebecca, adding, "I'm glad to see you looking much better than when I was last here. May I hope the improvement continues." He now bowed towards Jessica who, unusual for her, had not spoken one word during the time he had been in the room.

Now, to the surprise of them all, it was Rebecca who said, "Let me assure you, Mr. Harpcore, your kind offer has not caused any embarrassment, and as she has so spontaneously declared, Nancy Ann would be pleased to accept your invitation, as I'm sure will Peter when he returns." She drew in a short shuddering breath; then looking at her daughter, she said, "Would you see Mr. Harpcore out, Nancy Ann?"

"Yes, Mama." It was a mere whisper. And now with her head raised and eyes bright, she smiled at the visitor, then followed him after he had bowed his farewells to each of the company in turn.

In the hall, Nancy Ann handed him his greatcoat and waited for him to put it on before offering him his hat. Then smiling at him, she said bluntly, "It nearly didn't come off, did it? That's me; I should have kept quiet and let things take their drawing-room course." She now hunched her shoulders slightly as she added, "That was an expression of my teacher at school. It's a silly expression, isn't it?"

He wanted to put his head back and laugh; he wanted to

throw out his arms and hug her to him; he wanted . . . he wanted. But what he wanted, he realized by her manner towards him, was further away than ever, for she was treating him like a kindly uncle; she had no idea in that beautiful head of hers that he was acting as a suitor. He was tempted to put things right this very minute, but he warned himself, make haste slowly, especially in this household. So, in a conspiratorial whisper, he said, "Yes, you nearly did put your foot in it."

Suddenly, her face became straight and her voice serious as she said, "I've never been to a ball; I likely won't know how to behave. But then"—she shrugged her shoulders— "Peter will be with me. He has attended a number of balls, at least dances."

Again he spoke quietly: "Well, between Peter and myself," he said, "we will show you the ropes."

She smiled, then held out her hand, saying, "Goodbye, Mr. Harpcore. And may I take this opportunity to thank you for all your kindness to my mother in sending such beautiful food and fruit."

"Oh, that . . . that. Nothing. Nothing." He went quickly from her, shaking his head; but at the bottom of the steps he turned and looked at her again, then raised his hand in a little wave. And she responded in the same way.

She stood watching him walk towards the stable to get his horse, and when he reappeared, mounted, he looked pleased to see her still standing at the top of the steps. It was she who waved first; and he responded, holding the horse reined in for a moment before putting it into a trot.

After closing the door she stood looking towards the stairs. She liked him, he was nice, and she was going to a ball. She was actually going to a ball. . . .

As soon as Nancy Ann had left the room with the visitor, John looked at his wife with a pained look, and there was bewilderment in his tone as he said, "Rebecca. Why?"

She stared at him for a long moment before she said, "I . . . I have my reasons, John. I . . . I will talk about them later. And with you, too, Mother-in-law. But I think you know what they are already, don't you?"

"Yes, yes, Rebecca, I think I do." Jessica nodded at her

daughter-in-law, then looked at her son and said, "She'll be back in a minute. This matter needs mulling over; but in the meantime, John Howard, I would advise you to act as natural as you can. In fact, show her that you're pleased she can go to the ball, or dinner or dance, or whatever it is. And besides, whatever you think, remember that she's had very little pleasure in her young life and no fun, as I see it, whatever."

"Oh, Mother, she's happy."

"Up to a point. But what you don't realize, my son, is that your daughter's no longer a little girl, she's a budding woman."

"Nonsense. Nonsense. She is but sixteen."

"She is seventeen in a matter of weeks and you know it. And your bride"—she turned her head and nodded towards Rebecca—"was not yet eighteen when you married her. Think on't. Yes, think on't. Now here she comes. Be happy for her. It is a small thing as yet she is asking, but what she'll say when something greater is asked of her, I don't know."

"Greater? What do you mean, greater?" Her son looked at her, his face screwed up in enquiry, and to this his mother answered, "Rebecca will explain it all later."

Nancy Ann had prepared the couch for her father where he slept at night at the foot of his wife's bed, having flatly refused for weeks now to sleep upstairs.

She had taken up her grandmother's last drink of the day, hot milk with a sprinkling of ginger in it. She had said good night to her parents, then had gone into the kitchen and had said good night to the girls, and while doing so had imparted to them the wonderful news that she was going to a ball. And none of them gave away the fact that they already knew this. As Peggy said, Hilda had ears like a cuddy's lugs and through practice she could move from a keyhole with the lightning speed of a young colt, all of which Hilda took as praise. But they had all oohed! and aahed! and made a fuss of her. And now she had gone upstairs to bed, and Rebecca and John were alone.

John had been very quiet all evening. Of course, he had been sitting at a side table preparing his sermon for the coming Sunday. Nevertheless, he hadn't turned occasionally and smiled at her, as was his usual habit. And now she held out a thin hand to him, saying, "John. Come and sit near me."

Having obeyed her, he took her hand in his own and stroked it, and he looked tenderly into her face as she said, "Will you hear me out?"

"I've always heard you out, my dear."

"Yes, you have, John. Yes, you have. But I am sure you will want to interrupt what I am going to say to you now."

When he made no answer she leant back into her pillows and rested for a moment before, in a low voice, she began. "As you know only too well, John, my days are numbered. How many are left? I don't rightly know; that depends on the good God's will, but, of late, I have prayed to Him and asked Him to spare me until I see our daughter settled." When she felt his hand move she entwined her fingers in his, then went on. "When I go she will take over the household. Well, she has done that already, but she will think it her duty to look after Grandmama and you for the rest of your days. Our daughter, John, is a beautiful girl. She is intelligent and so full of spirit. I would hate to think that the loneliness of the future, that of an unmarried woman, would dim that spirit. I have searched in my mind of the men of our acquaintance, and who are they? Apart from Mr. Mercer, they are farmers and tradesmen, and farmers, as you know, both old and young, are notorious for using their wives as upper servants. Just think of the Bradfords, the Henleys, and the Fords; their women work harder than does our washerwoman. Anyway, the young farmers seem to be paired off immediately after they leave school, and usually it is to a robust daughter of another farmer. Then turn to the village. Which young man would be a suitable match for her? The Taylors? the Pollocks? the Nortons? They have seven sons among them, all worthy young men, but rough cast. And what is noticeable, at least to me, not one of them has yet turned his eyes in her direction."

"She is but a child."

"Please, John, let me finish. And I repeat what your mama said earlier, she's on seventeen; moreover, she is old for her years. The school did very good work on her: she is equipped for life, more so than many young girls of her age. Now, I come to the point. Mr. Harpcore has been very kind over these past months in sending me hampers. As you know their content has leant flavour to our diet, not, believe me, John, that I ever thought our way of eating was anything but good and wholesome.'' She paused now and drew two deep breaths before going on, ''Those hampers weren't really meant for me; they were a means of gaining entry, so to speak, into our home, and my illness has given him the excuse to call. No matter how kindly his thoughts were concerning me, his main intention was to see Nancy Ann. Please, don't bow your head like that, John. I know what you think of him. He is a man of the world, and not our world; he has been known to be a womanizer and a gambler, a man of high living, but, have you noticed for the past four months—no, indeed, five months—he has remained at The House? This is the longest he has stayed at home for many years. The man is changing, if he has not already changed. One thing I feel sure of with regard to his character, he is of kindly heart, and, John, sooner or later, in fact I think sooner, he is coming to ask for her hand.''

John lifted his head and looked at this woman who to him was a dear creature, one to whom at times he put the name pious; in fact, there were times when her righteousness had grated on him, for she had been adamant in adhering to the letter of the Good Book while he himself might have looked at it with a wider view. Yet, here she was willing to let her daughter marry a man like Harpcore, a roué, a man old enough to be her father. He couldn't really believe that she was the same person with whom he had spent almost thirty years. Could the approach of death alter a person so much? He would like to think that her mind had become affected; but no, her thinking was as clear as ever, yet not, to his mind, clean. Dear God, he mustn't put the term unclean to her thoughts. She was doing what she thought best for their child. And she voiced this with her next words.

''He is a man of substance. Undoubtedly he will take her into another world, but, and I am firmly convinced of this, she will eventually lead him into her world. Apart from such a marriage securing her future, it could, in a way, John''— she now moved her head slowly as she looked at her husband—"be the means of saving a soul. Think on that, John. Think on that."

He couldn't think on that. He gently withdrew his hand from hers and got to his feet, and he stood with his back to her when he said, "I cannot help but say it, Rebecca: I am amazed that you should wish for this match."

"I knew it would affect you, John, but it is my one wish before I go to see her settled. I'll . . . I'll die happy then. The boys, they can fend for themselves, but . . . but I have seen the result so often in the parishes where you have served of good women left in a lonely existence after having done their duty by their parents. I have never brought the subject up with you before, John, but it has pained me. Most women are made for marriage; I think the same applies to men. Look at poor Mr. Mercer. What a waste there, not only of his own life, but that of some good woman who could have shared it by now. John, I dread that kind of fate for my Nancy Ann, our Nancy Ann. All I ask is that you think on it, and when he comes to speak to you, as he will, deal with him as you would any man who is seeking a better way of life."

She watched him bow his head, then slowly turn down the lamp until the wick was a mere glimmer before undressing himself.

❧ 3 ❧

REBECCA GAZED AT HER DAUGHTER WEARING WHAT HAD
been her own wedding dress. Miss Waters from the village
had finished it only this morning, and even after three fittings
there were still some adjustments to be made by the little
dressmaker: for with the three petticoats underneath, the skirt
still didn't look really full enough, especially over the hips.
There had been the letting out of tucks here, the pulling in
of tucks there and, very important, the heightening of the
neckline in order to cover the breastbone.

The material looked as new as it had been when the dress
was first made, because, of course, it had been turned inside
out and so the pattern of the silver thread showed up much
more. The only new thing on the dress was the broad blue
ribbon that formed the sash; the original one had been too
faded. And then there were the satin slippers, a present from
Peter.

But the most surprising thing Rebecca noted about her child
was the fact that she no longer looked a child or a young girl,
but a young woman, for the hair style had transformed her
daughter.

For the first time Nancy Ann had put her hair up—at least
her grandmama and Peggy had put it up for her. Her ringlets
were arranged on the top of her head and a white silk flower

set in the midst of them, and when she looked at her reflection in the mirror, she couldn't believe what she saw.

For some years now she had told herself that she didn't want pretty clothes, that she didn't like frilly dresses, that she wasn't made for that kind of attire, but she also knew this way of thinking was because there was no money for pretty clothes, and, too, that her mother didn't approve of frills and furbelows. Yet here she was holding her hands out to her, tears in her yes, and saying, "Oh! my dear, my dear, you look so lovely, beautiful."

"Oh, Mama, it's . . . it's your dress."

She watched her mother shake her head slowly and look towards her husband who was standing at the foot of the bed, and she said one word, "John," and he nodded at her, saying, "Yes, my dear. Vanity of vanities, all is vanity, but you have a beautiful daughter, and so have I."

And now with a gallant gesture he held out his hand to Nancy Ann and said, "Your carriage is waiting, madam." There was a smile on his face that wasn't really a smile because it was the kind of smile she had seen on his countenance for some days now. There was a sadness in it, an acquiescence to something that puzzled her. As she took her father's hand, her grandmama appeared at the open door saying, "The horses are prancing; they'll be frozen stiff if you don't come this minute."

"Goodbye, Mama."

"Goodbye, my dear. Enjoy yourself."

"I will, Mama. I will."

She went to put her arms around her grandmother, but Jessica pushed her off, saying, "Stop it. You'll crush your ruche." And she pointed to the frill of lace hanging between the small breasts, then added, "Go on, get your cloak on."

Peter was holding out her hooded cloak; and the three maids were standing to the side, their faces expressing their admiration.

The sight of the young girl, who almost looked like a bride, was too much for Jane, and she blubbered, "Eeh! miss, I've never seen anything so beautiful. I can't believe it's you."

"Shut your mouth, you goat!" She had received a dig in the ribs from Peggy, who now said, "Enjoy yourself, miss."

Nancy Ann said again, "I will. I will."

"That's it," Hilda put in; "do that, miss. 'Tis your first ball an' you'll never forget it." Her voice had broken, and her words suggested that she was acquainted with balls and was recalling her own adventures.

Peter was the only one who had made no comment. Gently lifting the hood over the piled hair, he smiled softly at her, but as they made for the door, he turned and looked towards his father, saying quietly, "Don't wait up, Father, everything will be all right." And he inclined his head forward as if to emphasize his statement.

They were at the open door now; in fact, Nancy Ann was on the top step when suddenly she turned about, rushed back into the room, and, pushing her cape wide, she reached up her arms and put them around her father's neck and kissed him; then, turning as swiftly, she rejoined Peter, who now said, "That'll do your dress a lot of good."

The coachman was holding a lantern. He held it high with one hand, while with the other he kept the door of the carriage open. Peter helped her up the steep steps; then he followed her; the door closed on them, and the next minute they were off, and seemingly thrown into total darkness when the light from the vicarage door disappeared.

When she sought Peter's hand, he squeezed it and said, "Stop trembling. You'll enjoy it, you'll see."

"Yes, everyone keeps saying that, and it's all very well for you; you are used to these things."

"Oh no, I'm not, not affairs like this. A dance, yes. Believe me, I'm as nervous as you are."

"I don't believe you. Anyway, I'm so glad you're with me; I couldn't have come on my own. Oh"—she moved closer to him—"it's lovely to have you at home, Peter."

"Oops! a daisy." They were rocking from side to side as the wheels of the carriage hit a pothole, and he, assuming a lordly manner, said, "Disgraceful, holes in the road; I shall have them filled in tomorrow."

She giggled, then became quiet for a moment before she said, "Wouldn't it have been nice if James had come home for Christmas. I wrote to him and said we could put the babies in a special room and I would see that there was a fire on all the time. I . . . I told him how ill Mother was. Yet, what does he do? Writes a stiff letter back saying that Nicolette has a cold. That made me angry. Nicolette is not dying.''

"Now, now. Oh, for goodness' sake! Nancy Ann, don't start and weep. Remember where you're going. And listen. Listen; I'll tell you something. James and I met for a few hours before I came home. I didn't say anything to Father or Mother about this. Well, the fact is, James is not happy.''

"That doesn't surprise me.''

"No, it may not, but what might surprise you is, he is very unhappy. He doesn't think he can stand living with Nicolette much longer.''

"What!"

" 'Tis true. He doesn't see his own children; and her mother has practically taken over the house. As you know, they all live together in the schoolhouse. He works ten hours a day. He's in charge of the boarders. And . . . and there is something else which I can't explain, but which is making life impossible for him. You think Mama is strictly religious; well, by the sound of it, she can't hold a candle to Nicolette.''

"But . . . but why? What do you mean? Explain yourself.''

"I . . . I can't. It is a very delicate matter. I can only say that Nicolette considers marriage mainly for . . . oh dear me!'' She felt him move restlessly on the seat, then he finished off with the word, "Procreation.''

Procreation. Something to do with babies. Dear, dear. Her eyelids blinked rapidly.

"He badly wanted to come home and see Mother. You know what he said to me? Believe it or not, he said he was sorry he had scorned Eva McKeowan, for at least there would have been love on one side and perhaps on both sides, because love cannot but beget love. Then he contradicted that by saying, 'That's not right or I wouldn't be in the state I'm in now.' "

"Poor James.''

"Oops! Here we go again.'' They fell against each other now and laughed. Then presently Peter said, "I'll tell you something. I may come home. Oh, I don't mean, really home, but near Durham. You see, I'm another one who isn't very happy, at least in my work. Testing ingredients for food colouring isn't exactly an exciting occupation, and Graham Mercer has put a proposal to me. You know, or perhaps you don't, that his father endowed the Halton Grammar School outside Durham, and he is one of the governors and, as you can imagine, has some say in matters concerning the school. For some years he didn't bother with outside affairs, but now he's getting back to public life and taking an interest in the school once again. Apparently they are needing a man who can teach natural philosophy and a little mathematics and geography. I could manage a little mathematics, but the geography, oh! dear me. That's like asking me to find my way around Durham blindfold. Still, I think the post could be mine if I decide on it.''

"Oh Peter, do, do. Mother would be overjoyed. She misses you both, and I think she worries about James. You know, she didn't like his choice, no more than I did. I'm so sorry he's unhappy. Oh, but''—she squeezed his hand—"it would be lovely if you could be near.'' She paused a moment, then said, "It was so thoughtful of Mr. Mercer to offer you the post. He too has been so kind of late.''

"He's a good man, and he thinks a lot of you, you know.''

"Me?''

"Yes, you. He often speaks of you. He calls you a charming little girl, but if he was to see you now, he would drop the little girl.''

"Oh, Peter.'' She shook his hand up and down. "You are always making up compliments. Whom do you take after? Not Papa or Mama, and certainly not Grandmama.''

"I'm a special specimen, a throwback. But that was no compliment; at least what I mean is, I was recounting Graham's exact words. Oops!''

They were again jolted; but following this, they sat silent and Nancy Ann would have been surprised if she could have read her brother's thoughts, because he was asking himself: How did one suggest to another man, who had always been a benevolent friend, that he should propose marriage to his young sister before someone else got in. It might have been easy had he been otherwise than highly sensitive and not embittered by one rejection already. Likely the first thing he would say would be, I'm old enough to be her father. Well, so was this other person old enough to be her father. Of a sudden, he regretted he was taking this journey; it was like leading a lamb to the slaughter. Yet, Nancy Ann was no lamb. When it came to the push she would decide for herself. Or would she be influenced by their mama's wish, a dying wish? He knew his sister was a highly impressionable girl, she was all feelings. Oh, yes, there was no doubt about that, but she was also clear-headed and intelligent. Yet would her head rule her heart when she knew her mama's wishes? He doubted it.

"Oh, look!"

The coach was bowling between the iron gates now and on to the gravel drive which was lit by lanterns hanging from the trees, and showing here and there carriages, their shafts pointing to the ground, which meant their horses had been taken into the stables; then two or three times they were pulled to the side of the drive to allow other carriages to pass on their way out, these likely to return later. Suddenly the drive widened out into a huge forecourt brilliantly lit by lights from all the windows in the house.

The carriage stopped, the door was opened by a footman, and Peter descended, then helped her down. They were walking towards the broad steps that led to a stone terrace with a pillared portico . . . and there, coming through the wide open doors towards them, was their host. His hands outstretched, he said, "Welcome. I hope you've not had a rough ride. Everyone's complaining of the potholes and asking why I don't see to the road. I've told them that my stretch is perfectly flat, the potholes are fronting Mercer's land. Come away in."

He was walking by her side now, and when she entered the hall she stood blinking for a moment; she had never seen any place so brilliantly lit. Her eyes lifted to the glass chandeliers that looked to her like a galaxy of stars. Her cloak was taken from her by one of the liveried servants, who seemed to be all over the place. There was the sound of music in the distance and the buzz of voices; then a woman was standing in front of her. She was tall and was wearing a high goffered cap. Her dress was of black alpaca with a small white embroidered apron at the waist, around which was a belt supporting a chatelaine of keys.

"Mrs. Conway will show you to the ladies' room, my dear." He bowed slightly towards her and indicated that she should go with the tall person.

"This way, miss." The woman went on ahead, across the large hall, down a corridor, past numerous doors; then pushing one open, she allowed Nancy Ann to go before her, then closed it after her.

Nancy Ann stood for a moment, her back to the door, wondering what was expected of her. To the right of her, placed in a row, were a number of velvet-backed chairs, each facing a small dressing-table. Two of them were occupied, and the ladies who were powdering their faces turned and looked at her. It was a long inquisitive glance. Then they turned away again and proceeded with their toilet. She noticed immediately that one dress was blue and the other green and apparently made of silk taffeta; the skirts looked enormous.

Opposite her at the far end of the room, a huge fire was burning in a basket grate. To the left of her she saw a number of doors lining this wall. Then she felt the heat go to her face as one of the doors opened and a lady edged her way out while adjusting her skirt, and she continued to adjust it while making her way towards a table on which were two ewers and two basins, and to the side of it, a towel rack, each rail holding a number of towels.

The woman, after washing her hands, stood back and looked in the long mirror to the side of the table, then turned her gaze in the direction of the door. Her eyebrows were raised, the expression on her face saying plainly, What is the matter with you standing there?

There were long mirrors on the walls at each side of the fireplace, and now, her legs feeling like jelly, Nancy Ann made her way towards the one furthest from the ladies at the dressing-tables, and there, looking at herself, she thought, It's gone plain all of a sudden. She felt dowdy, out of place. She put her hand to her hair and pushed the curls here and there, all for something to do rather than with the intention of altering their position, then opened her vanity bag and took out a handkerchief and dabbed at her lips with it. And as she did so, there came to her the muttered voice of one of the ladies, saying, "Never! Never!" And the other answering, "Yes, I tell you, yes." There was a pause, then as Nancy Ann adjusted her sash one of the women spoke again, saying, "That's why the Crosbies or the Grahams aren't here."

"Nor the Taylors, nor you know who."

"Oh, she's still away; he was sent to Holland."

"But this, I . . . I can't believe it."

"You can believe it."

Nancy Ann could see in the mirror that they were both on their feet now. She also saw that they had turned and were surveying her, the while pretending to adjust their dresses.

The last words she heard one of them utter as they left the room were, "He's got a nerve. There'll be hell to pay." She didn't know whom they were talking about but she guessed they were pulling someone to shreds, and swearing at that, and they ladies.

The woman at the other mirror now turned around and amazed her with her next words: "Don't worry," she said; "they're a couple of bitches. You'll be all right." And at this she went out abruptly.

Nancy Ann stood with her hand held tightly against one cheek. Those ladies, they must have been in some way referring to her, but she couldn't even recall at the moment what they had said, only that it sounded spiteful. Of a sudden she wished she had never come, she wished she was home.

The door opened and there was the tall servant again, and the woman stared at her for some seconds before she said, "Are you ready, miss?"

"Yes. Yes, thank you."

She was surprised at the calm sound of her own voice. And she was further surprised that she could keep her shoulders back and her head up as she walked past the woman and into the corridor. It was, she told herself, as if she were preparing herself for a row, as she used to do years ago when any of the McLoughlins approached her. But it came to her now that this wasn't just a row she was facing, but a sort of covert battle. But why? Why? She was bewildered. Was it because Mr. Harpcore had shown kindness to her mother and the family? A parson's family, she knew, was considered lowly compared to those in this house.

As she entered the hall she was surprised to see Peter standing talking to the woman who had been sitting at the other mirror. He was laughing and she was wagging her finger at him. Then she saw Mr. Harpcore hurrying across the floor from the far side and before he reached them, he cried, "Don't believe a word she says, Mr. Hazel. She's a wicked woman."

"Ah, there you are." He turned his gaze on Nancy Ann and held it for some moments; then he put his hand out towards her while at the same time looking at the overdressed middle-aged woman, saying, "Pat, this is Miss Nancy Hazel, and this"—he now indicated the woman, saying—"is Lady Patricia Golding."

"How do you do?" Nancy Ann inclined her head and hesitated whether to dip her knee or not. Then Dennison said, "Well, let us join the others."

He now put his hand on Nancy Ann's elbow and led her across the hall and into a small anteroom, and from there into a ballroom, and such was the sight before her that she hesitated in her step, and he looked at her and she turned a quick glance on him, but didn't speak.

There was a dance in progress which she recognized as the Sir Roger de Coverley, and it was causing hoots of laughter. The dancers clapped as the end partners met in the middle of the two rows, swung round and danced away again. The orchestra, she could see, was on a raised balcony at the end of the room. There were couches and velvet seats arranged against the walls. And now, she was being led along between the seats and the dancers to the top of the room.

When she was seated on a single chair Dennison indicated the one next to her for Lady Golding, but she waved it away and, pointing to the couch to the right of Nancy Ann, she said, "I like to spread myself. You should know that. Anyway, your seats are not big enough to take me."

He laughed as he watched her seat herself on the couch and spread her russet-coloured gown to each side of her.

Peter had taken a stand to the side of Nancy Ann's chair, and he was gazing about him in as much wonderment as she, only his was more concealed.

"You told me you liked dancing." Dennison was bending towards her. "What is your favourite dance?"

She smiled up into his face, saying, "I like the waltz."

"Then waltz we shall." He now bowed to her, then to Lady Golding before threading his way towards the orchestra who had just finished playing. The dancers were dispersing and not a few of them cast their glances in Nancy Ann's direction. And one lady, preparing to take her seat further along the row, changed her mind and came up to them and, addressing Lady Golding, said, "Hello, my dear. I didn't expect to see you tonight. I understood you were going up to town to meet George."

"Did you, Grace? Now who could have told you that? because the last thing I heard from George was that he was chasing another bug in Africa. Well, I don't know if it was a bug or a rebel chief, but anyway I'll be lucky if I and the family see him before the end of March. Now who could have misinformed you to such an extent, Grace?"

"Oh, it was just . . . well, Alice happened to mention."

"Oh, Alice. Well, you should know by now, Grace, Alice doesn't know whether she's coming or going. She doesn't know if tomorrow is Pancake Tuesday or Whistle Cock Monday." A choking sound to her side caused Lady Golding to turn and glance at Nancy Ann, whose eyes were bright and whose finger tips were pressing her lips. Then looking at the woman again, she said, "I am sure you would like to meet Miss Hazel. Miss Hazel, Mrs. Grace Blenheim." Then waving her hand towards Peter, she added, "Mr. Peter Hazel." And as the lady now returned Peter's bow by slightly inclining her head, Lady Golding said, "Happy now, Grace?"

"Oh, Pat." The embarrassed woman turned away, her taffeta rustling as if with indignation.

Dennison, standing before them once more, was about to speak to Nancy Ann when Lady Golding said, "I had a visit from Grace."

"Oh, Grace." As they smiled at each other the band struck up, and Dennison, bending towards Nancy Ann, said, "May I have the pleasure?"

She rose, took the vanity bag from her wrist and placed it on the seat behind her, then extended her arms, placing the right one tentatively on his shoulder, and the tips of the fingers of her left hand in his palm. She felt his arm go round her waist and then she was swung into the waltz.

For the past few days she had been practising with Peter, but this was different. Her feet hardly seemed to touch the floor. This wasn't just one-two-three, one-two-three; she seemed to be lifted into the flow of the music. She smiled at him and he smiled back at her, and as they reached the end of the room she became aware for the first time that they had the floor to themselves. It wasn't until they had circled the room once that other couples joined them.

He was speaking to her, but she couldn't hear what he was saying. And so she said, "What?" when she should have said, "Pardon?"

His face came close to hers: "You dance beautifully."

"You do too."

"Thank you."

"Different from Peter."

"Different from Peter," he repeated on a laugh.

And now, her mouth wide, she laughed back at him, saying, "We've been practising." And she laughed louder now. She was no longer aware of the couples passing them or twirling round them; she was feeling happy in a most strange kind of way. This was what was meant by being at a ball, this being held in someone's arms and floating around and around and around.

When the music stopped she opened her eyes. She hadn't known she had had them closed during the last few minutes. And as he led her back to her seat she said, "That was lovely," then bit on her lip and, glancing at him, her voice low, muttered, "That was the wrong thing to say, wasn't it? My time at the Dame school was wasted."

His laughter drew eyes towards him, and when she had taken her seat, he bent over her and said, "That was lovely, Miss Hazel." And at this she suppressed her laughter. Then he said, "Excuse me, I will be back shortly." She watched him go and talk to a group of people standing in the middle of the room; then her gaze was brought from him by Lady Golding saying, "You enjoyed that?"

"Yes, my lady. He dances beautifully, very light."

"Yes, yes, he dances beautifully. And by the way, so do I." She had now turned to Peter who was sitting to her right on the couch, adding, "I may not look it, but I am very light on my feet, so what about you asking me for the next dance, young man? Or let us say the one after that, for the next is sure to be a polka and perhaps you'll be taking your sister."

"My sister I see every day, ma'am; she causes me no excitement. . . . I should consider it an honour to partner you in the polka, ma'am."

Her fan now came none too gently across Peter's knuckles as she murmured, "You may have been brought up in a vicarage, young man, but you are all there. I have gathered that much. As for you, young lady"—she turned now towards Nancy Ann and demanded—"what do you think of this setup?"

"You mean, the ballroom?"

"I mean, all of it: the extravaganza, the people, the servants you trip over everywhere."

Nancy Ann stared into the heavily powdered face before she said, and unsmiling now, "This is my first visit here. I cannot give you my opinion of the people or the servants, only that from what I have seen of it, it seems a very beautiful house."

"Ha! Ha! Ha!" The curled dyed hair bobbed backwards and forwards. "Couldn't have been better said. From whom did you learn diplomacy, girl? Certainly not from your father. I've heard him preach once or twice and it's a wonder his frankness didn't empty the church. How old are you really?"

Nancy Ann didn't know quite how to take this person: she wasn't her idea of a Lady, yet she had a title. Ladies, she imagined, didn't talk like her, nor did they put their finger in their ear and wag it about as she was doing now.

"Well, is it a secret?"

"No, my lady, it is no secret. I shall be seventeen years old in a fortnight's time."

"Seventeen. I was married when I was seventeen and one week. I had three children before I was twenty and that number had swollen to eight before I was thirty. What would have happened if George, that's my husband, hadn't decided to go and look for his bugs abroad, God alone knows. I wouldn't have been still light on my feet." The fan came once again across Peter's hands startling him now, but he laughed and looked across this amazing lady, as he thought of her, towards Nancy Ann. But there was no smile on her face and Lady Golding, noticing this, leant towards her and in a soft voice said, "You think I'm a queer old bird, don't you? I'm not really. But what I will tell you is, I am a friend of Dennison's, and he's a good chap at heart." Then raising her voice slightly, she said, "And speaking of queer birds, wait till you meet Beatrice . . . Beatrice Boswell his cousin . . . or half, whichever, with her entourage of dolls. Now there is a funny one. She's got the sniffles at present and is wrapped up to the eyes in her room, or perhaps she is having her daily bath. She has one every day, you know." She now turned towards Peter, saying, "A bath every day! Have you ever heard of it; it's enough to weaken a rhinoceros, that. But then she is a bit of a rhinoceros. Ah!" She bent forward and looked down the room to where a servant was standing in green, knee-breeched livery, white stockings and black shoes, and she exclaimed, "Controller of the menagerie." And without pause, and now slanting her eyes towards Nancy Ann, she went on, "I'm only putting you in the picture, dear."

In some bewilderment Nancy Ann's eyes were brought from the woman to the servant who was now saying, "Ladies and gentlemen, dinner is served."

There followed a slow rising from seats; and when the master of the house approached them, he did not stand before Nancy Ann but before Lady Golding, and it was to her he offered his arm, saying at the same time to Peter, "You'll take your sister in, Peter, will you, please?"

As he went to move away with Lady Golding on his arm, that strange lady muttered in an aside to Nancy Ann, "Keep close."

Nancy Ann stood up, and when Peter drew her hand through his arm she looked at him in slight apprehension, and he smiled at her and, bending his head towards her, whispered, " 'Tis as good as a play; enjoy it. Come on, into battle. Remember the McLoughlins."

It was odd he should say that when only a short while ago she had been thinking about them. So she smiled.

The tables were set in the shape of an open-ended square. The master of the house was seated at the middle place of the upper table. Lady Golding was seated immediately to his right, and next to her was Peter. The gentleman to her own right hand was apparently called Oswald, for as such he was being addressed by the lady sitting opposite to him on the inner side of the top table. There was a great deal of cross talk and chatter and every now and again, Lady Golding would lean in front of Peter and address some remark to her.

The food was of such variety that she could not eat half that was put on her plate. And by the time they came to the puddings, she politely put her hand up to wave them away, which she thought was a shame because she loved puddings.

And then there was the wine. There were four glasses before her and only one had been filled, and that was only half full now, and she wouldn't have touched it again only that Peter, nudging her slightly, said, "Sip on it, it's very nice. It will do you no harm." So she sipped on it until the glass was empty; and strangely it made her feel nice.

She noticed with some amazement that Peter ate everything put before him and drank all the different wines. Of course, she told herself, Peter had been out in the world; and yet he couldn't have experienced anything like this kind of life. But he had spoken of the grand dinners they sometimes had at Oxford, so perhaps this wasn't so strange to him after all.

She was feeling very hot: she wished she could get out into the air, even freezing as it was; the room was stifling and the noise and the chatter were incessant. How long had she . . . had they all been sitting here? Oh, more than an hour, nearer two. They couldn't possibly dance again immediately after such a meal. . . .

They didn't dance immediately after the meal. The ladies adjourned, some to the drawing-room, some to the powder-room. It was as she rose from the table that Lady Golding said under her breath, "Stay by me." And so, she stayed by her and found herself once again entering the powder-room.

Inside, Lady Golding, wending her way towards the closets, took her arm and said, "Wait there," then pushed unceremoniously past two ladies who themselves were waiting to enter a cubicle and who showed their annoyance at such high-handed treatment, and it was a natural reaction for them to look fully at Nancy Ann.

She stared back at them for she was becoming a little tired of the covert scrutiny that had been levelled at her during the evening, thinking as her grandmother might, with the aid of the wine, Who are they anyway? Most of them certainly didn't act like her idea of gentry.

There was loud laughter coming from the direction of one of the dressing-tables and a high voice exclaimed above the buzz, "In future, it'll be grace before meals. If Johnny had been here tonight he would have stood up and given it to us: For what we are about to receive may the devil and the vicarage take the hindmost."

Suddenly it became clear to her: it was because she was from the vicarage they were looking down on her; and, too, were jealous because Mr. Harpcore had danced with her. But then a strange thought came into her head, it was more of a muzzy feeling than a thought, but it centered around why her mother had raised no objection to her coming here tonight. And why Lady Golding had taken her under her wing. Whatever it was, her reaction must have astonished everyone in the room: as the door of the closet opened and Lady Golding emerged, Nancy Ann turned and, looking straight at the woman by the dressing-table, brought the room to silence by exclaiming in a loud high-falutin voice that was an exact replica of the lady who had made the statement, "In future it'll be grace before meals. If Johnny had been here tonight he would have stood up and given it to us: For what we are about to receive may the devil and the vicarage take the hindmost." Then in her own voice cried, "No doubt your Johnny would have done his best, but I can assure you my father would have made a better job of it and acted like a gentleman, just as my mama would, a real lady."

And on this, she turned from the astonished faces, almost pushing Lady Golding over, who was muttering under her breath, "Oh, my God!" and entered the closet where she stood with her eyes tightly closed for a moment. When at last she opened them it was to see two candles burning, one at each end of a narrow shelf on which there were a row of small bowls, very like the finger bowls that had been on the dining table, and on the shelf beneath, two small copper cans of water.

The closet consisted of a wooden box with a hole in the middle, the hole being surrounded by a leather pad.

She did not use it but she poured some water into a bowl, took a small finger towel from a pile placed next to the cans and, wetting the end of it, dabbed her brow with it. Then she sat down on the edge of the wooden seat and waited. She couldn't go out there and face them again. She wanted to go home. Oh, how she wished she was home.

How long she sat there she didn't know, but there were no further sounds or rustlings coming from the other cubicles now. When she heard the tap on the door and a voice say, "Come out, child, there's no one here," she rose slowly and pushed back the bolt. Then she was blinking rapidly in an endeavour to hold back the tears as she stared into the round and concerned face of this woman whom she thought of as old, but who had actually not yet reached fifty.

"It's all right; they're all gone." A smile now widened the powdered face. "They've learnt their lesson I think. Anyway, you sobered Betty Connor up. She couldn't believe the sound of her own voice. How did you do that?"

Nancy Ann gulped and said, "I'm . . . I'm quite good at mimicry."

"You are that. You are that. Now, come along. Stop blinking those long lashes of yours. No tears. You've won your first battle. Vicarage or no vicarage they'll not misjudge you, or him in the future. If they didn't understand why he's doing it, they will now."

"Doing what? Who?"

Lady Golding screwed up her face now, then said, "Oh, dear me." And she repeated, "Oh, dear me," before she added, "Come along, they'll be starting the dance again."

"Wait a moment." Nancy Ann put her hand tentatively on the older woman's arm. "Could you explain?"

"No, I can't. No, I can't, my dear. I've done all the explaining and meddling that I'm going to do for this evening."

"I . . . I would like to go home, Lady Golding."

"You are doing no such thing." The voice had changed. "You are going into that ballroom with your head as high as

it was a few minutes ago, and you are going to dance, and I don't think you'll be short of partners.''

A dance wasn't in progress as she entered the ballroom: the band was tuning up and people were standing in groups talking.

Following Lady Golding, she made her way to her seat where Peter was waiting. He had been talking to a lady, one of the few who had smiled at her kindly during the first part of the evening, and it was with an apprehensive look and a shaking of the head that he greeted his sister. However, the lady stretched out her hand and patted Nancy Ann's arm, saying in an undertone, ''That was the best bit of entertainment I've had in a long while. She needed that, she's been asking for it. I only wished I'd had the courage to do it myself.'' Then turning to Lady Golding, she said, ''What do you think, Pat?''

''The same as you, Flo. The same as you.''

''Ah, there they go.'' The band had struck up with a polka. ''And here comes the master of the house.'' The lady turned and left them, smiling and nodding her head.

As Nancy Ann went to seat herself, Dennison reached her and, thrusting out his arm towards her, said, ''No, you don't. No more sitting down for you,'' and without ceremony he whirled her towards the middle of the floor and they were lost amongst the other dancers.

''Did you enjoy your meal?'' he asked.

''Yes, yes, it was lovely.'' She looked into his face. It was flushed and his eyes were very bright, his lips looked red and he smiled all the while. He's drunk a lot of wine, she thought.

''You know something?''

''I know very little.'' And that was true, she thought; there was much explanation needed as to why she was here tonight.

''I think you are wonderful . . . a wonderful dancer.''

''It is because you are so good yourself, you make me dance.''

''I would like always to make you dance, and dance, and dance.''

Someone dunched into them, and there was much laughter and excusing; then they were off again. . . .

What Lady Golding had said turned out to be true: she

wasn't at a loss for partners. But no one danced as smoothly as Mr. Harpcore. Some held her too tightly, some she felt she herself had to guide.

And then came another interval during which there were more refreshments.

The woman whom she had imitated was quite drunk now and she was still drinking wine and talking loudly, and for the first time during the evening Nancy Ann found herself unprotected by either her host, Lady Golding, or Peter, for her last partner had paid his respects and left her settled near a door. The maids were handing round the refreshments, but all she herself wanted was some fresh air, or to get into a room that wasn't full of people, and one that hadn't a roaring fire in the grate.

Quietly, she sidled out of the door, crossed the anteroom, then made her way down a passage which she imagined would lead her into the main hall. It was a long passage, with a number of doors. One was open and she saw that it led into a library, and she sighed with relief as she said to herself: Nobody will think of coming into a library tonight, at least none of those guests, for most of them are much the worse for wine.

There was a fire in this room too, but it was low in the grate. She walked to the far end, where there was a desk, behind which hung two enormous curtains. To one side was a tall Chinese screen. She looked around it and saw a small chaise-longue upholstered in red velvet. As she thankfully sank on to it, she told herself she'd like to lie down on it, but she mustn't. Anyway, it was too small. She laid her head back and let out a long slow sigh. It was wonderful, to get away from the heat and the bustle, and the noise, because the music had ceased to be music for it could hardly be heard above the chatter.

How many people were here tonight, or this morning, or whatever time it was? Sixty, she would say. She had tried to count them at dinner, but the maids and waiting men had got in the way. What a lot of servants it took to run a house like this. It was another world. Oh, she could just go to sleep here.

The next second she was sitting bolt upright when she heard

the door open, then close, and a recognized voice saying, "Well, you should have explained." Then came Mr. Harpcore's voice answering, "There's nothing to explain so far."

"You mean, she has no inkling?"

"No, not really, Pat."

"Oh, my God!" There was a pause; then Lady Golding's voice came again, saying, "There have I been all night making a bloody fool of myself. I thought she must have had some inkling and I was trying to be helpful; I imagined this was a sort of breaking-in do."

"Breaking-in do, be damned!"

"Well, what else did you mean it to be?"

"Oh, I don't know, Pat. Quite candidly, I don't know where the hell I am. I only know I can't go on in the old way."

"You've been a long time thinking about changing."

"No, I haven't been a long time, only there were difficulties."

"Yes, indeed there were difficulties, and will be in the future. Does Rene know?"

"No."

"Well, I don't envy you the scene that lies ahead of you. Anyway, you should have put me in the picture. I only came tonight because you seemed to want me here specially."

"I did want you specially here."

"But what for?"

"Oh." He paused. "Well, to give a little balance to. . . ."

"Oh, Denny, what have you got yourself into! For years I've told you you should settle down. There was Angela Dearing. I thought. . . . Well, what happened there?"

"Nothing; it might seem irrational, but I didn't want a wife who had been worked over by at least two of my friends."

"Irrational! That is the word. Oh, you men! Well, we'd better be moving into the fray again. But the quicker you bring this into the open the better, I should say, because everyone seems to have an inkling of what is going on except the one concerned."

The door opened and closed again. She put her head on one side. What could she make of that conversation? Did it concern her? No, no. Why should it? Yet, what about those women in the toilet room scoffing. . . . Was he? *No, no;* that was impossible, absolutely impossible. But was it? She recalled the earlier instance when it had occurred to her the reason why her mother had allowed her to accept the invitation to come here. But thinking about it now, she poohpoohed the very idea that her mother would have such a thought in her head: her mother was a good woman, a very good woman, a God-fearing woman, and she knew that no matter how nice and kind Mr. Harpcore was, he was not what you would call a good man. She guessed that her father didn't consider him a good man. So her thoughts had been nothing but wild imaginings.

. . . Oh, she was tired. She wished she were home. Had she to go back into that ballroom? It was lovely to be quiet. But would anyone ever be able to be quiet in this house with so much coming and going? You practically bumped into servants at every step. Of course, they were all on duty tonight; in the usual way they would be spread all over the house, she supposed. She closed her eyes and had a mental picture of the ladies in the powder-room staring at her as she mimicked the lady at the dressing-table. Tomorrow she would make them all laugh at home by taking off some of the guests. And she would make the girls in the kitchen laugh their heads off. She'd barge in and pretend she was Lady Golding: she would stick her finger in her ear, then sniff, and nip the end of her nose between her finger and thumb, and take her tongue round her teeth and push her top lip out, and she would say, "Oh, my God! man," in that tone of voice. . . . Eeh! no, she mustn't say that, using God's name frivolously. It was blasphemy. But hadn't Lady Golding sworn? And Mr. Harpcore too? When she came to think about it, most people present here tonight weren't far removed from the McLoughlins. No, no; they weren't. And on this last thought she leaned her head against the back of the little couch and closed her eyes.

"My God! Where can she have got to?" Peter was sweating visibly, and for the countless time he was asking the question of Dennison, and he, with a hand on his brow, turned to Lady Golding, saying, "You are sure, Pat, that no one said anything to her to upset her?"

"No. I've told you, man. She was dancing with Gabriel

Chester when I left the room, and when I went back she wasn't there.''

Dennison now turned to his valet who was standing a little way behind him and said, ''You've searched the upper rooms, Staith?''

''Yes, sir. And the men have been up in the attics.''

Dennison gritted his teeth and walked away from the group to the far end of the hall where the housekeeper, Mrs. Amelia Conway, was standing, and he almost barked at her, ''You're sure her cape's in the cloakroom?''

''Yes, sir.''

''Fetch it here.''

The housekeeper was about to pass the order to the first housemaid who was standing in a group with other maids, but thought better of it, and hurried away. She returned within a minute and held the cloak out to him.

He took it from her, then walked back towards Peter, saying, ''She wouldn't have gone without her cloak, not in that flimsy dress; she'd get her death out there, it's below freezing.''

''Well, if she's not in the house, she must have gone out.'' Lady Golding let out a deep sigh. ''She's a young girl, she would run and she's likely reached home by now. Something must have happened after I left the ballroom. That's the best explanation I can give you.'' She now turned to Peter, saying, ''And I think if you're wise, young man, you'll ride back there and find out if she's done just that.''

''I can't see her doing it, not dressed as she was. However, I'll go.'' Then turning to Dennison, Peter asked, ''May I take the coach, sir?''

''Of course, of course, anything, only hurry. Get Mr. Hazel's coat.'' He waved to the first footman now, and the man, forgetting the dignity of his position, almost sprinted across the hall. And Dennison shouted to another liveried man, ''Take Mr. Hazel to the stable, the coach will be ready. Move! man.''

Without further words, Peter followed the scurrying servant out of the room. Dennison turned to where Lady Golding was sitting on a high, black-carved, hall chair, and, his voice holding concern, he said, ''You're tired.''

"Yes, I'm tired, Denny, but I'll wait until he comes back. In the meantime, though, I'll go into the drawing-room and put my feet up."

"Yes, yes, do that." He hurried forward and opened the door for her, then said, "Is there anything I can get you?"

"I think I would like a hot coffee with a little brandy."

Having given a servant this order, he saw her to the couch, and when she was seated, he said, "For it to end like this. But I'll tell you this much, Pat, if she has been upset by anyone and I find out who it is, they'll answer to me."

He went from the room now, and as he entered the hall the grandfather clock boomed three. It was more than half an hour since the last guest had departed, but it had been around two o'clock when Peter had first asked him where his sister was. And he had replied, "I thought she was with you. I have been looking for her." And he had laughed and said, "She's likely wandered upstairs and lost herself. She won't be the first one to have done that." But after the last carriage, with the exception of Lady Golding's, had rolled away down the drive and Nancy Ann had still not appeared, then the search had begun in earnest, and with each passing moment there had grown in him the fear, not that something dreadful had happened to her, but that she had run out into the night away from him because of something she had overheard. And it came to him that once again he was to lose someone that he loved.

Since losing his brother, he had never had any real feeling of love for anyone. He'd had the experience of three mistresses, but that wasn't love. However, since he had first set eyes on that child the day he had carried her back to the vicarage, she'd had an effect upon him. But now she was no longer a child, she was a blossoming woman and he wanted her and needed her more than he imagined he would ever want or need anyone in his life again.

Tim had been taken from him through scandal; and the aftermath of that was somewhere in this house still. And now he felt the scandal of his own past life had killed this second love.

He walked slowly along the corridor and into the library. The fire was dead but he sat down on a chair to the side of it. This was his favourite room. It was in this room he had spend wondrous days with his young brother during the holidays. Although there had been five years between them, they had talked as equals.

He had leant forward, his elbows on his knees, his hands dangling between them when he lifted his head with a jerk and peered down the long length of the room to the far corner where the Chinese screen stood. Slowly he rose to his feet. Again he heard the rustle, and then a slight cough.

He was standing now at the foot of the small couch staring wide-eyed down on the curled up sleeping figure. She was lying on her side, her knees up, one arm above her head. Her face was dim in the shadow of the screen.

There now arose in him a great gurgle of laughter that was almost hysterical. He wanted to throw his own arms wide, toss his head back and let out a bellow. It was impossible to stop his next reaction: he was on his knees by the side of the couch, his arms were about her, his cheek touching hers and his voice muttering, "Oh, Nancy Ann. Nancy Ann."

When her eyes opened wide and he saw the look in them he pulled himself upright, saying, "Please, my dear, my dear, don't be afraid. We've been looking all over for you. We . . . we thought you were lost."

Seeing the look still on her face, he withdrew further from her and, standing up and aiming to keep the emotion from his voice, he said, "Do you know what time it is?"

She pulled herself upright while pushing her dress over her ankles; then slowly swinging her feet to the floor, she blinked up at him, saying, "I . . . I must have fallen asleep."

"Yes, my dear, and . . . and you've given us all a scare."

"Why?"

"Well, no one could find you. We had searched the house from attic to cellar. Your brother has taken the coach back to the vicarage thinking you might have run out into the night. We . . . we surmised that someone must have upset you."

She pulled herself to her feet now, saying quietly, "Peter has gone back? Oh! my parents will be upset."

"Don't worry." He put his hand out and placed it on her shoulder. "He will be back within a matter of minutes." Suddenly he turned from her and put his hand to his head, and this action elicited from her an immediate query. Her voice full of concern, she said, "What is it? Are you ill?"

He did not answer straightaway. When he did, it was a mutter: "Just reaction at finding you alive and well. Oh! my dear." He turned to her again and now drew her from behind the screen and down the room and to the leather couch that was facing the dead fire, and he said, "Sit down for a moment."

She sat down, saying now, "Oh, I am sorry I have caused an upset, but it was the heat, and . . . and I ate too much and had wine. I'm . . . I'm sorry."

"Don't be sorry, my dear Nancy Ann." He had hold of both her hands now. "I'm going to ask you something and I want you to give me just a plain straight answer. Do you like me?"

She blinked rapidly before she answered, "Yes, yes, I like you."

"Nothing more?"

She considered for a moment, then said, "I . . . I hardly know you, do I? except through your kindness to Mama."

"No; that's true. But do you think you could ever come to . . . well, more than like me?"

She turned her gaze away from his, and she began to shiver inside. "I . . . I have never thought of you in that way," she said and slowly withdrew her hands from his.

"Well, would you consider thinking of me in that way from now on?"

She looked straight at him now, and after a moment she said softly, "Truthfully, I don't know. And there is Mama and Papa to consider."

"Yes, yes, of course, I understand, but would you consider it too precipitate of me if I were to speak to your father sometime soon? I . . . I don't want to rush you. We . . . we could be friends and get to know each other more."

She looked towards the dead ashes; then softly she said, "Am I not too young for you?"

As her face was turned from him, he could bite tight down on his lower lip; "No, my dear, the question is, am I too old for you? Do you consider me old?"

Slowly she turned her gaze on him once more. He was a

handsome man in a sort of way, but at the moment she just could not understand why he would want to marry her. Bluntly she asked, "How old are you?"

Unsmiling, he answered, "I am thirty-three next birthday which is close to your own."

"Thirty-three." She seemed to consider. It was old but not all that old. He was sixteen years older than her, almost twice her age.

"Do I appear so old to you?"

"No"—she gave him a small smile—"not all that old."

"I'm glad of that, Nancy Ann." His hands came out swiftly and caught hers again and he went on, his voice low and rapid, "I must tell you now, I love you. I feel I have loved you for a long time and I promise that if you will marry me, I'll make it my life's work to see that you are happy."

He could sense the increased trembling within her through her hands, and he said, "You are not afraid of me? Please say you are not afraid of me."

"Oh. Oh no, only I have never been . . . well, I mean no one has ever said they wanted to marry me, or that they"— she lowered her gaze—"loved me. It is all very strange; and it will all have to depend on Mama and Papa and. . . ."

Suddenly he left hold of her hands and, rising to his feet, he said, "Come. I think your brother must have returned, there is a commotion in the hall."

But before opening the library door to let her out, he caught her hand once more and, lifting it upwards, he did not kiss it but pressed it against her cheek for a moment as he stared into her flushed face. Then, taking her by the arm, he hurried her out along the corridor and into the hall, there to see not only her brother but her father too.

"Where was she?" It was Peter, his voice loud now and demanding; then not waiting for an answer he looked at Nancy Ann and cried, "Where have you been?"

"I . . . I fell asleep in . . . in the library behind a screen. I . . . I was so hot. Oh! Papa." She ran to John now and put her arms around his neck, and he patted her shoulder while he looked at the man who was now saying, "I couldn't believe my eyes. I had been in that room half a dozen times and never thought to look behind the screen. It is a small screen in the corner of the room and hides a still smaller couch, a miniature. That's why no one thought of looking behind it. I'm sorry, sir, that you have been troubled.''

John now looked at this man whom he saw was perturbed in some way, and naturally he would be, and he said, "I am sorry too, sir, that you have been put to so much trouble. It seems a weakness of my daughter to get into scrapes that enlist your help.''

"Father is right." Peter was nodding at Dennison now. ''She always manages to create a stir. And it was such a lovely evening; I enjoyed myself immensely, and so did she. Didn't you?'' He turned to her, and she nodded at him and, leaving her father's side, she walked the few steps until she was once again standing in front of Dennison and, holding out her hand, she said, ''Good night. And thank you for the evening and everything.''

Her words seemed to please him and he smiled warmly at her. Then going towards her father, he said, ''Couldn't I offer you something hot before you make the journey back?''

''No, thank you. Her mother is naturally perturbed, so we must make all haste and return home. And I must say again, I am sorry for the disturbance my daughter has caused. It was most inconsiderate of her, not to mention very ill-mannered. Good night, sir.''

Nancy Ann had been given her cloak by a very stiff-faced housekeeper, and her father now marshalled her before him out of the door, and down the steps to where the coach stood; but Peter, before following them, held out his hand to Dennison, saying, ''If she had been just a year younger, I would have boxed her ears.''

At this, both men laughed.

As Dennison stood on the top step and watched the coach door close on Peter, his valet came out and put a cape around his shoulders, and he made a motion of thanks with his hand, then continued to stand until the coach had disappeared into the lamplit trees bordering the drive. Presently he slowly turned and went indoors, and when he realized his valet was following him up the stairs he stopped and turned, saying, ''It's all right, Staith. Get to bed, I'll see to myself.''

''Are you sure, sir?''

"Yes, yes, I am sure."

In his room he tore off his cravat and his velvet jacket, threw off his patent leather shoes, then dropped into the easy chair that was placed to the side of a fire that was still burning brightly and, leaning back, he closed his eyes and muttered aloud, "Oh, Nancy Ann. Nancy Ann." And he saw again in his mind her sleeping face when he had first laid his head against hers. That was before the look of terror had come into her eyes. Then he muttered, "May all the gods that be, including the parson's, stand by me in this."

❧ PART FOUR ❧

The Engagement

❧ 1 ❧

THE FACT THAT DENNISON SHOULD ATTEND A CHURCH SER-
vice on New Year's morning suggested to the household staff
there was indeed something in the wind. The thought that he
might be serious about the chit from the vicarage was really
unbelievable to them; yet, all the signs pointed to the fact
there were changes in the air, and the top hierarchy of the
butler, the housekeeper, the valet, and the first footman were
greatly disturbed. It was they who ran the household; they
who, for the most part of the year, gave the orders, and especially did this apply to the valet and the housekeeper. But
what was significant to all the members of the household was
that this was the first New Year in the last ten that the master
had not welcomed in in Scotland, where, accompanied by a
number of his staff and a greater number of his friends, a
riotous time was wont to be had by one and all. And what
had happened here last night? The master's only company
had been Lady Beatrice and Lady Golding, and at one o'clock
Lady Golding had been able to walk straight to her coach
while Lady Beatrice had had to be helped upstairs. It was
well known she couldn't carry her drink. As for the master,
well, they just shook their heads: he had walked steady when
he had gone upstairs at two o'clock this morning. Of course,
he was used to carrying his drink; it was very rarely it floored
him. . . .

The fact that it had been the strangest New Year his staff had ever experienced wasn't lost on Dennison, and he wondered if the man who was sitting opposite to him now and who was attempting to cover his disapproval knew to what extent he himself had altered, if only by way of changing his life style, in order to bring himself to utter the words he had just spoken: "I hope it comes as no surprise to you, the reason for my visit this morning. I wish to ask for your daughter in marriage."

He watched the parson rise and then tower over him for a moment as if he were God himself; he watched the plain black-buttoned coat swell; he watched him turn away and stretch out his hand and grip the mantelpiece and look down into the fire. And when the man spoke, it seemed it was with an effort he said, "There, in a way, you are wrong, sir, for I fail to understand why a man of your position and"—there was a sound of a deep swallow before the next words came—"way of life, should wish to choose my daughter for a wife."

Dennison too now rose to his feet, and quietly he said, "May I answer that by saying, she's had such an effect upon me it has caused me to alter my way of life. I am well aware that that has not been blameless, but in defence of myself I can say that I have never knowingly hurt anyone. What I mean, if I may speak plainly, sir, is that what associations I have had have been with my own class; I have never given cause for pain or scandal to anyone below my station. It could be said of me, I have been a man of my time and class. Yet now I wish to change all that: my one desire is to settle down and have a family, and I've never met a woman in my life that I've had an affection for as for your daughter. I know she is young and I'm quite willing to wait a reasonable time if I have your permission to put my suit to her." He dare not state that he had already made evident his suit to her. "I promise you, sir, I shall cherish her."

It was a full minute filled with unease before John turned from the fireplace and said, "I must not lie to you about my feelings in this matter. You would not be my choice for a proper husband for my daughter, but my wife, who has only a certain time left to her, wishes to see her settled before that time expires. That is a factor in your favour. But finally, the choice lies with Nancy Ann herself. Naturally, I have not spoken to her of marriage so I don't know where her feelings lie, or even if she has given any thought to it at all. Young girls usually have romantic ideas, but she is of a very sensible turn of mind and older than her years, so in this matter I will trust her to make her own decision. If you will excuse me, sir, I shall send her in to you.''

Left alone, Dennison now stood with his back to the fire and looked around the room. To him it was the most depressing sight, showing not one sign of comfort. The furniture was heavy and ugly, in fact all he had seen of the rest of the house was depressing. Oh, what a different life he would open up for her. He would show her London, Paris, Rome. There was so much beauty to be seen. And how her own beauty would ripen in such surroundings.

He looked towards the door, waiting for it to open, and when after some moments it didn't, he not only became impatient, but worried. He moved from the fireplace and walked to the window, and found he was looking onto a vegetable garden that appeared full of cabbages, here and there their naked stumps standing petrified with the frost. The ground at one end was hacked into mounds as if someone had just finished digging. He swung round from the window when he heard a noise outside the door. But when it didn't open he walked quickly to the fireplace again, and now literally shivered. The room was cold and he couldn't expect a fire such as this one to heat it. He drew his lips tight in between his teeth. She wasn't coming.

When the door eventually opened, it was with an effort that he stopped himself from rushing forward; instead, smiling quietly, he went towards her and held out his hand.

Nancy Ann hesitated a second or so before placing her hand in his, and he held it whilst drawing her up the room towards the fireplace. Here, he took her other hand and they looked at each other without speaking.

Strangely, her mind wasn't in a whirl. It had stopped whirling yesterday after a talk with her grandmama who had said, ''Think hard. Forget about your mother for a moment. One thing is sure, you'll never in your life again get such an offer as he is making you. It doesn't, or very rarely does, happen to young girls in your position. Mating up with another young parson is the rule, and then, generally, bread and scrape for the rest of your life, as happened to your mother. But this, of course, is compensated for where love is. You say you like him. Well, that's a good start to any marriage. And liking, like pity, is the first cousin to love. But when you next meet him give yourself an answer to the question: Could you bear him to put his arms about you and hold you close? because marriage is made up of close proximity of the body, if not of the mind.''

Could she bear him to put his arms about her? He looked strong; there was a clean smell coming from him; he was, in a way, she supposed, handsome. His hair was thick and of a dark brown shade; his eyes were grey, his eyebrows were dark; he was clean-shaven, but there was a faint bluish hue about his chin.

She took her eyes from his face and looked down on their joined hands. His did not seem to match his body which was thick set and sturdy looking, because they were long, the fingers thin.

''Well, Nancy Ann, what is my answer?''

She looked at him, again holding his deep gaze for a moment before saying quietly, ''Yes, I will marry you.'' Then almost painfully, she went on, ''But there are conditions.'' His head moved, his face stretched slightly whilst waiting for her to state these. And she did: ''You will continue to attend church on a Sunday as you have been doing of late, but now you will accompany me,'' she said.

He wanted to throw back his head again and roar at her condition. She was such a child. But in the next moment she disabused him of this idea by adding, ''Because your presence there has only been a lead up to this moment, hasn't it?''

''Oh, Nancy Ann.'' His tone sounded as if he were offended. ''Do you think that?''

''Oh!'' Her hands were tugged from his in an impatient movement and, her voice loud, she cried, ''If . . . if we are to become acquainted, better acquainted, please don't treat me as a child and underestimate my . . . my intelligence.''

He looked at her in stupefied silence. She was right. Oh,

she was right. Good gracious. She had character. In this moment she put him in mind of Pat. Yet she looked so young, so . . . so . . .

"I'm sorry. Forgive me," he said. "And I assure you, from now on I shall not underestimate your intelligence. Oh no. And yes, you are right, it was all a lead up to this moment." There was a slight smile at the corner of his lips now. "What is more, I'll agree to your terms: whenever we are at home I'll accompany you to church. Is that the only term?"

Now she allowed a smile to touch her lips as she answered, "No; there are others, but all in due course." Her smile widened. She felt a wave of relief sweeping over her: she could talk to him like this; that must augur good for the future.

Again he caught her hands, and drawing them together now and to the front of his high-buttoned jacket, he said softly, "May I kiss you?" Even as he spoke the words he was thinking that it was the first time in his life he'd asked a woman if he had permission to kiss her.

When she made no reply but blinked her eyelids rapidly, he left hold of her hands, put his arms around her and gently drew her towards him, and when he put his mouth on her lips that made no response, he felt such a surge of feeling sweep over him that he warned himself: Steady. Steady. Go easy.

It was over. She had been kissed by a man on the mouth. And it had been quite a pleasant sensation. She couldn't remember being kissed on the mouth even by her mama or grandmama; the boys and her father, of course, always kissed her on the cheek.

"Nancy Ann, you have made me a very happy man, and so now I will make you a promise that I hope I shall be able to keep, and that is, I shall never willingly cause you distress."

That was nice of him. She liked him better the more she saw of him. And she had liked his arms about her too. . . . Oh, yes she had.

"I'm forgetting the most important thing," he said, putting his hand into the pocket of his three quarter length coat. He drew out a small box; then having opened it, he presented it to her.

She looked down on the sparkling ring. It was a gold band with a half hoop of six diamonds, and not small ones. She had never been one to wear jewellery, for the simple reason that she had only the gold pendant given to her on her last birthday by her mama, and a brooch that supposedly had belonged to her grandmother's grandmother.

He had taken the ring from its case and now, holding her hand gently, he slipped it onto the third finger of her left hand. Then, raising her hand to his lips, he kissed it, saying, "It is sealed." Then he added, "How say you, my dear?"

She gulped in her throat before, holding her hand in front of her face, she looked at the ring and whispered, "Yes, it is sealed."

"Now shall we go and show it to your mama and grand-mama and your brother?"

He did not mention her father, and this omission did not pass her unnoticed. Taking her hand now, he led her down the room, but at the door her drew her to a standstill, saying softly, "We shan't experience any privacy for some time, and so may I?" Again he was requesting that he kiss her.

She said nothing but bent slightly towards him; and this time, when he placed his mouth on hers, her lips were not as tight as they had been previously. And all the more he had to quell the urge to press her tightly to him.

On opening the door into the hall, the first person he saw was Peter, who stopped and looked towards them. And Dennison, still holding Nancy Ann's arm, led her forward, saying, "Well, my future brother-in-law, will you wish us happiness?"

Peter glanced at him for a moment; then he looked at his sister and, taking her into his arms, he hugged her in a way that Dennison envied, saying, "I wish you all happiness, Nancy Ann. You know that."

"Yes, Peter. Thank you."

Then he said, "You just missed Father. He's gone to the church."

"Well, we'll go and see him there after we've seen Mama and Grandmama."

She now walked hurriedly away across the hall and into

her mother's room, and it would seem that both her mother and grandmother were awaiting her entry.

At a run, she made for the bed and, without a word, bent forward and kissed her mother tenderly, then held out her hand with the ring on it.

Rebecca's thin white hands held the warm tinted one as she looked down on the ring. Then lifting her gaze to the man who was now standing at the foot of the bed, she said, "You will be good to her?" And he answered simply, "On my life, madam."

Nancy Ann had now turned to her grandmama, and Jessica, the tears running freely down her face, said nothing, but pulling herself up from the chair, she held her granddaughter tightly to her. Then, as was her way, she looked at Dennison, saying bluntly now, "You don't deserve her, you know, and I hope you realize how lucky you are."

"I do indeed. I do indeed, madam. No one realizes it more than I do." And bending slightly towards her, he smiled as he said, "Now I must raise the question of how long it is before I may take the liberty and have the honour of calling you Grandmama?"

"Oh." She flapped her hand at him. "Time enough for that; the proceedings have just begun."

Their attention was now drawn to the woman in the bed for she was saying softly, "June is a lovely month for a wedding. You can nearly always rely on the weather in June, at least towards the end."

Dennison's countenance stretched. Nancy Ann's mother's words had utterly amazed him. He had been prepared for a fight on his hands against a long engagement, with the parson suggesting two years, even three. But he wouldn't have had that: he would have beaten him down to a year, enough time to have the house refurbished to his bride's taste and the wedding preparations put into motion. Yet, here was the mother suggesting June.

He forced the look of surprise from his face and kept his tone flat as he said, "Yes, indeed, June is a good month," only to be slightly dismayed when Nancy Ann put in on a surprised note, "June? But Mama, that is not time. . . ." But she stopped as she stared at the thin face lying in the hollow of the pillow, and a great sadness overwhelmed her. She knew why her mother had proposed so early a time for the wedding and she wanted to fling herself on to her breast and cry out, "No! No! You will have much longer than that, so much longer." But her grandmama was deciding things for her: "Yes, I agree with you, Rebecca, June is the right month for a wedding," she was saying, and then she turned to Dennison: "Are you in agreement, sir?"

"Yes. Oh, yes. That is, if it's agreeable with Nancy Ann."

And Nancy Ann returned his look, saying, "Yes, I'm quite agreeable."

When Rebecca let out a thin long sigh, Jessica said, "Away with both of you now, and go and tell the girls."

"Oh, yes"—Nancy Ann smiled—"we must tell the girls. They won't believe it." And she glanced at Dennison and repeated, "They won't believe it, but we must tell them."

In the hall, Dennison drew her gently to a stop, saying, "The girls. Who are the girls?"

"Oh." She pulled in the left corner of her lip as she was wont to do when secretly amused, and now she said, "The maids. We have three, Peggy the cook, Jane her assistant, and Hilda the housemaid."

The quirk to her lips disappeared as he said, "Well, my dear, you go and break my glad news to them; I'll have a word with Peter." He pointed. "I can see him in the sitting-room."

"Very well." She stepped back from him, then walked slowly towards the kitchen door. It was understandable, she supposed, that he wouldn't want to meet the maids; he had a house full of servants, some of whom likely he couldn't recognize. . . . And she was to be mistress of them. The thought daunted her. Would she be able to go into the kitchen and chat with them? No, never; at least she supposed not, from what she had seen of them at the ball.

Peggy had been scraping the frame of a chicken, preparatory to mincing the bits and pieces to make patties for the evening meal, and those would be preceded by soup derived from the carcass; Hilda had been preparing vegetables, while Jane had been pulling up a wooden clotheshorse on which she had just hung some wet tea towels. But now they were all gathered round her. Peggy, wiping her greasy hands on her apron, was indeed reacting in the way Nancy Ann had forecast to Dennison: "I'll never believe it," she was saying, "that you're going up there to be mistress of that place. I'll never believe it."

"Nor me," cried Jane. "You're much too young for it," which brought a sharp rebuke from Peggy, "Shut your mouth, you!" while Hilda said, "Miss. Miss. 'Tis like a fairy tale. I wish you all the happiness in the world."

"And me an' all, miss, and me an' all," Jane put in. "Oh, yes, I wish you happiness. We all wish you happiness. Don't we, Cook?"

Her face unsmiling now, Peggy nodded, saying somewhat sadly, "Aye, Miss Nancy Ann, that's what we all wish you, happiness, long life, a big family, and happiness."

"Oh, aye, a big family, ten of 'em." Jane grinned now, and Hilda, pushing her, said, "Shut up, will you!"

"I must go."

"Is . . . is he still here?" asked Jane now, who was always quite undaunted by her superiors' rebuffs.

"Yes, yes, he's still here." Nancy Ann smiled at her.

"When d'you expect it to happen, miss?" Hilda asked, and when Nancy Ann answered, "June, towards the end," they all exclaimed loudly, "June! So soon?"

Her face straight now, Nancy Ann answered quietly, "Yes; Mother would like it in June."

"Oh, aye. Aye." Peggy nodded at her.

"Well"—Nancy Ann backed from them—"I'll be seeing you shortly."

"Yes, miss. Yes, miss." They nodded at her, then sent more good wishes to her as she walked up the kitchen. But once the door had closed on her, they looked at each other and Peggy said, "June. My God! And she not yet turned seventeen and he old enough . . . well, he's old enough to be her father."

"And with a name like he's got."

This time Peggy did not silence Jane, but it was Hilda who said, "Black sheep or white, under the skin I think there's good in him, and if there is she'll bring it out."

❧ 2 ❧

NANCY ANN DID NOT SEE HER INTENDED HUSBAND THE FOL-
lowing day, but in the early evening when it was already black
dark, the coach drew up at the door and the footman delivered
a very large cardboard box covered in fancy paper with a
letter attached to the bow of coloured tape tying the box.

Nancy Ann took the box to her mother's room, and there,
in the presence of her father and mother and grandmother,
she untied the tape, leaving the letter aside for the moment,
and after lifting the lid and parting the layers of fine paper,
she stood gaping down at the articles of fur lying there. It
was her grandmother who prompted, and in no small voice,
"Well, take them out, girl! Take them out. See what they
are."

There was a sable three-quarter length cape, a matching
hat, and a large muff. The hat had a crown but the back was
shaped like a bonnet and fell over the collar of the cape, and
from it there dangled four strips of fur; the same trimming
was on the front of the muff.

When she was attired in the outfit, her mother smiled and
moved her head backwards and forwards on the pillow as if
in amazement. And her grandmother's eyes glowed. Only her
father showed no appreciation.

Jessica, fingering the collar of the cape, said in awe, "Sable. Pure sable. Look at it, John Howard."

"I can see. I can see." And John Howard looked into his daughter's face bedecked with the fur hat and framed by the round fur collar, and he knew he should be happy for her. And he wished he could be. And in this moment he told himself, he must try, he must try. Perhaps, as Rebecca had said, their daughter could be the making of the man. He had already shown a form of courage in coming to church, for he must well know that this would have held him up to ridicule by many of his friends. Yes, he must, as his dear wife said, try to see the good in the man. And so now he smiled at his daughter, saying in as light a tone as he could muster, "Your vanity will no doubt be increased when everyone acclaims your beauty to be enhanced."

The compliment was precise, but nevertheless it was a compliment. Forgetting about her fine apparel, she flung a hand from the muff and her arms around the tall thin man; and he held her to him for a moment. Then, pressing her from him, he said, "It'll all be crushed."

"Fur doesn't crush, Papa."

"No, it only goes shiny and bald."

They all laughed now at Jessica's remark. And when she added, "Open the letter and see who it's from, girl," the laughter rose.

The letter was short.

My dear one,
   This, my first gift to you, I hope you find suitable.
   I shall call for you tomorrow about three o'clock, with the intention of taking you to The House and introducing you to the staff and the rest of your future home.

The letter ended,

   The library you are well acquainted with. If it complies with your wish I shall have a certain piece of furniture removed from there and set in your boudoir.
                    Ever your loving and grateful Dennison.

She folded up the sheet of paper and returned it to the envelope. It was her first love letter. She had the desire to press it tightly to her, but she told herself that would be silly, for she wasn't as yet in love with him. Yet what was love? Was it this excitement which the gift had filled her with? And more so, the tone of his letter? She liked him. Oh, she did, she did. . . . But tomorrow, having to meet the staff.

She looked from one to the other, saying now, "He wishes me to go tomorrow to The House to . . . to see what is to be done and to meet the staff." She shook her head, then added, in a small voice, "I'll . . . I'll be scared, so afraid. I . . . I won't know how to react."

"Don't you be so silly." It was her grandmama speaking again. "You will react as you always do, sensibly, with your shoulders back and your head held up."

The door opened as Jessica finished speaking and Hilda said, "Parson, Mr. Mercer has called. He'd liked a word with you."

"Oh, yes. Yes."

It seemed that John left the room with relief, and his greeting of Graham Mercer was hearty. He held out his hand, saying, "This is a pleasant surprise, Graham."

"I hope I am not disturbing you at this hour."

"Not at all. Not at all. You could never disturb me. Come in. Come in." He led the way into the sitting-room and immediately went to the table and turned up the wick of the lamp, then said, "Sit down, my friend. Sit down."

"I won't stay long. I . . . I just want to ask you a question, even while I already know the answer. Is it true that . . . that your daughter has become engaged to Harpcore?"

It was a moment before John answered him, for he was staring at the man whom he saw was agitated. And this was strange, because his manner could usually be called sedate, even more so than his own. And so it was quietly that he answered, "Yes. Yes, that's so."

"Why have you allowed it?"

Again he was taken aback, albeit slightly, by the forthright question, and it flummoxed him for a moment. However, before he could give an answer Graham said, "You know what kind of a man he is: he's an inveterate gambler; besides which . . . well, there are other things, but his gambling has made him notorious. He is, I know, a member of Tangents in Newcastle, a very unsavoury club. He also goes up to town, to London, where he is a member of one which is an absolute byword. And then there are the . . ." His head drooped forward and the words now seemed to come from between his teeth as he demanded, "Why did you do it? Why did you allow it?"

John was totally nonplussed now; yet there was a light dawning in his mind, and he said quietly, "Sit down." And when Graham shook his head, he appealed, "Please."

When they were seated opposite to each other at either side of the fireplace, it was Graham who spoke. "I'm . . . I'm sorry, but it came as rather a shock," he said. "If . . . if only I had known. You see, she is so young. I considered her so young. I was a fool, a slow fool. I've always been a fool." He raised his head and looked at John. "Right from the beginning of my life I've been a fool."

"Oh, no, no." John drew himself to the edge of his chair and put out his hand, saying, "You are no fool, Graham, but a gentleman of rare quality. My sons have always esteemed your friendship. No, never call yourself a fool."

"Then I can say I am fated never to know happiness because I never go about things in the right way: I always walk when I should leap; I remain dumb when I should speak. As you well know I hid myself away because I couldn't face life after one disappointment." He bowed his head, and John said, "I'm sorry. I can say this in all truth, I am sorry that you walked instead of leaping in this instant and remained dumb when you should have spoken. Yes, indeed, I am sorry."

A silence ensued between them for a moment; then Graham, raising his head, said, "Is she happy?"

"How can one say? To me she is still a child, but the womenfolk would impress that she is no longer a child but a young woman. And I suppose they are right because next week she will be seventeen years old. What she really feels, I must admit I don't know."

"She must care for him in some way."

"There are different shades of caring, and, as we all know, this period in a young person's life is made up of values that are often questionable. It is only later when one looks back

one is amazed at having escaped the consequences of such
wrong thinking. My dear Graham, I can honestly say at this
moment I am sad as to the future of my daughter, but I would
not have felt this in any way if I could have seen her future
joined to yours.''

"Thank you.'' Graham rose to his feet and John did likewise, and as they looked at each other Graham said quietly,
"You will not, of course, give her any hint of this?''

"No. No, never,'' John answered.

"Thank you.''

Together they walked down the room and out into the hall,
there to see Nancy Ann about to go upstairs. She was carrying the fur cape, muff, and hat across her arm. Turning,
she smiled widely at the visitor, and, taking a few steps towards him, she said, "Good-evening, Mr. Mercer.''

"Good-evening, Nancy Ann.''

He was looking at the furs across her arm, and she looked
down at them too, and, as if apologising for them, she said,
"They . . . they are a present.''

"Yes, yes, a present.''

Now she looked at her father before returning her gaze on
Graham Mercer and to ask quietly, "Did Papa tell you?''

Graham slanted his eyes towards John, then said, "Yes,
yes, your papa told me, and . . . and I wish you happiness,
Nancy Ann. I shall always wish you happiness.''

She watched him turn away and pick up his hat from a side
table. She too turned away and went slowly up the stairs.
What was the matter? What had they been talking about? He
looked sad, different. She liked Mr. Mercer. The boys thought
the world of him. He had wished her happiness, but it hadn't
sounded right. She hoped nothing was wrong with him. She
had always liked him; he was such a nice man, a good man.

She laid the furs on her bed and as she stroked the muff
her thoughts left Mr. Mercer. They were so beautiful. He . . .
he must have gone out today and bought them for her. He
was kind. She did like him; yes, she did.

It had just begun to snow when the carriage drew up at the
foot of The House's steps. The doors were open and two
footmen stood on the terrace, and when Dennison shouted,

"Bring an umbrella," one of them disappeared, to reappear within a few seconds with a large umbrella, which he pushed up as he ran down the steps. And as Dennison helped Nancy Ann down from the coach the footman held it over her, and she smiled at him whilst checking herself from saying, There was no need for this, I'm quite used to snow, for the man's actions immediately brought back to her all her grandmama had said earlier on this morning.

"Now I am not saying you should be stiff-necked with servants," she had said, "but that lot up there aren't like those three in our kitchen. They have been with you all your life: they are connected with the family, they seem part of it and you are familiar with them, too familiar at times. But now you are going into a different world, and those up there will likely all be lined up in the hall. And whatever you do, don't attempt to shake hands, or stop and speak to any individual one. And as for your countenance, keep it pleasant, but don't smile. Somebody, likely the housekeeper or the butler, will call out their names and give you their positions. Incline your head if it's necessary, but that's all. Now remember that. And if any of the upper hierarchy take a high hand with you, walk up the steps of your position and look down on them. You know what I mean?"

Oh, she knew what her grandmama meant all right, but she was going to find great difficulty in carrying out her instructions, especially the last piece of advice: she didn't like the idea of looking down on anyone; in fact, it was against her papa's teaching. Of course, he also said that God had placed each and every one of us in a certain position in life and we had to act in that position according to our capabilities. God expected nothing more of us.

She was inside the hall now, and the warmth struck her immediately, causing her to glance towards the roaring fire set in the deep stone fireplace at the end of the room. It was deep enough for suits of armour to be placed in the alcoves at each side of it..

The butler was taking her cloak and muff and woollen gloves. She knew that the woollen gloves didn't really match the fur, but they were her best ones; as was her plain grey winter coat, and only yesterday she had turned down the cuffs because her arms had grown too long for the sleeves. It was a very nice coat, made of Melton cloth, which her grandmama had bought for her two years ago. It was the nicest coat she had ever had, and she liked it, at least she had up to this moment. But now, divested of the furs, she glanced down at herself. Her whole body looked thin and long.

Having now unbuttoned her coat, she let the butler take it. She then smoothed down the front of her blue alpaca dress. She had always thought that this was pretty, but of a sudden, like her coat, it, too, felt dowdy set against the colours of the menservants' livery and the carpets and drapes in this hall. Somehow she was noticing things more now than she had done on the night of the ball.

"Come, my dear." Dennison took her by the elbow, saying in an aside to one of the menservants, "We will have tea in the pink drawing-room. I shall then ring when I want you to assemble them."

He led Nancy Ann across the hall, down a broad corridor, and into a room, which she saw immediately why it was so called: the drapes at the window were pink velvet with deep tasselled pelmets; the carpet, too, had once been a bright pink but was now faded in parts; as was also the upholstery of the two velvet couches and small chairs arranged here and there. But it was a lovely room, so warm and welcoming.

He drew her towards the couch that was placed opposite the fire, another large one, not so large perhaps as the one in the hall, but piled high with burning logs and coal, which she knew immediately was an extravagance because you shouldn't burn logs and coal together: coal didn't last half as long when it was mixed with wood. . . . Why was she thinking like this?

He was shaking her hands, saying now, "Don't look so far away, look at me."

Obediently she looked at him, and now he said, "This is a great occasion, our first tea together. I love this time of day, don't you?" And without waiting for an answer he went on, "No matter where I am, I always try to have a cup of tea about this time, even if—" he put his face so close to hers their noses almost touched and in a mere whisper he added, "even if I've indulged in overmuch wine."

She kept her lips tightly together to suppress a smile; then she actually laughed aloud when he added, "I consider it a great virtue, one I should be given recognition or an award for, that I should like tea."

He was saying, "I love to see you laugh," when the door opened and the butler entered, carrying a large silver tray, on which was placed a full silver tea service. A footman followed pushing a tea-trolley. It had two shelves and these were laden with plates, each holding an assortment of small sandwiches or a variety of pastries.

As the servants set about arranging the small tables to each side of them and preparing to serve tea, she was slightly embarrassed that he continued talking to her as if they weren't there, saying such things as, "Are you prepared for a two-mile walk around the house? I must confess there are parts I haven't seen for years. And we must discuss the engagement party. Yes, that is important."

When there came the sound of a teacup being rattled in a saucer, he turned his head abruptly, saying, "Leave them . . . leave it. We'll see to it."

Both men bowed towards him, then hastily went from the room. Smiling at her, Dennison rose from the couch, saying, "Men are clumsy with teacups. I am myself. Will you do the honours?"

She was quite used to serving the tea, but her hands trembled as she lifted the silver teapot. Then abruptly placing it back on its stand, she said, "If they made"—she nodded towards the door—"a tinkle with the cups, I'm going to make a clatter, because . . . well, I'm as nervous as a kitten. And . . . and look, there's a lemon here and milk, which do you want?"

The answer she was given was a loud laugh, almost a bellow, as he flopped back on to the couch, very like the boys would do when something amused them greatly. And it brought her from the table to stand looking down at him. He had one arm tightly around his waist and she noticed with amazement that tears of laughter were running down his cheeks. She herself couldn't really see anything at all very funny in what she had said; but then of a sudden she felt herself gripped and pulled down on to the couch, almost across his knees. And now he was holding her close and crying, "Nancy Ann, you are delightful. You're as fresh as the wind from the sea. Oh, I love you, I love you, my dear." And he hugged her to him tightly, kissing her face, not just her mouth, but her eyes, her cheeks, the tip of her nose, and then her lips. And when at last his face moved away from hers she was gasping for breath and his voice came to her softly now, saying, "Believe me, Nancy Ann, I love you. I love you so much I wonder just how I've lived without you for so long. Say that you will grow to love me. Come, say it."

There was a constriction in her throat, and there was a feeling inside of her that wasn't unpleasant: she was so relieved that his caress hadn't aroused fear in her. Her voice came very small as she said, "I . . . I think I might. I'll try." She croaked in her throat, then coughed, and he laughed and pulled her to him again, but gently now; then playfully, almost as one of the boys might have done, but less roughly, he pushed her away, saying, "I have lemon in my tea, woman. What do you have?"

"Milk."

She was at the table again and she noticed that there was a silver strainer resting on each cup. Dear, dear; they were afraid of a few tea-leaves. Well!

She poured out the tea, then said, "Do I squeeze the lemon in?"

Now he was standing beside her and pointing to a silver half-moon shaped object with two small handles attached to the middle. He picked it up, opened it out, took a half slice of lemon, placed it between the two silver half-moons; then, holding it over the tea, he pressed it, and the juice was squeezed out. Then looking sternly at her, he said, "Miss, you have a lot to learn before I can take you into my service."

And she, answering in what she thought a similar vein, and mimicking Peggy's voice, said, "I don't think I'll accept your service; it's too finicky, sir." And at this he swung her round towards him, almost upsetting the cup of tea, and, holding her by the shoulders, he said, "That was said in fun, but it frightens me."

"Oh, I'm sorry, mister, I am that, I am that." This was

said in Mrs. McLoughlin's voice, and she closed her eyes and tried to suppress a smile.

"Yes, you are a clever mime, aren't you? You've got it to a fine art. But don't you dare mimic me."

"No, Mr. Harpcore, I won't. I won't." She was enjoying herself when he said, "You've never called me by my name yet."

Her eyelids were blinking as she answered, "I know. It is Dennison."

"I can't stand the sound of that. I'm known as Denny to most of my friends, and I would like my wife to think of me as Denny."

His wife. The thought brought the colour flooding to her face, and she turned from him and picked up his cup of tea and handed it to him. But he waited until she had taken up hers too, and was seated, before he took his place beside her. Then reaching out and pulling the trolley towards him, he said, "Let's look at what they've given us," and he lifted the end of one sandwich, saying, "Salmon"; then another, saying, "Pâté"; and another, saying now, "I don't know what this is. But anyway, come along, let us eat, because you know, I haven't broken my fast since breakfast time. You, madam, have ruined my appetite. Do you know that?" . . .

It was almost half an hour later when he rang the bell. And when the butler appeared he said, "We shall be ready for you in five minutes, Trice."

"Very good, sir." The man closed the door, and Dennison, turning to Nancy Ann, said, "Well, are you ready for battle?"

"I'm . . . I'm afraid . . . really I am. There are so many of them. Why do you need so many servants?"

"Well, my dear, it is a very large establishment."

"Are there as many in your other houses?"

"Oh, no. There are only four permanently in the London house, and, really, that's a very ordinary place. It's one of a terrace, you know, and in three storeys. The only outstanding thing about it is it has a magnificent stairway. I . . . I think there are only ten rooms apart from the basement. If I'm staying there for any length of time, I take staff from here. Now Scotland. Oh well, that's a different kettle of fish altogether: it's a nice old place, not over large but it's got quite a bit of land. But once we got up there we could stay for a few months. It all depends upon the weather and the fishing and shooting and so on. . . . Don't look so concerned, my dear; you'll enjoy it all, I promise you. I'll make it my business to see that you do. Have you ever done any shooting?''

Her answer came prompt and from a straight face, ''No, and I never want to shoot. I . . . I think it's cruel.''

She watched him close his eyes and bow his head slightly. ''We must go into this question, my dear, concerning your likes and dislikes,'' he said; ''all our likes and dislikes . . .'' Then he asked the question, ''Do you like roast meat, roast lamb, roast pheasant, or chicken? I can see you do. Well, we'll talk about it later. What do you say?''

She could say nothing. She just wiped her mouth with a napkin, smoothed up the sides of her hair towards the rolls on the top, tugged at the waist of her dress, then smiling faintly at him, she said, ''I'm ready.''

''My dear, dear.'' He leant towards her and kissed her gently on the lips; then taking her hand, he led her down the room and into the passage. But there, he relinquished his hold. And now slanting his eyes towards her, he lifted his chin. But she had no need to take the hint for she was following her grandmama's instructions: her shoulders were back, her head up, her chin, not out, but drawn slightly into her neck. But then, her brave front almost dissolved when she entered the hall and saw the long line of servants stretching from one end of it to the other.

Two men were standing apart, together with the housekeeper, and Dennison turned towards them and indicated first the shorter of the two men, saying, ''This is Staith, my man, and Trice, the butler. You have met Mrs. Conway, the housekeeper.''

As the three people inclined their heads one after the other towards her, she moved hers slightly in recognition of the introduction. Then addressing the housekeeper, Dennison said, ''You may take over now, Mrs. Conway.''

The housekeeper stepped forward and, her manner matching her prim voice, pointed to the first man in the row, saying, ''John McTaggart, first footman.'' Then moving down

the line she went on, "Henry Robertson, second footman."
Now she came to the maids. "First housemaid, Jane Renton.
Second housemaid, Annie Fuller. Top floormaid, Pattie Anderson. Lily Sheeney, cook. Assistant cook, Sarah Brown.
Vegetable maid, Mary Carter. Scullery maid, Florie Kilpatrick. First seamstress, Mary White. Second seamstress, Lily
Davison. Third seamstress, Daisy Fulton. Boot-boy, Jimmy
Tool." The bowing of the heads and dipping of the knees
were deeper now as she got towards the end of the line.

At the name of the boot-boy she paused. This was certainly
not the child she had seen by the river all those years ago.
This boy had red hair and a small pinched face.

The stiff voice of the housekeeper went on: "Laundress,
Kathie Smart. Assistant laundress, May Stout. Washer, Jane
Cook."

They had come to the end of the line but, going off at right
angles, was another line of men. And now it was the butler
who came slowly down the hallway and, when he reached
Nancy Ann, in matching censorious tones he said as he
pointed to a man in his late fifties, "William Appleby, coachman." Then to the next man, middle-aged, this one: "David
Gillespie, groom." Then two men in their thirties: "Johnny
Winter, stable-boy. . . . Jimmy Pollock, second stable-boy."
And now turning to her, he looked her in the face, saying,
"The gardeners and the lodgekeepers come under the farm
management, miss."

She stood still for a moment looking fully back into the
face of this superior individual, whom she instinctively knew
would not have used that tone to her had he been at the other
end of the hall and still within hearing of his master. She was
quite good at remembering faces and names. It wasn't hard
to remember this man's name, Trice, because Peggy was wont
to say to Jane, "I don't want it in a minute, I want it in a
trice." And so, her voice cool and clear sounding, she said,
"Thank you, Trice," before turning to the housekeeper and
surprising her by adding, "And you, Mrs. Conway, thank
you also." Then she walked back up the line of staring faces
and here and there an open mouth, and when she reached
Dennison, she smiled at him and to his surprise and not a

little amazement, she said coolly, "That is over; shall we now look around the house?"

After a moment's pause and a successful attempt not to smile, he said, "Yes, my dear. Of course, of course." And with that they both walked away and towards the pink drawing-room again, and once inside, she leant against the door and closed her eyes, and he, standing before her, said, "You did perfectly, magnificently."

"They don't like me."

"What?"

"They don't like me, at least those at the top."

"Nonsense. What makes you think that?"

"I know. I somehow listen to voices, even when I'm not aware of doing so. I can sense what is behind their tone. It's to do with the mimicking, I think."

"Well, my dear, as clever as you are at mimicking, I think you are wrong here for they cannot help but like you. Just . . . just give them time. They've never had a mistress in this house since my mother died, and that is a long, long time ago. Come." His voice was quiet. He held out his hand and they turned and went through the doorway again, and she began her inspection of the house that was to be her home.

❧ 3 ❧

THE NEIGHBOURING GENTRY RESPONDED TO THE NEWS OF
Dennison Harpcore's engagement in various ways, but all
showed astonishment, except of course those who had attended the Christmas ball: "Well, we could have told you
so," was their comment.

Generally, the reactions came from those neighbours near
at hand who could not believe that the gambling, womanizing
owner of the Rossburn estate should take for a wife a parson's
daughter, and her just a slip of a girl. It was indecent, some
said; others, that they had heard of such men marrying their
housekeepers, but a parson's daughter! And the parson himself of such little account, for St. George's covered a very
sparse and indifferent parish. True, it had within its bounds
two estates, but you couldn't say either of them patronized
the church. A few of the staff might be sent from Rossburn,
but Graham Mercer of the manor had never darkened the
church's door for years, nor anybody else's door for that matter, until recently.

Particularly was it being asked by the wives how a chit like
that was going to manage such a household and staff. And
that same question was loudly asked in The House itself immediately after the inspection of the staff. There was a meeting in Mrs. Amelia Conway's sitting-room, and she demanded
of the butler, "Did you see the way she spoke to me, Ed-

ward? She was put up to it, I'm sure of that, because she looked like a scared kitten the night she came to the ball. And there she was, walking down the row as if she had been brought up among the best. My God! We're in for something.''

"Don't take on, Amelia." The first footman interposed. "There's ways and means of putting her in her place. And the wedding hasn't come off yet. Mr. Staith here''—he nodded towards the valet—"pointed that out to me." It was noticeable that John McTaggart didn't call the valet by his Christian name, but gave him his title.

"And what would they be?" asked the housekeeper.

Roger Staith stroked back the thinning hair on the top of his head, and his manner precise as always, he said, "Mrs. Poulter Myers should be returning soon. Can you imagine what her reaction will be to the news? But more so, the reaction of the vicarage sprite when she comes up against the formidable Rene. And you cannot imagine that plump little lady withdrawing her claws from the master, now can you? She's already lasted longer than any of them, and for the simple reason that she wouldn't let go, not because he still wants her. You remember Miss Honor Campbell? He seemed to favour her about three years ago when he made those frequent visits to Scotland and stayed with her people. We thought that might be serious, didn't we? But the fair Rene put an end to that. I happened to be there at the kill. It was a shoot in more ways than one. Madam Rene wasn't invited, but she landed, and was all charm to Miss Campbell. Even so she managed to make it evident that she was still warming his bed at night. So''—he spread out his hands, very much as a Frenchman might do—"I say leave it, and let us await events. And what is more, a little bird perched on the wings of Appleby while he's ploughed backwards and forwards with the coach to the vicarage these past few days has told me it would seem that the vicar himself, if one is to go by his countenance, is not the happiest of men over the arrangement.''

"Then why has he allowed it?"

The valet turned and looked at the housekeeper. "That I have yet to find out. The mother is sick unto death, they say, but there is a formidable grandmother in the background. And, from what I can gather, the parson is as poor as his own church mice and that it is his mother who has the money and has been the means of sending her two grandsons to university. So likely, she is the power behind the throne. However, we must all be patient, and we must all assume a front of acceptance, because''—he now rose to his feet—''we all know where we are well off, don't we?''

With this, the valet left the room, and the butler and the housekeeper looked at each other. Neither of them liked the man because they knew that he assumed, and this was a word he frequently used, that he ran the household, whereas they considered that the power behind the particular throne of the master of the house was themselves, each in his or her own way.

↘ 4 ↙

THE MORNING FOLLOWING THE INSPECTION NANCY ANN KEPT her mother and grandmother laughing as she mimicked the butler and the housekeeper, then began an imitation of herself walking down the line of servants. But in the middle of doing this she stopped and, looking towards her grandmother, she exclaimed, "That's odd, Grandmama."

"What is, dear?"

"That nice-looking young woman that comes to church every Sunday with the other two. She wasn't there."

"Oh, she must have been. She's one of the staff."

"She wasn't. Now I come to think of it, I recognized one of the women that usually accompanies her, but *she* wasn't there. I must ask him when. . . ."

"No, don't do that." Her grandmother's chin and finger were both raised.

"But why, Grandmama?"

It was her mother who answered now, saying, "Do as your grandmama says. She is, as your grandmama explained to you some long time ago, the mother of the little boy you saw by the river that day, and he is the cause of some embarrassment and hurt to . . . to Mr. Harpcore. You would be wise to leave that matter alone, dear. Anyway"—she drew in three short breaths before going on—"tell us more about the house, and then what your arrangements are for today."

152

"Oh." Nancy Ann sat down by the side of the bed and took her mother's hand, but she looked into space as she said, "The House. I . . . I don't know where to begin. And apparently I've only seen a portion of it. Well, there's the hall, with the biggest fireplace one could ever imagine. It's half as big as this room. Oh, yes, half as big. And it has a suit of armour standing in each alcove. You expect them to turn round and poke the fire." She shook her mother's hand gently and laughed. "And the walls of the hall inside are the same as outside, bare stone, but they are softened here and there with banners and tapestries."

"Oh? Banners and tapestries?" her grandmama put in. "But the family doesn't go all that far back. But go on; I'm sorry I stopped you."

And she went on: "The big drawing-room, that's mostly in blue: blue carpet, blue velvet couch and chairs, lots of little tables with knickknacks on them. Of course—" she now looked at her mother and nodded, "they won't be just knickknacks. I'll likely become better acquainted with them later. Then there is the room I told you about earlier on, the little pink drawing-room. That's pretty and cosy. Oh, what else?" She put her head back. "There is the ballroom, and the powder-room. Oh, yes, the powder-room." She did not go on to explain why she had emphasised the powder-room, but continued, "There is a huge dining-room; the centre table alone seats twenty-six, so Dennison . . . Denny informed me." She now turned towards her grandmama, explaining, "I have to call him that; he doesn't like Dennison."

"Well, it's a nice name . . . Denny. Yes, a very nice name."

"Then there was a breakfast-room and further along the corridor, the library. Oh, that's a splendid room, the library." She nodded to herself.

"What about the kitchens?"

"He . . . he didn't take me into that quarter; he said I'd be acquainted with them soon enough. I only know there's a servants' hall, and that the butler, the valet, and the housekeeper dine together, and that she has a bedroom and sitting-room of her own on the ground floor. I think most of the staff sleep in the attics, but three married ones have cottages in the grounds. Oh, there seem to be so many wings in the house. The east wing, the west wing," she said, waving her hand from side to side, then added on a laugh, "It's a wonder it doesn't take off." Then more soberly now she continued: "The bedrooms are a maze. There's a section of guest-rooms with dressing-rooms attached. I lost count; I think there must be twelve or more." She lowered her eyes now as if in some confusion, and her voice slowed as she went on, "I am to have a rest room, boudoir, he called it. It is to one side of the bedroom. At the other side there is a large dressing-room, then another smaller bedroom beyond, and then offices. These are on both sides of the bedrooms." She did not go on to explain what the offices were, but it was evident to the two older women, and both nodded their heads.

More brightly now, she said, "All the rooms were very pleasant. Well, really lovely. One of them has a balcony." She did not say, "It is to be our bedroom," but went on, "It is edged with beautiful wrought-iron railings. And the view from there is simply marvellous. I saw our chimneys."

"You didn't!"

"Yes, I did, Grandmama. You know we are in somewhat of a hollow here, and there were our chimneys just above the outline of the trees." She looked into space again for a moment and, more to herself than to them, she said, "Yes, I saw our chimneys."

"Well, go on."

She obeyed her grandmama's command and described the billiard room, the gentlemen's smoking-room, the endless flights of stairs, and when she came to the long steep ones that led to what used to be the nurseries, she said, "There is a rocking-horse still up there, and a great big iron fireguard around the fire. And there's a little schoolroom." Her smile widened. "The table is all marked where names have been cut out." She paused here, remembering that she had begun to read them out but Dennison had pulled her away, almost roughly, saying, "Leave that, leave that." And then, half in apology, he had added, "Some of those names go back fifty years; we could spend all day. Come."

Her mother said now, "Where are you going today?"

"Into Newcastle, Mama. You'll never guess what for."

"No, I'll never guess." The thin lips moved into a smile. "To choose satin material for the panels in my boudoir."

"Satin material for the panels?"

She turned to her grandmama. "Yes. The room isn't papered. The walls have narrow panels, wooden panels, made like long picture frames, but in between is satin. It is very faded, and torn in one or two places, so I am going to choose"—her head now moved in a deep obeisance as she added—"satin panels." Then she ended soberly, "Of all things in the world, satin panels."

"What do you think of the house as a whole?"

She didn't look at her grandmama but bit on her lip and looked down at the hand she was holding before she said, "It is beautiful, but . . . but much too large, and sort of . . . well—" She seemed to search for a word, then said, "Lonely, in a way."

"Well, it is a house that's been used to a lot of company and I'm sure it will be again."

She didn't answer her grandmama, but she thought: I hope not. And thinking back to the ball, she emphasized her thoughts: *Oh, I hope not.*

❧ 5 ❧

It was towards the end of January, and the arrangements for the wedding were already going ahead. A day never passed but he would go to the vicarage, always with the intent of bringing her over to The House for even a short time. Often she would say she had too much to do, or her mother wasn't well enough to be left, but nearly always Rebecca would give the final word, saying that she had five people running round after her, in one way or another, and that surely she could spare her daughter for an hour or two.

Dennison had come to like his future mother-in-law very much. She was an ally, had been, he recognized, from the beginning, as, too, was the grandmother. Oh, yes, the grandmother was for him. But in no way had he so far penetrated the reserve of the parson.

It was eleven o'clock in the morning. Dennison was preparing for yet another journey along the road that had become so familiar to him over the past weeks. His valet had just handed him a freshly cut cigar when there came a tap on the door and the first footman entered, saying, "Mrs. Poulter Myers has called, sir."

The cigar half-way to his lips, he looked from the footman to his valet, and for almost a full minute he remained silent. Then turning from the men, he walked to the window, saying, "Where have you put her?"

156

"She went into the drawing-room, sir."

Of course Rene wouldn't be put anywhere, she would go where she willed. "Give me two minutes," he said, "then tell her I am in the library. Bring her there."

"Yes, sir." The man departed, and Dennison stood for a moment looking out of the window. There was a cab on the drive, a hired cab. If she had come in the family coach someone would have warned him earlier, because the coach was distinctive, having the Myers's coat of arms on the panel, Myers being a man who liked to call attention to himself and his possessions. He now turned to the valet, saying, "If my visitor hasn't departed within the next half-hour, come and remind me that I shall not get to Durham in time for the London train. You understand?"

"Fully, sir."

Dennison passed the man and went quickly across the landing and down the broad stairs, turned at the foot, then made his way to the library.

He had hurried in his walk and run down the stairs yet wasn't out of breath. This pleased him greatly. He felt he had returned to his twenties these past few weeks: there was new life in him; and of course, he had cut down drastically on his wine.

But he walked slowly now up the long room to the fire and stood with his back to it, and not until the door opened, admitting his late mistress, did he move from it. Then without haste he advanced towards her, saying, "How nice to see you, Rene."

She took his outstretched hand but made no reply; then she passed him and, going to the couch, she lowered her plump body down into it.

She had discarded her outer coat and the blue cord velvet dress she was wearing was fitted to her ample figure. The bodice was plain, the waist nipped in, then billowed out into two overskirts edged with ruching. Her hat of three different shades of mauve velvet was turned up at both sides. It was high-crowned and set on the top was what resembled a flower made of feathers. The whole did nothing to add to her height. The skin of her face was what was termed warm peach. Her eyes were round and blue, shaded by curling dark lashes. Her nose was small, as was her mouth, but full-lipped. Yet, when it was open as it was now in a fixed smile, it appeared wide and showed two rows of quite large white teeth.

Her eyes were like slits as she looked up at him and said, "Well! Well! How long is it since I've seen you?"

In contrast to her plump figure her voice was thin and high. How high, he knew only too well when she got into a jealous rage. He put his head back as if he were counting, then said, "Five weeks, six weeks."

"You didn't count the days then?" Her lips came together and pursed themselves questioningly.

"I . . . I have been very busy."

"And otherwise engaged?" She now seemed to pay attention to her dress as her hands arranged the sides of her skirt and pulled it away from her small feet.

"Well, yes, you could say that, Rene. I don't have to be naive and tell you anything that you already know."

"You didn't think about writing and telling me." She continued to arrange her skirt.

"No; no, I didn't; I didn't want to disturb your holiday."

"Huh!" She was looking at him now and he saw her white teeth grinding over each other, in fact he heard them. Then her mouth was open and she was smiling again, and this made him more nervous than ever.

"When did you return?" he asked.

"A week yesterday."

The skin round his eyes crinkled, almost closing them. She had been home over a week and this was her first visit to him. Why hadn't Pat let him know? But what was he talking about? Pat was in London. But there were the Rylands and the Crombies and others. It was like a conspiracy. What was her game?

"That surprises you?"

He shrugged his shoulders while she stared at him without speaking now. The fact that she'd kept away from him for eight days not only surprised but amazed herself. Yet, she knew from what she had heard that he was absolutely infatuated with that vicarage chit; he had already introduced her to the household, and apparently was preparing her to become its mistress. Well, she felt she knew her Dennison and she could never imagine, not in this world, that little slip of a thing satisfying his needs, so many and varied. She also knew that if she caused a scene, in his autocratic way, he would say, "Enough is enough," as he had done to Larry, but were she to play her cards right, she could stay on the outskirts for the present and, with time, give that little snipe one hell of a life. And in taking this line she'd be killing two birds with one stone, because Arnold had become very testy since his own private affair had gone awry. As he was now always pointing out to her, he was a diplomat and there were limits even to the discretion of friends.

She said, "You don't expect me to congratulate you, do you, Denny?"

He shook his head, amazed at her control. He knew her well enough to know that she was worked up inside; the blue of her eyes had darkened so much as to become almost black. Yet here she was, adopting a pose, a philosophical pose to the whole affair.

And so he answered quickly, "No, I don't expect you to congratulate me, but I thank you for your understanding so far."

"Then I am not to be thrown to the dogs?"

"Oh, Rene, Rene, what an expression."

"That's how I feel at the moment"—she bowed her head—"thrown off, discarded. It's . . . it's hard to take because I was always there when you needed me."

"I . . . I know that, Rene." He walked to the couch and sat down beside her and, taking her hand, he said, "I shall be forever grateful for the past. You know that."

Her head was still bent when she said, "Then we can remain friends?"

"Certainly. Certainly."

She glanced at him sideways now, and there was a small deprecating smile on her lips as she said, "But I'll not put in an appearance very often. You will understand that?"

"Of course. Of course, my dear." He raised her hand to his lips, the while his mind shouted at him, "Thank God. Thank God for this."

"You won't expect me to meet her, will you, unless it is unavoidable?"

"Of course not, Rene. Of course not."

She wriggled her buttocks towards the front of the couch, and he quickly rose and helped her to her feet. "I'm not going to wish you happiness," she said, adjusting her hat. "It would be quite out of character, wouldn't it?"

He made no reply to this but smiled gently at her while shaking his head. Then his hand cupped her elbow and he led her down the room. But before reaching the door he stopped. "You haven't had any refreshment," he said. "I'm lax. Can I get you something?"

"No, thank you, Denny. No, thank you. It was refreshing enough to see you once again."

The sad note in her voice touched him and once more he said, "Oh, Rene."

He opened the door and to the amazement of the butler and the footman he led the visitor, not only across the hall, but also down the steps, preceded at a run now by the footman towards the hired vehicle. And there, as he helped her into the carriage, he was heard to say, "Thank you, my dear." And he stood bareheaded until the cabby had turned his horse about and driven it from the drive.

In the hall he passed the waiting butler, the two footmen, and his valet, their faces all aiming to remain expressionless, and as he now made for the drawing-room he said to the butler, "Fetch me the brandy."

He dropped heavily down on to the sofa and, laying his head back, he muttered aloud, "I can't believe it." And he couldn't believe that he had got off so lightly. She had really done the decent thing. People, when he came to think about it, were most unpredictable. He had imagined he knew her inside out and that she would have played merry hell and raised the house on him, but there, she went off like a lamb.

Quite suddenly he pulled himself up straight and bit down on his lip. That wasn't like her. Had she some scheme in her mind? No, no. He shook his head. She was genuine. Naturally, as she said, she wouldn't want to meet Nancy Ann. The only thing she wanted was to remain friends with him. And friends it would be. No further. Oh no, no further. Never, not again. Nancy Ann was his life from now on. He could swear on that. Look what she had done to him already. For two months now he had abstained. That was the longest he had gone since he was seventeen or eighteen—anyway, since very early on. And yet he could manage; just being with her was fulfillment enough, at least at the moment. But there were another four months or more to go. Oh, he'd get by. If things became too wearing he'd slip up to town; not Newcastle, no, that was too near. Anyway, he'd see. He'd get by.

He lifted the decanter that Trice had placed on a tray to his hand and poured himself out a good measure of brandy. He didn't usually drink so early in the day, but this was a special occasion, a kind of victory, but a victory that had sapped him somewhat. And—he smiled to himself as he watched his butler depart—it had surprised that lot out there too. They had expected a battle royal; likely been looking forward to it. He had no doubt but that every member of his staff had been awaiting the consequences. And now they were disappointed. Oh, yes, he knew human nature all right, at least his staff, and they were predictable. He threw off the remainder of the brandy, got to his feet, straightened his cravat, stroked his hair back, then marched from the room. He was going to his love.

⚹ 6 ⚹

JOHN HOWARD HAZEL WAS WELL AWARE OF HIS OWN WEAK-
nesses and of his lowly standing in the hierarchy of the
church, but he had always felt that he was worthy of a better
living than that of St. George's. The reforms introduced by
Parliament thirty or forty years before were supposed to have
applied to the Established Church too. For one thing, cathedral clergy had to give up certain benefices, and the money
saved should have been used to raise the stipends of the poorer
parsons. But it had yet to affect his stipend at St. George's.

And yet there still remained the plum livings where the
vicar passed his days almost in the style of the local gentry:
he rode to hounds, fished, and shot with them, and, as some
dissenters were wont to declare, was not always above shar-
ing their other sport of whoring. Moreover, it was questioned
why single parsons should have housekeepers. They should
either marry or have menservants. They were as bad as the
Catholics in this way.

John was well aware that it was the leading Conservatives
in towns and villages that supported the church, whereas the
Liberals and radicals tended, as did the working classes, especially those in the towns, towards the chapels. He knew it
was said, and rightly, there was more class-consciousness in
the upper and lower churches of England than there was between the rich and the poor, and that that order of things was

very prevalent in his parish, which was why his daughter's coming marriage to the Lord of the Manor, as it were, was causing such a furor.

There was much more snobbery and vying for positions in this parish than in any of the other three parishes he had held. Perhaps it was because it lay just outside the industrial mining area of Durham, on one side, and the shipbuilding and factory towns on the other. He often thought of his parish, not as an oasis, but as an island, its inhabitants barren of understanding of the frailties of human nature . . . not of each individual's own lack, but of his neighbours'. And he knew that he himself could not be counted as one apart from this company, because at present he was being tested above all others.

Why couldn't he recognize that the man who was soon to become his son-in-law was a changed individual? He had been a gambler, and yet he was giving himself very little time to gamble now. And the same applied, apparently, to his other needs, because he seemed to spend his time coming backwards and forwards to this house, if not just to see Nancy Ann, then to take her off to Durham or Newcastle in order to choose yet something more for the house of which she was to become mistress. . . . Mistress of that house? He could not imagine Nancy Ann as such. And what would happen when the mistress of *this* house was taken from him? Her days were running out fast, and with Nancy Ann gone his life would indeed be grey. Only one small piece of brightness was on his horizon: Peter would be returning; but not to live at home; like James, he would be attached to the school. Yet he would be near at hand. But what would it matter which of them was at hand when he lost his dear Rebecca?

His thoughts were checked when the door was pushed open unceremoniously and Hilda, in a whisper, said, "Lady Golding has called."

This wasn't the first time in the last few weeks that this lady had called upon them, and he supposed he should consider it an honour. His servants expressed awe at the mention of her name as if she was a holy visitation. But there was nothing holy about this woman: she was a robust, forthright individual, and likeable, but nevertheless, she was of Harpcore's class, a close friend of his and a woman of the world, and it would be with her like that Nancy Ann would have to associate, and learn . . . what? Yes, what would she learn?

Hilda's hushed tone came again, saying, "Miss Nancy Ann has taken her into the mistress."

"Well, that's all right." His voice was unduly sharp and the door closed abruptly.

It was a full ten minutes before he decided to go and greet the visitor. But when he entered the room she was apparently on the point of leaving for she was rising from her seat, saying, "Well, I won't tire you, Mrs. Hazel. I'm on my way to call on Denny. His head full of arrangements, he's obviously missing a mother and is treating me as such, and I consider it no compliment." She smiled broadly as she turned her glance on Jessica, who, being diplomatic and tactful for once, replied, "An elder sister perhaps, but certainly not his mother." And at this Pat Golding smiled more broadly still and, inclining her head towards the older woman, said, "I thank you. That remark is most kind and will buoy me up for the rest of the day." She turned again towards the bed, "Goodbye, Mrs. Hazel. I shall call upon you soon if I may."

"Please do, Lady Golding. You are very welcome. See Lady Golding out, Nancy Ann."

It was all very formal, and as her ladyship came up with John she merely inclined her head towards him, saying, "Vicar," then passed on. In the hall she pulled her fur cape tightly up to her neck as she muttered, "Don't you feel the cold, dear?"

"Not really; I prefer it to the heat."

Pat put out her hand and touched Nancy Ann's cheek, saying now, "What it is to be young. But wait till you get up there." She pointed towards the door. "It's like a hothouse; they have a coal mine delivered every week. And that daft creature is there again. Have you met her?"

"You mean Lady Beatrice?"

"That's who I mean."

Nancy Ann smiled. "Yes, I've met her and been introduced to her family."

"Oh, did you ever know such a thing? You can understand one or two dolls to compensate for a broken romance, but how many has she brought with her this time? Conway told me she had three bass hampers full. But—'' She leant towards Nancy Ann now, and in a low voice said, ''She's not as daft as she makes out. Oh, no, she's wily. She was wily before her head got muddled. I've known her since she was a girl. Do you think when she's down with her cousin she has maids waiting on her and a bath every day? No, of course not. If I could get into that room when she's taking a bath I'd be accompanied by a scrubbing brush, and use it. Believe me, Denny's a fool for putting up with her. And when you get up there, my girl, learn to put your foot down. And not only on her. There's lots of things behind the scenes in that house which want rectifying; half that lot wouldn't last five minutes under me. Well, I must away.''

At the open door she turned and, nodding at Nancy Ann, now said, ''I wish your wedding was over, my dear, I do that, I'm worn out already.'' Then she smiled broadly, put out her hand again and patted Nancy Ann's arm before stepping outside and hurrying through the frosty air to her coach. . . .

Lady Patricia Golding marched into Rossburn House and, almost throwing her cloak and fur stole at Robertson, she demanded, ''Where's your master?''

''He . . . he was in his study, m'lady.''

Without further ado she stalked across the hall and down the passage opposite, past the library, turned right along another short passage and, pushing open the end door, she walked in and surprised Dennison, who wasn't writing at his desk but sitting in a leather chair by the window. He had been gazing out on to the garden and thinking of the future, but now he was quickly on his feet, saying, ''My! my! Pat, you came in there like a devil in a gale of wind. What's your hurry? Sit down. Will you have a drink?''

''Yes, something hot. I've just come from your future wife's ice-box. My! how they exist in that house God alone knows. But I suppose''—she grinned—''He sees they survive because He needs the vicar. But enough of this. I've come to tell you something and it's just this, Denny. That woman in that bed is not going to last out till June if I know anything.''

"You think not?"

"I feel sure not. And you know what that implies: your wedding will certainly be postponed then. Can't you do anything about it to bring it forward if the invitations haven't gone out yet? And there's another thing. When the mother goes you'll have more opposition from the father; that man isn't for you."

"I'm well aware of that, Pat. But I can do nothing about bringing the wedding forward. Why, I was amazed when I knew it was to be June. If he'd had his way it could have been a village engagement going on for three or four years. No, I couldn't do anything about it."

"Well, that's up to you. . . . Get me that drink."

He rang the bell, and when the footman appeared he ordered hot coffee and brandy. A few minutes later, as they sat, one at each side of the fire, drinking the laced coffee, Pat said, "Have you seen anything of Rene lately?"

"Only once since she called here, all light and understanding, and that was at the Fentons' last Thursday. I understood from her that she was going up to town the following day."

"Oh, yes, she goes up to town quite a bit. And you know who she sees up there?"

"Is this a guessing game? She has many friends, as you know."

"Well, Larry Freeman wasn't one of her closest, was he? He was jealous of her association with you and she was jealous of the power he seemingly wielded over you. But it came out just in casual conversation on one particular night. I was having a word with Jim Boyle and he happened to turn the conversation in his undiplomatic way to you and her, and what your relationship was now, which led, as usual, to his dropping bits of tittle-tattle. And in this case it was that your late friend Larry and your late mistress Rene seemingly meet in London, and not infrequently. He had seen them once dining together and at another time riding in Rotten Row. Now what do you make of that?"

"I wouldn't know unless I gave it some thought."

"You don't need to think about that. Neither of them loves you now. No matter what kind of a front she puts on, the quieter she is, the smoother she is, the more dangerous I would sense her to be. By the way, how are your finances?''

"Oh! Pat. Pat.''

"Never mind, Oh! Pat. Pat. You can't have lost much lately because you haven't been playing, but last year by all accounts you went through a hell of an amount. Now, as I told you then and I'm telling you now, you can't keep it up.''

"I . . . I don't intend to, so don't worry.''

"Oh.'' She took a gulp from her cup, then wiped her lips with the back of her thumb before saying, "The instinct that has caused you to warm your bed in the past will soon be provided for legitimately; and how long you remain faithful, that depends. But the gaming is a different problem altogether. You're not a lucky gambler, you know, Denny.''

"I'm like everyone else, Pat, I have runs.''

"You had one winner with your horses last year. And that's an expensive business alone, but the cards can outdo it. You know I'm speaking the truth and I'm not going to apologize for taking the liberty of talking the way I'm doing; I've always done so since I first knew you, and I'm not changing now. I seem to have taken over from where your mother left off. I often used to wish I was a little younger. I would have made a damn sight better bed warmer than the one you picked.''

"Oh, my dear Pat.'' He turned away, his face screwed up with suppressed laughter. "What will you come out with next?''

"What I'll come out with next is to repeat the main cause of my visit here this morning when I should be with George in Newcastle supporting him supporting Roland who is determined to stand for the by-election in Fellburn. That son-in-law of mine hasn't got an ounce of sense in his head, yet he thinks he can beat the Tory candidate. Now that's something you should do, take up politics, get into Parliament. That would steady you up.''

"My dear Pat, I don't need any more steadying than I am at present. I've never felt steadier in my life.''

She drained the last of the coffee, then pulled herself to her feet, saying, "Say those same words to me after three years of marriage and I'll believe you're a changed man. Now I've got to go, but let me finish what I meant to say, marry that girl as soon as possible. The mother apparently wants to see her daughter settled, so that would be an excuse for bringing the wedding forward.''

''I couldn't do it, Pat.'' His tone was emphatic. ''That would be utterly cruel. It would be like saying to her: you were going to die in July after having seen your daughter settled, but now you won't last that long, so I would like to bring the marriage forward, that's if you wish to see it. No, no; things must stand as they are, I must take my chance.''

''Well, all I can say is, if she dies and the wedding is postponed, as it surely will be, prepare yourself for a fight with that man, because the girl's loyalties will be torn asunder. And from the way she talks she looks upon her father as someone special, an embryo saint. Anyway, I must be off. Think about what I've said, not only about her, but about your two friends. I never liked Larry Freeman and he never liked me. I used often to think, put a couple of horns on his head and you would have a good replica of the devil and someone just as smooth.''

''Go on with you.'' He pushed her gently in the back. ''You forget that he was a good companion to me for years.''

''Yes, anyone can be a good companion if they have board and lodgings free and their gambling debts and their bills paid. Oh—'' She was trotting towards the door as she said, ''I would be a friend to you myself if you would make me an allowance of two thousand a year, provide me with shooting and fishing for my married brood and grandchildren, travelling expenses, holidays abroad. Think about that an' all. I'm sure George wouldn't mind.''

''You're incorrigible. Get on your way, woman.''

In the hall the footman had helped her on with her cloak, and she flung her great fur stole over her shoulder, then saying, ''Don't see me off, you'll get your death,'' she turned to depart but he laughed at her suggestion and, taking her arm, led her towards the coach, and when she was seated he leant forward and said, ''Thanks for everything, Pat. I appreciate your concern and I'll think on it.''

''You do.'' She nodded at him.

He closed the door, gave a signal to the coachman, then stood for a moment watching her carriage being driven away before returning to the house and into the study again. And there, sitting down by the fire, once more he leant forward, one elbow on his knee, his closed fist supporting his chin, and as he stared into the flames he asked himself what he would do if the wedding was postponed. He had been firm with himself during the past weeks and had hoped his firmness would stand by him for the weeks ahead. They were now in the middle of April with only May to go. But what would happen if Pat were proved to be right? Well, in that case he would just have to go up to town every now and again and have a few days at the club. Anyway, he would have to go up next week; there was the business of the bank to see to.

❧ 7 ❧

Dennison had been away in London since Tuesday, and now it was Saturday and the letter she had received from him this morning had asked her to be at The House around four o'clock. He had begun his short letter with "My dearest one," and ended with "Your loving Denny."

She hadn't imagined she'd miss him so much. She had got used to seeing him every day even if it was for only a short time, and the thought had entered her mind that if she were never to see him again her life would become empty. She had spent most of the time in the sick room, but today her mother had insisted that Pratt drive her to The House and in good time to welcome her fiancé home.

When she stepped down from the dogcart she thanked Pratt, then walked across the gravel and up the steps to the terrace. She had learned not to knock on the door, and so, turning the big ebony handle she pushed the heavy oak door open, crossed the vestibule to the glass-fronted double doors that closed off the hall and, opening one of them, she entered. At first the hall appeared empty until, from the far corner, two surprised figures turned and stared at her. One was Robertson the second footman, the other was the pretty woman whom she saw in church on a Sunday, the one who hadn't been in the lineup when she was first introduced to the staff and whom she had not encountered since. The young woman was evidently flustered: she dipped her knee, bowed her head, then scurried away, while Henry Robertson came quickly forward, saying, "Good afternoon, miss."

"Good afternoon, Robertson." She had noticed before that of all the male staff he was the most pleasant and that his voice did not hold the stiff superior tone of the others.

"Has your master arrived yet?"

"No miss, but—" He glanced towards the big grandfather clock with the complicated face, whose strike boomed as loud as the church bell, and he said, "It's a little early. Can I get you some tea, miss?"

She stood uncertain for a moment. If she had tea it would be served by the butler or one of the housemaids, and, try as she would, she could not rid herself of the feeling of awkwardness in their presence. So, smiling at the man, she said, "No thank you. I think I shall take a walk. It's the first really fine day we've had for some time. The sun is quite warm. Should . . . should your master return before I get back, you can tell him I am walking in the direction of the farm."

"I'll do that, miss, yes." He hastily opened the glass door for her, then the front door, and he inclined his head in a bow as she walked past him. And as she went across the drive she told herself that if the attitude of the rest of the staff was like that of Robertson she would have no trepidation in becoming mistress of this vast establishment.

She turned the corner of the house and into the courtyard formed by the north side of the house and outbuildings along the other two sides. In going this way she wouldn't have to pass the kitchen quarters. Six horses were kept here for the carriages, the rest were in stables at the farm with their own men to look after them.

Two horses had their heads over their half-doors and she went towards one and held out her hand, and the horse rubbed its wet muzzle against her palm. She did the same with the second horse and was about to move away when, from the empty stable next door, a young man stepped, and at the sight of her, he raised his cap, then smiled, saying, "Good day to you, miss."

The unmistakable Irish voice caused her to pause and she looked at the man. He was a stranger in the yard, she hadn't seen him before; what was more strange still he looked like one of the McLoughlin boys, but he was a young man, well in his twenties.

She said, "You are new here?"

"Aye, miss, yes. Me name's Shane McLoughlin. I'm . . . I'm"—his face went into a huge grin—"I'm one of them Mc-Loughlins. You had notice, I understand, miss, of one or two of me brothers years gone by and put them rightly in their place."

She blushed even as she smiled and replied, "There were six and two threes of us in those days, I think."

"You could hold your own, miss, you could hold your own by all accounts. You see, me bein' the eldest, I was away in service. I was with Mr. McMahon, you know over in North-umberland way, but he died and the place was sold up. But I wanted to be with horses and when this job was going here and it was near me home, well, I thought, it's for me."

At the back of her mind she knew that she shouldn't stand here allowing this servant to chat to her like this, but it was so different, so refreshing.

"How is your family?"

"Oh, they are all doin' well, miss, especially since me da died. God rest him. There were fifteen of us at the end and not one of us sorry to see him go, 'cos, you know, he'd neither work nor want. Me ma's never been so happy in her troubled life, miss, an' we all stand by her."

She wanted to laugh out loud, really loud: there was an ache in her waist almost like a pain. She must go.

She was about to give him a last word when two men appeared from out of a door at the far end of the yard, and at the sight of her they stopped for a moment. Then one came forward. It was Gillespie the groom, and after casting a sharp glance at the Irishman, he looked at Nancy Ann, saying, "Is everything all right, miss?"

"Oh, yes, yes. I . . . I was just having a word with"—she almost said Shane—"McLoughlin here. I'm acquainted with his family. I'm pleased to see that he has come into Mr. Harpcore's service."

She inclined her head towards him; then looking at Shane who was now straight-faced and looking not a little apprehensive, she added, "Give my respects to your mother when you next see her. Tell her that I am so glad she is well."

A light spread over the man's face for a moment and, touching the forelock of his thick black hair, he said, "I'll do that, miss, with pleasure, I will, I will. Thank you, miss."

She now walked on, keeping her step as sedate as possible. She knew she had saved the man from at least a bullying reprimand, by claiming knowledge of his family, and she considered it a small price to pay for the enjoyment he had given her, for she had never wanted to laugh so much for a long time. Oh, when she got home she would *do him* for her mama and grandmama. She had the desire to skip and run.

The decorum and sedateness which she had been made to acquire over the past months was begging to be thrown off. And she threw it off, once she had left the precincts of the formal gardens and entered the woodland that formed a shield between the house and the river, for here, picking up her skirts, she ran along the narrow path before leaving it and winding her way between the trees. At one point she stopped and stood with her back leaning against a trunk and she looked up through the branches that were just beginning to show a spattering of green to where the white clouds were racing across the sky. And she thought, as she had often done after running when she was a child and stood puffing, Oh, that was lovely. Then she asked herself why it was that running was considered most unladylike. Men ran, then why not women? This question she had put to her grandmama some time ago and the answer she received was more puzzling still: "It's all because of the Queen," her grandmama had said.

She turned from the tree now and, walking slowly, she decided to have a look at the river before making for the farm. She was walking on the path again and as it was opening out on to a green bank she could see in the distance, sitting on a piece of rock near the water's edge, a boy. It was the sight of him that lifted her back years.

She was halfway across the green when he turned a startled look on her; and he jumped to his feet. Seeing he was about to run, she called to him, " 'Tis a nice day, isn't it?"

The tone of her voice checked him, and when she came up

to him she stood looking down into his face for a moment before she asked, "Were you fishing?"

He shook his head, then said, "No miss, just sittin'."

"Well, come and sit down again." And she held out her hand to him. But he didn't take it, yet he obeyed her as though she had given him an order and sat down on the long slab of rock. And she, seating herself some distance from him, said, "You won't remember me, but . . . but we have met before, and at this very spot. Do you remember a girl looking for her dog?"

He was gazing at her wide-eyed, his face unsmiling, but he answered her, "Yes, miss."

"Are you sure you remember? It's a long time ago."

"I remember, miss, 'cos I was kept in for a long time after."

"Kept in?" She screwed up her face, and he nodded, adding, "In the roof. I'm not now though; I work in the boot room with Jimmy." He turned his glance from her and, looking at the water, he said, "I like the river, but I can only come sometimes."

She did not question why he could come only sometimes. He was looking at her again, and as she stared back at him all the joy of the previous half-hour slipped from her. He had a most beautiful face. The great dark brown eyes held a depth of sadness that should never have been portrayed in one so young. His hair fell to the collar of his short navy blue jacket. It was quite brown at the ends and for some way up, and then it became streaky. But from where she was sitting she could see his parting, and the hair was silvery fair for about an inch on each side of it. "Do you often come down to the river?" she asked.

He shook his head, then said, "When Jennie lets me."

"Jennie?" Her voice was soft and enquiring, and he said, "She's . . . she's Jennie. I sleep with her. She works in the kitchen."

The sadness was deep within her now: she remembered he had called his mother Jennie before.

He rose suddenly from the slab, saying, "I must go back, Jennie'll be vexed."

She too rose, saying now, "I don't suppose she will if she allowed you to come out."

"No . . . no, she never, but the sun was out"—he looked upwards—"an' the breeze was blowin' an' they were all in the servants' hall, an' so I came." He stooped down now and retrieved something from the back of the stone, which she could see was a slate and a pencil, and she said brightly, "Oh, you do lessons?"

"No." He shook his head. "I just write."

"You can read?"

"Yes—" He nodded at her. "There are lots of books in the big attic, boxes of 'em."

"Who taught you to read and write?"

"Jennie."

"And what have you been writing today?"

"Just words."

She held out her hand and after a moment's hesitation, and reluctantly, he passed the slate to her. And she read in printed letters the words: Birds have wings, trees have leaves, and rabbits play, but they all die.

She raised her eyes slowly from the slate and looked at the boy. She was amazed, not so much by the words, but at the meaning behind them. Her voice soft, she asked, "How old are you now?"

"I am nine."

"And . . . and you have never been to the day school?"

"Day school? No."

She'd have to do something about this. She must do something about the child. It was strange, but it was as if she had first seen him only yesterday. He had made an impression on her then and it had remained, only now it was stronger. It had become an issue. She handed the slate back to him, saying, "You're a clever boy to be able to write words like that. Now, sit down again and write some more of those words."

As if partly mesmerized, the child sat down once more on the stone with the slate on his knee and his head turned towards her, and she nodded at him now, saying, "We'll be seeing each other again. Goodbye." He made no answer, but screwed round on the stone to watch her walking away into the wood.

A great deal of the light had gone from the day. It was wrong, very wrong that a child with that intelligence wasn't having some form of education. She'd talk to her father about it and ask his advice how best to broach the subject to Denny.

She had emerged from the wood and was on the main path again leading to the farm, and the outbuildings were actually in sight when she heard hurrying footsteps behind her. Turning, she saw Dennison and such was her feeling at the moment that the sight of him swept away the darkness surrounding her thoughts and she was in the light again, so much so that she picked up her skirts and ran to meet him. She had never imagined herself doing any such thing, but she was actually doing it now, and when they met his arms went around her and he lifted her from the ground and swung her round. Then he was kissing her. Hard and long he kissed her, and when at last he released her they were both breathing heavily. Her head strained back from him and resting in the circle of his arms, she gazed into his face. And when he said, "Oh, Nancy Ann, how many years ago is it since I last held you?"

She was gasping for breath, but, answering his mood, she said, "It must be all of ten."

"Oh, yes, yes, that long." Again his lips were on hers, and she was amazed at her own response and the enjoyment she was experiencing in his embrace. And her mind was telling her that she liked him. Oh, she liked him very much. And, as if picking up her thoughts, he said, "I'm glad I went away, because you've missed me, haven't you? Tell me you've missed me, and that you like me, even . . . even. . . ." He stopped and his head slightly bent, he waited while she admitted softly, "Yes, yes, I have missed you. And I do like you very much."

"Oh, my dear, my dear. All right, all right"—he wagged his hand between their faces—"I won't start again, because if I do, I won't be able to stop. Come." He put an arm around her, then added, "Look at me in my town clothes, I didn't even stop for a moment when they told me where you were bound for. And isn't this a beautiful day! and tell me what have you been doing with yourself."

And to this she answered, "Oh, you have a very good idea

of what fills my days, but I, in turn, haven't the slightest notion what fills yours. You tell me what *you* have been doing with yourself.''

They were walking into the wood again and he said, ''Well now, let me think. I went to the bank as was my intention and had a long talk with the head of that establishment. 'How are my affairs, sir?' I said, 'because I want to buy a piece of jewellery for my future wife.' But he said, 'What about those in the vault? There are two tiaras, a number of necklaces and rings.' But I said, 'I want something new and fresh, because it is for a very new and fresh young lady.' '' He squeezed her waist and pulled her into his side as she muttered, ''Oh, no, please. I don't want jewellery; I'm not fond of jewellery.''

''Be quiet. You want to know what I did with my days. Well then, I went to my tailor and ordered three suits, and then to the shoemaker to have shoes made to match them, but my main shopping was to a famous store that deals in silks and satins, brocades and taffetas, cords and velvets, and I chose a selection that had to be sent on to an establishment in Newcastle where this young lady that I have in mind will oblige me by being measured for several different outfits.''

She pulled herself from his grasp, saying, ''Oh, no, Denny, no. Papa wouldn't like that.''

His face losing its look of merriment for a moment, he said, ''Your papa, my dear, will shortly have no say in your life; we shall be travelling abroad after the wedding and you will need to be suitably attired.''

''Oh, dear.'' She sighed, then added, ''It is so good of you. But I am not used to lots of outfits, and . . . and. . . .''

In mock astonishment he now raised his arms above his head, crying, ''I'll swear to the gods you are the only young lady alive who spurns the thought of being well attired.'' They halted near a tree and he gripped her by the shoulders and, pressing her against it, he bent his face towards her, saying, ''Your education is going to be much more difficult than I imagined. After our marriage you will become a different being; you will have to.''

He was amazed at the strength of her hands that pushed him backwards; and now she was standing upright, facing him and saying, "I won't be a different being, Denny. I may be clothed differently, but I shall remain myself. I . . . I know I shall. And I don't want to be changed; I don't want to have my values and. . . ."

"My dear. My dear." He shook his head slowly from side to side. "Don't take the matter so seriously. You're the last person on earth I want to change, that way. I . . . I think that was what first attracted me, your independent spirit, and that is the person who I want to grow to love me. But you see, my dear, you'll be expected to attend functions and to dress accordingly. As for changing you, changing my Nancy Ann? Never! And"—he now pulled a comical face—"there's one thing I'll have to accept, and it is that my future wife was trained by her brothers in combat. Haven't I witnessed it! Those fragile-looking arms"—he looked from one shoulder to the other—"have proved the case in point. Oh, yes, a little bit further and I'd have been on my back."

"I'm . . . I'm sorry."

He held out his hands to her now, saying, "Never say you are sorry to me, my dear." His arms went about her again and he held her gently and they remained quiet, looking at each other. And then they were both startled and drew apart when there came the sound of running steps quite near, and out of the brushwood to their side scrambled the boy.

He was as astonished as they were and came to an abrupt gaping halt.

Nancy Ann opened her mouth to speak, then closed it again for she was looking at her companion's face which had suddenly flushed to a deep red. He was gazing at the boy and the boy at him, and his voice, like a loud bark, yelled, "Get away!"

As the child sped through the trees, Dennison turned from her, his hand pulling the skin tightly across his cheek. She did not speak until perhaps a full minute later after he had turned towards her again and, his voice a mutter, had said, "I can explain. I . . . I will sometime."

"You have no need to; I know all about it," she said.

His eyes widened, then narrowed, and he said, "Oh, you do?"

"Well—" She seemed embarrassed for a moment, then

said softly, "I know some of the circumstances, and . . . and I can understand your feelings in part, but not all."

"Not all. What do you mean?"

"The child is not to blame."

"Oh, please, my dear, don't take that tack. He's a reminder that I was deprived of someone I loved dearly."

"I . . . I still think you cannot lay the blame on him, and if you were to recognize . . ."

"What!" His interruption was in almost as loud a voice as when he had shouted at the boy. "You don't know what you're suggesting. You don't know what you're talking about. You know nothing whatever about it. One doesn't recognize the likes of him, flyblows. There's a lot you have to learn."

When she turned abruptly from him and walked hastily away, he stood nonplussed for a moment; then he was running after her, saying, "Nancy Ann! Nancy Ann! Please! Please!"

Once again he was holding her by the arms; but she remained stiff and unyielding, and when he bent his head and said, "I'm sorry I spoke like that, but this is a matter that has seared me over the years. Come, let us go to the bank and sit down by the river and . . . and I will try to explain." He took her gently by the arm, and they did not speak again until they had reached the river bank and he had sat her down on the very rock that she and the boy had sat on earlier. He did not take her hand or look at her but, placing his hands on his knees he looked down into the water and began quietly. "It was in this very river that my brother died. Whether he drowned himself or drowned accidentally, I'll never know. But I lost him at a time when I needed him most. My mother died when Tim was seven years old. I was twelve and at boarding school. My father never got over her going; they were very devoted. He was in such a state that I didn't want to leave him and go back to school, but he insisted I did. The school, though, was just in Newcastle and so, under the circumstances, the headmaster allowed me home at weekends. Each time I saw him he seemed to have let go a little more on life. I understood that he spent most of his days on horseback, riding until both he and the animal were exhausted. Then one day he didn't return and they found him at the bottom of the small gully: the horse had thrown him and broken its leg but my father had broken his neck.''

He straightened his back now and turned to her, then continued, ''Tim was alone in the house, that big rambling place. He was missing our parents very much. It was then I made a decision. Tim had a tutor; he was a good man and learned. He knew as much or more than any of the teachers at the school, so I decided to stay at home myself and join Tim in the classroom, and in a way I became mother and father to him. He was like my shadow. We did everything together. Although there were five years between us we enjoyed the same things; the only difference between us was that he was of a more emotional nature, more temperamental, I suppose. And his ideas tended that way. He could paint well, and he was already a great reader. He wrote poetry from an early age, and kept an extensive diary that read like a book. We travelled together too. Went through France; did the usual trip through Italy, museums and palaces. But most enjoyable was the time we spent in Scotland, riding and shooting, or just walking the hills. Mr. Bennett, of course, always accompanied us. Even though I was getting older I felt that Tim should continue his studies. I myself had always harboured the desire to go to university, Oxford by choice, but at twenty-two I imagined I was too late. However, Mr. Bennett had different ideas. He had a friend who was a don in the university and who, he was sure, could press my case as an older than usual student.

''Tim was nearing eighteen and, as Mr. Bennett pointed out, it was really time I stopped mothering him, and let him stand on his own feet. And so arrangements were finalized for me to go up to Oxford at the start of the next academic year. It was during this period that Tim was left to himself quite a bit, and at first I didn't notice the change in him, but when I did, I thought it was because of our coming separation and that he was already preparing himself for it by distancing himself from me. Then one day—'' He now turned from her again and, taking off his hard hat, he laid it on the stone to his side, then ran his fingers across his brow before going on, ''just as today as I espied you in the wood, there I saw him with a girl in his arms. Her face was familiar, as naturally it would be—she was a housemaid. What immediately followed I won't go into. When he told me he intended to marry her I imagined he had gone mad, but he assured me he hadn't as it was a matter of honour with him that he should marry her because she was heavy with his child. I remember laughing at this stage and attempting to put my arm around his shoulder while I explained that these things were happening every day in big houses all over the country, and what would happen if the sons of the house were to think it their duty to marry all the maids that fell to them during the course of their adolescence. But he threw off my hand and declared that he intended to marry this girl, that he had proposed to her sometime earlier, and what was more, he had put his intention in writing, and what was even more still, he had been to see her only living relative, an uncle, a carter in the village, and to whom he had given his solemn promise to take care of her, as the man apparently was about to emigrate to Australia. As you can imagine, I flatly refused to countenance even the idea of such an association, and the war between us raged for days. I called Bennett in to discuss the matter. Apparently, he had known about the association but hadn't told me in case it should arouse my anger. Anyway, he had imagined it was a young man's passing fancy and was, in a way, perfectly natural, because, as he said, in our society such licence wasn't afforded the women of our class until they were married."

At this point he sighed deeply and said in a different tone, "My dear, don't look so shocked. You are not coy, and you are so sensible. You know, it is this part of your character, I might as well tell you, that amazes me, because your upbringing I should imagine, has been on a par with that of a nun in a convent. Of course, there's your grandmama, who must have brought a little light from the outside into your existence at an early age. You should be very grateful for her. Anyway, do . . . do you wish me to continue?"

Her throat was too dry for speech, she merely inclined her head, and so he went on, "I gave him an ultimatum: he was to give up the idea at once, and I would see that the girl was decently taken care of, and if she didn't want the child it would be adopted, otherwise he'd have to face marriage as a working man, for he would have no help from me. As I told him, he had no money of his own, for the estates and all they held were in my name. Fortunately or unfortunately, my father had not made another will from the time I was born. This threw him into a state and gave me hope, because he was in no way able to earn his living. Apart from his pastimes of painting and writing, he had no other qualifications.''

He leant towards her now but did not touch her: with his two hands flat on the rock, he looked down towards them as he said in a low voice, ''The weather was bad, the river had swollen, the wooden bridge further down was blocked with debris. I didn't know he was out. But when night came and he hadn't returned I went looking for him with the men. Dawn the following morning, the rowing boat was found capsized near the bridge. The debris had gone through and must have taken him with it. Three days later his body was recovered.'' Still looking at his hands, he muttered, ''I was overwhelmed with sorrow and anger. I wanted to strangle that girl. I gave orders for her to leave the house, and these were carried out. Then, a day later, she appeared again, accompanied by this uncle of hers, who Tim had said was an intelligent man. He was also a cunning man. He demanded to see me and told me plainly that if I did not give her the shelter of my house, to which she was due, at least as a servant, then he would make the matter public and show the press the letters that my brother had written to the girl, telling of his sincerity and love for her and his desire to marry her; and that now he was gone I had thrown her out, and the only place for her would be the workhouse where her child would be born, for he himself was due to leave for abroad. But he promised, or rather threatened, that if I did not meet his demands he would put off his voyage and bring the matter to light to the public. He said he had friends who would support him in his crusade in exposing the legalized licence given to sons of the wealthy, where they could use their maids as training ground, with the result that the workhouses were packed with young girls and ba . . . illegitimate children.''

He now raised his head and looked at her, continuing, ''I knew he meant every word he said, and I am so made that I couldn't stand up to the scandal. There are times now when

I regret my weakness. Well, I think you know the rest. I gave orders that the girl could stay but that she must be kept out of my sight. And those orders have been carried out. Up till recently, up till I fell in love with you, I had never spent very much time here; in fact, the very thought of that woman and child kept me away. I could, I suppose, have made arrangements for them, and offered to place her in some comfort outside, but had I done so it would have been paramount to accepting responsibility for the child and that I would or will never do, and today is the first time I have seen him.''

Her voice came soft and sad as she said, ''He's still your brother's child, Denny.''

''I . . . I'm sorry, but I don't look at him in that light, and never will. You've got to understand me in this, my dear. And I don't want the subject brought up again. It is too painful for me. I only know the loss of Tim altered my life. It altered me. I asked the question, why I should be held responsible in this matter, held to ransom as it were, made a laughing stock of, when in every county in this country, where there is sited a large establishment, the surrounding farms and cottages are bespattered with the results of their sporting sons and only too willing serving girls.''

When she rose sharply from the stone, he caught at her hands, saying, ''I . . . I speak too freely and too soon. I'm . . . I'm sorry. . . . Oh, my dear. I had looked forward so much all the journey down just to see your face, and a little while ago your expression told me that you . . . you more than liked me; now it tells me that you dislike me.''

She swallowed deeply, then said, ''I . . . I don't dislike you, I . . . I'm only troubled by your way of thinking.''

He rose and, still holding her hands, he drew her stiff body to him, saying gently now, '' 'Tis the thinking of my class. You think as you were brought up, I as I was brought up. We are moulded by our environment. But from now on I want, I sincerely want our environments to mingle. You believe me?''

''Yes. Yes, I believe you.''

''Well, now, can you forget the last half-hour as if it had never happened and smile at me as you did before?''

''I can't smile to order.''

''No, no; of course not. That would mean you are like the

other ladies of my acquaintance, with the exception of course of Pat. You know you are very like Pat in some ways, and I like that, because I'm fond of Pat. She's a straight, honest, good friend. Well now, my dear, shall we go back to the house? Because I've not eaten since I breakfasted this morning, but apart from that I am very thirsty. And later this evening, I must call on your father because the banns can be called any time now. Then there are the wedding invitations to go out. Oh, there is so much to do. You know what I thought on my journey down?''

''No, I don't.''

''I thought, wouldn't it save all this trouble if we could slip into your church one morning early and your father could marry us. And we could board the train and go off, just like that, without bags of luggage, a valet, or a maid.''

She pulled him to a stop, saying, ''It's surprising, at least it will be to you, but I don't want a maid, Denny.''

''Oh, my dear, you must have a maid.''

''No. Why should I? I've always dressed myself. I couldn't imagine someone else in the room while I was dressing. And . . . and do we need to have people travelling with us?''

He stared at her for a moment; then putting his head on one side and a quizzical smile coming to his lips, he said, ''No, you're absolutely right, we don't. In London, Johnson could see to my wants, and his wife Mary could see to yours, and up in Scotland, James McBride would be only too pleased to attend me, and there's Agnes, and Nell, who would fall over themselves to see to you. No, my dear. No, you're right.'' His smile widened. ''Of course, you're right. And when we are abroad we shall see to each other.''

He now grabbed her by the arm and hurried her through the woodland. It was indeed as if the last half-hour had never happened and there was no such person as a little boy who lived in the roof of his house, and slept there with his mother and wrote on a slate: Birds have wings, trees have leaves, and rabbits play, but they all die.

❧ 8 ❧

THE BANNS HAD BEEN CALLED FOR THE THIRD TIME. THE villagers were getting used to seeing the master of Rossburn sitting in his pew and often looking down to where his future wife sat in the parson's family pew beneath and slightly to the left of the pulpit.

Most of the villagers were quite agog at the event of the coming wedding, for invitations had been flowing freely among the cottages and houses. There were to be refreshments in the vicarage for both villagers and guests after the wedding, but later in the day a dinner and ball were to be held for the bridegroom's friends up at The House. This was to be left in the capable hands of Lady Golding, for the bridal pair were to leave by the three o'clock train from Newcastle for London, where they were to spend the first three days of their married life before going across the Channel to France, and from there would return to finish their month of honeymooning in Scotland.

It was now the beginning of May and all the arrangements were in full swing. The weather was fine; everyone was in good spirits. Even Rebecca seemed to have a new lease on life, so much so that company didn't seem to tire her as of yore. So, on this particular evening, there were gathered in her sick room not only the family, including Peter, but Dennison too. And he was laughing loudly with the others as Nancy Ann, at the request of her grandmother, mimicked the conversations she'd had with Shane McLoughlin, starting with the first one.

"How is your family?"

Her voice now changed, her whole manner changed: she took up the pose of the young man and in his broad Irish accent she said, "Oh, they are doing well, miss, especially since me da died. God rest him. There were fifteen of us at the end, and not one of us sorry to see him go 'cos, you know, he'd neither work nor want. Me ma's never been so happy, miss, and we all stand by her." She paused for the laughter, and then . . .

"Oh, it's you, McLoughlin. You, you are in a hurry."

"Did I startle you, miss? It's like me ma says, a bull in a china shop can't hold a candle to me. I might have knocked you flying, an' I would have sooner kicked meself than hurt a hair of your head . . . excuse the liberty I'm takin' in saying it, ma'am . . . miss. And how is yourself these days?"

"I'm very well. Thank you."

"God be praised for that. Indeed yes. Indeed yes."

She now touched the front of her hair as if it were a forelock and, nodding her head, stepped back two paces.

Dennison had never really witnessed her mimicking, not at this length. She had, at times, repeated a phrase and taken up a pose and, in doing so, made him laugh. But this was acting, and so natural. He was both astonished and proud. He saw a picture of her entertaining his guests as no one else could. The usual accomplishments were to tap out a tune on the piano and sing in a soprano voice. But this was entertaining. His future wife would certainly be an asset in company, and moreover a beautiful asset, especially when she grew a little older and plumped out. Her figure was beautiful now, but boyishly so. Give her a year or two and children, oh yes, children, a son, his son. He wanted a son; above all things he wanted a son.

He now looked at his future father-in-law. He had never seen him laugh before. He had hardly ever seen him smile.

He looked a different being . . . even jolly. He wished he could get to know the man better. He wished he would trust him.

"Good day to you, miss. Good day to you." She was still pulling at the front of her hair now, when all of a sudden her papa said, "Whisht! whisht!" and she stopped abruptly, and they all looked towards the bed. Her mother's head had sunk into the pillow, her face had gone a deeper pallor. And then, to their horror, a trickle of blood began to seep from the corner of her mouth. . . .

Something near to pandemonium followed. Dennison himself rode into the village for the doctor, who at first couldn't be found as he was attending a birth at a farm some distance away. So it was almost an hour later when he arrived, and he was silent as he stood by the bed and looked on the unconscious woman.

After a slight examination he took the parson's arm and gently led him from the room, and when they were in the sitting-room, his voice sad, he said, "She will not regain consciousness. You should be thankful for that. She's in no pain."

At this John dropped into a chair and stared before him like a blind man. He had known this hour must come, but now it was here he felt he couldn't bear it, and he cried, "Oh! Rebecca. Oh! Rebecca," as Nancy Ann in the other room was crying, "Oh! Mama. Oh! Mama."

And in the hallway, about to take his departure, was Dennison, who was also crying, but in a different way inside. My God! for this to happen at this stage, for what did it portend? Postponement of the wedding. And for how long? How long, he didn't know, but he only knew he couldn't stand much more of this delay. His need of her in all ways was so great that at this moment he felt as desperate as the whole family did at the coming loss of the dying woman, for he felt that by her going he, too, would lose, he would lose the being that had begun to shape his life into a different pattern.

Of one thing he was fully aware, he would have a fight on his hands with the parson for, his wife gone, he would have more need to hold on to his daughter, and, using his bereavement, he would play on her feeling in every way possible, and without compassion: the Christian man would be forgiven in the tactics he would use in order that his child would never leave him, especially not to marry him, the man of whom he had never approved.

PART FIVE

The New Life

❈ 1 ❈

"PAPA, IT IS FIVE MONTHS NOW SINCE MAMA WENT, AND . . . and Dennison is becoming impatient."

"Dennison is becoming impatient." Her father's voice was high, every word stressing his indignation, and he repeated, "Dennison is becoming impatient. My child, he will be lucky if I allow you to marry after another year. Have you forgotten the fitness of things? A wedding you talk of and your mother hardly left this house!"

"It is five months, Papa. I shall be eighteen very shortly. . . ."

"I know what age you will be very shortly and I can tell you this, there are another three years before you are twenty-one, and I can withhold my consent."

"You wouldn't, Papa?"

"Oh, yes, I would, my child, for you well know I have never been in favour of this marriage. If it had been someone else, and there is someone else that would take care of you and honour you and provide you with a good and wholesome life . . . if it had been he . . . ?"

"What are you saying, Papa? I know of no one else who would wish to marry me."

"Then you are blind, my child, quite blind. He is the friend of your brothers and a man who has become my friend. . . ."

"What! You mean Mr. Mercer? Oh, Papa, you are mistaken; he has never been other than polite and courteous to me.''

''Of course he hasn't, child, because he is a gentleman in every sense of the word. But let me tell you, he was upset, very upset indeed when he knew of your engagement, and he blamed himself for being slow in approaching you. Your present fiancé had no compunction in that way. And so I say to you as I said a few minutes ago, think again, break off this engagement. Wait a little while and . . .''

''No, Papa, I shan't do any such thing, no matter how long you make us wait. I have grown fond, very fond of Dennison, and I couldn't be so cruel. He has been patient and more than kind. He has been very kind to you, and I'm amazed at your attitude towards him. And I must say this, Papa, if you don't give us your consent, then I'm afraid that Dennison might take it into his own hands and obtain what he calls a special licence. And I must tell you further, Papa, that Grandmama and Peter are not with you in this. Grandmama said six months would be decent, and it is close to that now and I hate to say this, Papa, because . . . because I love you so, but if you don't marry us then we must go elsewhere.''

He looked at her the while his mouth opened and shut but without any sound coming from it: he couldn't believe his ears. But then he had refused to recognize the change in her over the past year. She was no longer a little girl, she was no longer even a young woman. He had refused to recognize her maturity, and now face to face with it he was shocked by it. When he could, he muttered thickly, ''Leave me. Leave me.''

And so she left him, the tears raining down her face.

But the door had no sooner closed behind Nancy Ann when it was opened again and Jessica entered the room, saying immediately, ''John Howard, I'm going to tell you something. You are going the right way to lose her altogether. If you don't marry them, and soon, let me tell you, someone else will. She will go off with him and the bond between you will be severed forever. She is old enough for marriage; she knows her own mind.'' She did not add that which her thoughts dictated, that her granddaughter was ready for marriage. Contact with her future husband had made her eager for it, for he was a virile man and had the magnetism of such about him.

Her voice softer and her words slower, she went on, "John Howard, John Howard, don't lose her. You'll always regret it if you do. Marry them, because marry they will sooner or later. And what you are seeming to forget, John Howard, is that Rebecca wanted this marriage."

He came back at her sharply now saying, "She only wanted it because she saw him as the only one who could provide for her daughter; she didn't realize that Graham was just waiting until Nancy Ann was a little older."

"Graham? Graham Mercer?"

"Which other Graham is there, Mother? Yes, Graham, and he loves her dearly."

"Well then, it is a pity he was so slow. But that can never be now because, face it, John Howard, she has grown to love this man; and he adores her, be he what he may. And all right, your main feeling against him is because of his past and the women in it, but all that is behind him and he's shown it to be so over the past year. And for a man like that, it could not have been easy. Oh, no, it could not have been easy. So let us have no more of it. Marry them. It can be done quietly without any fuss. No receptions, no parties, invitations, all that has been cancelled and won't be revived, not even if you were to make them wait a year or two. But you mustn't do that, because if you do"—her voice sank low in her throat— "we could come down to breakfast one morning and find an empty space at the table. That man is strong, he has power; he has made her love him, because she didn't at first, and she's not a character that can be lightly swayed. I know that, because she takes after me. So, am I to tell her that you will marry them, say, on her eighteenth birthday?"

She watched her son close his eyes, then turn from her and lean for support on the table. He looked an old man. He was an old man, and he but fifty-three years old, and he was a broken man because he had lost his support. She had never been very fond of her daughter-in-law until the last year or so when she seemed to have shed a little of her pious manner. But she had to admit that she had been the stay that had kept this son of hers upright, and now she feared for his future, both mental and physical, for since her going, he seemed to have lost interest even in his vocation: his sermons were without spirit, and his interest in his parishioners had diminished to a point where it was as much as he could do to attend a deathbed.

Slowly she went from the room. She was tired; age at the moment was telling on her too. She had not counted her birthdays since she had turned a blind eye on seventy. The misery in the house of late had brought home to her the fact that there was nothing kept age at bay as much as happiness and a cheerful atmosphere around one, and that nothing made it gallop toward its end quicker than misery. Well, although she couldn't bear to think what the house would be like devoid of Nancy Ann, she was determined she at least should know happiness. And to this end she went to her, where she was sitting in her bedroom, still crying, and, putting her arms around her, she said, "Cry no more, but put on your cloak and hood and go over there and tell him that you can be married on your eighteenth birthday."

❧ 2 ❧

WHEN THE PARSON'S WIFE DIED A NUMBER OF STAFF AT THE
House were elated, albeit they hid their faces behind masks
of mournful sympathy. What did it matter if they had to fore-
go their own special "do" which had promised to equal that
of the wedding guests; the master was still free, and if they
knew anything about the vicarage and the protocol there, there
would be no wedding for a year or two at least. And what
would he do in the meantime? They knew what he would do:
visit London more often than he had done of late. And those
in the hierarchy had reminded one another that Mrs. Rene
Poulter Myers had not raised a storm at being thrown off, but
had played clever and remained his friend. According to Staith
she had visited the London house twice and had had tea with
him. She was a clever woman, Mrs. Rene, they all agreed.

Then in December came the news that he was to be married in January; as Mrs. Amelia Conway said bitterly, on the
parson's prig's birthday. But she, together with the butler and
the valet, thanked their master when, the day before his marriage, he told them they must have a wedding breakfast among
themselves, all the staff to be included, and that twenty bottles of wine and spirits could be taken from the cellar.

They thanked him most profusely and wished him happiness, to which he answered, "Thank you, but that is already
mine."

As the honeymoon was to be curtailed to a fortnight, he said he knew that everything would be in order when he returned with their mistress. It seemed to them as they said later, he stressed the last word. . . .

And now the valet was in the housekeeper's room, telling the butler and Mrs. Conway as well as the first footman McTaggart the details of, as he said, the shabbiest wedding he had ever attended. "The church was like an icebox," he said. "And there the master and her stood before her father, and the old fellow seemed to throw the service at them. Sometimes he mumbled and sometimes he almost barked. Her brother gave her away, and Sir George Golding was the best man, while Lady Golding attended the bride. And there was the grandmother and the three maids sitting in one pew and the churchwarden and his daughters sitting at the other side. When it was over they didn't go back into the vicarage so there wasn't a glass raised. There was some kissing and shaking hands all round, but when she came to her father, who was standing apart, she threw her arms around his neck and he held her for a moment, then pushed her away, only to grab her again and hug her as if he would never let her go. Oh—" The valet shook his head mockingly before going on, "It was all very touching, for as she was about to get into the carriage she turned and, taking the small bouquet she had been carrying and which was half crushed now with the encounter with her dear papa, she went up to the warden's daughter and gave it to her. Then, what do you think? she, the warden's daughter, began to cry. Oh my! Oh my! I tell you, it was all very touching. Then they were off, taking only two valises, a case and a trunk. That warden's daughter would have had as much. Well now"—he looked from one to the other— "let's make hay while the sun shines, for the harvest, from now on, is going to be very poor unless we put our heads together."

❧ 3 ❧

THE COUPLE SPENT THE FIRST NIGHT OF THEIR MARRIED LIFE
at their London house where they had been warmly welcomed
by the four servants, particularly by the man Johnson and his
wife. The house, as Dennison had described to her, was comparatively small, the rooms not as big as those in the vicarage, but so comfortably furnished and warm as to be called
homely. The dinner was not elaborate but they lingered over
it. Their talk was perfunctory and after dinner they sat on a
sofa before the fire to have their coffee. When this was cleared
away, he drew her into his arms and held her gently, saying,
"I can't believe it. I just can't believe it."

Nor could she believe it, for not only her mind but her
whole body seemed churned with a mixture of feelings: she
was sad because of her father's attitude; she was full of wonderment that she was now the wife of a rich landowner and
was mistress of two estates and a town house; but above all
these other feelings, she was fearful of what lay ahead in this
first night of marriage. Yet, childishly, she told herself, her
mama, and papa, had experienced such a night, and they
were good, even holy people, so what was there to be afraid
of?

She was still asking the same question when Mary Johnson
bid her good night and left her alone in the bedroom, after

having been told gently that she could manage in her undressing.

Her grandmama had bought her her nightdress and matching negligee. Both were of soft white lawn. The nightdress had a frilled lace collar threaded with pink satin ribbon; it had a ruched front and an extra full skirt. She had taken down her hair and, remembering her grandmama's instructions, had not plaited it but had tied it loosely with a ribbon that matched the nightdress.

She was standing looking at herself in the long cheval mirror and being surprised by her reflection when a tap came on the door and it opened. Instinctively, she wanted to scamper to the bed and seek cover beneath the bedclothes, but she remained still, looking across the room to where he stood for a moment surveying her. He was wearing a brown velvet dressing-gown with deep revers; his hair was brushed well behind his ears; his face had been newly shaved; his eyes seemed lost in their own light.

It was some seconds before he moved towards her, and then, taking her gently into his arms, he said softly, "Smile."

"I . . . I can't. I . . . I'm afraid."

"Oh, my dear, never be afraid of me. Just remember, I love you. Always remember, I love you, and from this night onwards you will love me."

Her first night of marriage proved to be a mixture of embarrassment, pain, and a strange new feeling that she had no word for, as yet, for it was beyond happiness, beyond the feeling of love her family had engendered in her. Its source was somewhere outside herself, yet deep within her being. It was elusive and couldn't be held. It was born of contact, born out of pain which was to lessen as the days of the honeymoon progressed. And they progressed in a maze of wonderment.

On the second day of their marriage during which he seemed to have grown younger, so boyish did he act, he played guide through the museums, took her to see Buckingham Palace and the Tower of London and lastly the Zoological Gardens, where at the entrance the hired cabby cried, "Mondays sixpence, every other day a shilling." He was a very jolly man, the cabby, and had seemed to enjoy driving them, on and off, all day through fine drifting snow.

In the evening, after a dinner served in a restaurant, the grandeur of which, she observed, outdid the ballroom at The House, she visited her first theatre and sat in a box, but could hardly keep her attention on the stage, where scantily dressed ladies danced and men sang funny songs and made jokes, the gist of which she was unable to laugh at because she could not understand them. What interested her was the galaxy of people and the way the audience was dressed, especially those in the boxes. The upper parts of many of the ladies were almost as bare as the ladies dancing on the stage. Her own dress of blue velvet had a lace top to it which ended in a blue velvet ribbon around her throat. Dennison had chosen that she should wear it.

The following day they crossed over to France. She had prided herself that she could speak French, that was until she heard the Parisians talking, and but for answering "merci" and "oui" she did not attempt to converse in their tongue. But not so Dennison, for he was very much at home with the language, and with the people.

The weather was cold and stormy, but did not keep them indoors. Again he played guide, but his manner now was not so much boyish as gay. They went in a rocketing cab to Versailles, to Notre-Dame, to the Conciergerie. The second evening they attended an opera and during the interval he proudly took her arm and paraded her among the packed throng in the comparatively small foyer and was not at all annoyed when gentlemen's eyes were turned on her.

It was nearly two in the morning when they drove back to their hotel. Later, as she lay in his arms, he asked her if she had enjoyed the opera, and she answered truthfully, "Not very much, not as much as the entertainment in London." And at this he had rolled her backwards and forwards as he laughed, saying, "Where has my little vicarage maiden gone?"

There had been times during their short stay in London when she was rudely jolted out of this fairy-tale existence into which she had been drawn, and jolted into life that was real and awful, such as when the cab driver had driven them along out of the way routes in the city and they passed through narrow streets where men lurked in doorways and women had hard and weary faces; even the very young ones looked old, and most of the children were ragged and barefoot. But of course she had seen ragged and barefoot children before; not so many, though, as seemed to swarm in London. And yet these London children were chirpy individuals, more so than those nearer to home. There was, she knew, great poverty in the towns round about Newcastle, even in their own village. Her papa had once got up a clog club and had asked the parishioners to subscribe whatever they could afford to provide for the needy children of the neighbourhood. And when the subscriptions had been thin, her papa had pointed out it was because the parishioners didn't like collections of any kind, especially the farming community who objected to the tithes and anything else that meant the laying out of money without visible return.

But overall the essence of the fairy-tale remained with her until what was to be their last evening in Paris when he took her to a casino. This experience would, he said, expunge the vicarage forever.

He often joked about her vicarage upbringing, but she didn't mind in the least because, in a way, she felt he was glad she'd had such a narrow experience for it gave him the opportunity to open up a new world for her.

But the visit to the casino was to have the opposite effect on her from that intended. In the first place, she was shocked at the sight of women gambling. Ladies all, at least so it was proclaimed by their dress, and the tone of their voices, and the arrogance of their manners.

She was further amazed when Dennison was greeted warmly by an immaculately dressed gentleman who was not a patron, but who seemed to be in charge of the establishment, for he greeted him by name and was enthusiastic in his welcome. But it was noticeable to her that she wasn't introduced to this gentleman. After he had left them she whispered, "You know him?" And he whispered back, mockery in his voice, "Yes, my dear; it is not the first time I have been in Paris." She remembered now her papa referring to him as a gambler. "And don't look so frightened; there are

no tigers about, they are all very nice people. Come!''
He took hold of her hand. "I shall show you my only
skill." . . .

For the next hour she watched him practising his skill: first
at a roulette table. And when, after twenty minutes or so, he
rose from it, she looked at him in something like horror as
she said, "You have lost the equivalent of fifty sovereigns?"

"Yes, my dear, I have lost the equivalent of fifty sovereigns. But the night is young. Please," he pleaded with her
now, "do not look so forbidding. I cannot recognize my Nancy Ann when you look like that. What is fifty sovereigns
anyway?"

He now led her to a corner of the room where four men
were sitting at a table, one of them rattling dice, and as they
approached it he said, "Give me three numbers."

"What kind of numbers? High numbers?"

"No; anything from one to six."

She blinked, thought a moment, then said, "Two, three,
six." It was as if she was back in the nursery finding it difficult to say twice, so she would always say, two, three, six,
instead of twice three are six.

"Two, three, six, it will be."

When a man vacated a chair, Dennison took it, and there
followed some quick exchanges in French between him and
another man.

She could not follow the game. She could only see that
three times out of four the die came up with a six for Dennison. After this there was more rapid exchange. One thing she
noticed was, there was no actual money on the table, only
small counters not unlike those she and the boys had used to
play ludo, except these were larger. She watched Dennison
push all the counters lying in front of him towards the middle
of the table. She saw the other men shrug their shoulders,
then push their counters likewise. Now Dennison glanced up
at her before taking up an ivory cup and putting the die in it.
There was silence round the table. When the die again turned
úp three there was a murmur of, "Trois, trois, un, deux,
trois."

He glanced at her again; then proceeded to make further
throws, the continued silence accentuating the ominous rat-

tling of the die in the cup. When, for the third time, it turned
up two there were exclamations of amazement from two of
the men, but the third one's face looked blank. This man was
sitting opposite and he now handed Dennison a bag.

Having put the counters in the bag, Dennison guided her
down the room.

At the touch of his arm, Dennison turned to the man of the
blank countenance who spoke rapidly at him. When Dennison shook his head and pointed to Nancy Ann, the man
shrugged his shoulders and turned away. And when Nancy
Ann asked, "What was he saying?" Dennison answered, "He
wanted to know if I had a special system, or was it a trick,
and I said, no, I just had a clever wife who gave me the
numbers."

The gentleman who had greeted them when they first entered was standing by the desk at which the counters were
exchanged, and, his manner still bright, he said in stilted
English, "It is your lucky night, Monsieur. You are staying
long?"

"Long enough to come back and lose my gains."

"You are a sportsman. Always a sportsman. It is a pleasure
both to see you and your lady." And as he inclined his head
towards Nancy Ann, Dennison said, "My wife, Monsieur."

"Ah! Ah!" His mouth opened wide on the exclamation
and, taking her hand, he bowed over it before raising it to
his lips, then saying, "Congratulations, and happiness, Ma-
dame, always happiness."

She was still blushing as they passed through the doors into
the cold night air. When the cab rolled up out of the darkness,
he helped her inside and gave the name of a restaurant on the
Champs Elysees.

"How . . . how much did you win?" she now asked in a
small voice. And when he, patting the pocket of his greatcoat, answered, "Five hundred guineas," she actually jumped
away from him along the seat, and her voice seemed to come
out of the top of her head as she muttered, *"Five* hundred
guineas!"

"Yes, my dear, five hundred guineas. But don't forget you
upbraided me for losing fifty guineas, so you can say I am
only four hundred and fifty guineas to the good, or at least

we are only four hundred and fifty guineas to the good, because you know, you did it.''

"I didn't. I didn't. I . . . I don't like gambling. I . . . I don't like to see you gambling.''

"Oh, my dear, it is a harmless pastime . . . when you can afford it.''

"And . . . and can you really afford to lose such sums?''

"I didn't lose, my dear, I won.''

"Do you always win?''

"No.'' He leaned forward and gave her a peck on the lips, then repeated, "No, madam, I don't always win.''

"But . . . but how did you manage to win on those numbers tonight?''

He did not answer her for a moment, but lay back against the smelly leather seat of the cab, and his voice seemed to come to her from a long distance, so soft was it as he replied, "I don't know. I'll never know. I only remember that I thought deeply, I wished deeply. It seemed as if there was another voice saying, 'I will lay a bet that I can turn the die up on the same number three times out of four.' It wasn't the usual game I realized now I was taking a big chance, yet not at that particular time. I willed it to happen and it did.'' He turned quickly to her now, saying, "I know what I'll do. Every time you accompany me to a game and I win—and I will if you are beside me—I will share the spoils. So tonight, madam, I owe you two hundred and fifty guineas.''

"No! No!" Her voice was emphatic. "I could never touch money got like that. No, no; never!''

In the dim light given off by the side lamps, she watched his expression change, his voice also as he said, "Then you are saying you will have nothing to do with my home or anything in it for, my dear, I come from a long line of gamblers. I am not as foolhardy as my ancestors who lost even the clothes from their backs. Nor will I ever make enough money or bet everything on a wager that would enable me to lose or build a house like my present home, or the lodge in Scotland, or that in London. It may further surprise you that my great-great-grandfather, one of the first chronicled in the early seventeen hundreds, was famous for running a gaming house in London. He is one of the men who lost his clothes, but he regained them again and it was his grandson who built Rossburn towards the end of the last century. My father was a moderate gambler, but he gambled. My grandfather was more daring, for he also bought the lodge and our London house.''

He had turned from her and was looking straight ahead, and she knew that she had annoyed him, not only annoyed, but made him angry. She didn't want to make him angry, ever; he was so kind, so good to her. She . . . she loved him.

The thought, like a spur, lifted her close to him. She put an arm across him, her head on his shoulder knocking her hat askew, and, the tears in her voice, she said, "I'm . . . I'm sorry, Denny, I am. I didn't understand. Please don't be annoyed with me."

His arms were about her now; he was holding her tight. His voice changed, he was soothing her, saying, "There, there. No, I'm not annoyed with you, of course not. How could I be? All I want is to make you happy."

She raised her head from his shoulder. Her eyes blinking, her lips trembling, she said softly, "I . . . I love you."

He didn't move: he did not hold her tighter; he just stared into her face in the dimness, then pressed her gently from him, took his silver mounted walking stick and rapped the roof of the cab and, when it stopped, spoke in rapid French. Then, sitting back, he drew her into his arms again, saying softly, "We are going home." There was something in his tone that made her repeat, "Home? You mean to the hotel?"

"No," he answered, "back to England, to London. We can stay there overnight, or longer if you wish, but . . . but we are on our way home."

❧ 4 ❧

NANCY ANN WAS FIVE MONTHS PREGNANT AND THE MOUND in her stomach definitely indicated this. For the first four months she had felt unwell, but over the past few weeks her feeling of well-being had returned. And tonight would be the third function she had attended in as many weeks; but she was once again complaining of the tightness of her corset.

Since returning home, she had refused to engage a personal maid, but had compromised by saying that she would have the assistance of Pattie Anderson, the top floor maid, when she felt it necessary. One of Anderson's functions, she had been told, was to attend to the needs of lady guests who were without maids. Lady Golding had already prompted her, she must never address her as Pattie, but give her her surname, as she must do with all her staff. This, at the beginning, she had found awkward, having been used to Peggy, Jane, and Hilda. Now she was saying, "It is much too tight, Anderson. I can hardly breathe."

"You'll not get into your mauve gown else, ma'am."

"Then I'll have to get into something else. Slacken the bottom tapes, please."

She didn't like Anderson. She was a woman in her mid-thirties and the tallest of all the female staff. And Nancy Ann compared her manner with that of a chamaeleon's change of colour, for she had the habit of putting on a superior tone when they were in the room together, but should her master come in, then her voice would change to a soft persuasive note and her manner suggest that of an older wiser woman only too eager to help the young mistress over the pitfalls in the way of dress.

The pale mauve brocade dress on, the myriad of small buttons fastened, Nancy Ann sat at the dressing-table, and when the woman went to touch her hair she flicked her hand away, saying, "Thank you. I can manage."

"What jewellery were you thinking about wearing . . . ma'am?"

Nancy Ann had noticed the pause before the use of the title "ma'am" not only with this woman, but with other members of the household too.

"I think I'll wear the pearls."

"Pearls, with brocade? I would have thought, ma'am, the diamond necklace."

She swung round the dressing-stool and, looking straight up at the woman now, she said, "I am wearing pearls, Anderson, and I can manage to put them on myself. Thank you. That is all."

The woman drew herself up. There was an almost imperceivable nod of the head, then, her voice stiff, she said, "Very good . . . ma'am," and on that she turned and walked out.

Alone in the bedroom again, Nancy Ann leant her elbow on the dressing-table and rested her head on her hands for a moment. There was a war going on in this house. She'd felt it from the moment she had come back after the honeymoon. It was understood she would see Mrs. Conway each morning and discuss with her the menu for the day, or the meal if they were entertaining company. But from the beginning the housekeeper had informed her, by a look, if not by words, that she was well capable of arranging the menus and for providing for any guests that might come.

The butler's manner to her was polite, as it would be to any guest. But there was one person on the staff that she actually disliked, and that was Dennison's man. She knew her grandmama's name for his manner would have been oily. She had even expressed her feelings about the valet to Dennison, and he had been surprised, saying in the man's defence that he was a very good valet and he had found no cause for complaint during the six years he had been with him. But he had gone on to explain to her that servants were a different breed altogether from . . . well, the class. They were brought up to be subservient, and this, at times, could give the impression that they were sly. This was the word she had used about Staith. And he had ended his little sermon by saying that she mustn't expect too much of them. Each of them had his appointed work and if this was done well, that was all she need worry about; in fact, she need not worry about the house at all; she could just leave it in the capable hands of Conway and Trice.

She often longed for the proximity of the girls back in the vicarage, and to be able to go into the kitchen any time she liked and talk to them. She had only once entered the kitchen of this house, which wasn't a kitchen, but kitchens, and she knew this had caused some consternation; especially to the young woman Mather who had stood at the doorway watching her as she spoke to the boy, David.

The morning following her visit, the housekeeper had said, "If you wish to visit the kitchen, ma'am, I will make arrangements."

And to this Nancy Ann had coolly replied, "It won't be necessary for I don't know when I shall be feeling so inclined. But should I do so, I think I can find my way there."

However, she had realized during the past month that although many of the staff looked upon her still as that chit from the vicarage, they were, nevertheless, coming to realize just what liberties they could take with her. There were just two of the house staff who had shown her small kindnesses since she had become their mistress, and these were Henry Robertson, the second footman, and Jane Renton, the first housemaid. Renton was small and thin with dark merry eyes, and her countenance was not always stiff. She put Nancy Ann in mind of Hilda.

Her mind on the vicarage, her thoughts dwelt on her papa. She was very worried about him, as were her grandmama and Peter. He had become very forgetful of late: only a week ago he had kept a congregation waiting; then, instead of a sermon, he had just read them the twenty-third psalm; and he had not afterwards stood at the church door to bid them good day, but had stridden away into the countryside and had not returned until late in the afternoon. The doctor was to call today, and she was anxious for the morrow to come so that she could slip over and find out what his advice was regarding her father. It was evident that there was something mentally wrong with him, yet, when he spoke, his words sounded reasonable enough. But he always had to recollect himself before he could give an answer, and that wasn't like her father.

Her toilet finished, she rose from the stool, passed the big high heavy satin-draped four-poster bed to where the open door led on to the balcony, and there she stood looking out over the gardens towards the village and the vicarage, and her thoughts weren't happy.

She turned now from the balcony railings when she heard Dennison come from his dressing-room. As he walked towards her his smile widened; and now, his hands on her shoulders, he looked down into her face, saying, "My dear, you look delightful. Curves suit you." Then he added softly and mischievously, "I must see that you are never without them."

"Oh, Denny." She turned her head away from him then, and, walking back into the room, she said, "Do you know how many are expected?"

"Not all that many; I don't think their table will hold more than a dozen or so. As Pat said, it's a breaking-in for Flo and Arthur. You would never think that Arthur and Pat were brother and sister; he's so retiring, can't get a word out of him at times."

"I rather liked him."

"Yes, I like them both."

"Who . . . who are likely to be there?"

"Oh, the Maddisons I suppose, and the Ridleys, and of course Jim and Maggie O'Toole. There's a pair for you. To listen to them you wouldn't think there were any troubles in Ireland. They are the funniest people I know. And . . . and likely Bunny and May Braithwaite. Well, that would make fourteen all told. That would be about the lot."

He picked up her silk coat from the back of the chair and

put it round her, and as he fastened the buckle at the neck he said, "If it's a cosy do, private, after dinner you must do them a mime. George loves to see you doing a mime."

"Do a mime, like this?" She patted her stomach.

"Why not?" His face was serious. "That's not going to object."

She pushed him and, laughing now, she turned away. And he was still smiling at his own joke when, some minutes later, he helped her into the landau.

The June night was warm, the air still clear, and as they drove over the bridge at Durham towards their destination, which was on the outskirts of the town, she looked down on the river, saying, "This is a most beautiful town, don't you think?" She was about to add, "Look at the river, isn't it lovely!" when she remembered he wasn't fond of the river, and with cause.

He answered, "Indeed it is, beautiful. The cathedral can hold its own against any other in the land."

She said now thoughtfully, "I would like to spend some time just wandering around it. My acquaintance with it is mostly what I read at school, yet Papa once spent his holiday in it."

"Your father spent his holiday in the cathedral. How on earth did he do that? Take services?"

"No. He came down every day and either strolled about or just sat, or chatted with the Dean." She added now, "I'm worried about Papa. I . . . I don't know what's going to happen. I . . . I don't think he can carry on much longer, even if he wanted to."

"Well, my dear"—he took her hand—"I've told you, he and your grandmama must come to us. There are rooms going begging in the east and west wings."

She looked at him, her face straight but the light in her eyes soft. He was so kind. But she couldn't say to him, "He will never come to live in your house . . . our house." Only last week her grandmama had said, "I think our time here is short, but there's one thing sure, he will never accept your offer to live at The House." And she'd had no need to add, "He would accept nothing from your husband, because his opinion of him has not changed."

This was something she couldn't understand about her father: he had always been such a forgiving man. Often of late she had recalled that Sunday long ago when he had cried from the pulpit, "Let him first cast a stone." That was the day she had suggested to James that she would tell Eva Mc-Keowan he was engaged. It was odd about Eva. In those days she had seemed such a flighty stupid young woman. But since she herself had known love she realized what Eva's feelings must have been at that time. Now she quite liked her. And apparently she wasn't the only one. But she could hardly take in the fact that Peter might be taking a fancy to her.

Peter spent every other Saturday afternoon and Sunday, which were his leave days, at the vicarage, and on a Sunday she would often see him stop and speak to Eva McKeowan. When the idea first entered her head she told herself that Eva was three years older than Peter, and surely Peter would never think about marrying a woman older than himself. But why not? Anyway, that was Peter's business.

She wished she weren't going to this party; yet she always enjoyed the company of Pat and her husband George. It had become routine over the past months for them and the Gold-ings to alternate in inviting each other to a card evening on Wednesday nights. The game they played was whist. She had become quite proficient at it, but always felt guilty when they played for money. The highest winning never exceeded five pounds which, except for herself, they found amusing. And if Dennison and she should win, for he always partnered her, he would ceremoniously divide the spoils when they returned home.

He had made one or two trips to London lately, and she knew that they were connected with business and that in all probability there would have been no gambling; nevertheless, his visits to Newcastle were always for that purpose alone. After one such visit he spilled seventy sovereigns into her lap, saying "You have nothing in writing so I'm not going to give you half, merely a percentage." On other occasions, on returning, he had either not mentioned his gaming or simply spread out his hands, smiled at her and said, "The gods weren't with me." . . .

A short drive led up to the Rowlands' residence, and to

one side of the house was a large lawn dotted with flower beds among which she could see a few people strolling.

Florence and Arthur Rowland were at the door to meet them. Their one manservant took her cloak and Dennison's hat, and then they were walking towards the open doors of the drawing room, behind which she could see a number of other people, among them, Pat and George Golding.

Pat immediately came towards them, talking rapidly as usual. "Hasn't it been a swelter! I can't stand the heat. How are you, my dear? Is it getting you down?" And without giving Nancy Ann time to say whether or not the heat was affecting her, Pat went on, "You know everybody, so come into the garden straightaway, it's cool out there."

As they made their way up the room, a lady came through an alcove, a gentleman on each side of her and laughing with her. But on the sight of the latest guests, the lady paused for a moment and in a high and almost childish voice that did not match her appearance she came towards them, crying, "Oh, Denny! Hello there. And what is this latest I've just heard about you, my boy . . . Parliament? Never! Never you!" And she dug him playfully now with her fan. "Arnold tells me you're trying to get your foot in."

It was evident that Dennison was both taken off his guard and embarrassed, but on a laugh he replied, "Not my foot; I always go head first," causing further laughter from the two gentlemen whom Nancy Ann knew to be Mr. Bunny Braithwaite and Mr. Edward Ridley. And it was Mr. Ridley who said in a loud voice as if he were shouting from the other end of the room, "That was an answer for you, Rene."

Nancy Ann was looking at the woman before her. She was small of stature, being only five foot three; she was plump—a more correct description would be fat—so that the flesh flowed out of the top of her gown showing the curve of her breasts. But the skin, a light cream colour with a blush to it, was perfect, as was that of her face. Her eyes were large and round and of a steely blue.

Nancy Ann felt a sickness riving her chest. Try as she might, she could not get the idea out of her head that, in some way, this woman menaced her life. She knew she had been a close friend of Dennison's, and once before when the woman, as now, was completely ignoring her, she had later said to him, "That woman dislikes me intensely. She cannot forget the episode on the road with the dog," and had then naively asked him, "What kind of a friend was she to you?" And she recalled it was a long moment before he answered, "She was a friend, like any other of my neighbours."

She watched her now thrust her hand through his arm, saying, "Come. I have something to show you. You think you have a fine garden, but you've never seen a specimen like this."

Dennison glanced at Nancy Ann as he left her side. His eyebrows were raised and there was a puckered smile on his face as if he was helpless in the situation.

Florence Rowland, happening now to come to her side, said, "Would you like a cool drink, Nancy Ann?" But before she had time to reply Pat put in, "Yes, she would, but I'll see to it, Flo. Come along, my dear, let us indulge ourselves."

Pat now led her through an archway and into a room, to a long table on which was an assortment of coloured drinks, with two maids standing behind the table ready to serve. But Pat did not guide her towards the table, but to the further end of the room where there was a deep window-seat and, gently pulling her down, she said, "Get that look off your face."

Nancy Ann made no reply but swallowed deeply, and Pat went on, "Flo did not invite them, not really. Arnold Myers is in the Diplomatic Service, the same as Arthur, and so, apparently, they occasionally meet, not only in town and abroad, but here and there. Well, Arnold had just come back from a trip and was pleased to find that Flo and Arthur had settled near here, and when they dropped in it was natural for Flo to ask them to stay on."

"That woman ignores me, Pat. I've told you before."

"Oh"—Pat wagged her head—"she ignores all women. She's a man-eater. Anyway, you have no need to worry about Denny." She patted Nancy Ann's hand as she now said, "I've never known Denny to be in love before, and now he is wallowing in it and with one whom I imagine to be a very sensible girl, even if she was incarcerated in a vicarage all her young days."

Nancy Ann smiled faintly as she replied, "There was no incarceration. From what I have noticed these last few months with regard to the upbringing of young ladies, I had extreme liberty; in fact, I realize now, I ran wild for most of my young days."

"Well, it certainly didn't do you any harm. And now, don't let that little bitch get under your skin, because, let's face it, she is a bitch. However, I must admit, not of the mongrel type: she comes from a thoroughbred stock and, like most thoroughbreds, she has been pampered and spoilt all her days. And like many of them coming under that category, her intelligence is not as bright as her pedigree."

Pat was now laughing widely at her similes; then pushing Nancy Ann gently, she ended, "If she was a common mongrel bitch one would know how to deal with her: you would grab her by the hair, kick her in the backside, and fling her out of the door, preferably naked. But with her special kind, you must use guile and finesse."

She was laughing loudly now and Nancy Ann was forced to join her. As they rose to their feet she put out her hand and said, "What would I have done in this situation, Pat, without you?"

"Followed the advice of your grandmama. Anyway, she and I think alike. I'm going to call in some day this week and see her. Now come on, let us not spoil Flo's little party, which I really did think promised to be dull until I saw Jim and Maggie O'Toole. When they start on their Irish yarns they make one forget all one's troubles. Chin up! Shoulders back, and stomach out." And on this last quip her laughter rang through the room as she led Nancy Ann out of it without allowing her to have the promised cooling drink. . . .

It could be said that the evening was a pleasant one. The conversation at the dinner table was merry, made so as Pat had foretold by the two Irish guests, with the husband and wife outdoing each other in telling tales of events that took place in their homes on the outskirts of Dublin. Rene Myers, too, seemed in very high spirits as she quipped across the table with the men opposite her, and more often than not including Dennison. Her husband, on the other hand, had little to say. He was a dour man with a long face, black hair

213

that lay flat on his head, and he had the disconcerting habit of staring fixedly at one without speaking. It was widely known that he was in love with his wife and that he put up with her foibles because he didn't want to lose her. It was also widely known that he was a very rich man. A millionaire twice over, some said.

There being no room to dance and no tables set out for cards, by eleven o'clock most of the guests had departed. The night had become cooler and the remaining company were seated in the drawing-room.

Dennison was sitting on a couch with Maggie O'Toole on one side of him and Rene Myers on the other. And every time Maggie O'Toole came out with some funny remark causing general laughter, Nancy Ann noticed that the woman, as she thought of her, lolled against Dennison, even going as far as putting her head on his shoulder.

She herself was sitting on one edge of a love seat, with George on the other side.

On another couch, Jim O'Toole sat beside Florence Rowland; and flanking Florence was Arnold Myers, with Arthur Rowland sitting perched on the end. And that was the company when Dennison leaning forward in Nancy Ann's direction, said, "Do us the McLoughlin fellow, dear."

"Oh no!" Nancy Ann shook her head. But when Pat and George put in together, "Yes, do, Nancy Ann. Come on," and Pat, turning to Maggie O'Toole, said, "She'll beat you at your own game."

"Well, let's see it. Let's see it," cried Maggie O'Toole. "What does she do?"

"She mimics. It's amazing. Come on, do." Pat thrust out her hand in a wagging movement as if she were lifting Nancy Ann from the chair. And when Dennison said again, softly, "Come on, dear," she said to herself, Why not? She had this one gift, and it was a gift because, as her grandmama said, no one in the family on either side had ever been on the stage. Anyway, it was unthinkable that they should have been, so her accomplishment must be in the nature of a gift. And she had practised it for years; even lately, in the privacy of her own room and for her own entertainment she had imitated the various members of her staff.

214

She got to her feet and by way of explanation she said, "I . . . I've known the McLoughlin family since I was a small girl, and I was surprised one day when I saw the eldest son in the courtyard, and this is the conversation that followed." She moved to stand in front of the flower-banked fireplace and, assuming a matronly dignity, her hands joined at her waist, she began, "You are one of the McLoughlins?"

Then, when her whole expression and her manner changed with very little movement of her body and there came out of her mouth the thick Irish vowels speaking the northern dialect, there was a gust of laughter from the company, and she had to stop until it subsided. And Pat's voice admonished them, "Be quiet now. Be quiet. Let her go on."

And they tried to let her go on, but there were tears of laughter running down the cheeks of Maggie O'Toole and that of her husband by the time she had finished.

Amid the clapping Maggie O'Toole cried, "I've never seen the likes. The Dublin Group couldn't have done any better, could they now, Jim?"

"They couldn't that. It's on the stage you should be, me girl, not stuck away in this backwater. Now if you ever want a career for yourself, I know the very. . . ."

"Be quiet! Jimmy."

She was about to go on when the thin voice of Arnold Myers cut in, saying, "Give us some other servant."

Unsmiling, Nancy Ann looked at him now from where she was still standing before the fireplace and in a cool voice she said, "I don't do servants. I only do Shane because, as I said, I have known his family for so long and because I am sure he would enjoy being mimicked."

"Give us the ticket collector."

She looked at Sir George and, smiling now, she said, "All right, the ticket collector." Then she went on to explain.

"It happened this way. I was in Newcastle station with my papa. We were to meet the boys, my two brothers coming back from university. When my papa went to the enquiry office I went to buy some platform tickets, and in front of me was a lady and her daughter who was about nine years old. She was a very prim lady and spoke precisely, and what she was saying was—" She now took up the stance of the lady and in a high mincing voice she said, "One and a half returns to Jayro." Then immediately her head seemed to sink into her shoulders, and it tilted to one side as if she were looking up under a grid and, her voice changing into the thick twang and dialect, she said, "What was that, missis? Where d'ya wanna go?"

Again she changed. *"Jayro,"* she said. "One and a half returns to *Jayro."*

Again she changed. "Jayroo? 'Taint on this line, missis."

"Don't be stupid, man."

"Tryin' not to be, missis."

Turning her head to the side and her mouth twisting, she said, "Willy! Here a tick. You know where this place *Jayroo* is?"

She had lifted her elbow as if nudging another man. Then quickly she again changed her stance. Her face stretched, her eyebrows went up, and this new character, Willy, turned its head slightly and apparently looked down on a child, saying, "Where does ya ma want to go, hinny?"

"Jarrer." The voice came out like that of a little girl.

Then with lightning speed she was once again the long-faced man turning to his companion and saying, "It's Jarrer, man, she's askin' for . . . Jarrer!"

"Oh, Jarrer. Well why couldn't she say that instead of talkin' like a bloomin' foreigner . . . Jayroo."

There followed enthusiastic applause, much laughter, from all present, except, Nancy Ann was quick to notice, that woman, who had never even smiled once during her performance. She had been aware of her attitude right from the start, when she had done Shane, and the advice her papa had laughingly given to James when they were discussing how to hold an audience, whether it be a congregation or a class in a schoolroom, had come to her: "Concentrate on the one that is about to go to sleep, or on a face that you know resents you, or, in my case, on someone who has been dragged to church unwillingly," her papa had said. "Get that one's attention and you needn't bother about the rest of the company."

But tonight she had been unable to apply that advice: that woman's determination not to be amused was too strong.

She now watched her pull herself to the end of the deep couch and attempt to rise, a signal for Dennison to get to his feet and offer her his hand. And now she was looking around her, saying, ''Well, we must be going because we are leaving early in the morning for London,'' and glancing at her husband while adding, ''I don't know why he's got to work when other people are on holiday. Town will be empty.''

It was Maggie O'Toole's voice that broke in now, saying, ''Well, we'll be passing through next week, Rene, for we're off to Rome; the Pope's giving a ceilidh.'' And she put her head back and laughed, the others also joining in. Then she turned to Rene again, saying, ''We'll look in on you and beg a meal.''

''Do. Do.''

And now Nancy Ann felt a restriction in her throat when the woman turned back to Dennison and said, ''Are you coming up, Denny?''

''I may do. I may do,'' he answered casually.

''Well, you'll drop in, won't you?''

''Thank you, yes. Thank you.''

''That's a promise. I'll expect you to honour it.''

She now turned and looked towards her husband and nodded.

There followed a chorus of goodbyes, and when Arthur Rowland said, ''I'll see you to your carriage,'' she flapped her hand at him, saying, ''Don't worry, we can see ourselves out.''

''Nonsense.''

Arthur and Flo went ahead; Arnold Myers followed, but his wife seemed to linger, saying a last word here and there, and when she eventually passed Nancy Ann, who was standing a little apart, she did so as if she weren't there.

Those remaining had seated themselves again, Jim and Maggie O'Toole, Pat and George, and Dennison. And to Nancy Ann they were like a family group. And with this feeling it seemed that the devil entered into her. She wanted to hit back in some way at the woman whose attitude towards her, she felt sure, had not escaped those present tonight, and so, as if she were indeed among her own family, she did another turn. Pointing her feet slightly outwards, and seem-

ing to pull her head down into her neck, her already promi-
nent stomach thrust further outwards, her arms held away
from her sides as if by fat, she waddled two or three steps up
the room, saying as she did so in an exact imitation of Rene
Myers's voice, "I'm off to London tomorrow to spread my
charms over the male population and there's enough of me to
cover them and plenty to spare."

She knew she was reacting spitefully, and she really did
not expect laughter from those present, but she felt they would
understand the reason for her retaliation, especially Pat and
George. But they were all staring at her, wide-eyed; and yet,
not at her, but beyond her. She turned her head slowly to see
standing there in the doorway the person she had been mimicking. She drew in a long deep breath as she watched the
woman walk slowly up the room to a side table, pick up a
vanity bag, turn as slowly about and walk down the room
again. But when she came to Nancy Ann's side she paused
for a moment but did not speak, yet the steely glint in her
eyes spoke for her. She was passing through the doorway into
the hall when Dennison's voice called, "Rene. Rene. Wait!"
And as he passed Nancy Ann almost at a run, the look he
too cast on her also spoke his thoughts.

She stood shivering, her eyes closed, until she felt Pat's
hand on her arm and heard her voice low, saying, "You
shouldn't have done that. Come and sit down."

"No, no. I . . . we'd better be going." She looked to where
the O'Tooles and George were standing, and she muttered,
"I'm sorry."

"Oh, away with you!" Maggie O'Toole was by her side
now. "Don't you be sorry for having said that. It's what we
all think but haven't the nerve to say it, me dear. You've got
no need to worry. You're a match for her, I can see. But I'll
tell you this"—and smiling, she leant forward close to Nancy
Ann as she whispered—"Having listened to you there, it surprises me that you come out of a vicarage."

At this point Dennison entered the room and said to
George, "We'll be away." That was all.

He did not look at or speak to her until five minutes later
when they were seated in the landau which now had the hood
up. They had been driving some distance when, from deep

in his throat, he said, "If that insult had come out of
a whore's mouth I could have understood it. You have made
an enemy tonight where you could have made a friend."

She had an answer to this, but she gritted her teeth and
decided to wait until they were in the privacy of their room.

Once they reached the house he did not follow her upstairs
as was his rule and have a drink brought up to him, but he
went into the library. And when she entered the bedroom and
saw Anderson waiting for her, she threw off her cloak, saying, "Just unbutton my dress, please, and undo the lace of
the corset; I will see to the rest." Then she added thoughtfully, "You . . . you must be tired. Get to bed."

"Thank you, ma'am." And the woman did as she was bid.

Half undressed, Nancy Ann sat down on the chaise-longue
and, bending forward, she buried her face in her hands.

Finally she finished her undressing and got into her dressing-gown, but she did not go to bed, she sat waiting for his
coming up. It was almost an hour later when she heard him
enter his dressing-room and talk to his man, and another half
an hour passed before he entered the bedroom. He stood
looking at her for a moment where she sat, not the picture of
dejection as he might have expected, but straight-backed and
stiff-faced. He seemed to be waiting for her to make some
comment, and when she didn't, he said, "What you might
not know, Nancy Ann, is that the O'Tooles, as charming as
they are, are chatterboxes and gossipers, and your spiteful
little charade will be around half the county by this time
tomorrow night."

She rose to her feet and, her voice controlled, she said, "I
shall ask you a question, Dennison"—she gave him his full
name now—"and for once I should like a really truthful answer. Was that woman your mistress?"

She watched the muscles of his face tighten, his cheeks
darken to a red hue, before the answer came, grimly, "Yes,
she was. But let me add that it was in the past, she is in the
past. I shouldn't have to explain to you that I have hardly left
your side since I first proposed marriage, and that my whole
way of life has altered. I don't even have the friends I once
had: I have dropped them, or, as has generally happened,
they have dropped me, because I wanted to fit in with your

type of life. And I have imagined I had achieved what I had set out to do. What is more, if I had married a woman of the world and she had suggested what you suggested at your little charade, I would have understood it. But that you, of all people, with your upbringing, and a guest in someone else's house, should imply that another guest was nothing more than a. . . .''

His teeth clamped together and he shook his head, but it was she who put in the word now: ''Whore?'' she suggested.

When he stared at her, she went on, ''You implied my words could have come from the mouth of a whore, and that I was implying something other than I was. What I was alluding to was her fat and her monopoly of all the men in the company. There was no deeper meaning in my mind. It was you who put the wrong construction on it.''

''Oh, my God!'' He put his hand to his brow and turned from her, muttering now, ''Your innocence is worse than your knowledge.'' Then he sprang round and faced her again as she cried at him, ''Then in my innocence I hit the truth, because she *is* a whore.''

''She is no such thing. And don't you dare say she is. And don't let me hear that word come out of your mouth again. She was a good friend to me, a good companion, and she took my marriage to you in a very civilized way, and I'm ashamed of your attitude. Let me tell you something, Nancy Ann, you have a lot to learn yet about this way of life. Good night.''

Her mouth dropped open, her eyes widened as she saw him walk into the closet room and close the door. She wanted to run after him and say, ''I'm sorry. Oh, I am sorry,'' but she couldn't. That woman had been his mistress: she had lain with him; she had. . . . She closed her eyes tightly on the thought, which provoked the reaction: It's just as well he sleeps alone, for I could not bear his touch tonight.

❧ 5 ❧

THE RIFT BETWEEN DENNISON AND HERSELF WAS MOMEN-
tarily forgotten the next afternoon when she arrived at the
vicarage and into a scene of some commotion, because Peter
was there, having got leave from school, as also was Mr.
Mercer. Peter met her in the hallway and immediately drew
her into the study, saying, "The Bishop's been. Father has to
retire."

"Well," she sighed, "that doesn't come as a great surprise. We've been expecting it, haven't we?"

"Yes, but the point is, they've got to leave here."

"Yes, I understand that too."

He looked at her closely, saying, "Are you not feeling
well?"

"Not too bright today, Peter." And his immediate as-
sumption was that her condition was causing her discomfort.

"Graham is in with Grandmama," he said. "What do you
think of the idea of them going to live in the little Dower
House?"

"Mr. Mercer's?"

"I wish you wouldn't keep calling him Mr. Mercer. He's
Graham."

"Well, yes, I think it's a marvellous idea."

"Come along then and let him explain." And now he led
the way to the sitting-room where, on their entering, Graham

Mercer rose from his seat beside Jessica who said, "Oh, there you are, my dear. There you are. Come and sit down. There is a lot to talk about."

"Good afternoon." She inclined her head towards Graham, and he said, "Good afternoon, Nancy Ann."

"Has Peter told you about the Bishop and . . . and the kind offer of Graham here?"

"Yes, yes he has, but . . . but what does Papa say?"

"Nothing much," her grandmama replied, "except that he seems quite willing to give up the living, and equally willing to take Graham's offer of living in the Dower House." She now turned and looked at Graham, saying, "I cannot tell you, Graham, what this means to me because, as I've already put my cards on the table to you, had we to buy a house it could, of necessity, have been little more than a cottage, and that of the meagre kind; you see, what money I had has gone. Oh, my dear." She turned now and thrust out her arm towards Nancy Ann whom she had seen was about to protest in some way, likely to say that Dennison would provide any monies necessary. And she went on, "I know what you're going to say, but you already know what your father thinks, and the solution that Graham here has offered is a real godsend. There's no other word for it." And she turned to him now, adding, "It is a beautiful little house. We are indeed fortunate."

He smiled from one to the other as he shook his head, saying, "Oh, I don't know that you'll still keep your opinion once you're settled. My steward used to live there until some years ago when he gave a number of reasons why he should leave. First of all, it was too big for his wife to keep up, there being eight rooms and offices. Secondly, all the chimneys smoked. Thirdly, no matter how you wedged the upper windows, they rattled. Fourthly, the well that supplied them with water would always run dry in the summer and they had to carry the water from the river. But the main reason seemed to be that it was in a lonely spot at the extreme end of the estate, adjoining your boundary." He now nodded towards Nancy Ann, then ended, "And no decent road within half a mile."

"I . . . I know the house. 'Tis very pretty, and it is most kind of you. I do appreciate it."

" 'Tis nothing, 'tis nothing." He waved his gesture away with a flick of his hand.

Nancy Ann now looked at her grandmother and asked, "What about the girls?"

"Oh, that's been settled too. Peggy and Hilda are to come with us, and Jane—" She now glanced towards Graham, adding, "Graham is taking her on in the kitchen; one of the maids has left." Then, her lips trembling, the lines of her face converging into folds under her eyes, she muttered, "They say God provides, but . . . but He's got to have an instrument." The tears were full in her eyes as she pulled herself upwards with Peter's help as she muttered, "Excuse me. Excuse me, Graham." Then Peter led her from the room. . . .

Graham Mercer was now thirty years old. He was of small stature, but being extremely thin, he looked more than his five feet six inches in height. His hair was dark and thick and he wore it short, trimmed well behind his ears and away from the back of his collar. His eyes too were dark, round and heavily black-lashed, which seemed to hide their expression. One was apt to gauge what he was thinking more from his voice, which was surprisingly deep coming out of such a thin frame. His mouth was wide, the corners drooping slightly. Altogether, his features gave off the appearance of sombreness.

Nancy Ann had rarely seen him smile and she had never heard him laugh, but nevertheless, she knew he was a kind and thoughtful man, and she said so now: "You are so kind. I . . . I don't know what to say, or how to thank you. You . . . you know that I would have gladly had my papa and grandmama with me but . . . well"—she shook her head slowly—"perhaps you know my father's views as well as I do. I cannot understand them, they trouble me; and so I am doubly grateful for your kindness."

He made the same impatient movement as before with his hand, saying, "If you only knew, I am acting out of selfish motives. I am very fond of your father, and it would be good to have someone near to whom I could talk. I feel sure, once he has rest he will regain all his faculties. Of course he hasn't really lost them, his present state has been brought about through the strain of losing your mama. I'm sure of that. And of course, at the same time he lost you too, and this, in a way, was another bereavement. Oh. Oh, please!'' He appealed to her now, his hand outstretched. ''I am not in the least apportioning any blame, but . . . but you know what I mean.''

''Yes, yes, Mr. Mercer, of course.''

He half-turned away from her, bowed his head and shook it vigorously. Then looking at her again, he said, ''If you feel in any way indebted to me, you can repay me. It is very simple.''

''How? How can I do that?''

''By forgetting that I am Mr. Mercer and remember that my name is Graham. The boys have always called me Graham. Your father, your mama, and grandmama, have always called me Graham; only you have persisted in being so formal.''

She watched him smile his rare smile, straightening out the corners of his mouth, and she smiled in return, saying, ''Very well, I will repay my debt . . . Graham.''

''Thank you, Nancy Ann.'' And they bowed to each other. Then quite suddenly she sat down on the horsehair sofa and, leaning forward, she put her hand to her brow.

Instantly he was bending over her, saying, ''What is it? Are you feeling unwell?''

After a moment she looked up at him. ''Yes and no,'' she said. ''Physically I am well, but . . . but the past few days have proved very trying.'' She didn't stick to the absolute truth and say, The past day.

''Well, now your father is settled, you need worry no more. I shall see to it personally that he is well looked after, and I shall visit him daily.''

She sighed, then said, ''Thank you. Thank you.''

For a moment he stared at her; then, flipping the tails of his long coat to each side, he sat down on the edge of the sofa and, staring into her face, he said, ''Is there anything else wrong?''

Her eyelids blinked rapidly, her mouth opened twice, then

closed tight, and she was about to shake her head when he said, "Is there anything wrong at Rossburn? Something happened that has upset you?"

She turned to him again. He was younger than Dennison and, in spite of the stern look he mostly carried, he was very presentable. Her father said that this man had loved her, had wanted to marry her. If she had married him he would not have said to her, Yes, I had a mistress. He would not have sat with the woman on the sofa and let her nestle against him. If she had married this man, her papa and grandmama would have come to the Manor House and they would have lived as a family.

She shuddered. What on earth was she thinking about? She loved Dennison in spite of his past.

When the hand came tentatively on hers she went to withdraw it, then let it lie. And when he looked into her face, saying, "Nancy Ann, if ever you feel you need a friend in any way whatever, will you remember that I am here for as long as God spares me just in order to help you?"

The hand lifted abruptly from hers and she was surprised to see him swing up from the sofa and walk hurriedly from the room. And she was more surprised at her thoughts as she lay back against the hard head of the sofa, saying to herself, Yes, yes, life would indeed have been different if I'd married him.

It was evening before she saw Dennison again. She was in the bedroom changing for dinner. This was another routine she'd had to get used to, why one had to change so many times a day and especially for dinner when they were dining alone. But, as Dennison had informed her when they first came home, it was expected of them; there was a certain standard to keep up before the servants.

There came a tap on the bedroom door. She expected Anderson to enter, and so was surprised when she saw Dennison, for he never knocked on doors. She was standing near the wardrobe and he came slowly towards her and, putting his hands on her shoulders, he looked into her face, then without a word he bent and kissed her gently on the lips.

"Are we friends again?" he asked softly.

She was weary. There was no fight in her. At the moment she didn't care what he had done in the past, she only knew she wanted his arms about her again. And when, without a word, she fell against him and was enfolded once more, and as his lips traced themselves over her face the thought came to her, in something akin to horror and amazement, that only a few hours ago she had been about to confide her unhappiness, and the reason for it, to Mr. Mercer . . . Graham. Really! Perhaps this is what carrying a child did to you: it weakened your reserves, for if she had felt inclined to confide in anyone, it should have been her grandmama, certainly not another man.

When she put her arms tight around Dennison's neck and returned his kisses, it was as if in relief that she had escaped some disaster. . . .

Certain members of the staff were puzzled, not to say the least, when the master and mistress exchanged pleasantries during dinner, and later walked out into the garden arm in arm, for hadn't Staith reported that the master had for the first time slept in the dressing-room bed, and had been in a vile temper this morning? And it had all become so clear after Appleby, the coachman, had passed the word in that the lady Rene had been at the do last night, and that after a quick exchange between the master and mistress when they had entered the landau they had sat in silence all the way home. And yet, here they were, back to lovey-doveying again.

Well, time would tell. They knew their master's weaknesses better than most, and they had faith in the lady Rene. But if she was going to play any cards at all, they hoped she would soon get going, because this one was pushing her nose in where it wasn't wanted. Asking for the quarterly accounts to be given to her now. That was something that would have to be looked into and manoeuvred. Oh, yes, yes, that indeed was something that would have to be manoeuvred.

✄ 6 ✄

NANCY ANN DID NOT CHOOSE HER NURSERY-MAID UNTIL three weeks before the child was due. She had interviewed five women from an agency in Newcastle. All had been over middle age, each had told her of her long history dealing with children. The one smelling strongly of spirits had related the longest history of all.

An advertisement in the *Newcastle Journal* brought twenty-two replies, and from these she chose four. And these she interviewed in her private sitting-room, Mrs. Conway ushering them in, giving preference to the eldest first.

By the time Nancy Ann had reached and dismissed the third one, telling her she would be informed of the choice later, she was somewhat in despair and wondered if she was really being too pernickety, as Mrs. Conway's manner suggested. The nurse for the confinement had been engaged, recommended by the doctor, but she was to stay only a month, and so the engaging of a nursery-maid was imperative.

She sighed deeply as the door opened once more and the housekeeper ushered in a young woman, saying, "Hetherington, ma'am."

Nancy Ann looked at the person crossing the room towards her: she could have been Hilda from the vicarage, but not so old; she was stockily built, with two bright brown eyes and a round face; she was dressed in a long blue serge coat buttoned up to the neck, and on top of a mass of brown hair she wore a straight brimmed felt hat; she carried a plaited raffia handbag and blue woollen gloves in one hand.

"Good afternoon, missis."

Mrs. Conway cast a sharp glance at her and it said, This one will never do. Speaking before she's spoken to!

"Good afternoon. Your name is?"

"Mary Hetherington, missis."

"Ma'am."

The young woman turned and looked at the housekeeper; then turning quickly back, she said to Nancy Ann, "Sorry, madam . . . ma'am."

"Sit down, please." As she spoke the words Nancy Ann was aware of the housekeeper's surprise and annoyance. Then the young woman was seated, her hands gripping the handbag on her lap, and Nancy Ann enquired, "Tell me what experience you've had with children, please."

The young woman drew in a deep breath. "Well, it goes back a long way, ma'am, because, you see, I'm the eldest of ten, and from I can remember I helped to bring them up till me father died when I was twelve, and then I went into service in the kitchen at Captain Dalton's house. I was thirteen when Mrs. Dalton's first baby was born, and"—she smiled a little—"it was a terror, missis . . . ma'am. Well, what I mean is, it cried night and day. She couldn't feed it, and the poor thing was hungry."

Her smile widened. "I think it was in desperation that they let me have it, I mean, to nurse. I used to put some treacle on my thumb and it would go off to sleep. Young Master Robbie, he's now seventeen and he still loves treacle."

A cough brought both their glances to the housekeeper. Her face was tight, but Nancy Ann, feeling more relaxed than she had done for a long time, looked at the young woman again and said, "Go on."

"Well, that's where it started, ma'am. When Miss Florrie came the next year, I . . . I was promoted to nursemaid, and from there it went on. There was five of them, and . . . and I brought them up. Young Mister Luke was the last one and he went to boarding-school some months ago. Mrs. Dalton wanted me to stay on and look after the house 'cos she now joins her husband in sailing trips. . . ."

"Which part of the county are you from?"

"North Shields, ma'am."

"North Shields? It's quite a way from here."

"Yes, ma'am, but . . . but I wouldn't mind that; I like the country. And . . . and I like dealin' with bairns . . . children, so Mrs. Dalton understands, what I mean is, me looking for another position where there are children."

Of a sudden Nancy Ann wanted to be rid of the housekeeper. She wanted to talk to this girl, this young woman. She had never felt so much at home with anyone in the way of staff since she had left the vicarage. She turned now and smiled at Mrs. Conway, saying, "Would you see to a tray being sent up?" Then instinctively she realized that the tray would be holding one cup only and she added, "I'm expecting the master in any moment; he'll have it here. And, Conway, I have made my choice. Will you see that the other applicants have some refreshment and their expenses paid before they take the brake back to the station. I shall make arrangements for"—she turned and glanced at the young woman—"Miss Hetherington to be sent on later."

The housekeeper's stature seemed to increase. Nancy Ann could almost read her thoughts as she watched her turn stiffly and march from the room.

After a moment she sighed and leant back against the couch and, looking at Mary Hetherington, she said, "By that you will have gathered, Miss Hetherington, that you are engaged."

"Oh, ma'am, thank you. Thank you very much. I . . . I hope I'll suit. I feel sure I will in the nursery, but . . . but this is a big place. I've never been in a big house like this afore; the captain's house is like a cottage compared with it. But I'll serve you well, ma'am."

"I feel sure you will. By the way, what was your wage?"

"Well"—Mary put her head to one side now as if apologizing for the statement she was about to make—"I had risen to six shillings a week, ma'am, all found, uniform an' all."

"Six shillings a week. Well, as I see it you were in a town and had access to shops and such. On your leave time here you would have to take a conveyance back to your home, which will cost you money, so shall we say eight shillings a week to begin with, this to be paid quarterly.''

"Oh, thank you, ma'am. Thank you very much indeed.''

Why was it, Nancy Ann wondered, that she was feeling more happy and contented than she had done for months past? Was it because she realized that here in this young woman she was to have an ally? She knew instinctively though that were she to make an ally of her, the young woman would have most of the household against her. There were things she would like to change in this house, and she promised herself that someday she would. Yes, she would. But she would be given no help in doing this from its master: what had happened when she had pointed out that fifty pounds of tea had been ordered during last quarter? Fifty pounds! Thirty pounds for the quarter would have been quite sufficient. When she had pointed this out to Dennison, telling him that he was being robbed, he had smiled and taken her face between his hands and said, "I know that, my dear prim vicarage lady. It is an understood thing in all establishments like this that the servants have their perks. Without them, I can assure you, my dear, the wheels of this house would not be so well oiled. It is little enough to pay for a contented staff. And what staff, I ask you, would put up with Beatrice and her invasion twice a year? Her daily bath? Her dolls?''

That is another thing she would love to alter: that woman, who ignored her almost as much as did the Myers woman, only in a different way, for when she arrived she would take to her bed and remain there for days, only getting up to bathe and attend to her dolls. She was supposed to be eccentric, but Nancy Ann felt strongly that this was merely a façade hiding a form of utter laziness. Oh, she'd like to do something about her an' all. . . . But here was this young woman, Mary Hetherington, a human being she could talk to.

She surprised the new nursery-maid by saying, "How did your late mistress address you?''

"She called me Mary, missis . . . ma'am.''

"Well, it is the rule in this house for the staff to be addressed by their surnames. I cannot say that I like it but with a large staff I suppose it is understandable. However, I think that in your case I would, as your last mistress did, prefer to call you Mary.''

''Oh, I'd like that, ma'am. I would, I would indeed.''

The door opened, and the first footman McTaggart and a housemaid entered, both carrying trays.

When they were set on tables to the side of the couch, the footman said, ''The master has just come into the yard, ma'am.''

''Thank you. Just leave the tea; I'll see to it.'' And when they were again alone she looked at Mary Hetherington and said, ''I'm sure you would like a cup of tea.''

''Me . . . ma'am? Oh yes. Thank you very much, ma'am.''

After handing the cup to Mary, Nancy Ann, pointing to the plates of sandwiches and pastries, said, ''Do help yourself,'' and Mary, now somewhat ill at ease, answered, ''Thank you very much, ma'am,'' but did not take up the offer. And when, a few seconds later, she was about to sip at the cup and the door opened and there entered a gentleman in riding outfit, she rose quickly, spilling the tea into the saucer as she did so.

''Ah, there you are, my dear. And . . . and don't tell me''—he pointed to Mary—''this is your choice of nursemaid.''

''Yes, yes, it is I'm pleased to say. This is Mary . . . Mary Hetherington. Mary, this is the master.''

Mary dipped her knee now, put down the cup on the table and said simply, ''Sir.''

''Mary is from North Shields.''

''Is she now?'' He turned and looked at her. ''That is some way off. Are you of a fishing family?''

''N . . . n . . . no, sir, not really: sea-going, but not fishing. My . . . my father was on cargoes.''

''Oh. Oh, cargoes. He would have gone all over the world then.''

''Yes. Yes, sir, he did.''

''Would . . . would you like a cup of tea, dear? I'll ring for another cup.''

''No, not really. I'm going to get changed; I've had a rough ride.'' He put out his hand and touched her hair, then turned away, giving Mary a brief nod as he did so.

''Would you like to see the nurseries?''

"I would, ma'am."

"Well, come along then." She swung her legs slowly from the couch, and Mary, solicitously now, said, "You feel able to, ma'am?"

"Oh, yes, yes; and the exercise does one good."

A few minutes later she was leading the way up the narrow staircase at the end of the long landing, and when they reached a further landing she stopped and, drawing in a deep breath, she said, "There should be a law passed that all stairs should be shallow."

They were now going along a narrow corridor and when it opened out on to another landing, Nancy Ann stopped, saying, "This is the nursery floor. But that corridor"—she pointed to her right—"leads to a maze of other corridors and the servants' quarters. And the staircase to the right leads to yet another floor made up of attics and store rooms. One can get lost up here, but you'll soon get used to it, I hope."

"Yes, yes, of course, ma'am."

Nancy Ann now led the way into the rooms that had been prepared as a day nursery, a night nursery, and nursery-maid's bedroom and sitting-room; also a washroom and closet.

After the inspection and out on the landing once more, Mary Hetherington said brightly, "It's a lovely set-up, ma'am, beautiful. Your baby will grow up happy here."

"I hope so. Yes, I hope so."

They were met in the main corridor by the housekeeper, who seemed to be having a hard job to contain herself. And the first thing she said under the guise of concern was, "Ma'am, do you think that was wise, all . . . all those stairs?"

"I'm perfectly all right, Conway, thank you. And I wanted to show Mary. . . ."

The very use of the young woman's Christian name seemed almost to make the housekeeper stagger. As she said later, you could have knocked her down with a feather, for if anything could have proved to her that the mistress would never fit into a place like this, it was this lowering herself to almost hob-nob with this new piece who came from one of the commonest parts of the area. What were things coming to!

Later that night, when they were sitting side by side in the drawing-room after dinner, Dennison told her that he'd had a few words with George before the hunt, and he had advised him to go up to London at the beginning of the following week to see Arthur, and he would introduce him as the candidate for Fellburn when the seat became vacant, which promised not to be very far in the future as Bradley, the present member, was known to be in a very poor state of health. He would only be gone a few days, he said. Did she think she would be all right?

Yes, she assured him, she would be perfectly all right. And if there came into her mind a suspicion that the proposed visit might not be merely political, but have two other strings to it, first, the gaming table, secondly . . . but she would not allow her thoughts to go further.

At the moment, she was, in a way, feeling strangely sure of herself, at least with regard to the household. It was as if, in engaging Mary Hetherington, she had won the first round of a battle, for in her she knew she would have an ally, and, as her father had been wont to say, "With one staunch friend you can face the devil."

⚛ 7 ⚛

ON THE LAST DAY OF OCTOBER EIGHTEEN AND EIGHTY-TWO, Nancy Ann gave birth to a daughter. Dennison was disappointed at the sex of the child, but did not show it. He had cradled the baby in his arms and, after gazing at her, he had looked at those present and said, "I have made a life." And there was laughter from the nurse when the doctor added, caustically, "With a little help."

The birth had been a difficult one, the labour long and hard, and Nancy Ann lay exhausted for some days following it. And such was her condition that the usual fortnight in bed after giving birth had to be extended to three weeks. . . .

The baby was two months old before it was christened, and then by the new vicar. Nancy Ann was well aware that her father was ill both mentally and physically now, yet she considered he could have made the journey to the church and christened her child, for she knew he often walked the grounds around the house by day and sometimes by night.

The christening party was attended by only close friends, so it was not all that large, perhaps amounting to thirty guests including Jessica and Peter.

Over the past months Jessica had very definitely made an impression on the staff of The House; in fact, she made it the first time she entered the place, the day the child was born. She had been driven up in the trap by Johnny Pratt. He had rung the doorbell for her, and when McTaggart enquired her business she had thrust him haughtily aside, saying, "Out of the way, man! Tell your master Mrs. Howard Hazel is here," only for McTaggart to intervene quickly and no less haughtily inform her that the master was at present upstairs with the mistress. "Then show me the way, man," she had demanded.

Slightly intimidated now, he had been about to designate this service to his second in command when she had interrupted with, "You!" and pointed towards the stairs, and he had gone up them without further hesitation.

And that had been the pattern the servants had adopted towards her whenever she deigned to visit The House, and it was said in the servants' hall if it had been someone like her from the vicarage with command and dignity who had become mistress of the house, they could have understood it, but as far as they could detect there was no resemblance between the grandmother and the granddaughter, not in the slightest. And they were amazed by the dissenting voice of the second footman, Robertson, who said enigmatically, "I wouldn't be too sure of that. I've known piebalds to turn out to be dark horses with a cuddy's kick."

The baby flourished under the care of the nursery-maid, and if ever the master of the house couldn't find the mistress, he made straight for the nursery floor.

Nancy Ann had now fully regained her health and her figure had blossomed out. Dennison was more loving towards her than ever, if that were possible. His trips to London were few and far between, but he did frequent his club in Newcastle. This, however, she didn't mind in the least. Sometimes he would return at night and throw ten guineas on to the bed cover, saying, "There, partner, that's your share." But she knew that whatever he had won it would be much more than twenty guineas, for he did not go in for small stakes. She had no idea of his real financial position, but once or twice lately he had spoken of selling the Scottish estate, because, as he said, getting into Parliament was an expensive business and if he got the seat he would have little time for going up there, and in consequence, it would be a responsibility.

He had been visiting Fellburn of late too, getting the lay of the land, as he put it; and his verdict after his first visit had been that it would be a difficult borough to hold, being three parts heavily working class. He also had told her that as soon as there was definite news of Bradley's retirement, she must accompany him and be seen round about the town as if they were taking an interest in people and things. She had wanted to remark on the implication ''as if,'' but she had refrained, for she had learned that he didn't like his ideas questioned, and certainly he wouldn't have been at all pleased if she had probed his meaning. . . .

It was in March of 'eighty-three that she fell pregnant again, and this time she promised him a son. It was about this time, too, that she discovered a happening on the nursery floor of which she had been unaware.

It should transpire this day that she was about to go into Fellburn with Dennison and was actually in the hall when Johnny Pratt came to the door and delivered a letter.

It was from her grandmother to say that James had come and apparently for only a very short visit. Would she come across?

Dennison had said, yes of course she must stay, and he would go to Fellburn as arranged for he was to meet members of a committee there.

She was dressed for town and so she went back up to her bedroom and changed her outer things. Then, being unable to resist another look at the baby, she went up to the nursery again, and when she pushed open the door of the day room she became still, for there, sitting on a low stool with her child on his lap, was the boy.

In springing up, the lad had almost dropped the child, but Mary took the baby from him and she, turning now with the child pressed close to her, said, ''I . . . I'm sorry, ma'am, but I can explain. It's my fault.''

'' 'Tisn't her fault, 'tis mine . . . ma'am. I'm . . . I'm up there.'' He thumbed towards the ceiling. ''I . . . I heard the baby crying, an' . . . an' I only come when I'm sent up to change.''

Nancy Ann stared at the boy. It was months since she had

last seen him, and then she had just glimpsed him that day on her first and only visit to the kitchen. He had grown much taller and, what was noticeable, the brown streaks in his hair were just at the ends now, the rest of it was of a golden fairness. His face was thin and pale, but his eyes were dark, large and deep-socketed. He ended now on a low note, "I wouldn't have dropped her."

Nancy Ann's hand went to her throat: she wanted to reassure him by saying she knew he wouldn't, but the thought came to her that Dennison might have come up and found him, not only in the nursery, but holding his child. He would, then, more than likely have laid hands on him. And this she voiced now by looking at Mary and saying, "If the master had come up. . . ." But her words were checked by the boy muttering, "I never come when he's in the house. I see from the yard when he's gone."

She noticed that he did not use the word master, and also that the fright and fear had gone from his face, although it showed some tightness. She wondered if he was aware of his relationship and, being aware, did he understand the implications, and why he was made to work in the boot room. He had often been on her mind, more so whilst she was carrying her first child: she couldn't help but think then that when it was born there would be in this house a cousin to it, illegitimate, but nevertheless, a cousin by blood.

She said quietly, "Go along: it will be all right."

The boy looked from her to Mary now, then back to her again, saying, "She won't get wrong, will she?"

"No"—Nancy Ann moved her head slowly—"she won't get wrong. Go along."

After hunching his shoulders almost up to his ears, the boy hurried from the room; and Nancy Ann looked at Mary, who was standing with her head bowed, still holding the child tightly to her, and she said quietly, "You shouldn't have let this happen, you know."

"I'm . . . I'm sorry, ma'am, but . . . but he's a lonely lad, and . . . and when I first saw him, he stood in the doorway there"—she inclined her head—"and . . . and he said, 'Can I see it?' And when he put his hand out the child gripped his finger, as is usual you know, ma'am . . . babies do, and the boy looked up at me and his face. . . . Well, I'd been used to children all me life, as I said, but I'd never seen a look on any boy's face like there was on his. I can't explain it. I've got no words in me to explain it, but . . . but when he asked if he could slip in at changing times if . . . if, that is, you and the master were out, I said yes. I didn't think it was all that wrong, ma'am.''

Nancy Ann went towards her and took the child from her arms and sat down on the wooden chair near the square table in the center of the room; then looking down on her daughter, she said softly, ''I . . . I suppose you know the history of the boy?''

There was a short space of time before Mary answered. ''Well, yes, ma'am, bits and pieces, from down below. I have spoken with his mother. But not about him,'' she put in quickly, ''only everyday things. She's . . . she's a nice woman. But I must say it, not treated right, ma'am.''

''What do you mean, not treated right?'' Nancy Ann looked up at her.

''Well—'' Mary bit on her lip and looked first to one side and then the other before saying, ''She's not given her place, ma'am. They keep her down, the housekeeper and most of them.''

Nancy Ann wanted to say, ''Well, she's at liberty to move on to another position and take her son with her,'' and she had thought this very same thought often, but she could see the woman's reason for staying: her son really belonged to this household, and likely there were hopes that, in some way, somehow and at sometime he would be recognized. Poor soul; she didn't know the futility of her dreams if she so dreamed.

At times she wondered what Dennison's reaction would be when the boy grew up into a man and, should he become so minded, try to openly state his claim to recognition. Yet, what could he hope to gain from that?

Her thoughts were interrupted by Mary's saying softly, ''I'm sorry if I vexed you, ma'am, but I'll promise not to let him hold the child again. But . . . but what will I do if he wants to see her?''

Nancy Ann rose to her feet and, handing her daughter back

to Mary, said, "Let things remain as they are, only please be careful. Do any of the staff know about his visits?"

"Oh, no, ma'am. If he hears anyone on the stairs he scurries out the far door. By the way, ma'am, have . . . have you seen where he sleeps . . . he and his mother?"

"In the servants' quarters, I suppose."

"Oh no, ma'am; they're in the far corner of the roof beyond the boxrooms."

"Beyond the boxrooms?"

Mary nodded.

Besides the unmarried servants' quarters up on the attic floors, there was a roof space crossed by beams that ran over most of the house. When she had first come to the house and had been alone one afternoon, she had made a tour of inspection of the warren of rooms above. She had walked for some distance under the roof and was amazed at the trunks and cases and pieces of odd furniture that was stored there. But she had never travelled the whole area.

Mary was saying now, with the liberty that was a natural part of her character and seemed in no way out of place, "It's enough to freeze you under that roof in the winter, ma'am, and boil you in the summer. And that's where, I understand, the lad spent most of his early days, that is, afore you came, ma'am. . . . I hope you don't mind me speaking like this?"

"No, Mary, not at all. I'm grateful to you." And after a moment she touched the smiling face of her daughter and said, "I must go now; my elder brother is paying a fleeting visit home. But I won't be all that long; I'll be back before it's time for her bath."

"I'll hold it until you return, ma'am. She won't mind." And she gently rocked the child backwards and forwards. . . .

A few minutes later Nancy Ann made her way out of the house, across the drive, through the ornamental gardens, and on to the wood path which led to the river. But a few yards along it, she branched off and zigzagged her way through the wood until she came to a small gate in the drystone boundary wall that separated the estates.

Graham had been kind enough to have this gate made in order to make it easier for her to visit the Dower House. In the ordinary way she would have had half an hour's walk from the house into the village, then on to the old coach road; or it would have meant getting the carriage out and keeping it waiting until she made her return. But this way, she could pop through the wood most days to visit her father and grandmama, now happily ensconced in the Dower House. She often asked herself, what would have happened to them if Graham had not made this offer, for had they gone to live in a village or a town her father's wanderings would have become a source of worry, especially to her grandmama.

The house lay about two hundred yards from the boundary, bordered on two adjacent sides by stretches of lawn, and on the other two by domestic outhouses. The comfort of the house given off by its furniture and carpets was like a palace compared with that of the vicarage. And even with its smoky chimneys, and they did indeed smoke, it was warm. And even when the well dried up in the summer the girls would laugh about this as they went to the river for the washing water. If any were more happy than the others in the house, they were Peggy and Hilda, for they had never had so much food to deal with. Every day there was a fresh supply of milk from the farm and every week butter and eggs, together with vegetables and fruit, in season. Graham's farm was small and kept solely to provide for the estate.

Nancy Ann pushed open the front door, and even before crossing the hall could hear raised voices. When she opened the sitting-room door her father and James and her grandmama looked towards her.

Rising quickly from his chair, James hurried to her; and then they were holding each other tightly. After a moment he pressed her from him, and she was amazed at the change she saw in him: his face looked haggard and drawn; his clothes looked anything but smart, in fact they looked rumpled.

Her father's voice separated them as he cried, "I am glad my Rebecca has gone; such a family would have broken her heart: one marrying into a house of sin, another stooping to court a warden's elderly daughter, and now another running away from his responsibilities." He glared from one to the other, then turned and shambled up the room, pulled open a French window and stalked out into the garden.

When Nancy Ann made to follow him her grandmama called, "Stay. Stay. It's no use. You won't get him to think otherwise. He's a changed man." Then she added, "Sit down and listen to what James has to say. So far"—she turned and looked at the tall figure of her grandson—"you've only been able to get out that you've left your family, and that was two days ago. Now let us have the reason."

James lowered himself slowly down on to the couch by the side of his grandmother and held his hands out to the fire, and remained like that for sometime before he said, "It was a mistake from the beginning, but I didn't know how much until she . . . she told me that she was to have a child. From then she slept in another room. In my ignorance, I thought it must be the habit of all women. When William was four months old she came back to me. Then the pattern was repeated. By that time I was no longer ignorant. She had told me openly that marriage was mainly for"—he wetted his lips and turned his head further away from them as he said the word—"procreation."

Nancy Ann stared at him in pity. She had heard that word before from Peter. She went on now listening to his voice low and hesitant: "But that wasn't all. Her mother took complete charge of the children. I could do nothing about it. Ours wasn't a real house; we only had apartments in her father's school house. I . . . I tried to talk to her father but he wouldn't listen. And then there was my salary. The second year, it was handed to her under the excuse that I had been wasteful, having bought a pair of boots and an overcoat, and both necessary. My children hardly know me. They refer to her or their grandparents all the time." He turned towards them again, and, his face blanched, his teeth ground together now, he seemed to spit out the words: "I've been made to feel like an animal, kept there for stock."

"Oh, Jamie. Jamie." Jessica put her arms around him, and he drooped his head on to her shoulder and hot tears sped down his face.

If it had been happening to herself, Nancy Ann could not have felt more anguish. She thought of the love that was showered on her by Dennison, and of her longing to be in his arms when he was gone from her.

James pulled himself upwards and turned away from his grandmother, rubbing at his face vigorously and saying, "I'm sorry." And when, presently, Nancy Ann said, "What do you intend to do, James?" he stood up and, his hands gripping the mantelpiece, he looked down into the fire, saying, quietly, "I . . . I want to go to Canada. Henry Bolton, a friend I knew up at Oxford, he's got a little business out there. Nothing very special from what I understand, but he'd be pleased to give me some kind of a job. It would be manual, but I wouldn't mind what I did. The only thing is"—he paused—"I haven't a penny. And yet that's not quite right. I've got fourpence. You could say I stole my railway fare; I took it from her cash box."

She noticed that he always referred to his wife as "her" or "she," never by name. He turned now and, gazing sorrowfully at Nancy Ann, he said, "Could you loan me enough to get across? I'll . . . I'll repay you. I promise you, Nancy Ann."

She too was on her feet and, going to him, she put her hands on his shoulders saying, "Oh, James, don't be silly, talking like that. Of course, I'll help you. How much do you want?"

"I . . . I don't know what the fare and all that would cost."

"Would two or three hundred be enough?"

"What!" Jessica was sitting bolt upright. "Where will you get two or three hundred without asking Dennison?"

"Grandmama"—Nancy Ann looked down into the wrinkled face—"I've got over six hundred pounds of my own. You see"—she paused—"Dennison always gives me part of his"—she did not like to say the word but was forced to—"winnings."

"Oh, Lordy! Lordy!" Jessica sat back in her chair with a flop. " 'Tis a good job your father isn't here at this moment, else that news would surely kill him. Although"—she nodded her head vigorously—"it doesn't affect me. And, yes, when I do have time to think about it, I'll surely consider it a nice gesture on Dennison's part. Yes, I will. Anyway"—she looked at her grandson—"there you are, that part's settled for you. But . . . but what will happen at that end—down in Bath? Will they follow you here and try to stop you?"

"Oh, very likely. I shouldn't wonder but her father will be on this doorstep very shortly; my absconding will be very bad for his school. You might think Father is narrow in his views but they're as wide as the ocean compared with my father-in-law's."

Suddenly becoming practical, Nancy Ann said, "Well, now, if that's the case, you want to get away from here. And get yourself a decent suit and travelling clothes. I'll go back to Rossburn. I've got over a hundred pounds in my cash box and I shall give you a cheque for the rest. But the quicker you make a start the better, for if your father-in-law should arrive, there'll be a scene, and I don't think Papa could stand it."

He nodded in agreement. "Yes, you are right, Nancy Ann. And . . . and thank you. I'll pay you. . . ."

"Oh, be quiet! Don't be silly. I have more money than I know what to do with." She smiled gently at him, then hurried from the room.

As she was going out of the front door she almost ran into the arms of Graham, who, before she could speak, asked, "Were you going in search of your father? Don't worry, he's in the library. He often drops in there."

"In your library?"

"Yes"—he smiled now—"in my library."

"He . . . he goes in without your knowledge?"

"Oh, I am so glad he makes use of it, and I'm pleased to have him there. At times he's very good company."

She noticed, the "at times." And now she said, "I wasn't about to look for him; I'm . . . I'm just going to run to the house. I'll be back. James has come. It's . . . it's to be a very flying visit. I'm . . . I'm sure he'd like to talk to you."

"James here? Oh, yes, yes." He moved to the side to let her pass, and as she hurried from him, she was aware that he remained standing on the step watching her. . . .

The parting between her and James was very painful; both knew they might never see each other again. For a moment they stood entwined and with their grandmother's hands on their shoulders, and they all cried.

Outside, a trap was waiting to drive James to the school to

see Peter. One of Graham's men was already seated in it, and Graham himself was shaking James's hand and saying, "I'm more than sorry to see you go like this. But keep in touch. You will, won't you?" Then nodding towards the man in the trap, he said, "John will take you to Peter's and wait for you there, and then see you to the station."

James was now too full of emotion to speak. He stepped up into the trap, then looked to where Nancy Ann and his grandmother were standing close together, and beyond them to Peggy and Hilda, but he did not even lift his hand in farewell, he just kept his eyes on them until he could no longer see them.

When the trap had disappeared from their sight, Jessica turned and walked slowly into the house; but Nancy Ann and Graham stood in silence looking along the short drive to where it turned into an avenue of trees.

When they entered the house it was to find that Jessica had gone to her room. In the sitting-room once more Nancy Ann looked at Graham who was seated opposite to her and said quietly, "It's strange what is happening to our family, isn't it? We were all so close just a short while ago. What has happened to us?" Her hands made an appealing motion towards him as if he could provide the answer.

"One of you died," he said, "and another couldn't stand the loss; the rest grew up."

She nodded at him. "Yes, yes, you're right," she said. Then sighing, she added, "It's been a strange day. I woke up this morning feeling happy and excited. I was to go with Dennison to Fellburn. He was to meet some committee members there, you know with regard to . . . well, as Grandmama says, getting his foot into politics, and we were then going down the river in one of the steamboats. But it was all changed when I got the note about James. But that wasn't all. I happened to go up to the nursery and there I saw my daughter being held in the arms of the boy. I suppose, Graham, you know all about Dennison's brother's son, David, because that's who he is. And it pains me that Dennison will not recognize him in any way. It's odd, a really weird situation, that the boy is still in the house and, from what I gather, has been brought up among the lumber in the attic. Well, there he was, sitting holding Rebecca. He's a lovely-looking boy. He must be eleven now and . . . and really speaks quite well. He's had no schooling, but his mother must have taught him to read and write, because once when I spoke to him, last year down by the river, he talked of reading books. He should be at school, Graham, a good school, but I cannot bring his name up with Dennison. He came across him once in the wood and his reaction towards the child was terrible. Can you understand it?''

It was some seconds before Graham replied, ''Yes, yes, I can understand it, strange as it may seem to you, for I know he loved his brother dearly. We all act in different ways when faced with the loss of loved ones. And I can see it would be impossible for Dennison to recognize the child. You mightn't like what I'm going to say, but I think it is to his credit that he allows him to stay there.''

When she gazed at him in silence he leaned towards her and said quietly, ''I myself have been through, you could say, a similar situation in that I . . . I lost someone I loved. I don't need to relate my story to you either, for it is common knowledge. But whereas, Dennison's loss made him take up a high wild life, because he is of an extrovert nature, I, being of the opposite, an introvert, scuttled into seclusion, because I couldn't bear what I thought of as the shame. I was a quiet young man, but when Miss Constance Beverley, a beautiful young girl, accepted my proposal, it was as if I had been endowed with the stature of a god. This is a small estate. We've never been enormously rich, though quite comfortable, but I went about as if I had become king of a country.'' He looked at his hands. They were lying palm down on his thighs, the fingers spread as if he were pressing something away from him. Then he added, ''When I was deposed, the day we were to marry, it was just after Tim's tragedy, and I nearly joined him. If I'd been anything of a strong character, I would have gone abroad, or even to London and found a new bride whether I loved her or not, and brought her back and flaunted her just to show my friends how little I had been affected. But no, being me, I had to make a tragedy out of it; although I must admit I didn't think at the time I was doing any such thing, nor for some years afterwards. My house, the seven hundred acres, my books and my cello became my life.''

She hadn't known he played the cello. She wanted to remark on it, but it would have been too trivial at this moment. Instinctively, she put her hand out towards him, and when both of his covered hers, their gaze held, hers soft with pity and understanding, his full of something that she recognized but would not put a name to. What she said now sounded inane: ''There's plenty of time for you to find happiness.''

He withdrew his hands from hers and, rising slowly, he said, ''The happiness you refer to, Nancy Ann, is past for me. I'm a dull fellow and quite stupid in a way: because I'm always looking inside, I'm blind to what's happening under my nose.''

''No, no. Good gracious, no. I don't see you like that, nor does anyone else, I should say.'' Her declaration sounded vehement.

''That's kind of you, Nancy Ann. And I must say one thing, I've felt much happier since your family have come here. I'm very fond of Mrs. Hazel, she's such a sensible person. And . . . and if I may say so, I value your friendship, Nancy Ann. Above everything else I value that. And, as I have said before, if ever you need a friend in any way and for whatever purpose, I should be happy to be that friend.''

Her eyelids blinked. She could feel the colour hot on her cheeks, and her voice was low as she murmured, ''Yes, yes, Graham, I know, and I could not imagine a better or firmer friend.''

After an ensuing few seconds of silent embarrassment, she put in, her words tumbling over each other, ''I . . . I'd better go. I'll . . . I'll just say goodbye to Grandmama. And . . . and thank you for being so kind and understanding to James. Poor James.'' She nodded at him now, then turned hastily away, forgetting that, in courtesy, she should have seen him to the door.

She ran up the stairs but did not go into her grandmama's room. There were two spare rooms on the opposite side of the landing and she went into one and closed the door. Then turning and leaning her forehead against it, she asked herself what was wrong with her; she was all wrought up inside.

Well . . . well, she would be, wouldn't she? James leaving his wife and family and going off to Canada. She turned now and leant her back against the door and stared across the room, and she knew that the turmoil inside her hadn't been caused so much by her brother's unconventional departure as by the conversation she'd had with a man who thought of himself as dull and of little consequence. And there arose in her mind the image of Dennison. Dennison would never consider himself dull or of little consequence: Dennison was outgoing, strong, forceful, and he knew it and impressed it on others.

She stood away from the door and felt a sense of guilt sweeping over her. It was as if she was criticizing her husband's character aloud. But that was silly—she shook her head at herself—she loved Dennison and everything about him . . . everything.

Then a thought obtruded into her mind: what had her father said? That Peter was proposing to marry Eva McKeowan? Oh no. Dennison wouldn't like that. No, he wouldn't. Did she like it? Well, now she came to think about it James would have been much happier had he married Eva. But did she like the possibility of Peter marrying her? Well, one thing was sure, it wouldn't enhance her family's standing in the eyes of the staff.

❧ 8 ❧

FOR THE LAST TWO MONTHS OF HER PREGNANCY NANCY ANN felt definitely unwell. The baby was due towards the end of December. She hoped it would come on Christmas Day; in fact, she was now almost willing it to come on Christmas Day. Hang on, her grandmama had said, and you'll get your wish.

It was the beginning of December and the weather was vile, as it had been during all of November and late October. There were days when she couldn't venture outdoors, even to go to the Dower House, and on these occasions she felt exceedingly lonely and especially so when Dennison was in London.

During the past six weeks he had made two longish visits to the city. He was negotiating the selling of the Scottish estate to help pay his election expenses. Elections, as he kept saying, were very costly businesses. When she tentatively questioned him as to what he did in the evening, he always replied, "What do you think, my dear? Take your choice: roulette, cards, or dice." And she left it at this, for she realized he did not favour this kind of questioning. Nevertheless, he always seemed so glad to be back in her company; and, of late, it was simply just her company, for he had not shared her bed for some weeks now, his reason being, and which he had put plainly to her, that he would be unable to bear being near her without loving her. . . .

She was in the nursery. Between them, she and Mary had bathed Rebecca and got her settled for the night. And now Mary, taking the high guard away from the fire, and pulling up an old button-backed upholstered chair, said, "Sit yourself down, ma'am, for a moment. You look a bit drawn. Are you all right?"

"To tell the truth, Mary, I'm . . . I'm not feeling too well. I haven't for the past day or so, but I suppose this is the pattern."

"No, no, it shouldn't be, ma'am, not if you're feeling bad like and it not due for another three weeks. Only once did ma feel bad when she was having them, and then it came a bit early."

Nancy Ann already knew the whole history of Mary's family, and she was going to become better acquainted with another one of them as soon as the baby was born because Mary's younger sister, Agnes, was coming to act as assistant nursery-maid. This last appointment to the staff had been made without consulting Mrs. Conway and so had not warmed the relationship between them. Nancy Ann did not feel any compunction in lessening the housekeeper's authority in this way, for she knew that the woman was lining her pockets, and doubtless those of the butler and valet, through co-operation with the tradesmen. She had learned a lot about housekeeping during the months of her mother's illness; the meagreness of the amount allotted to their daily needs had made her question the price of all commodities.

"Will I make you a cup of tea, ma'am?"

"No, thank you, Mary. I'd better be getting down; it's about time for Mrs. Conway's round."

"Yes." Mary looked at the brass-faced clock on the mantelpiece and they exchanged smiles and Nancy Ann, about to rise from the chair, suddenly opened her mouth wide and gasped at the air as her two hands grabbed at the mound of her stomach.

"Oh, my goodness! No!" Mary was bending over her,

saying now, "Lie back. Take it easy. That's it. That's it. Has it gone?"

Nancy Ann let out a long shuddering breath as she said, "Yes . . . but"—she looked up into Mary's face—"it can't be, can it?"

"It could, ma'am, it could. What was it like? sharp like?"

"Oh, yes, yes."

"I . . . I think you had better get down to bed, ma'am."

"Yes, I think so, Mary."

As Mary helped her from the couch the door opened, and the housekeeper stood there, a look of disapproval on her face, and Mary, turning her head towards her, unceremoniously said, "She's started."

"What?"

"I said, Madam's started."

"Nonsense, woman. It's not. . . ."

"I know it's not due, but I tell you, anyway, it's comin'. Give a hand; get the other side of Madam."

For the moment the housekeeper was too flustered to put the upstart maid in her place, but going towards Nancy Ann, she said, "Do you think it has, ma'am?"

"I . . . I don't know, Mrs. Conway, but . . . but I shouldn't be surprised." She had hardly got the last word out before she doubled up again and they were both supporting her.

A minute later, the housekeeper left her to go to the cord at the side of the fireplace, and she pulled on it vigorously. "The men must help," she said; "those stairs are steep. She . . . she shouldn't be up here."

Nancy Ann, straightening her body as much as she could, gasped and, looking at the housekeeper, she said, "It's . . . it's all right. I'll manage the stairs. Just . . . just let me get down." . . .

She got down the stairs, but just in time before another spasm attacked her; and from then on she did not know much about the evening that followed, only that her grandmama was at one side of the bed with Pat, and the doctor and Mary were at the other.

Three messages had been sent off to London: one to the house and, at Pat's suggestion, one to Dennison's club, and the third to Reilly's, the private gaming-house.

By midnight Nancy Ann was in a state of collapse. Although the excruciating pains were coming at regular intervals, the child showed no sign of emerging into life.

At half-past three in the morning, Doctor McCann consulted with Doctor Maydice whom he had called in earlier, and they decided that if they didn't want to lose both the mother and the baby something definite must be done. So by four o'clock a wooden table had been brought up into the bedroom. Nancy Ann had been lifted on to it, and dishes of hot water were standing ready. Mary, Pat, and the housekeeper stood at hand, and Jessica, in a state of collapse, had been made to rest in the adjoining room.

Chloroform had been administered to Nancy Ann, and so she made no sound as the knife was put into the top of her stomach and drawn right across it, and within a short space of time a strong-limbed-and-lunged male child was taken from her body.

It seemed eons of time later when Nancy Ann emerged through the white heat of pain into a bright light. The sun was shining; and there was a well-remembered smell in her nostrils. Slowly she turned her head on the pillow and looked at the face a few inches from hers, and she thought, What is Denny kneeling on the bedstep for? And when his voice, low and broken, came to her ears, saying, "I will love you till the day I die. Do you hear, my love? You have given me a son, a beautiful son, and I swear to you again, I will love you till the day I die."

When he was happy he always said nice things. He would love her till the day she died. Well, he wouldn't have to wait long—would he?—because she was ready to die at any time; such pain as she was enduring killed love and the desire for life. She turned her head away from the face and looked towards the end of the bed where she saw her mother standing, and she was reprimanding her, saying, "Go to sleep now, go to sleep. You'll be better tomorrow. And remember, never shelve a responsibility."

PART SIX

The Woman

❧ 1 ❧

AFTER THE BIRTH OF THE CHILD NANCY ANN LAY FOR ALmost a week between life and death. Her wound would not heal and she was delirious most of the time. Then came a period when the crisis passed and for two weeks following she lay in a state of calm and showed no interest in anything, not even her son. There followed a long convalescence while she sat with her feet up on the couch fronting the fire, and all the while Dennison was never far from her side, except when he made quick sorties into Newcastle or Fellburn.

He had become very interested in the political situation, about which he talked and he talked. He laughingly said that as she couldn't yet go out into the world, he was bringing it to her. And she listened patiently because she liked to hear him talk; and when he was talking to her he was near to her.

Gladstone was now Prime Minister and apparently he was making as many mistakes as had Disraeli. He was having the same old trouble with Ireland, Egypt, and now South Africa.

Once she had said to him, "You are too Liberal to be a Tory and too Toryish to be a Liberal; you should start a party of your own." And at that he had laughed and hugged her.

Although at times she became tired of political talk, she had to admit that she had learned a great deal during the past months by just listening to him. She also knew that Dennison himself had learned a great deal since he had first delved into politics.

From April onwards her strength increased daily. She walked in the woods, sometimes accompanied by Dennison, but more often she was alone, and at such times she went through the gate and to the Dower House. She found it strange that as soon as she had passed through into Graham's estate she experienced a sense of peace.

Her daughter, now eighteen months old, was trotting about the nursery and jabbering in a language all her own. And her son was already showing elements of a strong character in that he was never still. That he was the joy of his father's life was plain to everyone in the house, for Dennison visited the nursery now almost as often as she herself. And such was that atmosphere of the nursery floor that he even joked with Mary and her young sister Agnes.

All this should have made her extremely happy, but there were two worries in her mind. Her father was fast losing all his reasoning faculties. What is more he had developed a heavy hacking cough, and she feared he might go the same way as her mama. Then there was this other thing that had taken on a deeper penetration than the anxiety about her father: she could understand Dennison leaving her bed during the latter part of her pregnancy, and also in the months following the birth of the child, but for the past month or so she had never felt better physically. The trauma of the birth, although not forgotten, was well in the background, and although Doctor McCann had told them both that for her safety's sake there should be no more children, that, she felt, should not have kept him away from her side.

Now that she had given Dennison a son and a daughter, particularly a son, he was more than content, he said, that this should be the limit of their family. What she had been too embarrassed to discuss with him but felt quite unable to bring up with Pat was the question: Did this mean an end to loving? at which Pat had pushed her and laughed loudly.

Then why did he not come to her bed? Oh, he came, to lie near her for a while and hug her, but such embraces were short. Other times he lay on the top of the bed quilt and talked to her while he stroked her hair and fondled her face;

then kissing her good night, he would retire to the dressing-room.

Knowing his ardent nature, it was impossible for her to imagine that he abstained from satisfying his need. Then came the question, But with whom? and always at this point there loomed up in her mind the picture of the Myers woman, the fat slug, as she sometimes termed her.

Since the night she had mimicked her, they had met three times, and on each occasion the woman had openly ignored her while making a fuss of Dennison. And this never went unnoticed by the company they happened to be in. Pat had advised her that on such occasions she should smile and talk, and on no account stick close to her husband. Leave the field apparently open, Pat had said, which would show that she had nothing to fear.

This latter advice, however, she found difficult to follow for, strangely, the very sight of the woman aroused in her the almost overwhelming desire to strike out at this lump of flowing pink flesh. And she had said so to Pat: "I have a great desire to push her on her back and see if she can rise without assistance. I imagine her rolling from side to side."

And there was that time last year when she was greatly perturbed when Dennison was in London. George and Pat had insisted on taking her to a house-party and there she had overheard the end of a conversation: "She's gone up to town. Well, you couldn't expect her to stay here, could you?" Then another voice saying, "She's determined, I'll say that for her," had completed the conversation.

She did not have to think twice to whom they were referring. Mrs. Myers was not at the party.

Dennison never mentioned the woman's name, but she herself often wanted to yell it at him, especially when he returned from London full of life and high spirits. He always brought back a gift for her: a diamond brooch, a ruby-studded bangle, an ornamental hair-clip; once, a beautiful tiara, which she never wore.

June came, and the weather turned exceedingly hot. Day after day the sun shone. Thunderstorms cleared the air for a short time but the heat persisted.

During one thunderstorm, John had roamed the grounds,

and when Graham found him he was soaked to the skin. His cough was worse. The doctor was called and bronchitis was diagnosed. That was towards the middle of the month. The weather cooled, but John's condition had worsened so much that Nancy Ann was now taking her turn sitting up with him at nights; her grandmother and the girls were exhausted with their day's routine. Graham, as always, was being very good, and on alternate nights he took his place by the bedside. But last night he had insisted on staying again because her grandmother had been so concerned at the sight of Nancy Ann's white drawn face that they both said she should return home. As Graham pointed out, a couch had been brought into the bedroom and so he could rest on it if necessary. Later, on looking back at the events leading up to the explosion that took place, she recalled that Dennison seemed surprised to see her that night. He had been in the library and after a moment had come towards her, saying, "He has gone?"

When she had assured him that her father had not died he had made a fuss of her, taken her upstairs, and seen her into bed.

Today was Sunday. It had begun hot and the heat seemed to increase with the hour. She had gone to morning service, but alone, Dennison having made his excuses: not only had he an enormous amount of work to attend to, but he was sorry he couldn't stand the new parson: he was too young, too unripe, and too pious for him altogether.

In her mind Nancy Ann agreed with him, but as she said, it wasn't the parson, it was the service that mattered. She went in the open landau, and those servants who could be relieved of their duties followed behind in the brake, but the housekeeper, the butler, the first footman, and the valet were not among them.

During the day she paid two visits to the Dower House. Her father's bronchitis had worsened somewhat and the oppressive heat was not helping him.

When she emerged from the wood into the gardens after her second visit of the day, she saw Dennison at the far end of the rockery lawn. He was lying on a lounge chair in the shade of the big oak. As she approached him she saw that he was asleep, a book and some newspapers were lying to the side of the chair and his hand was dangling above them. She smiled as she looked down on him. He looked so relaxed and always much younger when in sleep. He certainly didn't look anywhere near his thirty-seven years; in fact, he prided himself on his figure for as yet he had no paunch.

She went on into the house and, after sluicing her face and hands in cold water, went up into the nursery. The children were fractious. Although Mary had all the windows open, the room was stifling.

Mary, cradling William in her arms and rocking him backwards and forwards in a way she termed giving him a shuggy, said, "By, when this breaks, ma'am, the heavens will open. I've never known anything like it. We're not used to heat like this."

Nancy Ann agreed with her.

At dinner, she thought that his afternoon siesta must have refreshed Dennison greatly for he was quite gay, making her laugh about some of the men associated with the coming election and whom he had met in Fellburn. "The next time you come with me you must study them and add them to your repertoire," he had said.

It was a long twilight, heavy and foreboding. Earlier in the evening the wind had risen, but it had died down again. She opened the library door. Dennison was sitting at his desk at the window, dressed only in a pair of breeches, carpet slippers, and a white shirt that was open down to his waist and showed the dark hair of his chest. In spite of the heat he appeared to be still in a bright mood for, rising from the desk, he bent and kissed her; then, smiling down at her, he said, "You know, in spite of all your nursing and the heat, you are looking quite robust these days." And she answered, "Yes, I'm feeling quite well again."

"That's good news. How much longer do you think your father will need nursing?"

"Just till he gets over this bad bout," she answered.

He now turned from her and walked towards the desk, saying, "You know, as I suggested in the first place, he should have a nurse. There's no reason why not." He had his back to her as he ended softly, "I miss you, you know."

Her heart warmed to him, and she answered just as softly, "And I miss you too."

He turned and looked at her; then walked back to her again and kissed her on the brow now. Then, pushing her away from him, he said, "Go on and do your ministering angel act."

She went, but reluctantly. She had the feeling that he needed her tonight in the same way as she needed him.

She walked slowly through the gardens and the wood, but at the gate she stopped and came to a decision. She would ask Hilda if she would take her place for tonight. She could sleep on the couch and, of course, would call Peggy or her grandmama if needed. Yes, that's what she would do.

And she did this, explaining the situation to her grandmama who understood as always.

As she was returning through the gate into the grounds there was a distant rolling of thunder. The wood appeared black dark now, but through use she was able to find her way. As she emerged into the comparative light of the gardens, she saw in the distance the sky split by lightning.

A plan had formed in her mind: she would not go in by the front entrance but by the side door, make her way into her bedroom, get undressed, and surprise him when he came up. Of course, that is, if he wasn't upstairs already. This she doubted, for he rarely now came up before eleven at night.

So thinking, she skirted the large lawn and made her way along by the creeper-covered wall that bordered the back of the stable yard and outhouses to where the archway led into the yard.

She had just stepped off the grassy path on to the cobbles that paved the archway and the yard when the sound of a man swearing brought her to a halt. Her fingers went to her lips: the man was saying, "It's a bloody shame. She should be put wise."

Now another voice came to her from the end of the archway, harsh and low, replying, "If you know what's good for you, Irish, you'll mind your own bloody business."

"Don't call me Irish, I've got a name. And as for me own bloody business, somebody should take it on, because that lot in there are swines of the first water. To think they would have a hand in such a game. My God! I'm glad I am Irish at this minute, 'cos it's a rotten, stinkin' English trick that, if ever I knew of one.''

"Look"—the voice came conciliatory now—"I'm only saying this for your own good. They're a power in there, that lot. I don't like it meself, but a man's got to eat, to keep his family, and they are damn good jobs here, you must admit, no matter who's dippin' their fingers into pies and pullin' out plums.''

"That's one thing, dippin' your fingers into pies, but this other . . . the mistress is a decent young body and why the hell can't he be satisfied with her? Or go off to London as he usually does for his whorin'? But to have that drab coming to the house when they know the coast's clear. My God! I've heard it all now. The gentry are rotten, that's me opinion, rotten to the core. Anyway, how would they know she wouldn't be in the house the night?''

"Oh, are you blind, man? Didn't the plump lady ride past the main gate yesterday, and didn't she stop and have a word with Benton or his missis. They're both in it. And the mighty man Staith would have got word down to them that the coast wasn't clear. Now there's a rat if ever there was one. I've only ever seen another like him, and that was the master's so-called friend, a Mr. Freeman. He was afore your time, but a real snake in the grass he was. Couldn't stand the master getting married, and up and offed it. But Staith is the leader of the big four and what they say goes, right through this whole system, and down to the farm at that. Old Taylor's getting on, and he has to keep his nose clean, but young Billy I understand's got a mind of his own, as has Frank. They don't toe the line.''

"But d'you mean to say that fat piece is comin' here the night?''

"It seems like it. She came last night right enough. Half-way through the grounds. She left her horse at the east lodge. There's nobody in there now, you know, but there's a stable at the back.''

"God Almighty! D'you know, I've got a smell in me nose that stinks. Appleby must be in this up to his neck.''

"Oh, aye, Appleby is. He passed on the message to her

coachman. And it could quite easily be your Jim that could be drivin' her; he's second there now, isn't he?''

"I'd break his bloody neck if I thought Jim was in on this. That's swearin' to God."

Nancy Ann was now leaning against the wall, her hand pressed tight across her mouth, her eyes staring wide into the darkness, and her whole being was yelling, *No! No! No!* He wouldn't! He wouldn't do that. Oh no! And they all knowing. Oh, dear God!

"You know somethin'? I always had a sneakin' likin' for the master, although I know he didn't leave her to go up to London just to take the air, or to do his bettin', or gamblin'. Anyway, he could have done that in Newcastle, 'cos there's big money floatin' around there, so I understand. Anyway, in spite of that, I always judged him to be a man with a bit of honour in him. But to bring that fat whore into his bed and his missis not a few strides away from him. Oh, my God and His Holy Mother! that to me is a sin beyond sins. I'll tell you one thing, I'm gettin' out of here shortly. This racket's too strong for me; it turns me stomach."

"Don't be such a bloody fool. It's got nothin' to do with you. We live our lives and they live theirs. Let them sort it out. And you can sort lots of things out when you've got money. Aye, and lot of things can be forgiven you if you've got money. Money is power, lad."

"Power be damned! You can keep it. I'd rather be back in the old country grubbin' taties, rotten at that, but even they smell sweeter than the stink that's in me nose at this minute. What's more, and this really maddens me, all that lot when they'll be laughin' up their sleeves at the young mistress."

"Well, that's her own fault, I suppose: she can't carry them, she hasn't got the presence. Well, you couldn't expect it, being brought up in a vicarage as she was; a bit prim, she is, priggish. Well, that's what they call her in there, Parson's Prig."

"She's no prig; she's a decent kindly young soul."

"Well, I can say this, she's got one follower in you, Irish. All right! All right! Shane. But, enough of this; we're goin' to have our hands full the night with those animals, 'cos just listen, that thunder's comin' closer. The big fella an' young Prince will kick hell out of their stalls if there's any more of it. . . .

How long she had remained standing by the wall she didn't know, but she found herself walking back through the garden towards the wood, and in the darkness she groped towards a tree and, putting her arms around it and leaning her forehead against the bark, she moaned aloud as the tears thrust up from her being and flooded her face. She was overwhelmed as if the waters of a dam had burst over her head and she were drowning, dying, while still conscious of the agony of the process. . . .

At some time she must have slipped down the tree to the ground. Her back was against the trunk, her legs tucked under her, her arms about her waist. She was no longer crying, nor was there present in her that dreadful feeling of humiliation, but what was in her was a white flame of anger. It was a new emotion, and was burning her up inside. It wasn't debilitating. On the contrary, it had a strength all its own, a separate mind of its own, and it was telling her what to do. Step by step it presented her with a plan, and on the blackness of the night about her she saw it unfolding, right up to the time when he would present her with an explanation.

When a flash of lightning lit up the woodland around her, she did not jump to her feet, telling herself that it was most dangerous to be under trees in a storm, and when the burst of thunder startled her, that's all it did. She did not run for shelter from the storm that it heralded; the storm inside her was far more frightening, for it was demanding retribution: she wanted to rend something, someone; she wanted to throw things, break things, claw, fight. She was no longer her father's daughter. "Let him without sin cast the first stone." Well, she was without sin in that way and there was righteousness in the stone that she was about to cast.

As she got to her feet, she thought of her father. He was the only one who had been right: he had known the nature of the man who had sought her hand; he had seen through the hypocrisy of his changed character, as had, no doubt, the staff of that house, which was why they had never accepted her as mistress, laughing at her behind her back. The Parson's

Prig. Well, she would show them what a Parson's Prig could do. And for the first time in her life she blasphemed: by God! yes, she would this night.

There came another flash of lightning, then a deep roll of thunder. Still she didn't move from under the tree, but asked herself how long it was since she had heard the voices of those two men. An hour? Oh yes, it must be.

Slowly now she groped her way among the trees. Once she stopped when she heard a rustling in the undergrowth some distance away, and she asked herself what would happen were she to come face to face with someone, a poacher. And such was her strength at this moment that she told herself he would certainly get a bigger shock than she would. It was as she neared the wall again that she heard the chimes of the stable clock. They told her it was eleven o'clock. Away from the wood the night seemed light, yet the sky was low and black.

As if already following her plan, she passed the archway and walked to where the wall ended and a high hedge began. The path beside it led to the middens, but there was a gap some distance along it, wide enough to take the flat cart that carried the drums and buckets of household refuse of all kinds to the tip.

She passed through the gap and into the yard. At the far end of the buildings was a doorway that led to what was called the maids' passage, and when it opened to her touch, it appeared to be all the confirming proof that she needed, for it was the first footman's duty to go round the house and see that all doors were bolted. Apparently this had been the practice since, a few years previously, robbers had simply walked into the house and helped themselves to a quantity of silver.

She had no fear of meeting any of the staff: those who weren't in bed would, no doubt, be ensconced discreetly in the housekeeper's room. She had no difficulty in mounting the stairs going up from the passage for they were lit by the glow of a night candle on the landing above. From here another flight of stairs led to the attics, whilst a door opened on to the gallery. This too she found was softly lit here and there by candles, which was not the rule.

How dare they! How dare they! All prepared to light my

lady in and out. She'd "my lady" her. And him. By God! she would. A small voice from some depth in her that had the echo of her mother said, "Oh, Nancy Ann. Nancy Ann." And she made an actual physical movement with her hand as if flinging it aside. She was past niceties of thought or action; she felt she had really come of age.

There were three ways into the bedroom: through the main door, through his dressing-room, and through hers. He had likely turned the key in the main door. But why should he, for that was hardly ever used except by herself and him, the staff customarily using one of the dressing-room approaches.

She had crossed the gallery and was in the corridor now; the thick piled carpet hushed her footsteps. She stopped at his dressing-room door, and as she did so a streak of lightning flashed past the long window at the end, lighting the space as if in daylight. This was followed immediately by a crash of thunder that brought her shoulders up to her ears. But before its vibrations had trailed away, she had turned the handle of the dressing-room door, was inside and had closed the door. Strange, there was no light here, but from under the door leading to the bedroom there was a beam showing.

As her hand gently sought the handle of the door she heard her husband's voice saying, "Rene. Rene"; then the woman's tone, soft and laughter-filled, saying, "Denny. Denny. What I've braved for you."

She did not thrust open the door but turned the handle gently; then she stepped into the room that was lit by the two pink glass shaded lamps, and there, lying on the high bed on top of the covers, stark naked, lay her husband and the woman. For a moment the sight seemed to blind her. All she could see was the pink flesh which appeared to encompass the bed, and the long fair hair spread over the pillows.

There was a moment of utter silence: then Dennison was sitting bolt upright, crying, *"Nancy Ann! My God!* No! No! Listen! Nancy Ann."

Slowly she walked towards the foot of the bed, and there, over the chaise-longue, she saw the clothes, dress, corset, petticoat, fancy bloomers, stockings, all in a jumble, and by the side of them his dressing-gown, with his small clothes on top. Her mind registered this, for he always changed into his night things in his dressing-room.

As if it was part of the plan she glanced towards the doors leading on to the balcony. They were wide open. Almost as quick as the lightning that further lit the room her arms spread out and within seconds they were full of the clothes; then dashing now through the open doors, she flung them over the balcony, but did not stay to see some of them fall to the ground and others come to rest on the cherry tree whose branches extended to within a few feet of the house wall.

Dennison was on his feet now, yelling, but his words were unintelligible to her. She saw him run into the dressing-room; then she looked at the woman on the bed. There had been a triumphant smile on her face when she had first looked at her lying there by the side of her husband; now that was gone and she was tugging at the quilt in order to cover herself. But the quilt was tucked into the bottom of the bed and, being unable to loosen it, she swung her fat legs over the side of the high bed. As she did so her upper body came forward, bringing her hair over her shoulders. When Nancy Ann grabbed it, the woman let out a high squeal; and then they were grappling like any fishwives. But Mrs. Rene Myers had never sparred with brothers, nor had she fought with the McLoughlins, and when one of her soft breasts was suddenly punched she squealed again, but had no time for anything more before she was swung round and a shoe contacted her buttocks and sent her sprawling on to the balcony where her soft body coming in contact with the iron railings wrenched from her a high-pitched scream. The next instant Nancy Ann had banged the doors closed and turned the key. And she was running to the window at the other end of the room when Dennison rushed out of the dressing-room, a towel round his middle, seemingly having been unable to find any of his clothes; even if there had been a light in the dressing-room, he wouldn't have even known in which drawer his handkerchiefs were kept, so well had he been taken care of all his life.

As her hand raised and flung the key into the night, he yelled at her, *"Have you gone mad, woman? Have you gone mad?"*

She made no answer whatsoever. She was aware that he had tucked the towel into itself in order to form a hold and when his hands now came out as if to grip her shoulders the fury in her reached its peak and almost simultaneously, just as she had seen the McLoughlins do when fighting, and not infrequently men coming out of the inn on a Saturday in the summer, she doubled her fist and levelled it at his face, at the same time lifting her knee into his stomach.

Neither of these blows had the force behind them as they would have had had they been delivered by a man, but nevertheless they staggered him and brought him bent double and wrenched a groan from his lips which was drowned by the screams coming from the balcony, added to now by the commotion in the corridor.

It needed only the gesture of her wiping her hands to say that the episode was over, for now she turned from the mêlée in the room, and as she opened the door into the corridor and looked into the horrified faces of the butler, the housekeeper, the valet, she spoke for the first time. Her voice sounded dead calm even to herself. "The storm's breaking," she said. Then as she went to move away, she turned to the valet and added, "The keys to the bedroom and the dressing-room doors don't fit that of the balcony doors; I'm afraid you'll have to break it down."

They said nothing. They could not have been more astounded if, before their eyes, she had turned into the devil himself.

She was slightly surprised to see Mary on the nursery floor landing, fully dressed, and to be greeted with, "Oh, ma'am. Ma'am." And then, as if giving an explanation why she wasn't in bed, saying, "They were uneasy. It's the storm. They were so hot. I didn't wake Agnes, she sleeps through anything."

Nancy Ann went into the day nursery and here the rain was now hitting the roof so hard that she had to almost shout to make herself heard. "There are some boxes and hampers in the store cupboard," she said. "Will you bring them, Mary?"

"Sit down, ma'am. Yes, yes, I'll bring them, but sit down. Would you like a cup of tea?"

"Yes, thank you, Mary. But bring the boxes first, please."

Mary made three journeys to the store cupboard, and when the floor was littered with soft travelling bags and boxes, Nancy Ann said, "We'll pack all the children's body clothes first, and then the bedding."

"But ma'am." Mary stood hovering over her, her face crumpled with enquiry, and Nancy Ann, looking up at her, said, "I'm taking the children to my father's . . . the Dower House. Did you hear the commotion downstairs?"

"I . . . I felt something was afoot, ma'am." Then she pointed to the window. "I could see from the store room window the lights in the yard, and I made out in the rain a carriage there. Are you going by carriage, ma'am?"

"No, Mary, that carriage won't be for me or the children. We . . . we shall wait till dawn, when I'll get you to go down to the yard and seek out McLoughlin. What time exactly do the men rise?"

"Oh"—Mary hesitated for a moment—"some of them are in the yard at half-past five, ma'am."

"Well, I'm sure McLoughlin will be one of them. Try to take him to the side, then tell him I would like his assistance, and bring him up the back way. Will you do that?"

"Anything. Anything, ma'am. But, oh, 'tis sorry I am to the heart that . . . that you are troubled like this."

Nancy Ann lay back in the chair and let a long drawn breath out before she said, " 'Tis sorry I am too, Mary, to the heart, that I find myself like this. There's an old saying, We live and learn, but I have been very slow to learn. I did not listen to people wiser than myself. But then, it is all experience, and if we learn anything, we never make the same mistake twice."

No, well, it would be an impossibility, wouldn't it, to make her mistake twice, to again marry a man like Dennison? It *would be* the act of a fool. Yet, hadn't she already been a fool? No, no, she hadn't. She denied her accusation. She had been, or had tried to be, a trusting wife. She had tried, oh yes, she had tried, not to imagine how he spent part of his time when in London, or even in Newcastle. Well, she need wonder no more.

It was strange, but all the anger had gone from her. There

was a coldness in her, an empty coldness, as if her whole being was a room without furniture or decoration of any kind. She could look back at the events of the last hour and picture each movement she had made from the time she saw the naked bodies on the bed, and it was like looking at an album. Turning the pages, she felt her fist digging into the soft flesh of the woman's breast, then the feel of her hair as she entwined her fingers in it, and the strength that came into her arm and foot as she swung her on to the balcony. Then over a page, she saw the clenched fist going into Dennison's face and her knee into his stomach. Years ago, the boys would have inwardly applauded her antics while outwardly expressing disapproval. Yet, in the rough play she'd had with them, or while defending herself against the McLoughlins, only once before had she used her knee. From whom had she inherited such traits? Her grandmama? Yes, she could see her grandmama acting in the same way, given the same provocation.

"Thank you." She took the cup of tea from Mary, then said, "Once you get the bags packed you must go to bed. I will sit here."

"Oh no, ma'am, no. If you sit up, I sit up. I'll take that chair an' you put your feet up on the couch there." She pointed to the old horsehair couch that was set under the window.

Nancy Ann made no protest at this because of a sudden it seemed that all her strength was draining out of her. She did not feel the need to cry, but a great need to sleep, to shut out life and dream that she was back in the vicarage where the pennies had to be counted and the food was always plain, but where the days were filled with happiness, and she had never come across the man called Dennison Harpcore.

Shane McLoughlin stood in the nursery looking at the cases and bundles on the floor. He then raised his eyes to where the young mistress stood, and, as he was to say to his mother when he visited her on his next leave day, he had never seen a change in anybody come about so quickly, for although her face was as white as death she seemed to have grown in stature, so straight did she hold herself. And her manner, too, was no longer that of the smiling young woman but was firm and in command of herself and her intentions.

After she had finished speaking, he touched his forelock and said, "Yes, ma'am, don't worry about this lot. You go ahead and I will see they get to the gate—I'll take the flat cart—and from there I'll carry them to the house. Don't worry yourself, ma'am. And ma'am"—he looked into her face—"I take this liberty of speaking as someone who has known of you for many years, and to who you've shown kindness since I came into this service. And I'll say this, ma'am, I'm your servant any day in the week."

"Thank you. Thank you, Shane."

At the mention of his Christian name, his eyelids blinked rapidly, and he jerked his chin and moved aside to let her pass.

She now went into the night nursery and, taking the baby from Agnes's arms, she went out, followed by Mary who was now carrying Rebecca.

Their advent into the yard and their crossing of it did not go unnoticed, but none of the male staff approached them, simply stared wide-eyed at the mistress of the house followed by her nursery-maids, one carrying a child, the other two cases.

The morning was bright, the air was fresh, the garden was giving off varied scents, but Nancy Ann neither saw the beauty nor smelt its fragrance; her future ahead appeared like a battlefield, for she knew she would have to fight for the custody of her children, but fight she would.

Her entry into the Dower House at the early hour brought her grandmother from sleep, and Peggy also. Hilda was already awake and busying herself in the sick room.

In the sitting-room, Jessica immediately dropped on to a chair and stared at her granddaughter as she gave her an outline of what had transpired, and for once she could find nothing to say. And after Nancy Ann had finished, she continued to gaze at her, and when she did speak, it was in an unbelieving mutter: "You threw her out on to the balcony in the storm stark naked? And . . . and you struck Dennison?"

"Yes; I did both these things."

"You actually used your knee and fist on him?"

"Yes, I did."

"Huh! Huh! If the whole thing wasn't so tragic, child, I would laugh my head off and pat you on the back, for in your place I would have reacted in exactly the same way."

The words of understanding, even of approval of her actions, was almost too much. She flung herself down on the carpet and buried her head in her grandmother's lap. And Jessica, stroking her hair, bent over her, muttering half to herself now, "I never thought that of him, no, no. No matter what his vices, I always gave him credit for gentlemanly instincts. But that . . . that was coarse, and blatant, and degrading." She lifted Nancy Ann's head and was surprised to see that her cheeks were dry. She asked softly, "Have you done any thinking beyond this moment?"

"Yes, yes, Grandmama, I've done a lot of thinking, in fact, I've thought all night. I'm divorcing him."

"Oh, child, your father would never . . . Oh, then"—she sighed—"what does John Howard know or care what happens now? But perhaps he, Dennison, won't let you."

"He'll not be able to stop me. Which judge, in a court of law, could pass over an incident like that and not call it reason for divorce? There are those in the house who would deny that they knew anything about the matter. There are also those who would stand by me, a few. And anyway, those who did not witness her entry or departure from the house will have been given evidence of her having been there from some of her garments still hanging from the highest branches of the cherry tree; I noticed her blue silk under-drawers and a matching waist petticoat. They'll be awkward to get at, even with a ladder, and until they are down they'll be in full view of anyone coming up the drive."

"Oh, Nancy Ann. I do wish it was possible to laugh. But my dear"—her tone changed—"you look so deadly pale and tired. You haven't slept?"

"No, not at all."

"Well, you know what you are going to do. My bed is still warm, you are going into it and have a couple of hours rest. Now, no more talk, just do what you're told. The girls and Mary will see to the children. You have a treasure in that young woman."

Nancy Ann did not need any further persuasion to go to her grandmama's room, and, after undressing, she put on one of her grandmama's nightdresses. But as she was about to get into bed, she paused and did what she hadn't done for almost three years, since Dennison had laughed at her when she knelt down by the bed to say her night prayers. From that time she had said them just before going to sleep. But this morning, her face buried in her hands, she found that, although she was kneeling in a suppliant attitude, she could not pray, especially could she not say, "Our Father . . . forgive us our trespasses as we forgive them that trespass against us." So she rose from her knees, got into bed and, turning on her side, she buried her face in the pillow. But still she did not cry. And it came to her that last night in the wood she had cried all she was ever going to cry again.

When she awoke she lay quietly for some time with her eyes closed, imagining that she had really dreamed all that had happened last night. But when it was borne in upon her that it was no dream but stark reality, she opened her eyes and looked round the room. It was almost a replica of her grandmama's room at the vicarage, cluttered, but homely.

The door opened and her grandmama came in and she stood by the bed and said, "There now, you've had a nice long rest."

"What time is it?"

"Just on noon. Coming up twelve o'clock."

"That late?"

As she made to rise, Jessica put her hand on her shoulder, saying, "There's no hurry, everything is arranged. Mary and Agnes have the children on the lawn and Rebecca is running around yelling her head off, as usual. By! she has a pair of lungs on her, that one. But you have a visitor. . . .No, no, it isn't him, it's Graham. He's been here this hour past; he's been playing with the children. He seemed to know all about it before I opened my mouth. Funny, how things get about. They'll likely try to hush this up over there, but it's too late already. It appears that one of Graham's gardeners was courting a kitchen maid up at The House and was paying a late visit. He was about to make his way back, apparently using your pathway, when he heard the screams between the clashes of thunder, and he ran towards them, which brought him out on the lower lawn below the balcony. And there, in a flash of lightning, he sees, what he told Graham's butler, a spectacle that you would only expect to see in a madhouse. Graham didn't go into details, he didn't need to. But he's concerned for you. Anyway, don't hurry, just take it easy. Get yourself washed and dressed, then we'll see about arranging rooms. And, my dear''—she put her hand on Nancy Ann's shoulder—''you've got to be prepared for the other visitor.''

Nancy Ann made no reply, but the thought of the coming meeting sent a tremor through her. . . .

Strangely, she felt shy of meeting Graham. She was aware of the high regard in which he held her, and she wondered if he would associate the Nancy Ann she had been with the one she had become, this brawling person who had used her fists and knees like some drunken washerwoman.

As she went down the stairs, she was asking herself if she were ashamed of what she had done, and the answer came back even before the thought had ended: *No, no, she wasn't. Not a bit. Not one bit.*

''My dear.'' Graham was holding her hands. ''I'm sorry, so sorry. I mean that, I really am.''

''These things happen, Graham. They were bound to happen to someone like me, silly, gullible.''

''You were never silly nor gullible.''

She had withdrawn her hands from his and was leading the way into the sitting room, and there he went on, ''I cannot believe it of him. I must admit I was never very fond of him, but I imagined you were happy with him and that was enough for me. Or let us say''—his voice trailed off into a mutter, and then he said quietly—''he'll never let you keep the children, especially his son, and, things being what they are, I'm afraid the law will be on his side.''

''Not after I explain my case.''

He now walked away from her to the far end of the room and looked out of the window. Then turning, he said, ''This will ruin him, you know, especially when he's aiming to get into Parliament.'' He smiled sadly, saying, ''The moral code men demand of those who are in the public eye is really laughable: their lives must appear beyond reproach. That the majority of them lead double lives is overlooked. The surface one must be righteous in the eyes of the people, yet the so-righteous ones can make no secret of their incompatibility. The lack of tolerance of our dear Queen and our Prime Minister are two good examples, don't you think? Both righteous people, yet cannot stand the sight of each other.''

She looked at him. She hadn't known that, about the Queen and Mr. Gladstone. But there he was, this kind, good, and faithful friend, speaking up for a man that he didn't really like, and whose place he would have filled if he hadn't been so slow, to use his own words. She was finding it strange that she could let her thoughts flow free like this. No longer did she admonish herself: I mustn't think like that, I am a married woman. It is a sin to think such things as another man being in love with you. . . . Where had the girl gone who had thought like that? She didn't know, except that she had died last night.

He returned to her now, saying, "If there's anything you want, anything at all I can do, you must tell me. One thing I fear, you are going to be hard pressed for room here."

"No, no. It will be all right once I can arrange things. And I'm so grateful that I have this house to come to. What I would have done otherwise I don't know. I shall always be grateful to you, Graham."

She thought that he was about to say something, but instead he gulped in his throat, jerked his chin out of his soft collar, then turned from her, saying, "You know where I am if you need me." And then he was gone.

As she stood looking down the room, she recalled what he had said about the law being on Dennison's side with regard to the children, and the thought turned her sharply around and she hurried through the French window and onto the lawn where Rebecca came running on her stubby legs to meet her, crying, "Mama! Mama! A bunny! Bunny!" She pointed.

"Yes, darling, yes, a bunny." But there was no rabbit in sight. Lifting the child up, she called to Agnes: "Bring William in, Agnes. And, Mary, will you come along a moment?"

A few minutes later, in the makeshift nursery, she gave Mary an explanation for her order, saying, "Keep them indoors until—" She paused, dithering between using the master, my husband, their father, or Mr. Harpcore; when she could use none of these terms, she added lamely, "Just keep them in until later, Mary. You . . . you understand?"

Mary understood.

She next went into her father's bedroom, and her grandmother turned from bending anxiously over the bed and said abruptly, "We'd better call the doctor, he's had a turn for the worse. Send Johnny straightaway."

Nancy Ann left the room hastily and she had reached the hall when she saw Hilda opening the front door, and there stood Dennison.

She looked away from him and to Hilda, saying now, "Would you tell Johnny to go for the doctor as quickly as possible?"

"Yes, miss . . . ma'am."

She now turned about and walked quickly into the sitting-room, conscious that he was close behind her, and once more she was standing where she had been a few minutes earlier. But now her heart was racing, her throat was dry, her eyes were wise and unblinking. She noted without surprise that there was a slight discolouring on his cheekbone. She also noted that only his chin and lips had been shaved, the dark stubble having been left no doubt to diminish the evidence of her blow.

He was the first to speak. "What is the meaning of this," he said, "taking the children?"

When she did not answer, he said, "You will bring them back to the house at once. That is an order."

When she still did not speak he cried louder now, "You heard what I said?"

And now she answered him in like voice: "Yes, I heard what you said. And now you hear what I say. I will not take my children back to your house, nor will I enter it again, and if you had any common sense you would not be standing there putting on the act of an aggrieved party. Even the mentally lowest of your band of spies would have more sense than take up that attitude."

"How dare you!"

"Oh, I dare, I dare, and will dare more than that before this business is ended."

He gazed at her, his lips slightly apart, his eyes narrowed, because he could not link the figure standing before him with his sweet young wife, with his pliable young wife; a transition had taken place. Here stood a woman, a woman who felt she had been grievously wronged. But if only she would listen. His voice low, and with a plea in it, he said, "Nancy Ann, will you listen to me? There is an explanation."

"Oh, please"—she shook her head slowly from side to side—"I beg you, don't lower my estimation of you any further. I find you naked in bed with your whore. . . ."

"Nancy Ann!" His voice was a bawl. But she continued and repeated her words, "I say with your whore. Your clothes are lying together on the couch, and not for the first time, as you've admitted. And you expect me to believe there is an explanation, when your underlings had made the way clear for her, even to putting candlelights on the stairway and the gallery."

His face stretched and his voice came rapidly: "I tell you I knew nothing of this. She came unawares."

"And I suppose she undressed unawares, and got into your bed unawares, and she lay by your side unawares. Don't, I beg of you, go on any further."

He turned from her and sat down heavily on a chair and, leaning his elbow on his knee, he dropped his head on to his hand, and like that he muttered, "It looked bad, I know, but if you would only listen. In any case, I beg of you, come back to the house, bring the children. I . . . I miss you. I need you."

She was quite unmoved by his plea, and her voice was low and cool as she said, "I've already told you, I have no intention of ever coming back to your house. I am going to divorce you."

Her words did not cause him to spring up from the chair, but his hands slowly left his face, he straightened his back and he looked at her, and there was even a suspicion of a smile on his face as he said, "Don't be silly."

"I am going to divorce you, Dennison." The very fact that

she had given him his full name now brought him to his feet and, his face darkening, he said, ''You can't do that.''

''I can. You must admit I have a very good case: that woman was your mistress before we were married; and since, she has laughed up my sleeve at me over the past years, insulted me; then she dares to come into my home, into my bed. That is enough, I should imagine, to win my case.''

''Win your case!'' He was bawling again. ''Well, the lady in question could bring a case against you for damages to her person.''

''She is a slut, and she got the deserts of a slut.''

''Then, in a way, last night, there was a pair of you, for your actions were not those of any lady or vicarage miss, more like those of a fishwife, a drunken one at that. You, in turn, should be ashamed of yourself.''

''It may surprise you that I am not in the least ashamed of myself. My only regret now is that I didn't go further and let you join your slut on the balcony. Your staff then could have witnessed the result of their preparations.''

''Oh, God Almighty!'' He now began to pace the room, his hand to his head. Then stopping abruptly, he cried, ''I don't know what's come over you, woman. I expected retaliation, of course I did, but not this. And this divorce business, you can't do it, you mustn't do it.''

''I can do it, and I will do it.''

She watched his head move forward, his shoulders rise. His whole attitude spelt of incredulity. And now he muttered, ''But the election, it . . . it would ruin me.''

''You should have thought of that and put your political life before that of your private desires.''

His whole body moved from side to side as if he were struggling against fetters. Suddenly, it stopped. For a moment he stared at her; then his face became convulsed and, an arm outstretched and its fingers stabbing at her, he cried, ''You'll never get the children! You will never get my son! No court of law would give you custody because every man worth his salt has his mistress, and those trying the case could have too. You, my prim little vicarage maiden, don't know of the times you live in. I took you as an amusing child out of that stifling atmosphere and I imagined I could teach you how to live a full life, which, in part, meant meeting the traumas of life, particularly marriage, with dignity. But I recognize now, you never had dignity. You never will. Now, here's my last word on the subject: I'm going to London for a few days. You know where to reach me. By the time I return I expect you to have changed your plans and returned to the house. Good day to you.''

She sank down on the sofa. She was trembling from head to foot; she could not even keep her teeth from chattering; it was more as if she were being affected by a great chill. Presently, the cold turned to a numbness; and the sensation frightened her, as it was to do until later in the day when the doctor called and said he was afraid that John had now contracted pneumonia and was a very sick man.

Such was the hurrying and scurrying now that her own troubles were pushed into the background, at least by others in the house. In her own mind, however, they remained very much to the fore.

It was on the third day, when John's condition became somewhat stationary, that Nancy Ann went into Durham, there to see her father's solicitor; and when she returned, there was a visitor awaiting her, and immediately she put her arms around her, crying, ''Oh! Pat, Pat. I'm so pleased you are back.''

Sitting on the sofa side by side, their hands gripped, Pat said, ''I shouldn't be here. We returned from Holland to London where George had business he wanted to tie up, then we were off to France. But there, yesterday morning, we had hardly got indoors when I had a visit from Denny. I couldn't believe it. I just couldn't believe what he had to tell me. My dear, you have got to go back to the house, and quickly.''

''Oh, no, Pat, no. I'm never going back there. In fact, I've just been into Durham and seen a solicitor and told him what I intend to do. I'm divorcing him, Pat.''

''Oh, no, by God! girl, you're not, not if I can help it. You didn't listen to him and what happened. And, now, *be quiet!''* She shook Nancy Ann's arms none too gently. ''That bitch of a woman had been working up to this ever since the day you married; in fact, ever since the day she realized that he

had an interest in you. I saw it as a danger signal when she offered him friendship after he had become engaged to you. The only person she could ever be friendly with would be the devil, and then she has enough wiles to trick him. Now, I'm telling you, this is what she's been waiting for, just this situation. And her cronies over there, who should be kicked out of the place, have made it possible for her to carry it out. At this time of the year she would usually be abroad, exposing her fat to the sun and bragging about it never changing colour. But no, she's sitting there, tight. And let me tell you, girl, that Dennison loves you as he's never loved anybody in his life. He wants you, girl. He needs you. You've been a bulwark to him, you've changed his life. But if you throw him out of your life, he's a man and if he's going to be blamed for cohabiting with her, then that's just what he will do, he'll take up the idea that if he's blamed for it he might as well earn it. And she'll have won. Nancy Ann''—Pat shook her arm—*"she will have won.* She's had men in her life since she gained puberty, but he became an obsession with her. He still is. Now look, don't turn your face away like that. And listen to me, listen closely. You wouldn't hear his side of the story as to how it happened. Well, he told it to me detail for detail, and I'm giving it to you now. It was like this. It was a hot thundery night. He had been working late on his papers. That's another thing, this Parliamentary business was the best thing next to yourself that ever happened to him. It could have been a steadying influence and you mustn't ruin it, you mustn't. Anyway, as I say, he had been working late. He was very hot and tired, and, this is the point, he was missing you, even if he hadn't been in your bed for some time. And that, by the way, was through the doctor's suggestion: he told him it would be dangerous if you had any more children. Oh, yes, yes, I know, and he knows''—she flapped her hand—''there are ways and means. But he was being considerate, over considerate, he realizes now. Well, anyway, let me come to the point. He went upstairs, and the heat was so oppressive that he decided not to go straight to bed, but to sit on the balcony for a time. So he dismissed Staith. Then after a while he undressed, not in the dressing-room, but in the bedroom, and threw himself on top of the bed. And that storm brewing didn't prevent him from dropping into an exhausted sleep. The next thing he knew was, he thought you had come back and he put his arm around you, and then, to use his own words when he saw who was lying there, 'God, I couldn't believe it. I thought I must be dreaming.' Whatever madam's intention was in coming to the house in the first place, the end must surely have been what she saw presented from the bed, and she must have undressed there and then. Anyway, he remonstrated with her quietly and gently, because you must remember, Nancy Ann, and face up to the fact that that woman was once his mistress. But that was before he knew you, and he swears to God and he swore to me that he has never touched her since, although I know myself she followed him to London. I was in a London house once when she called and we all had tea together. Anyway, you can imagine he didn't go into exact detail over what followed; I could only gather as well as assume that she must have become very persuasive, to say the least, and except for kicking her out of the bed, the only thing he could do was . . . well, to be counter-persuasive. And he was doing just that when, as if, again to use his own words, his conscience had conjured you up and placed you at the foot of the bed, because he was never so shocked in his life as when he saw you standing there, and for a moment he became paralysed until he saw you grabbing up all the clothes and rushing towards the balcony. He said there was no light in the dressing-room and he couldn't put his hand on anything but a towel, and there was the thunder and lightning punctuated by the screaming of Rene. When he rushed back into the room, there you were throwing the key of the balcony doors out of the window. And the next bit . . . well really! my dear"—she smiled now—"if this business hadn't been so serious, I would have laughed my head off, to think that the little vicarage piece could use her fists and knee on her lord and master. You didn't exactly give him a black eye, but it was a beautiful blue one. The outline of it was still there when I saw him. But the knee, I thought I'd heard everything then. Katie Lynshaw. You know Katie Lynshaw who lives over Jesmond way. You met her at the Tollys. Well, she's not the size of twopennorth of copper, but she almost brained Harry with the chamberpot. She cracked it over the side of his head, and was left holding the handle. The poor fellow was never the same afterwards . . . well, you know he died last year. I'm not surprised. But to use the knee''—she tut-tutted, she was smiling now—''it was most unladylike.''

"I've never been ladylike, Pat." There was no smile on Nancy Ann's face.

"Don't be ridiculous. You were the most ladylike individual I ever came across, at least on the surface. But we're getting from the point." Her voice took on a sober note again. "You've got to believe what I've told you. He had no hand in this. He wasn't to blame. And there would have been nothing more to it that night, I can tell you that. He was so upset and so sincere. I know when a man is speaking the truth and I'd put my life on bail that every word he said was just as it happened. And what is more he's no fool; he knew that she couldn't have got in there without assistance, and he dismissed Staith straightaway.''

Nancy Ann's eyes opened slightly and she said, "He did?"

"Yes, he did. And when he comes back he's going to sort out the others, too. Of course, he'll have to stand the racket when he does return, and you will too, because this escapade will keep the county laughing for some time. Those who are abroad will regret not having been here; but the story will be renewed and extended in the telling for some time to come. And if it wasn't for Arnold Myers's career I would like to bet that Rene would have had you up in court, because from what I can gather, her middle . . . huh! . . . her middle was badly bruised and she had to keep to her bed for a couple of days; she even called in the doctor. Well, flesh like hers can't be banged against iron railings without leaving some mark.'' She now put her hand out and gripped Nancy Ann's knee, saying, "You are a mixture, my girl, aren't you?"

"Yes, perhaps I am a mixture, but . . . but I'm no longer a girl. At this moment I have the feeling that I will never grow older, I feel I know all about life, its façades and its undercurrents, and I detest it all.''

Pat sighed deeply, then smiled faintly as she said, "In the mood you're in it would be useless to try to contradict you or dare to say you still have a lot to learn. But there, I've said it. The sun, the moon, and the stars are a mystery, but to my mind they are nothing to the mystery of human nature; its agonies, its ecstasies; why one is driven to strive for something, then regrets attaining it; why one loves the most unlikely partner—now that is a mystery to me—and why one can hate one or other of one's parents. We are admonished to love our father and our mother, but I can tell you this and I have never voiced it before, Nancy Ann, I hated my mother. She is now eighty-three years old, lively and lording it over her third husband down in Dorset, but I retain memories of her in my early days, humiliating my father who was a quiet, unobtrusive man and who, I know, was glad to die. I was nineteen years old when he died, and I told her that day that I hated her and I don't retract one word. But I ask again, why did they marry in the first place? What is this attraction between two people? Which brings me back to you. What attracted Dennison to you? Yet the answer seems simple and plain: you were so different from all the women he knew, without guile, straightforward, so young, untouched. You could say that was the attraction, but there was something deeper in this case, I feel sure. And I say again, Nancy Ann, he loves you, he needs you. Do this one big thing, give him another chance. Go back to his house, rule it as you should have done from the beginning and I'm sure now you are capable of doing just that. You have the power in your hands either to make him or break him and, knowing a little about you, if you break him, you'll have him on your conscience to the day you die, even if you were to marry again to that nice Graham Mercer, honourable gentleman that he is. Oh''—she flapped her hand once more—''don't be abashed and don't look like that. I'm no fool, and certainly Dennison is no fool, and he knows in what regard Graham holds you and why he has been so kind to the family.''

''Oh! Pat, don't say such things.''

''Oh, dear, dear, dear; I thought we had reached womanhood just a moment ago. So you know as well as I do what I say is true. But even if you were to marry him you wouldn't know a moment's happiness because your first love would be forever there, and the fact would grow on you that this business that has separated you was none of his doing.'' She now

heaved herself up from the couch, saying, "I'll away now.
I've said enough, more than enough, but know this, Nancy
Ann, I'm your friend, I'm your true friend. At a pinch I'm
old enough to be your grandmama. I'm one already and I
have the nerve to say at a pinch. Vanity, vanity, all is vanity. . . . By the way, what is her opinion of all this?"

Nancy Ann considered for a moment before saying quietly,
"She hasn't given me her opinion; she hasn't said a word one
way or the other."

"That's a good sign. She's a wise woman. Look, I'm returning to London tomorrow; what message may I take?"

Nancy Ann turned away saying, and still quietly, "It's done.
I told you I've been to the solicitor."

"Oh, don't be so stupid, woman; they won't have ordered
the clerk to write a letter yet." She now came towards Nancy
Ann and, putting her arms about her, she said, "Let me tell
him he may come back and talk and . . . all right, you can
make your own terms. Quite candidly, he would agree to
anything as long as you return. Swallow your pride, my dear,
we all have to." And her voice became low as she ended,
"We all have to do it sooner or later in this life. Being women,
our power lies in doing just that." She lowered her head for
a moment; then, jerking up her chin, she said, "I'm away.
Get out of the house; take a walk and think seriously of what
I've said. Bye-bye, my dear."

She bent forward and kissed Nancy Ann on the cheek before turning and walking out with the gait that spoke of authority in itself.

Nancy Ann went to the window and watched the carriage
rolling away. Her mind was in a turmoil, for she believed
what Pat had told her was indeed the truth of the matter, yet
she couldn't go back to that house and face that hostile staff.
You can make your own terms. The words were to the fore-
front of her mind. Oh, if she could make her own terms, she
knew what she would do over there.

But to live with Dennison again.

Yet what would life be like living without him? Pat had
been right. Oh, what was she to do? What was she to do?

She started as the door was thrust open and Jessica called,
"Come! Come quickly!"

A moment later she was standing beside her father's bed. He was propped high up on his pillows. His eyes, deep in their sockets, gazed at her for a moment before he murmured, "Look after your grandmother now. Bring the children up in God. Stand up against . . . Promise. . . ."

Again, she was startled when Jessica, thrusting her to the side, took up her son's waving hand, saying, "There you are, my dear. There you are. Rest now. Rest."

"Nan . . . cy Ann."

"She will be all right. Don't you worry."

"Promise. He. . . ."

"I promise, yes, I promise to see to the children."

The mother and son stared at each other for some seconds. Then John Howard Hazel closed his eyes and his head drooped to the side, and Jessica made a small sound in her throat. Then she turned and looked at Nancy Ann and, tears streaming down her face, she said, "Well, 'tis over."

"No, no! Not like that, not so. . . ."

"Yes, my dear, like that, as quick as that. Once death calls it doesn't linger, and it's just as well."

Jessica turned from Nancy Ann and looked down on her son's parchment-skin face again; then slowly she drew the sheet up over his head, and from his half-sitting position it looked as if he were playfully hiding behind it. She turned and, taking Nancy Ann's arms, she said, "Come; Peggy and Hilda will see to things."

Nancy Ann allowed herself one backward glance before she was led from the room. When her mother had died they had knelt in prayer around the bed; it seemed wrong somehow that they were walking out like this. And . . . and he had wanted to say something more to her when her grandmama had pulled her away from his side.

"Oh, Papa. Papa." Slowly, and hard now, she began to cry. They had not seen eye to eye for a long time, but at the end she should have given him some word, some reassurance that she knew he had been right all the time.

Yet had he been right? Oh, what would happen next? She was tired. If it wasn't for the children she could wish she was lying with him now.

* * *

It was forty-eight hours later. The house had become one where death lay: the blinds were drawn shutting out the bright sunlight; people had come to the door, leaving words of condolence, some having used their sympathy as a means of penetrating the manor grounds.

Peter had been given leave to be here yesterday, and was coming again tomorrow. But it was Graham who had seen to the arrangements, even to asking Nancy Ann if she had informed her husband, and when she said no, he himself had sent off a wire to the address she gave him.

It was at the end of the day; a lamp had been lit to brighten the gloom, and as Nancy Ann looked at her grandmother sitting straightbacked in a chair in which she could have reclined, she was made to wonder yet again at the calmness she had shown over the last two days, for had she not lost her only son? Then she was further surprised by her reply to a statement she herself made voicing something that had been worrying her. "You know, Grandmama," she said, "I feel Papa wanted to say something more to me before he went." She did not say, "before you pulled me aside." And Jessica answered, "Yes, I know he did, my dear, and I prevented him. And why? Because I do not believe in deathbed promises, and I knew that my dear boy wanted to extract a promise from you, and you being made as you are would likely have suffered for it for the rest of your life."

"What . . . what promise could I have made that would have caused me to suffer, Grandmama?"

Jessica's voice was quiet now as she said, "He wanted you to promise to bring the children up in a God-fearing way and to look after me, but what he meant was that you should stay here."

Their glances held for some seconds before Nancy Ann said, "Would that have been a bad thing?"

"Yes; yes, it would in more ways than one. I must say this to you now: no matter what has happened, and what did happen wasn't his fault. I, too, had a talk with Pat. The point is this, your place is back in that house, by his side to help him, because what you must realize, Nancy Ann, he is not a parson like your father was, he is not a man of God, he is a man of the world and, let's do some plain talking, he had two believe Pat, that since he married you he has been faithful. Of course, there again, that might be only up to a point, but it is a fact that he has not taken a mistress. And now, having said that, this is where I come in. I love my grandchildren . . . when I see them from time to time. You see, you must understand that for years I've lived in a house without children and that, until your father became strange in his mind, there has been a sense of peace and quiet around me. And you might find what I'm saying may sound hard, even callous, but I can no longer put up with the constant, and that is the word, constant chatter and busyness that children create in a house. And it is their right to chatter and be busy-busy, and those who look after them to be busy-busy, too. But I am past being able to live in such an atmosphere, that is not to say that I feel I am nearing my end, but what I will say is that my patience is not what it used to be. Oh, please, my dear, don't look like that. Don't bow your head. We have been honest with each other all our years together; let us continue in that way. Peter said to me yesterday that I must go and live with them when he marries. My dear, can you see me living with Miss Eva McKeowan, as nice and as affable as she has turned out to be? He said I should likely be lonely here. But how could I be lonely with you and the children a walk away? And there is Graham. Who could want a better friend than Graham? And what's more, Peggy and Hilda have become very important to me. They are servants, I know, but one ceases to think of them as such, more like caring friends. I say all this to you to put your mind at rest concerning me, because I know, like Peter, and like my dear John Howard, you will think it is wrong that I should be on my own. But, my dear, I am going to say something to you that I've never said to anyone in my life before, and that is, there has been a longing in me for years to be on my own. Even when my dear husband was alive, and I loved him, yes, I loved him dearly, there were times when I just longed for him to go out, go away on a journey so I could have the house to myself and be on my own. We are all very complex creatures, dear. We never know what is really going on in each other's head, as I don't know what is in yours at this moment, except

perhaps that you are thinking that you have discovered I am
cold-blooded, nay, even cruel.''

"Oh, no, no, Grandmama, never that. And . . . and I understand, I do, I really do. But at the same time, I must tell
you that . . . that I am deeply hurt. Oh, not at what you have
said, but about the cause that brought me and the children
here.''

"I can understand that, dear. Oh yes, I can understand that
fully. But there's one way to deal with it. Treat it as a lesson
and it will give you strength to face whatever happens in the
future, because your life has just begun, and there could be
other trials ahead of you.''

Other trials ahead of her. Nancy Ann thought of these words
over the next two days for she knew that one of these trials
was imminent.

Because of her grandmother's frankness about the children
she had told Mary to keep them outside as much as possible
when the weather was fine. So it was towards five o'clock the
day before the funeral that the first of the trials took place.
Mary and Agnes were giving the children a little picnic under
the beech tree at the bottom of the lawn, and Nancy Ann had
joined them and they were all sitting on the grass. It was as
Mary was saying to Rebecca, "No, my dear, another piece
of bread and butter and then you may have your cake,'' that
the child's eyes sprang wide and she bounded up, crying,
"Papa! Papa!"

Nancy Ann did not turn as the child ran past her. Outwardly her body stiffened, while inside it was as if all her
muscles had become fluid. Slowly, she rose to her feet and
turned to see him standing some distance away along the path
that led to the gate. The child was in his arms, her arms tight
about his neck, her voice prattling unintelligibly.

He was standing now in front of her, and she noticed immediately that his face looked grey and that he wasn't dressed
as sprucely as usual. His voice was low and level as he said,
"I came as soon as I heard. I've just got in.''

She could find no words and was saved from embarrassment by the child saying, "Tea, Papa?"

"Yes, yes, that would be nice, a cup of tea.''

It was Mary who came forward, saying naturally, "Come along, my dear, your papa would like a cup of tea."

She took the child from his arms; then turning to her sister, she said, "Go and tell Cook that the master's here and would like tea."

At this, Nancy Ann turned away from them, and he followed her, and the protests of the children followed them.

In the dim light of the sitting-room she placed herself some distance away from him after indicating that he should be seated. And when he said, "It was very sudden?" she spoke for the first time, saying, "Not really. He was very ill."

"When is the funeral?"

"Tomorrow."

"All arrangements have been made?"

"Yes."

He did not ask who had seen to them. But now, bowing his head, he joined his hands between his knees and looked down on them as his stretched fingers interplayed with each other as if intent on pulling them apart. Then he asked quietly, "Have you seen Pat?"

"Yes. Yes, I have seen Pat."

"Did she give you my explanation?" He was still not looking at her.

"Yes."

"And you believe it?"

When she did not answer immediately he raised his head quickly, saying, "It is the truth, absolutely. I swear on it. You must believe me, my dear."

What happened next happened so quickly that it gave her no time to escape from his touch, for he sprang from the chair and dropped down by her side on the couch and was gripping her hands. His face close to hers, his eyes pleading, as was his voice, he said, "Come back, Nancy Ann. Please. Please. I need you. Dear, dear God, how I need you, I'm lost without you. I'll . . . I'll do anything you ask. Make . . . make your own terms, only come back to me."

Her lips were trembling, her eyes were moist as she looked at him; part of her was urging her to throw herself into his arms, the other, the new born part that had emerged over the

last week, was telling her there would never again be another
opportunity like this.

Withdrawing her hands from his and easing herself along
the couch, she rose to her feet, turned her back on him and
walked to the fireplace; and there she stood for a while before
she said quickly, "Very well, but only, as you said, on my
own terms."

She knew he had risen to his feet and that he was standing
some way behind her, and was waiting. Swinging round now,
she said, "If I'm to go back into that house, I shall only go
back as its mistress."

"You have always been its mistress."

"No, no, I have not." She only just prevented herself from
putting her hands up to her lips because she knew she had
shouted and in the presence of death laid out in the adjoining
room. And she went on, more quietly now, "Of your large
staff, no more than two or three have given me my place, and
surely the events of the past week have shown you how little
they consider me. Well, I want a clean sweep. If I am to be
a real mistress in that house I don't want to live among spies
and traitors. I shall want to reorganize the whole staff."

His voice, too, came quietly to her, saying, "Very well,
my dear, you do that. If that is all."

"That isn't all. There is something that has worried me
since I have been in that house. You are not going to like
this, but I must say it, it is the boy. He is a bright intelligent
boy, he should be sent away to school."

Even in the dimness of the room she saw his face darken
and his jaws clench, and after a moment he said, "You ask
too much, Nancy Ann. You know my feelings in that way. I
. . . I could never bring myself to see to that boy's education.
It would be a concession, an acknowledgment that I have
fought against."

She broke in now, saying, "Would you object to someone
else educating him?"

He paused for a moment as if thinking, then said sharply,
"Not Mercer. I wouldn't have that."

"Nor would I. I hadn't thought in that direction."

He knew in what direction she was thinking, and again she
saw the muscles in his cheekbones tighten, but he said noth-

ing, only half turned from her, muttering now, "Is that the sum total of your demands?"

"No." Even the syllable trembled as it passed her lips. Now he was facing her again, staring at her, waiting, and when, her head down, she said, "Our life together cannot . . . cannot be the same."

There was a long pause that went into a full minute before he said, "You mean you will not come back as my wife?"

When she made no answer he asked quietly, "For how long do you intend such a situation to continue?"

"I don't know."

Again there was a pause; and then, his words seeming to come from deep in his throat, he said, "You know me, Nancy Ann, I would find that situation impossible were it to be . . . be permanent. Let us be frank when we have got this far. I want a wife. I need a wife. I need you."

Why at this moment should she see the face of James and hear his voice saying, "Procreation; that was all I was needed for"? And then came Peter and a wisp of the conversation on the night they were driving to the ball, and his words, "That is no marriage."

Her voice was small now as it came, saying, "You'll have to give me time."

"How much time? I gave you too much time after William was born. That's where I made the mistake."

When she turned and again looked into the empty grate, he said, "I shall stay for your father's funeral, after which I shall return to London. The house is being redecorated; I . . . I am thinking about selling that too. Anyway, in the meantime I am staying with Pat and George. They have made arrangements to tour through Northern France and have left it open for me to join them if I so wish. I shall do so, and in that case I will be away for about three weeks. When I come back we will talk again. Will that suit you?"

She forced herself to say, "Yes, thank you."

"Then I will take my leave of you until tomorrow. What time is the funeral?"

"Eleven o'clock."

"I shall be there."

As he turned from her she said, "Dennison." And at this he swung round to her, waiting.

"May I ask you to inform the staff that I will now be in sole charge of the house and the yard staff?"

She saw his face stretch slightly, and he repeated, "The yard staff?"

"Yes, the yard staff."

"Very well." His head moved slowly. "I will do as you wish. When will you return?"

"The day after tomorrow."

"I will inform them."

Almost with military precision now, he turned and marched from the room. And she, going to the sofa again, sat down and leant her head in the corner of it while her hands gripped the back, and so mixed were her emotions that she couldn't tell whether she was happy at the turn of events or desperately sad.

❧ 2 ❧

THE FUNERAL OF JOHN HOWARD HAZEL WAS WELL ATtended. Most of the men from the village joined the cortège outside the gates of the Manor House. And the new parson, the Reverend Michael Nesbit, spoke very kindly of his predecessor.

Those villagers who came back to the Dower House were given refreshments in the barn; the few carriage people who returned were received in the house. Dennison was not among them. But Pat and George, and her sister Florence and her husband did return. But within three hours of John Howard Hazel being laid in the ground the house was back to normal, except it lacked his presence.

And now Graham, who had stayed after all had gone, was bidding Nancy Ann goodbye. He did not offer any word of condolence; in fact, his words throughout the week had been few, although she had seen him every day. And she herself gave him no word of thanks, but she took his hand in between hers while her tear-filled eyes spoke for her.

They had reached the door when he said, "You are going back then?" He did not look at her as he spoke and he had to wait for an answer: "Yes, yes, I am going back."

Now he did look at her while saying, "You could do nothing else. He could, as I've said before, have claimed the children even if you had got a divorce."

292

She was surprised that he could speak like this, and she was asking herself how he should know about the divorce, but then she remembered that he too was a friend of George and Pat, although he never went visiting there.

Without waiting for her to make any comment, he went on, "Don't worry about your grandmama; she is not afraid to be on her own. But then, she won't be entirely. When are you leaving?"

She had to wet her lips before she said, "Tomorrow."

"Oh." He was walking away from her when he turned his head slightly and said, "If you want any help, just let me know."

She watched him disappear along the path and she did not check herself as she thought, Why are there so many different kinds of love?

She did not move back to the house the following day, for the weather changed and it poured with rain. But the morning after, the sun was bright and warm and at mid-morning she sent Mary and Agnes across with the children. Agnes was to stay in the nursery to see to them and Mary was to return, bringing McLoughlin with her to carry back the things he had brought over in the first place.

This morning Jessica appeared to be her old brusque self, saying, as she watched the gangling Irishman shouldering the cases and bundles like a pack horse, "He's a McLoughlin all right." Then as Mary picked up the last soft bag and went out the door Nancy Ann kissed the old woman and felt herself being hugged in arms that were still strong. She returned the embrace, then hurriedly followed Mary.

It was as they entered the path through the trees that Mary, slowing her pace, said, "Ma'am, I've heard something that I think you should know."

"Yes?"

"Well, McLoughlin, he . . . he told me something that he . . . he thinks you should know."

"Yes?"

"Well. Well, Jennie. . . . Well, really, it wasn't her at first, it was young David. Well, as usual the boy was where he shouldn't have been; he prowls around, ma'am, and worries

Jennie to death. But anyway, he saw them, the housekeeper and her sister, in one of the empty rooms upstairs and, as he described it to Jennie, Mrs. Conway was putting silver things and little framed pictures like cameos into a cloth bag. And then they went down the back way. It isn't the first time, ma'am, I understand. You see, they, by what McLoughlin said, they . . . well, they didn't expect you back, so some of them must have been helping themselves, Jennie told McLoughlin, and he thought you had better know, ma'am.''

"Thank you, Mary. At least it would appear I have one loyal servant in the house.''

"Oh, you have more than that, ma'am. But . . . but, you know, folks are frightened for their jobs, and those in a position at the top of a household like yours . . . well, ma'am, well, you know what I mean.''

"Yes, Mary, I know what you mean. But there's going to be a great change in my household.'' She noticed that she said, "my'' household, and for the first time it was to be her household, and she ended, "It will start this very day.''

The change in the staff's attitude was very apparent when McTaggart came down the steps and relieved her of her bag. And at the top of the steps there was Trice waiting, and slightly behind was Mrs. Conway.

It was evident to her that they had definitely been informed who was now in charge of the house and them. She passed them without moving a muscle of her face. She did not, as she usually had done, thank the footman for his assistance, but at the foot of the stairs she turned to Mrs. Conway, saying, "I would like you, and you Trice and McTaggart, to await me in my office immediately. Also call Appleby and Gillespie, and have the rest of the staff assemble in the hall.''

The tone was one that neither Mrs. Conway nor the others had ever heard her use and the woman even dipped her knee and replied smarmingly, "Yes, ma'am.''

In her sitting-room she sat down heavily in a gold-framed Louis chair, and the long drawn breath she let escape seemed to deflate her body. Up to this moment she had felt strong in her determination to clear the household of those she now considered her enemies, and she still meant to get rid of them, but, nevertheless, she was finding it a strain to keep up this new pose. What was more, she was alone as never before: there was no Dennison to lay her head against; nor was there a grandmama to give her earthy advice and spur her on; nor yet, Graham, to tell her he was behind her waiting to be used. No, here she was, in this huge establishment, about to rule it. But there was something she must do before she went downstairs and confronted those people.

She pulled herself up from the chair and, going to the wall, she rang the nursery bell. Within a few minutes Mary appeared in the room, and she said to her, "Will you fetch the boy up, Mary, please? Do it as unobtrusively as you can. Come up the back way. If he should be in the boot room, the best way to come would be to approach it from the yard and take him quietly out that way again."

"Leave it to me, ma'am. I'll do that."

She now went into the closet room and cooled her face and hands with water from the ewer. Then seated at the small dressing-table, she gazed at her reflection and asked herself if she looked the same as she had done ten days ago, and the answer was, no, the bright sparkle had gone. There was no colour in her cheeks, the light in her eyes showed a pain in their depth. No, she was not the girl she had been ten days ago. She was no longer a girl. That period of her life was over.

When she heard the door opening in the other room she went back, and there was the boy. Mary had her hand on his shoulder pressing him forward, and when she was seated and he stood before her, she said, "Hello, David."

And he answered, "Hello, ma'am."

"Would you like to tell me, David, what you saw the housekeeper doing, and which room she and her friend were in?"

He blinked his eyes, then glanced up at Mary. She nodded at him, and then he said, "Will they get wrong?"

To this she answered truthfully, "Not more than they deserve if they have been doing wrong. What kind of things were they putting in the case? Can you describe them? Were they little pictures like this?" She reached out and took a miniature from the table standing to her side which showed a hand-painting of Rebecca at six months old. Dennison had commissioned it. And now the boy nodded and said, "Yes, that size. Some were bigger."

"And what else were they putting in the case?"

His eyelids blinked again before he said, "Just bits, ma'am, bits of silver like are on the breakfast trays."

"How did you manage to see them doing this, David?"

"Oh." His head wagged, then he muttered, "I was looking around, 'cos you and the master were gone and . . . and I was in the bedroom in the far wing . . . and I heard somebody coming and I hid behind one like that." He pointed now to her dressing-table and went on, "And I could see through the space atween the glass and the top what they were doin'."

"Did you tell anybody about what you saw?"

"Yes. Yes, I told . . . I told our Jennie."

"And what did she say?"

"She was vexed." He smiled now, a slow smile that lit up his face and seemed to spread to the bright gold of his hair that had no brown streaks in it now, as he added, "She's pleased you're back, ma'am, and so am I, an' the cook an' all. She says. . . ."

He had stopped abruptly and hung his head, and Nancy Ann, smiling gently at him, said, "I'm pleased to hear that, David. Now go back with Mary and if you should be asked why I wanted to see you, just say I wanted to know if you had been a good boy. Will you remember that, David?"

"Yes, ma'am. Oh, yes, ma'am."

She now turned to Mary, saying, "After you have taken him downstairs, go straight to my office and await me there."

She let a full fifteen minutes elapse before she left her sitting room. From the gallery she could see the whole staff assembled and the sight of them en masse brought that quivering feeling to her stomach. But, her head held high and her gaze directed straight ahead, she slowly descended the stairs, passed the end of the two ranks they had formed, went through the arch, along the passage and into her office. There, Mary pulled out the chair for her and she sat down at her desk. Then after a moment, looking up at the kindly face of the young woman who had become closer to her than even her grandmother or Pat, she said on a sigh, "I hate doing this, Mary, but it's got to be done."

"Yes, ma'am, an' you're quite right. The captain used to say, you know where I worked afore, whenever he had to face anything that was disagreeable, and such times were when he had to stop the mistress overspending, he would say, 'Clear the decks ready for action!' "

"Oh, Mary." She pressed her lips together, closed her eyes and shook her head for a moment; then she said, "Well, here we go, clear the decks ready for action. Go and tell Trice, McTaggart, and Mrs. Conway to come in."

It seemed that Mary almost skipped from the room to carry out this duty, and a few minutes later the three people who had considered themselves to be heads of the house under the valet, walked quietly into the room and stood before the desk.

Nancy Ann had a pen in her hand. She was writing names on a sheet of paper and she finished the last one with a flourish before looking up at them and saying without any lead up, "Your wages are paid by the quarter: there are three weeks to go, you will be paid in full. But you will now all pack your bags and leave this house within the next hour."

They were so stunned that not one of them said a word, but simultaneously their lower jaws had dropped. She had never seen the butler's mouth open so wide for he always seemed to talk through his teeth. But it was he who spoke first, saying, "But, ma'am, you can't do this, we were engaged by. . . ."

"To my knowledge the master has told you that I am now in sole charge. I am dismissing you all. But there is one more thing. Unless you want to find yourselves in court, the articles you have stolen must be returned within the next two days or else the police will be informed. Particularly you, Mrs. Conway, you had better tell your relative to return the bag of miniatures et cetera you filled for her just recently, or you might find yourself in a dire situation."

For a moment she thought the woman was going to faint. She saw the colour drain from her sallow face leaving it grey and her throat expand as if she was aiming to draw breath into her body.

She now looked at the butler. His countenance looked evil,

but she faced him, saying, "You have all, for years, lined your pockets at the master's expense. You have done deals with every tradesman who has called here. This I have proved from the order books. And so I need have no worry that I am turning you out destitute. Nor shall I worry that you will all find it difficult to obtain good employment; it would be impossible for me to foist any of you onto another family. . . . This is all I've got to say."

Not one of them moved, until the footman, McTaggart, muttered, "No reference?"

"No reference."

"We could make you prove what you say."

"Oh, I can prove what I say, and witnesses would come forward." They seemed about to glance at each other but changed their minds; instead they glared at her with such ferocity that she wouldn't have been surprised if one of them had lifted his hand to strike her.

Mary was holding the door open for them and they turned on her baneful glances as they passed.

After closing the door, Mary came back to the desk and looked at Nancy Ann sitting now with her head leaning against the back of the tall leather chair, and she said, "You did splendid, ma'am. The main battle's over. Who's next?"

"Anderson."

When the top floor maid was ushered into the room she did not show any sign of the civil insolence that had dictated her earlier manner when dealing with the mistress of the house, but she stood before the desk and said meekly, "Yes, ma'am?"

Nancy Ann did not beat about the bush here, she said immediately, "You are being dismissed, Anderson. You'll have your money in advance. It will be ready for you by the time you have your bag packed."

"Ma'am." The woman's voice trembled. "What . . . what have I done?"

"You needn't ask what you have done, Anderson, you know what you have done. Apart from everything else, your manner has been offensive at times. But that is just by the way. I won't embarrass you further by describing your disloyalty; you know only too well how far that went."

She now looked at Mary, saying, "Send in Appleby and Gillespie."

The woman did not take the hint that she had been dismissed but still stood, and then she said, "A reference, ma'am?"

"I cannot give you a reference, Anderson. If it had just been your manner to me then I might have reconsidered, but you were in league with those who were above you and planned my destruction and unhappiness."

She felt a tinge of regret as she saw the woman almost stumble out of the room, yet she forced herself to remember how she had been treated by this servant.

When the coachman and groom entered the room their faces were stiff and, as Mary might have put it, in their turn, looked ready for battle. But the wind was taken out of their sails immediately by Nancy Ann saying, "You two men were the means of bringing a person to this house unknown to the master of it. You showed no loyalty to your master and certainly none to me. Well now, you are both at liberty to find employment with the person who engaged you. You are dismissed as from now. You will have your wages in advance. That is all."

"But, my God! it isn't." It was Appleby speaking. "I've worked for the master twenty years, he wouldn't have. . . ."

She silenced him by lifting her hand, and, her voice raised high now, she said, "He would have. He dismissed his valet for the same offence and has given me permission to dismiss you."

William Appleby was a small thin man with a wiry body. Now he seemed to swell as he leant across the table towards her and he almost barked at her, "You won't reign long. Parson's Prig they call you and Parson's Prig you are. His whore was worth a dozen of you and she'll be in your place afore the end, God willin'."

Both the groom and Mary had now to hold the man and thrust him out of the door, and after Mary had banged the door shut she leant against it and looked to where Nancy Ann was sitting with her hand pressed tight across her mouth. Then she went to her and, patting her shoulder, she said, "There now. There now. Don't upset yourself, ma'am. He was bound to go on like that. He's had it easy for years, that one. They say he used to valet the master at odd times afore Staith came on the scene; and he was also hand in glove with Trice, especially where the wine cellar was concerned. You're well rid of that one, ma'am. Is that the lot you want rid of, ma'am?"

Nancy Ann shuddered. The man's words were ringing in her ears "And she'll be in your place afore the end." After a moment she said, "Yes, Mary. Now . . . now I want you to go and bring Robertson here. No; wait. First of all I must talk with you. Sit down." She pointed to a chair, then looked at the young woman, her hands joined in her lap, and she said, "Do you think Agnes would be capable of controlling the nursery if she had someone there to help her?"

Mary's eyes crinkled at the corners for a moment. "Oh, yes," she said; "she's capable enough, ma'am. Like me, she had training with our squad, the lot of them, as I said. But . . . but . . . ?"

Nancy Ann leant over the desk towards her, saying, "Do you think you could take the position of housekeeper? I'm sure you could, but do you think so? And would you like it?"

"Me?" Mary was now thumping her chest with her thumb. "Housekeeper, here?"

"Well—" Nancy Ann allowed herself to smile a small smile while saying, "I have no other house."

"Oh, but, ma'am, 'tis a big job and responsibilities. And would they accept me?"

"Oh, they'll accept you or they'll go." There was a definite note of authority in Nancy Ann's voice now, and she straightened herself up as she said further, "When I speak to the rest of them they will be given their choice. But we're having no more Judases here if I can help it. Well, what do you say? There is nothing, as I see it, to the position except ordering the victuals and supervising the staff, and I'm sure you can do that. Anyone who can control children like you is capable of giving an order and seeing that it is obeyed. Then there is the salary. It would be almost doubled."

"Oh, it doesn't matter about that, but I'm not going to be a hypocrite and say it wouldn't be welcome, especially at home. But, as for help up in the nursery"—Mary smiled widely now—"I have another sister, Alice, ready to be placed out."

"Oh, that would be excellent. So shall we say that's settled?"

"Oh, ma'am." Now Mary put her flat hands on the desk and, bending over towards Nancy Ann, she said, "I bless the day I came under your care, I do that, ma'am." There was a break in her voice, and Nancy Ann, deeply touched, said, "It was a good day for me too, Mary. Now go and call in Robertson, please."

Mary walked towards the door but stood there a minute fumbling with her handkerchief; then, with a slight sniff, she went out.

When Henry Robertson came into the office Nancy Ann wanted to say immediately to him, "Don't look so perturbed, it's all right." He was standing now before her desk, a man of medium height with reddish hair which seemed to clash with the nut brown of his uniform. This man had always been civil towards her and helpful when he could. She spoke again without preamble: "Do you think you can carry out the duties of butler, Robertson?"

There was a second's pause and a stiffening of the shoulders and a pulling in of the chin before the man replied, "I could, ma'am, I could, and serve you with loyalty."

"Thank you, Robertson." And now she asked, "Do we need two footmen?"

"No, ma'am, not really, one would be ample."

"I will see one is engaged for you. Thank you, Robertson."

"Thank you, ma'am, and it's obliged I am to you. Thank you." He turned smartly and marched out.

When the door had closed on him Mary said, "One loyal soldier, or sailor," she smiled, then added, "Ma'am."

"Well, let's have the other loyal one, Mary—McLoughlin."

"Oh yes, ma'am, but he's already enlisted on your side. . . ."

When Shane McLoughlin stood at the other side of the desk, she said to him, "You will have already heard that Appleby and Gillespie have been dismissed."

His voice was low when he replied, "I have, ma'am."

"Would you like the position of coachman?"

She saw the broad chest expand, and on a breath that he slowly let out, he said, "I would that, ma'am. I would that."

"It might entail other duties. As my husband has not now got a valet, you might be called upon to stand in and assist him, such as at those times when he goes away on a shoot."

She now saw the man hesitate, and then he said candidly, "Valet the master, ma'am? Oh, I doubt if I'd be any good at that. I'm fumble-fisted. A horse now, I could handle, but to dress somebody . . . well."

"You would not be expected to dress the master, only lay out his clothes and things like that. It's something that you can soon learn. Mary there would help you."

At this, Mary looked at her wide-eyed. But when Mc-Loughlin turned towards her, she said to him blithely, " 'Twill be all right. You'll soon get into the way."

"Well, if you think so, I'd be only too pleased."

Now he turned and looked at Nancy Ann, saying in a characteristic Irish way that placed all human beings on a level, "You'll not regret this day, ma'am; and you can tell the master so. I'll likely make a mess of everything at first, inside that is, not outside. No, no; those stables'll be run as they've never been run afore, and the carriage horses will be a credit, I promise you that. But upstairs. Well, once I get the hang of it, the master will never have been better served. You can tell him that from me. As for yourself, ma'am, I'm your servant from this day on. An' I have been since I came into the place. But what you've done for me the day has made me sign me cross at the bottom of a document." . . .

He was in full spate and would have gone on had not Mary, looking at Nancy Ann, prompted, "There's Winter and Pollock, ma'am. Are you makin' one or t'other of them a groom?"

"Oh, yes, Winter and Pollock. Whom do you suggest, Mc-Loughlin?"

· It seemed that now Shane was considering, and then he said, "Winter's the first stable lad. He's a good fellow is Winter, though he's not as old as Pollock, and Pollock's been here, so I understand, some longer time. He's forty if he's a day, but he's not as bright up top as Johnny. I would say, raise the first stable boy, ma'am.''

"Then it is Winter. Well, when you go out, you can tell him to come and see me. But that will leave you short of a stable boy.''

Almost before she had finished speaking he put in, "I can soon rectify that, ma'am, with one of our lot, I mean me younger brother, Benny by name and bright up top. He's very good with dogs, training them that is. He'll fall into the ways of the horses. Can I tell him, ma'am? He's already helping out a bit in the yard.''

"Yes, do. He may come and see me tomorrow.''

" 'Tis settled then, ma'am, 'tis settled.'' He jerked his head twice at her, a grin on his face from ear to ear; and then he said, "Will that be all at present, ma'am?''

As the door closed on him both Mary and Nancy Ann looked at each other, and Nancy Ann knew that Mary was about to give vent to one of her body-shaking laughs, and she wagged her finger at her; but the admonition was directed towards herself, too, for she knew full well that if she gave vent to laughter it might become hysterical and end in a torrent of tears. And so she turned her attention to the list on the table.

"Do you know anything objectionable about any of the others?'' she asked.

Mary thought for a moment, then said, "No, ma'am, except that, to keep their jobs, as I said, they've had to run with the hare and hunt with the hounds. No, I think you will find all the rest all right, ma'am. But there's Benton the lodge-keeper and his wife. They keep to themselves. And yet they were in with the other lot. But they and the gardeners and the farmhands come under Mr. Taylor the Ground Manager.''

Nancy Ann was considering again; and then she said, "The cottages. Those of Trice and Appleby are already furnished; they will have only their personal belongings to take with them. But there might be some quantity of these, so you can inform them they may stay on till the end of the week, until they find some other place to live. Appleby's cottage can then be taken over by McLoughlin and his brother. As for the other one, it was a very nice cottage, Trice's, wasn't it?''

"Very nice indeed, ma'am, being for married quarters."

"Well, I have ideas about who will occupy that one." She now rose from her chair, saying as if to herself, "Let us get it over."

When she entered the hall it was to be confronted by what appeared to be a sea of troubled eyes. As she remarked later to Mary, it was as if they were expecting the devil.

She began immediately. Standing with her hands joined at her waist, her head held well back on her shoulders, she said, "You are all aware by now what has taken place. If any one of you wishes to leave my service you can report to me in my office tomorrow morning. That is all. Oh . . . just one thing." She had half turned from them. Now she was looking down the hallway to where, at the far end, was a green-baized door which opened into the corridor leading to the kitchen and the staff quarters. And near this door stood Jennie Mather, and she said, "I would like to see you in my office for a moment, please."

Jennie Mather looked about her, then took one step forward and, pointing to herself, she said, "Me, ma'am?"

"Yes. Yes, you." And on this Nancy Ann turned away and went back into her office; and Jennie Mather slowly followed her.

Jennie Mather was now a woman nearing thirty. She had been a beautiful young girl. There were still traces of the beauty on her face because sorrow and humiliation does not alter the bone formation, merely the skin and the look in the eyes. Her skin was pale, colourless; her eyes were large and of a deep-sea blue, but they held no light, there was a dull subdued look in them.

She was doubtless surprised when her mistress said to her, "Please, sit down."

Before Nancy Ann could continue, Mary interrupted quietly, "You won't be requiring me anymore, ma'am, for the time being?" It was a very tactful question, and Nancy Ann, looking at her, said, "No, thank you, Mary. That will be all for the present. I will be up in the nursery shortly."

"Very good, ma'am."

Left alone, the older woman looked at her mistress whom she considered a young girl, her slim body almost lost in the great leather chair. That was until she spoke; and what she said caused her whole expression to change, her eyes to widen, her lips to move one against the other as if they were speaking silent words, and the colour to flood her pale skin, for this young mistress was saying to her: "I've wanted to speak about this matter for a long time, Jennie." She did not say "Mather" but "Jennie," then went on. "I think that you have been treated badly in this house. If I'd had my say when I first came here, I would have had your son recognized in some way. But it wasn't to be. That is, up till now. Your boy is highly intelligent. It's a credit to you that he can read and write. Some weeks ago I was looking at the books that I suppose he had been reading up in the attic and I marvelled at his advancement. But that is only one side of education. In the ordinary way he would already have been at a boarding school for some years now, so I intend the wrong to be rectified, at least in that way. Would you agree to this?"

Jennie Mather couldn't speak. She had been sitting upright in the straight-backed chair, now she was slumped, her head was bowed on her chest. And as Nancy Ann watched the tears rain down the young woman's face, she had great difficulty in restraining her own. And she said softly, "Please, please, don't upset yourself. Come. Come now. Let us talk about this. We both have his welfare at heart."

It was some minutes before Jennie could say, "Oh, ma'am, I never thought to live to see the day when I should hear someone speak for us . . . because I have been made to suffer." Her voice now broke again and, her head drooping forward once more, she shook it from side to side as she muttered, "Oh, God, how I have been made to suffer."

"There, there. Please don't distress yourself. Come; dry your eyes, and answer me this. Why, when you have been humiliated so, did you stay? You could have taken your boy and gone, surely?"

Again it was some time before Jennie answered, and then she asked simply, "Where, ma'am? Where could I have gone? I had only one living relative, an uncle, and he in Australia. I had no money except my wage and that a pittance, because my son had to be paid for out of it."

"What!"

"Yes, ma'am. I had to pay for his keep until he was able to work in the boot room."

"Who ordered that?"

"The housekeeper, ma'am."

It was on the point of Nancy Ann's tongue now to say, Dear God! But, as if her tongue was loosened, Jennie Mather began to talk. Looking across the table, the tears still raining down her face, she said, "It was either the workhouse or the attic. And it wasn't even an attic, it was right under the roof. And I couldn't bear the thought of the workhouse at that time, because I used to think I'd be in for fourteen years before I could leave. You see they don't allow you to leave until your child can work for himself. Little did I know then that I would do almost fourteen years of hard labour here. It couldn't have been worse there, it couldn't. Yet I must admit, ma'am, I hoped against hope that the master would relent. I thought that once he saw my son who looked the spit of his father, who was his own brother, he would forgive and accept the boy. I would have been quite willing to leave, to go away altogether as long as my son was recognized in some way. But no, he hates the sight of him. And my only wonder is, feeling as he does, he has allowed us to stay. It is only because we have hidden away as it were. But now . . . but now, ma'am, you were saying you would send him to school, a proper school. Oh, at this moment, I feel there is a God after all."

"Well now, listen to me. I would rather it weren't known that I shall be paying for the boy's education. It will have nothing to do with the master, and I couldn't see how this could be hidden until a moment ago when you said that your only living relative was an uncle in Australia. Does he write . . . correspond with you?"

"Yes, ma'am, now and again I get a letter. He moved around when he first went out, but for some years now he's been settled in a place called Kalgoorlie. He and another man have set up a grocery business. And in his last letter he talked about buying some land. He even said that when David was old enough he would send for him."

"Well, that has solved the problem, at least my problem.

You can say that your uncle has sent you the money with which to educate your son. How about that?''

"Oh, ma'am, I'll do anything you say."

"And it can be known to the rest of the staff that the reason why I called you in is to offer you the cottage, Trice's cottage, and your previous work back."

"Trice's cottage! And my. . . ." There was a look of wonderment in the young woman's face now, for it was well known that Trice's cottage was better than the other four on the estate having, besides the loft, a sitting-room and a kitchen. But then this wonderment turned to dismay as she said, "But the master, if he were to see me."

"Oh, I've thought about that. But I doubt if he'd recognize you now. Anyway, he is out most of the time and you could arrange your work accordingly. . . . Oh, now! now!" Nancy Ann rose from her seat, saying, "You mustn't cry any more. . We will talk again tomorrow when we'll discuss which school will be suitable for David. Then you must go into Newcastle and make arrangements. I shall give you a letter of recommendation."

Jennie had risen to her feet. She could not speak now, but what she did do was bend her knee deeply, then stumble towards the door.

Her entry into the kitchen interrupted a buzz of conversation among the entire kitchen staff, and it was the cook who said, "My God! girl, not you an' all?"

"No." Jennie shook her head before saying thickly, "Me and David are to have a cottage, Trice's."

There was complete silence for a moment; then Cook said, "Oh, well. But not afore time I'd say. I'm glad for you, Jennie, I am that. And I'm glad a day of reckoning has come in this house; it has been long awaited.'Tis meself that says it, although I've had to close me eyes and shut me mouth this many a long year."

As Jennie passed the group standing between the long wooden kitchen table and the great fireplace with the big black ovens to the side, she said in an offhand way, "And I'm to go upstairs again into my old job." Then, without waiting for any response, she went quickly out of the kitchen, along a corridor, and into the cold meat store, where previous to being called into the hall she had been slicing bacon for the next morning's breakfast, and boning breasts of lamb ready for rolling. However, she did not immediately begin her work again, but, her teeth clenched tightly, she looked around this room where, summer and winter for years now as part of her duty, she'd had the thankless job of standing in this cold cell preparing meats. Even on the hottest day it could make you shiver. Now all that was over. Dear God! She moved slowly round to a butcher's block and, resting her buttocks against it, she bent her body forward and covered her face with her hands. . . .

There followed a busy day. Much coming and going inside and outside the house. But there were to be two more incidents before this chapter of her life would close.

It happened in the late evening. She'd had her supper served on a tray in her sitting-room, after which she went upstairs and paid her last visit to the nursery to see the children already tucked up in their cots and fast asleep. Agnes was tidying the nursery and she reported that William had been a little fractious. "Cutting his teeth, ma'am, he is," she said, her manner giving the impression she knew all about the cutting of front teeth—which she did—but more so, did it point out that she was capable of carrying out the duties of her new position.

Nancy Ann had looked down on her daughter's round pink face. She was growing fast and already her features were beginning to resemble her own, whereas the chubby baby showed marked traces of his father in the nose and lips.

She bade Agnes good night. Then at the foot of the stairs she passed Mary, and she said to her, "It's a lovely night. I'm going for a stroll as far as the river."

"That'll be nice, ma'am. The air's cool now; 'twill make you sleep."

When she reached the drive she did not go straight across the sunken garden and make for the river, but she turned to her left and made her way round the side of the house and through the yard. The men were still busy moving in and out of the stables and the tack-room. When they saw her, they stopped and raised their caps to her. And she smiled at them.

One whom she hadn't seen before came out of the barn carrying a bale of hay which, on seeing her, he almost let slide from his shoulder. But, standing still, he managed to grip it with one hand while touching his forelock with the other, and in an unmistakeable Irish voice, he said, "Evenin' to you, ma'am."

This was definitely another McLoughlin. And without her enquiring he answered a question when he added, "I'm Benny, ma'am. Shane's me brother. I'm new."

She had stopped. And it was in this moment more than any other that she longed for Dennison to be by her side, for, had he been, once they gained the privacy of the gardens, she would have taken on the voice and the manner of the young fellow, saying, "Evenin' to you, ma'am. I'm Benny, ma'am. Shane's me brother." And he would have laughed, then shaken his head and put his arm about her shoulders and hugged her to him, saying, "You are a clever little puss, aren't you?" He often used this term after she had mimicked someone: a clever little puss. But would she ever again feel like mimicking anyone? Now she came to think of it, she had not done an imitation since the night she had taken off that woman.

The sun had set, the long twilight had begun. She emerged from the wood and on to the green sward that bordered the river here, and there she saw the boy, sitting on the very stone where she had espied him all those years ago. And as if he had sensed her presence, because he couldn't have heard her footsteps, he turned his head quickly, then rose to his feet. But he did not move towards her.

When she reached him, she said, "Good evening, David."

"Good evening, ma'am."

She noticed that he had a pencil in his hand and that he had been writing. Some loose pages were lying on the flat rock to his side. She now watched him rub the pencil up and down between his fingers.

"It is a beautiful evening, isn't it?"

In answer to her remark, he said, "Am I really to go to school, ma'am?"

"Yes. Yes, David, you are really to go to school."

She was quite unprepared for what happened next, for the

boy now flung his arms about her and laid his head on her breast and, his voice rising to almost a falsetto note, he cried, "I love you. I do, I do. I love you."

After taking a gasping breath, her arms went about him, and she placed one hand on his hair and stroked it. And when, in almost a gabble, he went on, "I'll always love you. I'll love you till I die. I love you better than anyone in the world," she pressed him from her and, holding his face between her hands and seeing that his eyes were wet, which almost brought the tears to her own, she said, "I . . . I am very honoured that you should like me, David, but . . . but you must not say anything like that again, except to your mother. You must love your mother."

"I do. I do. I love Jennie."

She stopped him here by saying, "You should call her Mother, not Jennie."

"I . . . I think of her as Jennie, because I've always called her Jennie, because everybody calls her Jennie. And . . . and yes, I love her, but not like I love you."

"Now David." There was a stern note in her voice. "You are grateful to me because I . . . I am the means of sending you to school."

"Oh, no, no, ma'am, it isn't just that. I've always loved you."

She closed her eyes and bit on her lip. Here was a situation for which she wasn't prepared. She drew him down on to the rock seat and, taking his hand, she said, "Now promise me something, David."

"I'll promise you anything, ma'am, anything."

"Well, promise me that you will not say—" She paused. How was she to put this? Then she went on slowly, "You will not repeat or express your feelings again because, you know, they will change." When he shook his head, she shook his hand, saying, "Oh yes they will. How old are you now?"

"I'm . . . I'm twelve, ma'am."

"Yes, you are twelve, and you are a very sensible boy, and so let us now change the subject. Tell me, what would you like to be when you grow up?"

Without hesitation he said, "I'm going to write stories, ma'am, like those up in the attic."

"That is good. So you are going to be a writer." She glanced down at the sheets of paper lying to her side on the rock, and she added, "Do you write much?"

"Oh, yes, ma'am, when I can at night, or in my free time. I write poetry, ma'am. I wrote that one last year." He pointed down to the papers. "But I have altered it, made it better." He picked up the piece of paper and handed it to her, and she smiled before she read what was written on it.

Softly, softly, the dove coos to me,
Softly, softly, from the branch of the big oak tree.
Would I had wings I'd fly to it there,
Then together we'd gently take to the air
And soar on the wind to the end of the sky.
O dove of the grey breast, why can't I fly?

My feet touch the ground,
But my heart's in the sky
And it sighs as it asks for the reason why
You, my dove, can travel the earth
While only my mind can know its worth.
Softly, softly, dove, coo to me
From your throne on the branch of the big oak tree.

After she had finished reading she sat staring into his face, and she told herself that he hadn't written those words, he had copied them from some book upstairs. Then she realised she was looking at a boy who was twelve years old and who had spent most of his time, apart from his work, on his own, solitary, up in that space under the roof where were stored all kinds of things, most being boxes of books and stacks of papers. She had seen these herself. She had even read the first edition of *The Newcastle Chronicle* or the *General Weekly Advertiser*, as it was called in 1764. It was dated March 24th, and she remembered being very amused at the advertisements in it, especially the one for Mr. Bank's Ball at the Assembly Rooms, tickets to be had from his dwelling house in the *Flesh* market. She also remembered shuddering at the advertisements for Mr. Mole's fighting cock pit in the Bigg Market, and offering a prize of £50; another prize was a dark brown horse. Oh yes, there was all kinds of reading stored in the attics, so why shouldn't he have imbibed enough knowledge to be able to write like this? Yet at twelve years old she was sure that neither of her brothers would have even thought like this. As for herself, who was supposed to be bright where her reading was concerned, she wouldn't have been able to compose a similar piece of poetry. Constructively it had its faults, the metre was not quite right, but the essence was that of a thinker. Oh, what a shame it was that this boy had missed so much good schooling. Yet would he have learned anything more than that which he had taught himself with the help of his mother? Yes; yes, he would have had a wider knowledge. But all that was now going to be rectified.

"Do you like it, ma'am?"

"I . . . I think it is a very fine poem, and you will undoubtedly be a writer some day. But you must make up your mind to learn all you can about . . . well, all kinds of things."

The boy was staring at her, but it was some seconds before he said, "Why does the master hate me?"

She was completely nonplussed by the question and she made to rise from the rock, but his penetrating gaze still on her forced her to remain looking back at him. And now with almost a stammer she said, "He . . . he . . . the master doesn't hate you."

"He does, ma'am. He is my uncle, so the men say."

Oh, dear. Oh, dear.

"I know all about it, ma'am. I know that my father was drowned in this river." He turned his head and nodded towards the water. "This is why I like to come down here; I feel I am near him. There are many pictures of him in the attics. He was beautiful. I look like him." There was no suggestion of pride in the words for he went on, "That's why they tried to dye my hair with tea. I hated it here until you came, ma'am. I was going to run away many times. I'm glad I didn't. . . . But why does he hate me so . . . the master?"

"He . . . he doesn't hate you, David. It is just because he is sad. He lost his brother, you see."

The boy now screwed round on the shelf of rock and, lean-

ing forward, he rested his forearms on his knees as he said,
" 'Tisn't that. No, 'tisn't that.''

As she looked at his bent head and the position in which
he was sitting, it came to her like a revelation and not a
pleasant one, that although the boy looked like his father, his
manner, his slight arrogance even at this age, and the position
he was sitting in now, all spoke plainly that his nature was
derived from the man who actually did hate him, for except
for his fairness he was now as Dennison must have been at
his age.

She rose hastily to her feet, saying, "I must be going,
David. We . . . we will talk again once the matter of the
school is settled.''

He was standing now and looking at her, and he made a
small movement with his head but did not speak. And as she
walked away she knew he was watching her, and she felt as
she might have done had a mature man been in his place.

The meeting with the boy last night had disturbed her, for
she could see that his strength of character would in the future, in some way, create trouble.

It was half-past ten in the morning and she was sitting in
the drawing-room drinking a cup of chocolate when there was
a knock at the door and Robertson entered, saying hurriedly,
"Lady Beatrice has arrived, ma'am.''

Nancy Ann only just prevented herself from saying aloud
the words that were running through her mind. Oh, no; not
her. But she got up and went hastily through the door Robertson was holding open for her, and there, already entering the
hall, was Lady Beatrice Boswell, who, ignoring for the moment Nancy Ann and looking at Robertson, said, "Pay the
cab, man.''

Robertson looked at his mistress and made a small movement with his hand as if to say that he hadn't any money, and
Nancy Ann turned to where Mary was standing at the bottom
of the stairs and said, "Take some money from my cash box,
Mary, and pay the cabman.''

The cabbie was now coming through the hall door laden
down with packages, and as he began to drop them one after

the other with a thud, Lady Beatrice cried, "Be careful! man. Be careful!"

The man sighed and turned away, saying to Robertson as he did so, "That's only half of it."

Still ignoring Nancy Ann, Lady Beatrice looked at Robertson and demanded, "Where is Trice?" And the man, glancing from Nancy Ann to the newcomer, muttered, "He is no longer in service here, ma'am."

"What! Oh, well, take these upstairs to my rooms."

As the man hesitated, Nancy Ann said quietly, "Leave them where they are, Robertson." And now looking fully at Lady Beatrice, she said, "Will you kindly come this way?" She motioned towards the drawing-room, and to this Lady Beatrice replied, "I'll see you later when I am refreshed."

"You will see me *now,* Lady Beatrice."

The tone stretched the painted face, the eyes widened, the mouth fell into a polite gape. She glanced from the butler to Mary who had re-entered the hall, then to a maid who was descending the stairs, and now letting out a long and seemingly placatory breath, she stalked haughtily past Nancy Ann and into the drawing-room.

Slowly, Nancy Ann closed the door behind her. Then passing the indignant figure, she seated herself on a single chair and, her hands joined in her lap, she looked at the woman. She had not seen her for over a year because her last entry into the house had been during the week the baby was born. And on that visit she stayed only a short time because the household was in an uproar. Previously her visits had often been of a month's duration; but even then she had generally kept to her bed, the while demanding the servants be at her beck and call. And so she herself had seen very little of her. Dennison always laughed about her. He was sorry for her, he said, because she had to live with her cousin, the Honourable Delia Ferguson, whom he jokingly described as being a horse minus two legs and a tail.

"I wish to say to you, Lady Beatrice, that you cannot stay here."

"Wh . . . *at!*" The word was drawn out; the painted cheeks that looked as if they had been tinted with enamel moved into deep creases. Then the voice demanded, "Where is Dennison?'' And she looked around as if she expected him to appear from behind the furniture.

''Dennison is in London. I am now in complete charge of the house and the staff, which has lately become depleted. I have retained enough for the comfortable running of the house, but this does not provide for a guest to have servants at her beck and call fourteen hours of the day.''

''This is outrageous. How dare you! You know who I am? I'm related to your husband, much closer to him than you are. Dennison would never countenance this.''

''For your information, Lady Beatrice, Dennison has given me a free hand. For the future I may arrange my staff and invite whom I like into my house.''

''Your house? Your house? Oh, I've heard about you and the fracas you caused. I stayed overnight in Newcastle at the Barringtons. It's a scandal. Do you know your actions were scandalous? Not those of a lady, even if you were provoked. Oh, I know all about it.''

Now Nancy Ann rose to her feet and, forcing herself to remain calm, she said, ''Then if you know all about it, you will have gauged that I'm of a character capable of removing obstacles I find in my way. Now, Lady Beatrice, I have much to do. You may remain until tomorrow morning or even longer, say a week, if you will conform to the rules of the house. Breakfast is served in the small dining-room at nine o'clock, dinner at two, afternoon tea at five, and supper at seven. You will have no one to maid you . . . I don't. If you wish for a bath you can take it in one of the ground-floor closets so the maids won't have so far to carry the water. If you agree with these arrangements then, as I said, you may stay for a week. But I'd be obliged if, in any case, you did not unload your dolls.''

The woman's face had altered yet again. For a moment Nancy Ann thought it was going to crumple into tears, but then, she couldn't imagine this person giving way to tears; she was such a dominant, selfish, arrogant individual. There was only one other person she disliked more. She watched her turn about now and walk down the room. Her carriage was no longer upright. It appeared to Nancy Ann that she had lost inches. It could have been that she had taken off her brown leather buttoned boots and was in slippers, or removed the old-fashioned high silk and flower-bedecked bonnet. The attitude of the woman now brought another of Mary's nautical sayings to mind: The wind had certainly been taken out of her sails, and that, she reckoned, was a very good thing, which would mean she would soon leave. Just the thought of having her in the household for weeks on end brought tense-ness to her whole body.

After a moment she followed the lady into the hall where there were at least twelve packages and boxes still remaining. Most of the boxes looked light, being made of cardboard, but amongst them were three soft travelling bags, their contents bulging the sides.

Robertson was standing looking down on the array and she said to him, "Take the dressing-case up but put the remainder of the bags in the store-room, please." . . .

She was somewhat surprised when Lady Beatrice did not show herself at dinner, nor yet at tea, nor yet at supper. And becoming a little apprehensive, she sent Mary up to find out if she was all right. A few minutes later Mary came down and, standing before her, she shook her head from side to side, saying, "She's all right, ma'am, but—" And she paused so long that Nancy Ann prompted, "But what, Mary?"

"Well, ma'am, if I may say so, if I hadn't seen the lady that came in this morning I would not have . . . well, linked her up with the one that is sittin' upstairs now."

"Why not?"

"She's . . . well, she's like an old woman; there's no sprite-liness about her. I asked her if she would like to come down for a meal and she thanked me civilly and said she wasn't hungry."

"Were her things unpacked?"

"Not that I could see, ma'am. She was sitting by the win-dow looking out. And . . . and. . . ."

"Yes?"

"Well, she had washed her face. You know, it . . . it was no longer painted, and it was just as if she had wiped off the other person that came in this morning. It was a kind of a shock, ma'am. She's old. Well, what I mean is, I would have taken her to be in her forties when I've seen her afore, but she always had her war paint on so to speak, and her manner was . . . well, not pleasant, as you know, ma'am. But there's a different woman upstairs tonight. If . . . if I hadn't seen it for meself I wouldn't have believed it.''

"Could . . . could she be acting? I mean, playing for sympathy?''

"No, no, ma'am. I came on her unawares like. I tapped on the door, and then went in because she hadn't bid me enter and I thought she might have been out, gone for a walk in the grounds or something. But there she was, sitting by the window like a lost soul.''

Nancy Ann thought for a while, then said, "Get Cook to make a tray up with something light and send it up to her, will you, Mary?''

"Yes; yes, I'll do that, ma'am.''

Nancy Ann wondered if she should pay the guest a visit, then decided, No, she must not show any softening in that direction, for Mary, even with her keen insight into human nature, might have been taken in. . . .

It was turned ten o'clock. She was already undressed for bed and was sitting in her dressing-gown at the open balcony door. The night was cool, the moon was rising, and as she looked into the night she was again overwhelmed by the feeling of aloneness. She had no desire to go to bed because every time she lay on that bed she could see the two figures lying side by side; yet, even so, she was wishing he was here at this moment.

When the tap came on the door, she thought it might be Mary and said, "Come in." She was slow to turn about, but then she found herself stationary, twisted in her chair, for there, within the circle of the lamplight, stood Lady Beatrice. And it really did seem that only the name remained, for this person was far removed from the lady with the grand arrogant manners she had encountered this morning. Slowly, she rose from the chair as the woman, stepping towards her, said, "May I talk to you?''

"Yes. Yes, if you wish." Nancy Ann pointed to the chaise-longue, and then she watched the woman turn and look down on the couch as if she was hesitant to sit. When she did sit down, she placed her joined hands between her knees and rocked herself backwards and forwards two or three times before she said, "I'm . . . I'm not the same, am I? This person you are seeing now, I'm not the same."

"No, you are not the same." Nancy Ann had seated herself on the chair some little distance from the couch. "No, I am not the same." Lady Beatrice shook her head again, then said, "But this is me, this is the real me. Will you listen?"

"Yes, yes. If you wish I will listen."

"You know why I come here and stay in bed for days on end, for weeks on end?"

"No. No, I don't."

"I . . . I come to have a rest, to be waited on, like my mother was waited on. Has Dennison told you about me?"

"Very little, only that you had a broken romance."

"Ha-ha!" Now she put her head back and the "ha-ha!" she emitted this time was much louder. "Dennison is kind. He's always been kind to me, right from the beginning, and tolerant. Of course, it cost him nothing and made him laugh at times. And of course he knows what Delia's like, Delia Ferguson, the Honourable Delia Ferguson." She stressed the last three words. "I've lived with her for twenty-six years. Shall I start at the beginning?"

"If . . . if you wish."

"You are sure you don't know the facts already?"

"Only what I've already told you, Dennison said you had a broken romance."

Lady Beatrice did not repeat the "ha-ha!" but she put a hand up to her brow and with her two middle fingers, she rubbed the furrows that were now evident there backwards and forwards as if trying to erase them.

"My mother was a very extravagant lady," she said. "She and my father travelled a lot. When they returned she always brought me dolls, sometimes six, one from each country they would have visited. I never went to school; I had a governess and a nurse. By the time I was twelve I had at least forty dolls, ranging from the size of my finger"—she held up the first finger of her right hand—"to a cloth one that was four foot long and is so made that it can double up into a small parcel. When my mother was at home there were balls and parties. I was never allowed downstairs to enjoy them, but was promised that when I was sixteen I would be brought out. But my mother died before I was sixteen, two months before my birthday. After her death my father went travelling. He was away a year. When he came back I was carrying a child.''

Nancy Ann now watched her blink her eyelids rapidly, then turn her head and look round the room. It was in much the same manner as she had used in the drawing-room when she asked where Dennison was. Then, in a low voice, and her head bent forward, she continued, ''My only recreation was riding. My governess and nurse didn't bother with me much, they were engrossed in their friendship. Anyway, they thought I was grown up. My daily companion was the groom. He was married to one of the housemaids. He was thirty years of age. He was very presentable, but above all he was kind, too kind. I fell in love with him, and he promised to leave his housemaid and we would run away together. He did run away, but not with me. But he didn't run far enough, only to a village a few miles away. My father went looking for him with a gun; but it was supposed he didn't find him, that he had run further away this time.'' She paused again, gasped at the air, then said, ''My baby was born and it lived a month, and I went out of my mind. My father put me into an asylum. It wasn't a really bad place. Apparently he had to pay quite a great deal of money for my care and they were kind to me. When at last I was well, I didn't want to leave; it had become a form of shell, I felt secure. Then my father died and I had to go home. And what did I find? That nothing was mine except the furniture; the house and land was mortgaged. But the sale of the estate wasn't enough to meet the creditors, so some of the furniture had to be sold. But still there was quite a bit left and some good silver and china. So, my dear cousin Delia came forward with the offer of storing it for me. Her house was large and rambling. Like her parents, she hadn't bothered very much about the interior, her main concern was the yard and the horses. So I went to reside with Delia. I had no money, nothing personal except my dolls and my clothes. And over the twenty-five years I have been with her I have been forced, as Cook would say, to earn me keep, because Delia has a very sparse staff. There is a cook and scullery

maid, and one housemaid. I earn my keep, so to speak, by
doing the needlework; I'm very good with my needle. I . . .
I also clean the silver, my silver which Delia now considers
her own, having kept me all these years, as she pointed out.
The furniture, too, she considers part payment for my existence. Are . . . are you beginning to see?''

Nancy Ann could find no words to express her feelings at
this moment. She was so astonished, so bewildered by this
story that she felt from one moment to the next that she
couldn't believe it. Yet, she had only to look at this person
before her to know that every word she was saying was the
truth, and that it was being painfully dragged from her.

''When Dennison came to my father's funeral he said, 'You
must come and stay with me,' so I grabbed at the opportunity. And when I saw the number of servants lazing about the
place, and there were more years ago than recently, I took
the opportunity to make the best of them because I found that
my mental trauma had left me, in some way, physically weak,
and the demands that Delia made on me exhausted me, because as time went on I became little better than a housemaid
. . . I am still little better than a housemaid. I've had a dream
all these years of someone dying and leaving me their empty
house, and I pictured myself bringing vans to the door and
directing my furniture and plate and china into those vans,
because my possessions filled two full vans when I arrived
there, and I would derive pleasure from seeing Delia's house
denuded. But of late that picture has faded, and all I have to
look forward to is my sojourn in those two rooms upstairs
and hot baths, and my family around me. Yes''—she made
two deep obeisances—''my dolls are my family. I love them.
I talk to them. Because of them I am classed as an eccentric,
but that troubles me no more. Now . . . well, you have
stripped off my disguise. There will be one person, however,
pleased about this and that is Delia herself, because when I
take my jaunts, as she calls them, to Dennison's, she loses a
maid, a personal one now because she suffers with her back
and it has to be rubbed. So when I return she will be happy
knowing that my route of escape is now closed. Well, I've
said what it has taken me all day to gather courage to say,
and I might as well finish by adding, I scorned Dennison's

choice when he married you, while at the same time knowing that if he had kept up his association in other quarters my visits would have been cut drastically short long before now.''

She now rose to her feet, drawing on two sharp breaths before she continued, ''You seemed so young, and you appeared typically vicarage bred. But this morning I saw you as no longer young, and I realized that Dennison had seen what I and likely others had been blind to, that you possess strength of character, for which I admire and envy you at the same time. Well now, I will leave you. I'm sorry I've intruded. I'm also sorry I played the high-born lady with you. I've been a stupid woman not being capable of differentiating. I will leave in the morning. Good night.''

Nancy Ann was incapable of speech until the figure reached the door and was about to open it, when she said, ''Wait a moment, please!'' She went hastily towards the older woman and there was no hesitation when she extended her hand and said, ''You're not the only one who has been blind; I too have been quite as blind in my own way. Come and sit down.'' She drew her back to the couch and now, sitting side by side, their hands still clasped, she said, ''I shall be pleased if you will stay for as long as you intended. The only thing is, as I said, I have cut down on the staff. As you have said yourself, it was wasteful. And I would be grateful if you will take your meals with me downstairs.''

She watched the face that looked almost as old as her grandmother's crumple into a mass of small lines. The eyes were lost in puffed flesh, the trembling lips looked colourless, the flesh under the chin hung in a loose round sack. She had never noticed this before, because when she had seen her, the strings of her bonnet, definitely drawn tight, had ended in a bow there. And now she said softly, ''Please, please, don't distress yourself.'' Then, again to her surprise, for the second time in twenty-four hours a head was laid against her breast. But unlike the tears of the boy, this crying had the appearance of a river in spate, for the emotion shook them both, and as she held the bony frame tightly to her and muttered soothing words, a section of her mind was telling her that indeed she was now a woman, being a confidante of both young and old. Yet another section was longing that she herself could lay her head upon another breast and feel strong arms about her, and hear a voice murmur, "My Nancy Ann."

When at last Lady Beatrice's tears were dried and Nancy Ann had led her to the door and along the corridor to her own room and bade her good night and told her to worry no more, that they would talk more on the morrow, she had already made up her mind that on the morrow, too, she would write to her husband and tell him what had transpired during the week he had been away, without, of course, mentioning the boy, and she would indicate between the lines that she would be pleased to see him return.

PART SEVEN

The Pattern of Life

❧ 1 ❧

It was Rebecca's fifth birthday. The sun was shining for the first time in a week. The rain that had been pouring down for days and had flooded fields and roads, had ceased two days ago. The water had drained from the land and only the streams and rivers were running high.

Everything was planned for the afternoon party. Ten children altogether were invited from the families of the Maddisons, the Ridleys, and the Cartwrights, together with their nurses. And, among them, were seven of Pat's grandchildren. The children's parents were to come later to join a dinner party.

A happy feeling of excitement pervaded the house; not an unusual feeling nowadays, for it could be said that the house had been happy for two or more years now. The master rarely journeyed to London since the town house had been sold. But that didn't mean he had given up his gambling, as the household well knew; on two nights a week at least he would go to his club in Newcastle. At other times he visited the O'Tooles without taking his wife there. They were the evenings when the men got together. Only three months ago he had not returned until three o'clock in the morning from one of the "O'Toole sessions," as he called them. And he had woken her, kissed her, then scattered a great handful of sovereigns around her on the bed, saying, "Five per cent of a thousand."

She could not believe that he had won a thousand pounds in an evening, and among friends, and for the first time since their honeymoon he had talked about gambling. Some evenings a thousand was pin money, he had told her; on a Newcastle night some men could lose five or ten thousand.

When she had enquired where any man could have so much money to be able to lose that amount, he had laughed at her and said, "Some of the richest men in the country live in the three counties of Durham, Northumberland and Westmorland, not mentioning Yorkshire. Why! only take the Tyne. Look at the shipyard owned by the Palmers. Look at the glass works. Although they might have changed hands over the years, the Cooksons made a fortune out of them. Then there are the chemical works, the foundries, all owned by local men. And the offshoots from these, it's unbelievable: Candle factories, blacking factories, nails, bolts and screws factories. You think hard of any commodity, and this area produces it. What's more, some of the owners hardly leave the district. They take their wives abroad once a year but can't wait to get back in case someone might be duping them. And yet there are other factories and businesses round about that never see their owners, men who consider this part of the country too dirty to stick their noses in, at least their wives do."

But when she had said, "If there is so much money why don't they distribute more to the workers who are now on strike in the mines?" he had chucked her under the chin and laughed as he replied, "Miners and such are only happy when they are opposing something. They get better wages now than they have ever had in their lives and still they are not satisfied. It is the malaise of the working class, to grab."

She remembered thinking later that night, or early in the morning, when he lay breathing heavily by her side: this was why he had lost the election eighteen months ago; he lacked sympathy for the poorer classes.

Since she was very young she had mixed with the poor of the village. Most were lacking in higher education, but in craftsmanship many of them were artists, like the blacksmith, and Mr. Kell the shoemaker. His shoes lasted people for

years. Her father had always said they were works of art.
Then down in the hamlet there was Mr. and Mrs. Cooper.
He was a marvellous tailor. Huntsmen often went to him to
have the leather in their breeches renewed or to order a new
pair rather than go to the breeches maker in Newcastle. His
wife knitted stockings that you couldn't buy at the hosiers in
any town, for they seemed to last a lifetime.

In a way she had detected a pride in all these people, but
Dennison seemed blind to this side of the workers. Yet, had
he not for years overpaid his staff and allowed them to pam-
per themselves? He was a strange mixture, was her Dennison.
She had ceased trying to understand his deeper motives. And
she had told herself she mustn't worry about them any more,
because the house was at peace. Everyone seemed to be
happy.

Over in the Dower House, her grandmama was more
spritely than she had seen her in years. She had taken to
walking and visiting Graham, which seemed to please him.
She herself had kept out of Graham's way as much as possible. And she would not allow herself to dwell on why she
did so; she would just not allow her mind to ask questions
concerning him.

Then there was Peter. He had married his Eva a year ago
and they now had a little house in Durham outside the school,
and both appeared extremely happy. But their marriage had
caused an irritation, at least to Dennison, for it seemed to
have given Mr. Harry McKeowan the idea he was now connected with The House, was of the family, and, given the
slightest excuse, he made it his business to call, sometimes
accompanied by his wife.

She herself often worried about James. She had had only
four letters from him since he'd gone to Canada. In the last
two he had mentioned he had a companion. He did not say
whether man or woman, but she guessed it was a woman,
and she didn't feel at all shocked.

The letters had all come from Toronto. Apparently he was
teaching in a school there, and from what she could gather it
was in a comparatively poor quarter of the town.

In her replies to him she never told him that she'd had two
visits from his father-in-law Mr. Hobson, demanding to know

his whereabouts. The first time she had lied and said she had not heard from him. The second time she had said she had no intention of telling him where her brother was.

She was never to forget that second visit, because Dennison had been present, and after he had told Mr. Hobson that his visits would not be welcome here again, he had further shocked him, and herself a little too, by saying, "What have you decided to do with your daughter? Put her in a convent, or send her out to stud when necessary?" The man had looked as if he was about to explode, but had then left their presence without further words. And he could hardly have reached the hall door when Dennison threw himself on to the couch, his head back and let out a great bellow of laugh, crying, "I enjoyed that. I bet nobody's ever hit the mark before with that fellow." . . .

She was in the bedroom finishing dressing: she was winding a silk scarf around her hair because they were going out for a walk in the grounds. It was a daily routine when the weather was fine, and whenever Dennison was accompanying them the children were apt to run wild, and he with them, especially with his son for he simply adored the boy. She always enjoyed watching them; but she rarely joined in the romps, she who had loved romping.

This morning, she was feeling a little tired. Yesterday had been a busy day. In answer to an urgent call, Beatrice had returned to her cousin's: apparently Miss Delia Ferguson had taken a bad fall from a horse and hurt her leg; she would be obliged if Beatrice would come home as soon as possible.

Beatrice had pointed out those words to Nancy Ann, saying, "Note, obliged if I would return home. Well, what can I do? But I hate to leave here, and you."

Strangely, it would seem, Nancy Ann had answered, "And I shall hate to see you go, Beatrice. We all shall." But it was really true: Beatrice's visits were welcomed now by the whole household; the children loved her, the staff respected her. This Lady Beatrice was no longer a painted lady who had to be waited on hand and foot, but one who would go into the kitchen and chat with the cook and discuss recipes, one who arranged flowers, one who did exquisite needlework. Even her dolls were accepted and spoken of as people by such a thoughtful person as Jennie: Lady Jane was the tall clouty one, Miss Priscilla was a pretty china-faced one, Sambo was the little black boy, the larger black doll was Mrs. Sambo, and so on.

Jennie had become very fond of Lady Beatrice. And Nancy Ann knew she did special things for her on the side. Jennie, too, had become a different person.

Whether or not Dennison had recognized her, Nancy Ann did not know: he never remarked on her, but then he very rarely saw her; she had learned the art of disappearing when he was about. Jennie's life had changed in more ways than one in the last two years. Happenings had taken place that had not only altered her life, but had freed Nancy Ann from providing for David's schooling. The boy had been in the Newcastle House school only three months when Jennie received a letter from her uncle enclosing a bank note for fifty pounds. The grocery business was apparently doing so well that he and his partner had invested in pieces of land, supposedly a good thing to do out there.

But apart from the money, the main point of the letter was about David. As soon as he had built a decent house, the uncle said, David could go out and join him.

Jennie had shown some concern when telling Nancy Ann of her breaking the good news to David. Apparently he had been emphatic in stating that he didn't want to go to Australia, that he would never go to Australia.

Jennie couldn't understand his attitude, but Nancy Ann, herself, had a glimmering of it. The boy was so full of affection and, because of the circumstances, he had had very little open love from Jennie, although there was no doubt about her feeling for him, and so he sought it from other quarters. His continued visits to the nursery were confined nowadays to the times when he was on holiday and knew that the coast was clear, which meant when the master was out. He was particularly fond of Rebecca, and she adored him and would prattle on about him.

It had been a worry to Nancy Ann at first, and then a bit of a mystery that her daughter didn't mention the boy's name to her father. But this was cleared up when Mary told her that Agnes had explained to Rebecca if she once mentioned

David's name to her father he would stop David coming up to the nursery, because, after all, he belonged to the kitchen quarters. And apparently this had been enough to make even such a young child use discretion. It was all part of a game, Mary said.

Last night, Pat and George had been here for their weekly supper and card session, and their visit had lasted longer than usual, in fact, until nearly one o'clock in the morning. George and Dennison had become involved in the state of the country. George, though retired, still endeavoured to keep up with the times. His views, however, did not coincide with those of Dennison, and some wrangling had taken place.

She recalled there was some heated talk over a man called Alexander MacDonald who was in Parliament and who supported the working classes but who apparently seemed to lean towards the Conservatives for, he had said, they had done more for the working classes in five years than the Liberals had done in fifty.

This was from George. Then Dennison had put in that it was the Liberals who had made parents responsible for their children's attendance at the board schools, and when Pat had laughed at him, saying, "Don't be daft, Denny, working-class parents don't want their broods to waste a full day at school, it'll cut down their earning time," neither of the men had welcomed the interruption.

As Nancy Ann tied the knot of the silk scarf under her chin, she recalled the heated exchanges of the early morning, and she wondered why women were never taken seriously. The height of a woman's intellect, in Dennison's mind she knew, was the playing of an instrument, singing, being good with her needle, a confident hostess, a devoted mother . . . and, of course, a pleasing wife. Well, for herself, she couldn't sing, and her efforts on the piano were mediocre; she questioned herself as being a competent hostess for, try as she might, she found she couldn't appear overjoyed at greeting people she didn't like, and unfortunately Dennison had a number of friends in this category; she could, however, give herself points on being a loving mother, and also congratulate herself on being an entertainer when in the company of those she classed as friends. Yet, these days, Dennison rarely asked her to show off her prowess. As for being a pleasing wife. . . . Her innate modesty forbade her to take this further.

The thin voices of the children carried to her from the hall which meant they must be yelling at the tops of their voices. She went out of the room smiling and when she reached the top of the stairs she looked down on to the two shining faces and demanded in mock sternness, "Who is that who is making all that noise?"

"Come on, Mama, Papa is waiting. We are going down to the river."

When she reached the bottom of the stairs, she held her hands out and both the children tugged at them, William more strongly than Rebecca, although he appeared to be a head shorter.

Rebecca was growing into a beautiful child: her skin was a warm peach tint; her eyes were large and appeared to lie flat on the skin at the top of her cheeks; her mouth was well shaped, but the evenness of her teeth was marred by an overlapping tooth at each side of the upper jaw, both of which became evident when she laughed.

Her brother was not what one would call a pretty child: his face was a compressed replica of his father's; his body was sturdy and seemed unsuited to the petticoats, dress, and short coat in which he was attired. Although he was fourteen months younger than Rebecca his appearance and boisterous vitality made him appear quite as old, if not older than her in many ways.

They were pulling her towards the door when Mary came quickly to her side, saying, "Could I have a word with you, ma'am?"

Such was Mary's tone that Nancy Ann, releasing her hold on the children, tapped them towards the porch door, saying, "Go to Papa. I'll be there in a moment."

She turned, asking now, "What is it, Mary?"

"I thought, I'd better tell you, ma'am, David has arrived."

"But he's only been back at school two weeks. Why?"

"I don't know, ma'am, only Jennie told me just a moment ago. She seemed agitated. She seemed to know the reason but she didn't stop to tell me. I think she wanted to get back to him."

"Well—" Nancy Ann looked perplexed for a moment, then said, "Tell Jennie to . . . to keep him out of the way."

"Oh, she'll do that, ma'am, if possible, but you know he's been stubborn of late."

"Yes, yes, I'm well aware of that, Mary. Anyway, see what you can do." And she turned from Mary and went slowly out through the hall doors and into the porch. But there she stood for a moment. Yes, indeed, the boy had become stubborn of late, in fact he had ceased to be a boy. He was nearing sixteen, but an onlooker could be forgiven for thinking that he was a youth of eighteen. He was of striking appearance, being tall for his age and so very fair. As her own son took after his father, so did the boy take after his father, whose portraits had been banished to the attics years ago. She remembered seeing four of them lined up against a row of boxes. They had definitely been placed there so they could be viewed.

Over the past years the boy had not made evident his feeling for her in any way, but he had openly expressed a deep affection for Rebecca. It was understandable to her that he did not bother so much with William, no doubt seeing him as the son of his father.

There had been glowing reports of the boy's progress from the school, especially in French and Latin. The headmaster's report stated that he took naturally to languages; mathematics was not his strong point, nevertheless, he persevered with this subject and the results were quite good. The report went on to state that there was every possibility of his reaching university entrance standards.

But why had he come today?

"Mama!"

She answered the call and went out. Rebecca was at the bottom of the steps and she pointed to where Dennison, with William by the hand, was running him across the sunken garden. Then she gripped her mother's hand and endeavoured to make her run after them, shouting all the time, "Papa! Papa!"

Her high-trebled voice stopped Dennison and he turned around, laughing, then swung the boy up into his arms and held him above his head, shaking him the while.

Now Rebecca had let loose of Nancy Ann's hands and was climbing to Dennison's side, crying, "Lift me! Papa. Lift me!"

He dropped the boy to the ground; then, putting his hand to his back and stumbling a few steps, he said, "Oh, you're too big and I'm a very old man," at which both the children started to laugh and tugged him forward.

By the time they had left the garden and reached the woodland she was walking by Dennison's side and the children were scampering ahead, chasing each other around the boles of the trees.

Nancy Ann smiled as she watched them, saying, "The weather has kept them in the house so long the air seems to have intoxicated them." Then she shouted, "Be careful! Rebecca. Don't be so rough; you will pull his arms out."

"That'll take some doing. He's as sturdy as a little bull. He'll have a fine figure as he grows." There was pride in Dennison's words and there was pride in his face. Quickly now, he took her arm and pulled her close, saying, "You know, Nancy Ann, I've never been so contented in my life before as I have been of late."

They had reached the edge of the wood, but the river being high, the grassy area sloping to the little bay was mostly under water. The children were running round them both and he cried at them, "Now! now! that's enough. Calm down." And as they sped away, he said to her, "I was about to say, 'Thank you, Mrs. Harpcore, for giving me such a son . . . and a daughter, and making life worth living' . . ."

What happened next Dennison described some long time later as: The devil had heard what he said, had opened the gates of hell and dragged him in, for Rebecca's voice came to them on a high scream, yelling, "William! William! No! Leave it! Leave it!"

They both turned sharply and looked to where the children were. William was standing on a piece of rock that normally formed a seat. The water was lapping over it. He was bending forward as if trying to pick up something, while Rebecca was standing to the side above the rock. They could see a long black piece of wood in the water, one end of it jutting against the rock, and it was this that the child was trying to pull in.

Then a higher scream rent the air as he toppled forward on to the piece of wood, and his impact on it caused it to swing around and into the fast-moving water.

Dennison, leaping down the bank, reached the river's edge and plunged unheeding into the river, his arms outstretched to grab the plank of wood to which his son was now clinging and screaming. Although the river here was running fast the surface was not turbulent and the boy's head and shoulders were well above it with his arms tight round the plank. Twice, Dennison's hand was within grasping distance of the child, but each time the river whirled him away.

The water had been up to Dennison's waist and then up to his chest, when all of a sudden, he himself gave a cry and disappeared for a moment under the fast-running water, to reappear, thrashing wildly. And it was only Nancy Ann's hands gripping his hair that saved him, too, from being swept down the river.

Her reaction to follow him had been as instantaneous as his: that he was unable to swim and she herself could manage only a few strokes had not been considered. Now she was dragging Dennison to the bank, but no sooner had he reached it and had stumbled to his feet than he turned about and, sweeping the wet hair from his face, he peered down the river to see his son now well into the thick of the current, still clinging to the plank.

Now he was running swiftly, with Nancy Ann stumbling behind him and Rebecca behind her still screaming at the top of her voice.

It was at this moment, further down the river, that Jennie was standing arguing with her son. She had just been saying to him, "They are out walking. What are you asking for: trouble? What's the matter with you, boy?" And he had answered sullenly, "It's her birthday. I . . . I wanted to give her something." And to this Jennie had hissed at him, "You must be mad. You would know that he would be here and there would be a party on." And in answer he had thumbed behind him to where some thirty yards away stood the bridge that formed part of the estate's boundary at this end. And he said, "He's not likely to come this far, he never does. And he couldn't get through the wood." Now his thumb jerked at the right of him and up the bank where the woodland looked dense with undergrowth; and he finished, "He wouldn't go through there, would he, and soil his pretty clothes?" The last words were said in disdain. And it was at that moment they both heard the scream which caused them to glance at each other, and when it came again, he muttered, "That's Rebecca."

"She must be playing a chasing game likely."

When the scream came once more he said, "That's no chasing scream."

They both hurried to the water's edge and looked towards the slight bend of the river. Almost immediately they saw the figures racing along the bank, all yelling, and then their eyes were directed to the middle of the river.

"Oh, my God!" Jennie exclaimed. "It's . . . it's the child. It's the child." She now glanced backwards towards the bridge, crying, "He'll be swept through there, it's free."

She looked at her son. He seemed frozen. Then she watched him tear off his elastic-sided boots, then his short coat and muffler, and his mouth opened into a gape as he dashed from her and plunged into the river. Her eyes never left him as he swam strongly against the now turbulent water. The cries on the bank had ceased, even Rebecca's screams, for their attention was on the strongly swimming boy, who himself was being swept down stream but not as fast as the oncoming plank of wood. They had all reached Jennie's side now and like a combined body they seemed to hold their breath as they watched David's arm come out of the water to grab the end of the plank. Then there was a concerted gasp of dismay as the wood, being caught in the turbulence caused by the water converging towards the arch of the wooden bridge which was half blocked by a square structure, swung round, but on a high hysterical note Rebecca's shrill tones voiced their relief as she cried, "He's got him? David's got him."

Now they were all again running towards the bridge, and it must have entered David's mind, as it did that of Nancy Ann and Dennison, that he mustn't allow himself to be swept through the archway, for, beyond, the river widened considerably and ran for a good way between steep wooded banks.

David's face was near that of the child's. Its eyes were

closed, and when he gripped the top of its coat, meaning to drag it from the plank, the child slipped easily from it as if it had not been gripping the plank, merely lying over it.

Now David was striking out with one arm, and with his other was aiming to hold the child's head above the water. He could see they were within yards of the archway, the water had turned into deep churning frothy waves. He saw the structure ahead. It was some kind of a coop; he could just make out the wire netting, and because of its height and the rise of the river it had become caught in the arch of the bridge.

It was looming over him now, like a house. He gasped and spluttered as the water entered his gullet, and he and the child would have been swept round the structure and through the archway, but with one great effort he brought his arm over his head and his fingers clutched the wire netting, but even as they did so the force of the water swept his body towards the gap. If he could have used his other arm he could have clawed his way quite easily to safety, but within its grasp he held the child.

His face now was pressed against the netting, but when he felt the hands on him he forced his head back and looked into the eyes of his mother. She too was clinging to the wire netting, and with her free hand she was aiming to pull him and his burden backwards, but without success.

Then another face appeared close to his. For a second he stared into its eyes; then the weight of the child was suddenly taken from his grip. His arm was stiff, but he lifted it and dug his fingers into the wire netting. Then, as one body, they were all moving slowly backwards. He could now feel the ground beneath his feet, but the water was still swirling strongly round him.

He didn't remember reaching the bank, for quite suddenly he felt sick and everything went black. When he came to, he was on his face and spewing out water. And when he turned his head to the side he saw that the child, too, was lying on its face and its father was pressing its back while his wife was holding its head up from the ground.

His mother was kneeling by him. She looked strange: her hair was hanging down her shoulders in flat strips and there were some bits of twigs sticking out of the side of it. In a cracked voice, she asked, "You . . . you all right?"

He didn't answer but pulled himself upwards to hear the man bawling, "Fetch a doctor!" and the voice of one of the three men standing near him answering, "Yes, sir. Yes, sir," before turning on his heel and running to do the bidding.

"Lift him up and bend him over." Nancy Ann's voice was just a whisper, but Dennison obeyed it. He lifted the limp figure of his son and bent him forward from the waist, but when no water came from his mouth and the head and shoulders just drooped forward, he almost thrust him on to the ground again, face downwards, and began to pound his back.

After a few minutes, when the child showed no signs of reviving, Nancy Ann's voice, still small, said, "Hot water. Get him into a bath of hot water." She now turned her face up to one of the men: "Tell them in the kitchen to get ready a bath of hot water," she said.

The man scampered away, and Dennison raised his head and looked at Nancy Ann who was shivering, and he went to say something but, swiftly changing his mind and bouncing to his feet, he bent again and picked up the child in his arms. And now he was running with Nancy Ann by his side, her hand on the small dangling legs sticking out from the wet dress.

The third gardener too was running; only Jennie and David walked, he supporting his mother now, for she was in a paroxysm of coughing.

The party was met in the middle of the wood by most of the male staff from the yard, but they said nothing, they just followed the master and mistress through the gardens to the kitchens.

The bemused kitchen staff, obeying orders, had a tin bath before the fire, and Florrie Kilpatrick was in the process of scooping hot water from the boiler to the side of the fireplace into it while Mary Carter added scoop for scoop of cold water from a bucket.

There were some rough towels lying to the side of the bath and Dennison laid the boy on these. And Mary, her face twisted with anxiety, thrust Nancy Ann unceremoniously aside, tore off the child's clothes, then lifted him into the bath. But it was Dennison's hands that rubbed him while the steam rose, not only from the bath, but from his and Nancy Ann's drenched bodies.

Mary was now supporting the lolling head and her own head was deeply bowed over the child's as she watched her master's hands massaging the child's heart, but to no avail.

Time passed. Once Dennison cried for more hot water, and some time passed again before, of a sudden, he sat back on his heels and, his teeth clenched and his lips wide apart, he made a sound like the distant cry of an animal in pain. It was echoed by a moan that ran through all those present in the kitchen.

Mary lifted the child from the water and laid it on a towel and gently folded the ends over it. Then she turned to where Nancy Ann, who was still on her knees, looked as if she was going to topple sideways. She helped her upwards. Dennison too rose, but with the child in his arms now. And those in the room parted and made way for him as, with his son hugged to him and head bowed over him, he stumbled from the room, with Mary supporting Nancy Ann following him . . .

Outside the kitchen door a crowd had gathered: the yard men, the workers from the farm, the four gardeners, and the lodge people. Standing on the outskirts of them was David. He had changed from his wet long trousers into a pair of breeches, and he was now also wearing a striped shirt. He looked no different from the rest of the men, but that he was different was made apparent when one of them said quietly, "It's like a curse. His brother, and now his son, both in the same river. Both male heirs. Like a curse on him."

When David turned slowly away and walked from the yard, the men's eyes followed him and the man who had been speaking ended, "Aye, like a curse."

It was at this moment that the doctor rode into the yard. But he had come too late. It had even been too late when the child's father had grabbed him from the boy who was his nephew, legal or not.

* * *

The child was laid out on Dennison's bed in the dressing-room, and for nine hours after he sat beside him, without eating or drinking or saying a word.

To Nancy Ann, during this time, the loss of her child was becoming unbearable. And her own inward screams of protest were almost audibly added to those of Rebecca who had become quite hysterical, so much so, that the doctor had to be called again to put her to sleep with a dose of laudanum. But as the hours of the day wore into night, her concern for her daughter and her sorrow for her dead son was diverted to an anxiety over Dennison, an anxiety which at one stage became threaded with resentment and anger. And she wanted to cry at him, "I have lost a son too. Put your arms around me. Comfort me. I can't bear this." But she found no response in him. . . .

At what time of the night she fell asleep on the couch in the bedroom, she didn't know, but when she woke and went to straighten herself, her whole body was cramped because of the way she had slumped into the end of the couch.

She stumbled into the dressing-room, but to her surprise she found that Dennison was no longer there. She looked at the clock. It was quarter to six. She stood for a time staring down on her son who looked peacefully asleep, and as she cupped his face with her hands she asked herself why her body wasn't being rent asunder with tears. But there seemed to be nothing in her but a great lonely void, a dry lonely void, no sap of life anywhere in it.

On the landing she met Jennie, and for the first time she thought of the boy and she put her hand out to her, but found herself unable to express any words of gratitude for what David had done.

Slowly she went down the stairs and into the library. Dennison wasn't there; nor did she find him in any other part of the house downstairs. But meeting Robertson, she asked, "Have you seen the master?" and he answered, "Not since he went out first thing, ma'am, just on light. I . . . I think he took his horse."

When she returned upstairs she knelt by her bed and drooped her head on to it. But she did not pray, she couldn't. He hadn't shared his despair, not by seeking comfort from her or comforting her, nor had he spoken one word to her or touched her hand. It was as if, in some strange way, he was holding her responsible for their son's death.

And Dennison did not speak to anyone during the following three days. There was a constant coming and going in the house but he would see no one, not even Pat and George. Pat consoled Nancy Ann by saying, "It is understandable. He has lost his only son, and he was quite crazy about the child. Yes, it is understandable. But don't worry, this phase will pass. You will be all he wants or needs during this time."

She did not enlighten Pat that her husband didn't seem to need her as she needed him; that, in fact, he needed no one.

When Rebecca had run to him, crying, "Papa! Papa!" he had thrust her aside, turned his back on her and walked away, leaving the child to have another of her screaming fits. It was strange, but the only person who seemed to have any control over these was the boy. He did not cosset her or pet her, but, to her amazement, she witnessed his tactics of harshness. And she was for preventing him when he shook her daughter by the shoulders, saying, "No more of that now, or else I walk out of here and you won't see me again, ever. And I mean it this time." At this her daughter's screams had subsided to sobs and sniffles and she had laid her head against the boy's shoulder as the boy had once laid his head against hers. It was strange, strange. But she was thankful that at least someone could quieten her daughter's spasms of hysteria.

Peter came, and, of course, Eva came with him. That was another strange thing: Peter never visited without his wife. He seemed to need her by him all the time. And, in a way, she envied their relationship. Eva, she had to admit, was a nice person and seemed to have grown younger since her marriage. This must be what happiness did for one. Yes, she envied her.

Her grandmama came and took charge of the house. She seemed to be able to rise to any occasion. Lady Beatrice arrived only a few hours before the funeral, having come as soon as she heard the tragic news. Then there were those who left their cards of sympathy; and of these, those who came in were received by Jessica or Beatrice. Graham had come on the day of the disaster, but had not been since.

The funeral was to take place at eleven o'clock on this Friday morning. She was already dressed in deep black. She was sitting looking out of the window, her coat, hat, and long veil laid out on the couch ready for her to don. She stared into the distance, not thinking so much about the burial of her son at this moment as of the effect his death had had on her husband. At times she felt he must have lost his mind, for he had not spoken half a dozen words to her since the tragedy. In fact, he had avoided her. And if his manner continued like this she dreaded to look into the future. She wanted to cry, how she wanted to cry, but it seemed as if a wall of sand had built up between her heart and her eyes.

When she heard the dressing-room door open she turned her head. Dennison walked slowly up the room towards her. He did not look at her as he drew a chair up at the other side of the window, but just as she had been doing only a moment before so he now looked out into the grey day. She waited for him to speak, stilling her tongue and forbidding her hand to go out towards him. His neglect of her over the past few days had created in her a feeling of humiliation and deep hurt to add to the grief of her loss.

He was still looking out of the window when he said, "Try to understand the reason for what I am about to say."

She waited, while he still kept his gaze concentrated on the window. But when his voice came low, the words that it spoke chilled her with foreboding, for he said, "I . . . I have made arrangements to go away for a time." What he said next was blotted out by the scream in her head almost as loud as any made by her daughter over the past few days, and through it she was yelling, You can't! You won't! You can't be so callous. Oh no. No. What am I to do? I can suffer your silence, but not your absence. Don't do this to me, please.

She had lost some of his words, but when she heard him say, "The Fergusons have been kind enough to invite me," her mind yelled again: The Fergusons, at the lodge in Scotland. He sold it to the Fergusons. He's never been there since. He . . . he must have been in correspondence with them right

. . . right from the . . . She could not even let her thoughts go on and say, The day my darling boy died.

"This house," he was saying now, "and everything around will . . . will drive me mad. You . . . you can't understand. I see him everywhere, running . . . running, jumping, always running and jumping."

He had said, "You can't understand." He was now looking at her: his grey eyes appeared colourless, his skin seemed as if it had been drawn tight over the bones of his face and looked like dull parchment. She could see that he was suffering, but so was she. Oh, so was she. She heard her voice, sounding to her own ears like that of a little girl, saying, "Don't leave me. Please, please, Denny, don't go. Not right away. Later perhaps, we . . . we could all go."

When he shook his head vigorously and got to his feet, she stared up at him, then watched him walk from her half-way down the room before he stopped, saying, "Try to understand, Nancy Ann. I'm on the verge of despair. I'm at breaking point. Don't you understand I have lost my son, my only son? I will never have another."

When she heard the scream she couldn't believe it was from her own throat, and the words just spewed out of her as she cried, "What you seem to forget is that he was my son too. I bore him and, as I understand, at peril of my own life. You are so made you imagine that you are the only one that's suffering. There is your daughter upstairs, the shock could affect her for the rest of her life. *Your* son. *Your* son. Always *your* son. He was *my* son too. And there were days, yes, even weeks when you never saw him; you were too busy at your gaming table and other pursuits." And she closed her mouth on the last words: the thought that always strove to the surface of her mind concerning his London visits and which she would not give place to was aired now.

He had turned and was looking at her, but he did not say, "What are you suggesting?" he said, "Please lower your voice; the household will hear you."

"Does that matter? They all know that you have hardly spoken to me; and that when you haven't been sitting in vigil, you have slept alone. These are things that do not escape the household which you seem so anxious should not hear me raise my voice in protest at your treatment, and this treatment from one who is supposed to love me. 'I shall love you till the day I die,' you once said; no, not once, but many times.''

She watched him draw in a deep breath: his waistcoat expanded, his cravat was pressed out; then they slowly sank back into place and, as if on a sigh, he said, "I do love you, Nancy Ann. But that is from another part of me. It is no use trying to explain the conflict of emotions that is tearing me at the moment. I only know that I must get away from these surroundings.''

"And me?''

He bowed his head, shaking it slowly now. "Try to understand, Nancy Ann, try to understand the turmoil I am in. You, most of all, are connected with what I have lost. At the moment, I haven't the power or the words to explain, or even to sort out my feelings.'' He now looked at her fully for the first time, saying, "Talk to your grandmama. She's a wise woman. She will no doubt help you to understand my motive. Anyway—'' He looked downwards now, pulled out from his waistcoat pocket a gold watch that was attached to a gold chain lying across his chest, then, his voice a mere mutter, he ended, "The time is almost on us. I . . . will see you downstairs.'' And with that he turned from her, and she clasped her hands, one on top of the other, tightly over her mouth. She had been unable to take in the tragedy of the loss of her child for days. It still wasn't believable. But this scene just enacted was certainly unbelievable. This man, who had been so full of love for her five days ago, this man who the night previous to the awful day had knelt in this very room, his arms about her, his head buried in her breast, and in between repeating and repeating her name had told her she was the most beautiful thing that had ever happened to him in his life, and that she was now more desirable than on the day he first married her, this was the same man who was leaving her to bear her loss alone. The loss that should have brought them even closer together had opened a great chasm between them, and she was falling into it, down, down down. . . . Oh my God, no. She said it as a prayer, joined her hands, looked upwards now and appealed, Help me through this day.

* * *

Mary watched the cortège from the nursery window. The black-plumed prancing horses, the black carriages, the black-clothed people were all smudged together because her face was aflood with tears. He had been her baby too. She had been the first to handle him, to wash him. And although, during these last two years since she had been made house-keeper, she hadn't spent as much time up here, nevertheless, she considered this her domain rather than the housekeeper's comfortable apartments.

The cry of, ''I want my mama,'' turned her head to where Agnes was cradling Rebecca in her arms, and Agnes said, ''It's starting again. She's trembling like a leaf. Has he gone . . . David, this mornin'?''

''I don't know; Jennie's still in bed. She was feverish last night. That river nearly did for her an' all. Anyway, I'll go and see if he's still around and bring him up.'' Then turning from the window, she said, ''Oh dear God. Dear God. What a day! And how she's going to survive this, an' the master the way he is, I don't know.'' . . .

It was ten minutes later when she returned, the boy with her. He was dressed in a navy-blue suit. The tight trousers came down to the well-polished boots. His coat was double-breasted. It had no revers, but the starched white linen collar he wore stood up stiffly beyond the rim of the jacket, almost giving the appearance of a parson's insignia. Although he appeared older than his years, he still looked a schoolboy, except when he spoke; then his voice sounded that of a man.

He walked straight across the nursery to Agnes who was holding Rebecca's shuddering body to her. The tears were running down the child's face and she was gabbling. Gently, David put his hands on her shoulders and pulled the dazed child on to her feet, then dropping on to his hunkers before her, he said, ''What's this?''

She went to lean against him, her sobs shaking her body, but almost roughly now, he gripped her shoulders and held her up straight, saying, ''Now, no more of that! Do you hear? No more of that! because if there's another whimper out of you, I'm off. Do you hear? And for good this time mind, and I mean it.''

The child blinked her eyes. Her head was bobbing, her body shaking, and she muttered, "Davey. Davey. I want my mama. I want William."

"Now we've been through all this, haven't we?" His voice was quiet and steady, and he was about to go on when Agnes, her own voice trembling now with weariness and agitation, said, "I've told her till I'm tired, Master William's gone to heaven; she won't see him again. I've told her till I'm blue in the face."

"Shut up!"

"How dare . . . ! Who are you to . . . ?"

Mary had moved forward now saying harshly, "That's enough of that kind of talk." And the boy twisted round and looked up at her, saying, "Then tell her to talk sense."

"David, you've gone too far this time. You've . . ."

"I haven't gone far enough."

He turned now from the two astonished faces and, looking at the small girl again and his voice changing, he said, "You remember Snuff . . . you know, the puppy?"

When she nodded tearfully, he said, "Well, you know what happened to Snuff? Prince didn't mean to kick him, Snuff ran under his feet. And what happened to Snuff?"

The small lips trembled, the eyelids blinked, the voice whimpered, "He died."

"Yes, he died. And what did we do? Where did we put him?"

"In . . . in a box, on . . . on a blanket."

"Yes, in a box on a blanket, to keep him nice and warm. And we buried him, didn't we, in a nice grassy part in the wood, didn't we?"

"Yes, yes, in a nice grassy part, yes."

"Well now, when William died and they put him in a box. . . ."

"Get up out of that!" Mary's hand was on his shoulder, and he swung round and glared at her, saying, "Leave me alone, I'm telling you. Leave me alone." And the look in his eye caused her to step back from him.

He turned his attention to the child again, saying, "As I said, William died and they put him in a box and he's nice and warm, and when you stop crying and having tantrums we'll go and see him, like we used to do with Snuff, you remember?''

"Yes, yes, Davey, but . . . but when will he go to heaven?"

He stopped for a moment and glanced, first to the right of him, then to the left where the two faces were glaring down on him. Then looking at Rebecca again, he said, "Well now, that depends upon you. When you stop crying and stop having tantrums, because he'll never get to heaven if you keep crying; your crying upsets everybody, you know, your mama"—he didn't add papa—"your great-grandmama, and . . . oh . . . oh, everybody." He shook his head slowly, then went on. "Now, if you promise me you'll stop crying and be a good girl, I'll come back next weekend and I'll take you to see William's lying nice and warm, all covered with flowers. Now, is that a promise?"

She sniffed and sniffed and at each sniff Agnes bent over her and wiped her nose; then the child muttered, "Promise."

"And you'll be a good girl?"

"Yes, Davey. You . . . you won't go away though, will you? You won't go?"

"I'll not go very far. Look, put up your hand." She put up her hand. "And the other one." She put up the other one. "Now, count me seven on your fingers." She counted seven on her fingers. He took the first finger of her left hand and wagged it, saying, "I'll be back on that day. Now, you count all those days until I come back. All right? No more screaming."

She shuddered and paused, then said, "No more screaming."

"And you'll be a good girl?"

"I'll be a good girl."

"Well, on that promise you deserve a shuggy. Come on in and get on Neddy." He straightened himself, then pulled her upwards and walked with her into the day nursery. And there, lifting her on to the rocking-horse, he rocked her backwards and forwards.

After a time he sat her on a low chair before an equally low table, put some paper and coloured pencils in her hand, and said, "I'm going now, but mind, I want to see all the numbers up to twenty and all the letters of the alphabet down there when I come back.''

"But . . . but I can only write up to 'F,' Davey."

"Yes, I know you can. But I want to see that you've written all the other ones down, and that means that you've got to work hard.''

He bent down now, his face on a level with hers and looked into her eyes. They were deep dark brown. Her hair was a shining brown with red lights in it. Her skin was like flowing milk. He touched her cheek with his finger as he said softly, "Be a good girl for me." Then of a sudden, her arms came up and went round his neck, and she was clinging to him. But she did not cry or make any sound, and he held her pressed to him for a moment, before pushing her gently back into the chair.

Mary and Agnes were standing at the door. When he passed between them they turned and also walked back to the middle of the room, and there, swinging round, he addressed himself to Agnes, saying, "Drop all this stuff about William being in heaven." But before Agnes could retort Mary put in, "Now you look here, young man, I think you've gone far enough in this quarter of the house. Who do you think you are, anyway?''

It was a silly question to ask and she knew it immediately. And when he came back, saying those same words, "That's a silly question to ask, isn't it?" she spluttered, "You're . . . you're getting above yourself.''

"No, not above myself, Mary, not yet anyway. But I'll still say to Agnes," and now he nodded to the younger woman, "stop pumping the heaven stuff into her. Just think. It's so stupid anyway. Ask yourself a simple question. How can everybody get up there? Do you know what air consists of?" He shook his head. "No, you don't. It's a fairy tale, this heaven business. Anyway, I've got some news for you . . . I'm rich.''

"What?"

"You heard what I said, Mary, I'm rich."

The two sisters exchanged glances, then Mary fixed her gaze on the face before her, which was already a handsome face and topped by the mass of fair hair. It could have been representative of the haloed angel in the stained glass window of the village church. The eyes, though, certainly weren't those of any angel, except perhaps when he was talking to the child. But generally they gave off a cold hard stare that had been nurtured on a bed of bitterness, animosity, and shame, the shame that lay deep in all born such as he. She said quietly, ''What d'you mean by rich?''

''*Rich . . . rich.* You've no doubt heard, haven't you, of the uncle who created a place for my mother in this household, by blackmail as far as I can understand? Well, we'd been hearing a lot from him of late, and his idea was for me to go out to Australia, where he was doing well, he and another man. But now he's dead, and the other man, an honest man apparently, has sent us his fortune, together with the deeds of three pieces of land.''

The sisters turned and looked at each other in amazement, and it was Agnes who said, ''You're not just making this up?''

He almost barked at her, saying, ''I never make things up. I'm what you would call a realist, if you know what that means, a realist; I see things as they are. I've been made to, haven't I? right from along there.'' He thrust his hand out towards the door indicating the attics and the space under the roof, and he repeated, ''Yes, right from along there. I don't imagine things. I never had the chance. My only mirror was the polish that I put on boots. *Boots, boots, boots,* leggings, shoes, gaiters and boots . . . *boots . . . his boots.*''

They both looked at him almost with fear in their eyes. This was no boy, this was a man, and there was something familiar about him. He stood before them, tall, exceedingly fair, yet dark. His words made him appear dark, and menacing.

Mary, aiming to bring things down to a normal natural level, wagged her head as she said, ''So you are rich, but what d'you mean by rich? Fifty pounds? A hundred?''

''Thousands.'' His voice was quiet. ''Five thousand four hundred pounds. There was much more but the solicitor here and a solicitor over there took their share. But that is what is in the bank, five thousand four hundred pounds.''

Mary was disbelieving. ''Out of a grocery shop? A share

in a grocery shop, five thousand four hundred, or more?"
She curled her lip.

"No, not completely out of a grocery shop. Your calcula-
tion is good, Mary. Apparently the thing to do out there is to
buy or lease land. He had done that, five pieces of it, and
just before he died he sold two, and the others could turn out
to be valuable. Mr. Barrow, his partner, has told me that if
I wish I can sell the land to him, or keep it, or come out
there and take up where my uncle left off."

There was silence in the room. They stared at each other:
a triangle, triumph at one vertex, amazement and disbelief at
the other two. Yet, no sooner had he turned away and walked
out than the disbelief vanished as they looked at each other.
And it was Agnes who said, "God Almighty! What'll happen
now? What'll he do?"

"God knows, him being who he is."

"D'you know something, Mary?"

"What, Agnes?"

Agnes swallowed deeply, moistened her lips, then said,
"Who d'you think he . . . well, he appeared like, standing
there talkin', even him being the colour he is? Who d'you
think?"

"Well, yes, you're right. I thought that an' all. He might
have the colour of his father, but his father's brother's in him
right up to the look in his eyes. It was as if it was the master
himself talking." They nodded at each other.

"Eeh! What's going to happen next in this house? Eeh! this
house." Agnes shook her head, and Mary answered, "God
alone knows."

❧ 2 ❧

THE CLOSE FRIENDS AND SYMPATHIZERS HAD ALL LEFT. FOR
Nancy Ann it had been a day like an eternity. She was in the
evening of it, but she knew it would never end, because there
could be no finality to the emotions that were tearing her into
shreds. She saw them spreading down the years all radiating
from their centre, a deep burning place just below her ribs:
the sand wall that had prevented her crying had spread and
formed a desert. She was aware in a half-ashamed fashion
that the overriding emotion in that centre did not emanate
from sorrow for her dead son. It was there. Oh yes, it was
there. And it was the foundation for the other emotions, for
it had bred them. Yet, emanating from the core was the most
frightening emotion, an emotion that was new to her and
terrifying in its intensity, for, apart from everything else, her
Christian religion had forbidden hate. She had disliked, and
strongly, but hated never. Although she'd had no previous
acquaintance with it, she certainly recognized it when it
flashed into her being an hour ago as her husband stood before her, dressed for his journey, saying, ''I shall write to
you.'' She hadn't heard herself asking how long he intended
to be away, for there was a great whirling in her head; yet,
she heard his answer: ''A few weeks. I . . . I may stay for
the shoot.''

Nor did she hear herself say, ''What will people say, leaving me like this?'' because she imagined the question had been only in her mind and she hadn't voiced it. But he had answered it. ''Our friends understand,'' he had said: ''Pat and George and the others will visit you regularly. I have spoken to them. Try to understand my feelings, dear.'' And he had bent towards her but she had shrunk from him as he placed his lips on her cheek. And a dreadful thought sprang into her mind, but she throttled it before it escaped her lips, for it would have said, ''Have you made arrangements to meet up with your past mistress?'' For she had the picture of the woman making her way towards him in the churchyard, where he stood apart with two gentlemen and George. She saw her take his hand and he nod his head as she spoke. Then they were joined by Larry Freeman. They shook hands, and she had noticed that Dennison put his other hand out and clasped that of his one-time friend. Then the Myers woman had patted the lapel of Dennison's coat before she turned from him to be accompanied by the man Freeman to her carriage.

It was as Dennison walked away from her that the hate consumed her. And if, in that terrifying moment, it had become tangible it would have felled him to the ground. And when the door closed on him she had felt the desire to scream as her daughter had screamed.

Then, as if a hand had been laid gently on her shoulder and turned her about, she found herself walking to the couch on which she sat slowly down, and her mind became filled with the presence of her father, and, as if he were sitting by her side, she said, ''You were right. Oh, you were right. You could always read inside a man. You used to say that gambling was bred of greed, and licentiousness of selfishness, and that selfish people dug their own graves, and when they lay in them no one mourned their loss and no sincere tear softened the clay.''

Yet, she asked herself, how she could have loved someone these past six years without coming to know his selfishness? It was true she could recollect countless incidents that should have pointed to his self-centredness, but, loving him as she did, she had accepted them as part of his strong character. Anyway, weren't we all selfish in different ways?

But this, this desertion, this thrusting her aside at the moment when she needed him most. . . . Never again in her life would she know such suffering; her whole being and spirit were devastated. She was in such trauma it was almost too much to bear; it was as if she had lost not only her son but her husband, too, in one fell blow.

She did not witness his departure, but when her grandmama came and, putting her arms around her, said, "He won't stay away long, my dear. He is in torture at the moment, try to understand. Yet I know how you feel," then she knew he had gone.

Dry-eyed and white faced she looked at Jessica and asked, "Would my father have left my mother? Would your husband have left you at such a time?"

And after a moment's silence, Jessica's answer was, "All men are different; it's how they are brought up, the environment: some expect little from life and are glad to pay for that little; it all depends on where the Lord placed you when you were born."

Beatrice, in a way, was more understanding, for she had flounced into the room and, nodding first at Jessica and then at Nancy Ann, she had cried in a high-pitched voice, "I wouldn't have believed it of him. Callousness, that's what it is, callousness. All men are callous. I'm . . . I'm sorry for you, Nancy Ann. I am. I am. Now I'm going to bed before I say any more, I'm going to bed. Good night, Jessica. Good night, Nancy Ann." . . .

The house was quiet. Rebecca was asleep in the nursery, her grandmama and Lady Beatrice were in their rooms. The household, too, was quiet; except for Robertson and Mary, the staff had retired.

Mary had just left the room. She had tried to persuade her to eat, but eating was something, she felt, that she would never want to do again. She couldn't force the food down her gullet—liquid yes, but no solid food. Mary had sat by her and held her hand and, supposedly to divert her thoughts, she had told her the strange news about David and Jennie and the money coming from Australia. But Nancy Ann had made no comment on it, merely nodded her head to signify that she had heard. But as Mary was about to leave, carrying the tray, she had said to her, "Go to bed, Mary." And Mary had turned and said, "Not until I see you there, ma'am," then she had gone out.

As she sat, her gaze fixed mostly on her hands lying in her lap, she kept telling herself, I must go upstairs; I cannot keep her waiting. Yet she didn't move. She didn't want to go upstairs. She didn't want to lie in the bed alone, yet she didn't long for his presence; she felt she would never long for his presence again, either in bed or out of it.

She lay back and stared into the flames and in them she saw her son. He was waiting at the top of the nursery stairs, hanging over the gate that had been placed there for his safety since the day he had tumbled half-way down them. His arms were about her neck and he was crying, "Mama. Mama. Good morning, Mama. Good morning, Mama." She could see Rebecca, too, in the background, but just as a shadow. Her son was to the fore, his face close to hers demanding, "Going for ride. Papa taking us for ride." Then, "Come play with Neddy. Watch me gallop."

She watched him gallop high up on the rocking-horse, high up among the flames of the fire. Suddenly she closed her eyes to shut out the sight because the picture in the flames had changed from the nursery to the cemetery.

She opened her eyes when there was a tap on the door and Robertson entered, saying, "Mr. Mercer, ma'am. He asks if it is too late for you to see him?"

"No, no. Show him in."

Graham came slowly up the room towards her. She had not stood up to meet him; Graham was Graham and there was no need for ceremony. She had seen little of him this past week. In fact, not since . . . that day. Dennison and he had nothing in common and so he had never been a regular visitor.

He sat down on the couch at an arm's length from her, and he looked at her, and she at him, and neither of them spoke for a full minute. Then he said, "Forgive me for intruding at this late hour, and . . . and I didn't really expect to see you, I thought you might have retired." He did not add that it was only ten minutes ago that he heard from one of his men that his counterpart had driven her husband to the station to begin his journey to Scotland, and that he couldn't believe it. But he said, "I . . . I won't stay; I just wanted you . . . well, to know how deeply I feel for you at this moment."

She had laid her head against the back of the couch. Her face was turned towards him; her mind was saying, He would never have left you at a time like this; he would have put his arms around you and comforted you and said, "We'll have another son. Don't worry, my love, we'll have another son." Those were more or less the words she had spoken to her husband: "I . . . I could give you another son," but he had wiped the idea away with one violent movement of his hand as he cried at her, "You couldn't, unless I was prepared to sacrifice your life for him. You know as well as I do what happened the last time. The next would be fatal. Don't talk such rubbish. I've had one son. I'll never have another." And with his next words he had then seemed to disown both her and his daughter: "You had your daughter. I had my son," he said. "Now I have lost him I have nothing. I cannot expect you to understand; only a man knows what it is to lose a son, a legitimate son, the essence of his very being."

A strange thing was happening somewhere inside, in that big knot below her ribs. It was disintegrating. She had the most odd feeling that pieces of herself were flying off in all directions, and as they left their base, they melted. And their melting caused a flood of emotion to rise inside her. It pushed out her ribs, it widened her throat. Then, such was its eagerness to spurt from her mouth, that it blocked its own outlet, and she gasped and moaned: she was choking. Then an agonised cry escaped her, and with it all her melted emotions swept through every duct they could find: her eyes, her nose, her mouth, even her ears seemed to be an outlet. She was drowning in her emotions, yet she was being held firmly and a voice was repeating, "There, there, my dear. That's it, cry, cry. There, there, my love. Don't worry. Don't worry. That's it, cry. Oh, yes, cry."

She clung to the voice. She pressed it close to her, yet she could not stop her crying. And now she began to wail. She wailed for the loss of her son. She wailed for the loss of her husband. She wailed for her father whose words she had not heeded. She wailed for her mother who, she knew now, and had known for some time, had pressed her against her own instincts into security, the security that had led her to this agony. Her wailing reached the hall and brought Mary and Robertson into the drawing-room to stand, mute for a moment, to see their mistress being held in the arms of Mr. Mercer, while clinging tightly to him.

Graham turned his head in the direction of the servants and cried at them one word, "Bromide!"

"Bromide," Mary repeated; then turning, she flew from the room and up the stairs and to the medicine cupboard. And from the top shelf she took a bottle of laudanum, then ran downstairs again. Mr. Mercer was still holding her mistress, and she was still clinging to him.

It took all Robertson's and Mary's efforts to disengage her hold on Graham. And when at last she was lying slumped in the corner of the couch and still crying, still wailing, Graham, turning to Robertson, said, "I think you had better fetch the doctor. . . ."

It was almost an hour and a half later when the doctor came into the house. He had been away on another call and his never even temper was at its lowest point. "What now? What now?" he said, as he entered the room. He was well aware of the tragedy that had come upon this family, but in his line of work there was very rarely a day passed he didn't come face to face with tragedy. Yet when he looked upon the mother of the child that had been buried this day, his innate kindness and professionalism overcame his irritability, and, sitting down beside Nancy Ann, he took her hand and while patting it said, "Now, now, my dear. Now, now. Come along, we must stop this crying, or it will only make you ill. And you know, you have a daughter to see to. By the way—" He turned his head upwards and looked to where Graham was standing, and through a puzzled frown he asked him, "Where's he, the husband?" And Graham answered bitterly, "He's gone on a shooting trip, I understand."

The two men exchanged glances for a moment and then the doctor said bluntly, "Then all I can say is, I hope his gun backfires," and rising to his feet, he addressed a shocked Mary and an equally shocked Robertson with a command: "Well now, let's get her upstairs to bed. She'll need to be

carried. You, Mr. Mercer, will kindly, I'm sure, give a helping hand.''

"I'll manage her myself,'' Graham said. "It will be easier.'' And bending, he put one arm under her knees and the
other under her armpits, and with Mary supporting her head,
he carried the woman he loved, the girl he had loved and
whom he had lost because he was too considerate to plead
his cause.

Consideration, he had learnt, was a vice, not a virtue. Yet,
if her husband had been considerate he himself would not
now have been holding his beloved in his arms for the one
and only time.

⚡ 3 ⚡

WHEN DOES THE FALL OF ANY HOUSE BEGIN? NOT NECESsarily when the rot is discovered, for then it can be too late: the timbers may have been attacked, eaten away with worm; the bricks beginning to crumble; the foundations starting to sink into bog, with walls taking on crazy angles. The whole place becomes so rotten that nothing can save it.

That is the deterioration of a house.

But what if it's the owner who has disintegrated? Where did the rot start in him? With the loss of his son? Or, before that, the loss of his brother? Or, going back further still did it begin with the fantasy created in him by his father that he was someone special? That God had seen fit to place him in a position of wealth which spelt power? That he was bred specifically to be a member of that society that believes itself privileged because privilege had been the right of its ancestors, right back to the time when they were thieves and vagabonds, traitors and sycophants, their loyalty given only where it would show good return?

Coming down the line from that, could the descendant then be blamed for his traits? Not if he was a good loser; not if he was the kind of real sporting fellow who would bet on a fly crawling up a window. Not if he was Dennison Moorland Harpcore, and not if the said Dennison Moorland Harpcore had still a well from which to draw. There was no disgrace in owing money to a bank, but there was deep disgrace in being unable to settle your gambling debts, and the disgrace at the moment was weighing heavily not only on Dennison Harpcore, but also on his whole household.

Many things had happened in the years since the day of the child's funeral.

Dennison's stay in Scotland had lasted five weeks. And following on from the day of his return Nancy Ann had known that another phase of life had begun. He had remained at home for four days, during which time he showed no desire to see his daughter. On one occasion when Rebecca, seeing him, had flown to him and grabbed his hand, he had patted her on the head; and when the child cried, "Oh, Papa, I'm glad you are home," he had pressed her aside, saying, "Be a good girl now," and left her standing mute with tears in her eyes. To Nancy Ann herself, his manner was coolly polite. When he had asked after her health she had answered, "I have been rather unwell." And he had replied, "That's to be understood"; then had added, "We have both been rather unwell, and are likely to be for some time."

During his short stay he did not seek her bed, for which she was thankful; nor did he sleep in the dressing-room, but had ordered his things to be moved to a guest suite. This action had created deep humiliation in her: although she did not desire any bodily contact with him, the fact that he was moving himself from the proximity of her emphasized in some tortured way that he was blaming her for the loss of their son. And yet, she asked herself again and again, how could that be? If it hadn't been for her timely rescue of himself, he, too, might have been drowned.

How near she was to the reason for his behaviour she wasn't to know till some years later.

Looking back on that year, Nancy Ann saw it as a nightmare in which she had become a young girl again, telling herself she couldn't go on, that she wasn't able to cope with these changed circumstances and begging her grandmama to let her take Rebecca and stay with her, and then being upset by Jessica's blunt refusal: the emphasis on it being that she was a wife and mother, that life was full of ups and downs.

A tragedy had been experienced. This would pass; time was the healer.

But time did not prove to be the healer. When Dennison was at home he spent most of his time in the library. What he read she did not know; she wondered if he was once again aiming for a place in Parliament, even though his first attempt had ended in an ignominious defeat. Such was the wall he had put up between them that she could not have penetrated it even if she had so wished. She rarely saw him after he left the dinner table, at which his efforts at conversation would almost drive her to yell at him, ''Your small talk is not fooling the servants. They know the position. They know everything. Why bother? You are only fooling yourself.'' But she never raised her voice; she would answer him politely. However, she made a point of never opening the conversation or asking a question.

Pat had said, ''Patience. I know Denny; this phase will pass.'' She said that in the first year. She didn't say it so often in the second. And there were times now when she called that she never mentioned his name.

It was towards the end of the second year that a number of things happened. Jennie died. David, at seventeen, left school and went to Australia, from where she had since received four letters. He was working hard and he was making money; life was rough and men from all over the world were flooding the country. In his first letter to her he had spoken of Mr. Barrow, that he had been greatly surprised on meeting him, expecting a very old man, but he was only middle-aged. . . . He seemed to get on well with this Mr. Barrow, as his uncle had evidently done, too. The fourth letter she had received some months ago, and in it he had spoken of coming back for a holiday. He had not said coming home.

It was during the third year that she had to ask Dennison to meet the tradesmen's bills, for some were pressing. It was after that he sold the hunters that were kept at the farm and, seemingly in consequence, his drinking became heavier.

Then at one period last year he had come to her somewhat shamefacedly and asked her if she had any loose cash as he had run out and he wanted to get up to London to see his banker. She had given him all that was in her cash box, nine pounds ten shillings. That time he had been in London a week and when he returned he seemed greatly agitated. It was then he asked her if she would loan him one or two pieces of her jewellery, and she had replied, "They are yours."

As she did not often wear jewellery and had no great fancy for it, it was all kept in the safe which was situated behind a picture in the library. On that occasion he showed her the pieces he was taking, a diamond and ruby studded tiara, three rings, and two brooches. At that moment she had been sorry for him, for he had stood with his head bowed, muttering, "You shall have them back. I promise you, you'll have them back." She wanted to cry, "I don't want them, it's you I want back," only a second later, to ask herself: Did she? Did she want this man back? This man who had killed all love within her, for nothing could wipe out his neglect which, over the past years, had amounted to cruelty.

Now had come the spring of 'ninety-two, and she felt strongly that an end to her present existence was looming near. Things could not go on as they had been. He was having to sell the farm and five hundred acres of land. Last week she had forced herself to confront him and say that some of the tradesmen had stopped delivering. At the same time she had reminded him that next month the staff wages were due. But it was during this evening that a happening would take place which would lead to final severance.

He had been in the library for some hours. He didn't go there to work anymore, but to drink.

She was crossing the hall on her way to say good night to Rebecca when she saw Robertson coming from the direction of the servants' quarters. He was carrying a tray on which was a decanter, and just as she put her foot on the bottom stair, he stopped and said, "Ma'am, may I have a word with you?"

"Yes, Robertson, of course."

The man looked down at the decanter as he said, "I'm sorry, ma'am, but I have decanted the last bottle of whisky. I . . . I put the order in some weeks ago but they haven't as yet sent it."

She swallowed deeply and gripped the bottom of the bannister tightly before saying, "What about the wine and the older stock?"

"There are only half a dozen bottles of wine left, ma'am."

"But the vintage?"

The man was still looking down at the decanter, and it was a moment or so before he said, "The master has been taking them with him to . . . to town, ma'am."

She turned her gaze from him and looked up the stairs. The humiliations. To what depths had her husband sunk when he had to sell, or bribe, with the contents of the cellar. She very rarely went down into the wine cellar, but she remembered it as she had first seen it, stacked from floor to ceiling, rows and rows of bottles, one particular section with the cobwebs of years on them. Dennison had proudly pointed out to her that some of these bottles had been laid down in his father's youth. Swiftly now she turned about and, putting out her hand, she said, "I will take the tray."

The man held on to the salver, looking her in the face now and saying, "Are you sure, ma'am?"

"Yes, yes, Robertson, I'm sure."

At this he relinquished his hold and watched her walk across the hall, her gait wavering as if she too had been drinking.

Without knocking at the library door she went straight in. He was sitting to the side of the fire in a deep chair, his legs sprawled out. On a small table to his side was another decanter and glass. He had not turned his head, and when she reached his side he said, "Put it there." It was only when she said, her voice grim, "This, so I have been informed, is the last of your cellar," that he lumbered round in his seat and blinked at her, then said, "That's nonsense, nonsense. Get out! Go to bed!"

"I shall not go to bed." She walked round to the front of the chair and faced him, and there, her face tight, her hands clenched at her waist, she cried at him, "You are a disgrace to your house, your name, me, everything."

He thrust himself back in the chair and peered at her. His whole face was bloated, his skin blotched; his neck was thick and his paunch bulged. There was very little left of the man he had been five years ago, and the picture he presented caused her lip to curl as she said, "You are disgusting."

Her words acted on him like an injection, for so quickly did he pull himself up from the chair that she jumped back in some fright. And now he was yelling at the top of his voice, "Disgusting, am I? Disgusting. And who's to blame for that? Eh? Have you asked yourself who's to blame for that? Disgusting, you say. I would have believed it if you had said I was a fool, yes, a fool, to have ever married you. Do you know that? I haven't had a day's luck since I married you. They told me it was a mistake. But would I listen? No. No. Parson's Prig they nicknamed you, and by God they were right, for you've brought the vicarage with you. And from the day you entered the door of this house—" He now took his hand and wiped the saliva from his mouth before spluttering, "My luck went down. I could lose before, but I could win twice as much, and things might have levelled out. Aye. Aye, they might have. But you had to go and strip Rene, and I, like the bloody fool I was, threw her off. But she's got her own back. By God! she has. Because, you know what, my little lady? 'Tis her man that has stripped me, with the assistance of my dear friend Larry. Oh, yes. Oh, yes. Funny that, funny." He paused, as if thinking now, before he went on, muttering, "Bloody underhand game somewhere. Can't put a finger on it. All honourable. Huh! All honourable play. Skillful, not cheating. Oh, no, not cheating, just skillful. But it's cheating." His voice had suddenly risen to a scream, and now he was pointing at her. "They are bloody well cheating me. Do you hear? They've cheated me out of everything, and all through you. If I'd only had the sense to make it up in town everything would have been all right. But I was thinking of you, you, my little prig, and told myself, whoever warmed my bed it mustn't be her . . . thinking of you. I must have been mad. And she went mad. Aye, aye, she did, in a different way." He had turned and flung his hand out towards the decanter, and he stared at it for a moment before looking back at her again, and, his voice lower now and each word coming as if sieved through his teeth, he growled, "And you humiliated me. I could have saved my son, but you had to put your pious little hands out and stop me."

When her face stretched in amazement he nodded at her, then went on, "I couldn't swim, but a dog thrown in the water will paddle, and I just needed one more arm's stretch and I would have had him. But no, my wife had to humiliate me, save me from drowning. God! How I hated you that day. You look amazed, and so right you are to look amazed. You will say, I could never have saved him, but in my heart I know I could. I am strong. It only needed another split second and I could have conquered that bloody river. But no. . . ."

"You shan't, you shan't put the blame on me. You . . . you sank, you went under. You were thrashing like a mad dog. You could never have saved him. You just told yourself that to ease your conscience, because since your brother drowned in the river you have been afraid of it. Yes, you have."

As his hand came up to strike her she sprang back and watched his doubled fist hover in the air. Then he screamed at her, "Get out of my sight before I do you an injury."

And she had got out of his sight, stumbling, as if she herself was drunk.

Robertson and Mary met her in the hall. They had made no pretence they were there by accident, and Mary had helped her up the stairs to her room. And there she had given way and cried in Mary's arms, and asked of the woman who had become her friend, "What's to be done? Where's it going to end?" And Mary had said, "God knows, ma'am, but it must have an end soon. You can't go on like this. You'll kill yourself."

Two further incidents took place before the end actually came. The first occurred on a pleasant evening when she had taken Rebecca for a walk. She no longer walked by the river bank; the paths from the garden were overgrown. The usually daily walk was to the Dower House to visit Jessica or, if the day was bright and dry and she wanted to exercise, she would walk to the village. But she hadn't taken that road for some time now, because she could not face the tradesmen to whom money was owing. So, if they went out of the main gates, she would walk along the coach road in the opposite direction. And this is what she was doing this evening.

She was holding Rebecca's hand and her daughter startled her by saying, "You know something, Mama?"

363

"No," she had answered. "What is the something that I should know?"

"I was just going to say, wouldn't it be lovely if we could live with Great-Grandmama."

She had remained silent for a moment; then she had said, "Yes, my dear, it would be lovely if we could live with her."

She did not treat her daughter as a child: Rebecca at ten might still look a child of ten, a beautiful child, but her mind and disposition seemed at times almost adult.

The day her brother had drowned had changed her too. She'd had intermittent screaming fits for a year afterwards, but when they stopped, so stopped her childish games. She had in a way become a sedate little girl. She had stopped running to her father when she saw him. She had not laughed much, except with David, and when he had gone to Australia, she had cried for days afterwards.

Her daughter was saying now, "It is always bright there, Mama. Great-Grandmama is always cheery."

"Yes, yes, she is, my dear, she is always cheery. She's a wonderful woman."

"You know what she said to me yesterday?"

"No; what did she say?"

"She said that when I was sixteen I would be married and live happy ever after."

Nancy Ann came to a dead stop and looked down on her daughter. She could not believe that her grandmama had said that, but she must have, for her daughter didn't lie, nor was she given to making up fairy tales.

"Grandmama said that to you?"

"Yes, yes, she did."

"What a strange thing to say."

"Not really, Mama, because I had been asking her about Great-Grandpapa, and if she had a happy life, and was that why she was happy now?"

"Oh. Oh, I see." They were walking on again when she saw, coming round the curve of the road, a carriage approaching. As the vehicle came nearer she could see there were two people seated in it. Then, to her consternation she recognized one of them, the fat face under the high hat, the voluptuous body. She also recognized instantly that the woman had espied her, for she was now leaning over the side of the carriage, her mouth wide open, one hand waving.

When the carriage came abreast of Nancy Ann, the woman cried at her, "You know nothing yet. There's more to come. I promised you. By God! I promised you."

The carriage passed on but the fat body twisted round and was still hanging over the side, her words loud but unintelligible now.

Nancy Ann was shaking from head to foot. There was a high grass bank behind her, and she leant against it. The last time she had looked on that woman's face she had been aware of the beauty of the skin and that it hadn't been painted. But the face that had just thrown hate at her was like a mask, with deep pink cheeks, red lips, and darkened eyes. And there was proof that she was on the same escape route as Dennison for she was drunk.

"What is it, Mama? Who is that lady? Are you all right, Mama?"

Nancy Ann pulled herself up from the bank and stepped onto the road again and, looking down into her daughter's concerned face, she said, "It's all right. Let us go home."

"But the lady, who is she?"

"Oh, she is a person who lives some distance away and she . . . she is ill."

"Ill?" The girl frowned. "Like Nelly Sand in the village?"

"No, no, not that kind of ill. She . . . she is just unwell. Come. Come, my dear." And she began to hurry now back towards the house, each step seeming to beat out the woman's words: There is more to come. . . .

The second happening brought surprise and pleasure . . . at first. She was in her office going over yet again the accounts and the bills. She was worrying about not only the staff's wages and how they were to be met, but also the fact that she would have to dismiss some of them, either the first or second housemaid, either the vegetable maid or the scullery maid, and, too, one of the laundresses. They were already down to one seamstress. When two had left to go to America with their parents she had not replaced them. There were now only two gardeners, and three of the men from the farm had been dismissed since the horses had gone. She was telling herself that when he returned from town and whether he was drunk or sober, she would insist that he find some means of paying the staff when her thoughts were interrupted by the excited voice of her daughter, crying, "Mama! Mama!" and before the office door had opened she was on her feet and moving towards it.

"What is it? What is it?" She held Rebecca by her shoulders and looked into the beaming face.

"It's . . . it's David. He's come by cab. I . . . I saw him from the window. Come. Come." She was pulling her mother forward; but there was really no need, for Nancy Ann too was hurrying.

At the open door she looked on to the drive where a man was handing boxes and packages to Robertson, who, laden down but smiling, carried them up the steps. She watched the cabby raise his hat to his passenger, and then there he was, striding towards them, a tall handsome man, no vestige of the youth or boy left.

She put her hand firmly on Rebecca's shoulder to stop her running forward, and under her breath she said, "Wait. Wait."

Then he was standing in front of them, looking from one to the other, and her being was filled with a mixture of emotions that was impossible to sort out, at least at the moment. And she could restrain Rebecca no longer, for her daughter now had her arms tight about his waist and was looking up at him, saying over and over again, "Oh, Davey, Davey. Oh, Davey, Davey."

"Well, let me in. Am I permitted?" Even his voice had changed. It was deep, so pleasant-sounding, and he had said, "Let me in." It was the first time he had entered this house by the front door. He had made no attempt to go round the back. Evidently he had told the cabby to stop on the drive. Thank God Dennison was away. Did David know he was away? How could he? He had just arrived. Or had he?

She motioned with her hand towards the door, asking the question now, "When did you arrive?"

"Oh"—he was walking into the hall now, his arm around Rebecca's shoulders—"six days ago. No . . . no, a week."

"A week?" she repeated questioningly. And he turned fully

366

and looked at her, saying, "Yes, a week. I've been doing business in Newcastle. But yesterday I booked into an hotel in Durham, and . . . and here I am." He turned from her and looked round the hall, his head back. But when Robertson's voice came, saying, "Can I take your coat, Dav . . . Mr. David?"

The two men exchanged glances for a moment. Then smiling, David said, "Yes, Henry, you can take my coat."

The fact that Robertson had addressed him as if he were the young master of the house was not lost on Nancy Ann. And again she thought, Thank God Dennison is not here, for she realized she was being confronted by someone who would not be confined to the kitchen quarters ever again. But where should she receive him? In the drawing-room of course.

As she attempted to speak casually, saying, "Well, come along in, and let me hear all your news," he turned from her and, going to where the parcels and boxes stood on the floor, he picked up two of the largest and, handing them to Robertson, said, "Pass them around, will you, please? There's a number inside; they've all got names on. Are all the old ones still here?"

The man hesitated, glanced at Nancy Ann, then said, "One or two have left."

"Oh well, you'll have to raffle those. And these two"—he pointed down to two small packages—"these are for Mary and Agnes. Where are they?"

It was Rebecca who answered, saying, "It's Mary's time off. I think she has gone to the village. Agnes is upstairs. Shall I take them up?"

"Yes, you can. But first of all, this one's for you. Take that too. Can you manage it? Or perhaps Henry here will take it up for you. Open it upstairs, then let me see how they look."

She went to take the parcel but, first, reaching up, she threw her arms around his neck and, pulling his head down to her, she kissed him; then, grabbing the long box, she ran from him. Robertson followed her, and he followed Nancy Ann into the drawing-room.

Inside the room he put his hand behind him to close the door, then stood in that position for a full minute while he looked round the room. She was already standing at the fireplace when he moved slowly towards her, saying, "This is the first time I've seen this room. Splendid, isn't it?"

"It's a nice room. Sit down." She pointed to a seat, an armchair, while she sat down at the end of the couch. And when he stared at her without speaking, she said, "If you've been back a week, why didn't you call in before?"

"As I said, I had business to do and, you may as well know, I have been here before, at least as far as the lodge. But—" His face lost its pleasant look and now he said stiffly, "Your lord and master was at home and I was determined that this time I wasn't going to crawl in through the kitchen."

"Oh, David."

"Why do you say, 'Oh David' like that? Do you wish me always to keep to the kitchen quarters? In London I have a suite of rooms. In Newcastle I have a suite of rooms. In Durham I have booked into something similar. But here I have to crawl through the back door. No more. No more." He looked hard at her for a moment then said, "I'm a comparatively rich man—do you know that?—and hope to be richer."

"I'm glad for you."

"Are you?"

"Yes, of course."

"Knowing how things stand with him and that he's on the verge of bankruptcy, you can honestly say the tables have turned, and you're glad for . . . ?"

"Who said he was on the verge of bankruptcy?"

"Who said? It's a well-known fact. If you don't know it, you must be the last person not to."

When she bowed her head, he went on, "I can't say I'm sorry, except that I wish you weren't involved in it, that it wasn't going to have repercussions on you. But his state of affairs is like salve on the sores that he inflicted on me. Can you understand that?"

Yes, she could understand it. But she couldn't tell him so; she had to defend Dennison in some small way, so she said, "You can't blame him entirely for what happened to you. It was your father's doing in the first place."

"By all accounts my father would have been willing to marry Jennie, my mother. That was something, too, that was painful to discover. I knew from the beginning that I was different because I hadn't a mother and father like other people. I was tied up in the corner of that roof; I wasn't allowed out; I mustn't go in the yard when the master was about; the master mustn't set eyes on me or on Jennie. And who was Jennie? Jennie was the woman who slept with me. Jennie was the woman who cried herself to sleep night after night and who took me in her arms and hugged me to give herself comfort. But where were my mother and father? I got the answer to this when I was seven. One of the maids told me. For a long time after that I didn't like Jennie. She was my mother and she hadn't told me that she was my mother. But even then it hadn't dawned on me that we were kept in that state because he ordained it. And you tell me he wasn't to blame.''

She bowed her head now, saying softly, "I'm sorry. I . . . I blame myself. I should have done more.''

"No, no.'' He put his hand out towards her. "Anyway, you saved my life. Before we had a penny you sent me to school. I don't know what would have happened to me if you hadn't taken that brave step, because at that stage I was ready to do something desperate, even setting fire to this house.'' He poked his head towards her now and smiled, a wide smile, showing a mouthful of even white teeth. "Yes, yes''—he nodded at her—"I had considered it. And I was situated in the best place to do it, wasn't I? Up in the roof among all that junk and debris of years. But it would have been such a pity if I had, because I wouldn't be sitting here now.''

When he paused and kept his eyes fixed on her, she said, "How long do you intend to stay?''

"Oh, a week or so, perhaps a month. I must get back because things are moving so fast out there they could run away with me. And to think that I am where I am this day because my uncle was persuaded to buy three pieces of land, arid stretches of nothing. Fools' land, they called it. Some of the sages laughed and said it would only show profit when the rains came, and, as everyone knew, water was rarer than gold, and still is in that part of the world. Oh, if a man could dig a well and find water, he'd be a millionaire overnight. Then shortly after my uncle died, in eighteen eighty-seven and eighty-eight gold was discovered. Oh, not in one of his patches, but not so far away. And from then the fever started. And now they're rushing in like lemmings, but not to death, to life. It's sad to think though that where one man will strike it rich a hundred might go on digging until their beards grow down to their pants.''

"Has gold been found on your land?"

"A little, on a bit I sold, but they expect more. Of course until recently, a man didn't actually buy the land, he leased it. But it's the same thing, because when the ore runs out it's not worth the ownership.''

"What do they call the place again?"

"Kalgoorlie. It's situated in the western part.''

"What is it like to live there? Have you nice houses?"

He laughed at this. "Not what you would call nice." He stretched the word. "But they'll come. You wouldn't think much of it as a town if you were to see it: beer halls, dance halls, Chinese washhouses. But civilization is definitely making an inroad. We have our preachers . . . oh, of all denominations, and they're going to build a big hospital there which will take care of the whole district, a certain religious order called Saint John of God. Oh''—he made a face now—''we will soon be civilized. Our only real need is water, but that'll come. Nothing can deter an Australian once he has set his mind on it. I've learned that much. They're rough, tough, coarse individuals, but get on the right side of them and you couldn't wish for better men; get on the wrong side of them, though, and God help you. But then, you look around and you ask who are the real Australians, for there's Irish, Scots, Germans, Swedes, French, Chinese. Oh yes, Chinese. And, of course, our breed, and among our lot you'll find the most experienced tricksters and swindlers.''

When he stopped talking he continued to stare at her, and after a while she said, "You seem to enjoy the life.''

"I do. Yes, I do. It's free; there's no restriction. That's the best part of it for me." The bitterness had come back into his voice, and he asked again, "Can you understand that? Being able to walk where I like, and now do as I like. Money is power. Before I had any I recognized that truth and determined, in some way, to get it. Through writing, I thought. And I still might: I'm half-way through a book on my particular small section of that vast country. Who knows but that someday it, too, may bring me fortune, and perhaps fame?''

She looked away from him towards the fire. She didn't know if she liked this new David, this cocksure man. Yet, he wasn't new: the facets of his character showing now had been there years ago, and were but replicas of his despised uncle, but with strength attached to them and an honesty that likely had been part of his own father's character, a young man who would have gladly married beneath him for love.

She was startled when he jumped up from the chair, saying, ''What's the matter with me! Your present is still in the hall.''

She watched him stride down the room, pull open the door and disappear for a moment; then he was walking back towards her, an oblong parcel in his hand. And bending over her, he placed it on her knees, saying, ''I hope you like it.''

Slowly, she undid the wrapping to disclose a fancy striped-coloured box done up with ribbon. When she undid this and lifted the lid she stared down at the brilliant rose and blue patterned garment lying there. When she took it out she had to raise her arms well up in front of her, but even then the bottom of it fell in folds on the carpet. But now she stood up and held the garment to the side.

''Well, do you like it?''

''It's . . . it's beautiful. I . . . I've never seen anything like it. Is it a dressing-gown?''

''No, it is what is called a kimono, a Japanese kimono. All the work on it is hand-done. I bought the silk and an old Chinese woman did the work. It took her many months.''

The garment had a high collar, and now her fingers touched what looked at first like a buckle attached to it. Then she saw it was a brooch, and she turned her gaze on him and said, ''This . . . this is a brooch?''

''Yes, it is a brooch.''

She unpinned it, then let the garment drop across one arm while she examined the brooch where it lay in the palm of her hand.

It was of an intricate design in filigree bands of gold, and on them were two ruby-studded hearts. ''Oh! David.'' She looked up at him. ''I couldn't accept. . . .''

"Don't"—he jerked his head to the side—"don't for goodness sake be coy, not you. The question is, do you like it?"

Her lips trembled; she felt her teeth chattering against each other. She had to steady her whole body before she could say, "Yes, yes, of course I like it. Who wouldn't?"

"Well then, that's done."

She had to sit down. As she sank on to the couch she knew he was about to take a seat beside her. But she was saved from whatever this might lead to when the door burst open and Rebecca stood there poised.

The girl was wearing a white fur hat and a matching necklet and muff. Then, on a gurgling laugh, she flew up the room and once more flung her arms about David, crying, "Oh, they're beautiful! Beautiful, David. Thank you so much. You are kind. Oh, I am glad to see you back. You'll stay? You're going to stay? Oh, Mama"—she turned her head towards Nancy Ann—"do make him stay."

"Rebecca, now, now, behave yourself and let David alone for a moment. Where is Mary?"

Rebecca now swung round and pirouetted with her hands held out before her and tucked into her muff, and she almost sang, "She's in the kitchen. They're all in the kitchen, and everybody is very excited. It's like Christmas, only better." She turned again to David and was once more about to embrace him when Nancy Ann said sternly, "Now, now, no more; let David sit down. And behave yourself. You're not a little girl any more. And she's acting like one, isn't she, David?"

He said nothing to this but he put out his hand and gently touched Rebecca's cheek. The gesture caused her to remain still while she stared at him. And then, he said softly, "She's going to be a beautiful woman like her mother."

"Will I? Will I be beautiful like Mama?"

"Yes, yes, you will." The question had been quiet and the answer was equally quiet. Then they both looked at Nancy Ann folding up the kimono and seemingly unaware of what they had been saying. But her voice, too, was quiet as she said, "Go and ask Mary to bring us tea, will you, dear?"

"Yes, yes, Mama."

"But first of all, go upstairs and put those beautiful furs away. You don't want to soil them, do you?"

"No, Mama." Sedately now the girl walked from the room.

Left alone, there was silence between them, except for the rustling of the tissue paper that she placed over the garment before putting the striped lid on the box again. She had pinned the brooch back on to the neck of the garment and, after a while, she raised her head and looked towards him. But he wasn't looking at her now; his gaze was directed towards the fire. And it stayed so for an embarrassingly long time, for neither of them spoke until, his voice hardly audible now, he said, "You know what I'd like to do?"

"No, David, I've . . . I've no idea."

"Well, I'd like to take you into Newcastle to a theatre. I'd like to sit beside you in a box and see you laugh at the antics of those on the stage. Then after that, I'd like to take you to supper in a discreet restaurant. There we'd have a table to ourselves and we'd drink wine and have a good meal. And then—" His voice stopped.

Her lips were trembling again, her teeth chattering and, like the percussions given off from a drum, the vibration was passing through her whole body and a voice was saying to her, Oh, no, no, don't be ridiculous, when he turned and looked at her and said, "But I can't, can I? Because you are married, and because I'm David, the garret creature, as Staith once called me."

She looked down at her joined hands as she said, "I'm sorry you should feel like that, and I'm sorry it was necessary for you to keep to the kitchen quarters, but . . . but then you lived in the cottage for . . ."

"For how long? And that came too late. My home, as you know, wasn't even the garret, it was a corner under the roof. You know, when I think of it now I want to lash out, break something." He looked around, before adding quietly but bitterly, "But most of all I want to break him."

"Please, please." She went to rise, then changed her mind. "Please don't say things like that. He . . . he allowed you and your mother to stay and, knowing him as I do, that was a big concession. It may not appear so to you."

"Oh, don't talk to me like that, my dear." He had called her "my dear," not ma'am anymore. "He was forced into that by my uncle. Although just a common working man, he was an intelligent one, and if my mother had been thrown out he would have blazoned it in the main papers of the day. And you say your husband allowed us to stay. But how did he allow it? It was all right, I understand, if I could be strapped in the basket, but once I began to toddle around and cry, that was another thing. I was put on a lead. Did you know that? Like an animal. A circle was cleared on the floor and, like an ox, I could walk or crawl round it. And should I cry, then I was administered drops of laudanum. I look back now and think it was very strange that I should, at the age of three, have learned not to cry, because even then, something in me rebelled at my mind being dulled. And at an early age, too, I learned cunning. I could undo the buckle and straps and wander round the attics. It was in one of them that I first saw the picture of my father. But I only saw him as a man with golden hair, while mine was streaked with tea."

He paused here, and his look and voice altering, he said, "During one of the days I escaped I made my way down to the river and I sat on a stone and a dog came and sat beside me; then a fairy came out of the wood looking for it. That day is as clear in my mind as this moment."

Her eyelids were blinking. She was near to tears, but she told herself she must not allow them to flow, because once she allowed the water gate to open, God knows what would happen, especially with this man sitting there looking at her the way Graham looked at her, and as Dennison once had. She forced herself to smile and say lightly, "I never thought of myself as a fairy, and I'm sure my parents didn't. I know I was a source of worry to my mother because I was such a tomboy. I had two good tutors." Her voice trailed away and they were left staring at each other. And she was searching in her mind for something to say to break the deadlock and alter that look in his eyes when the door burst open and Mary stood there, and in a hoarse whisper she said, "The master . . . the master's just come into the yard."

Then she was gone again, banging the door behind her.

They were both on their feet and she was gasping now,

"Oh, David, David, please, please come out this way, and go to the . . . and go to . . . I mean, please. . . ."

"Why should I? We've got to meet sometime."

"David—" She was standing in front of him, her hands joined tightly together, imploring him now, "He . . . he's a sick man. He . . . he's half demented with worry. And, please, I beg of you."

When he still didn't move, she put her hands out and gripped the lapels of his coat and, her voice a mere hissing whisper now, she said, "If you love me, do what I ask. Please go." There was a pause while their gaze held fast; then she had hold of his hand, drawing him up the room and through the far door which led into the dining-room. Still holding his hand, she pulled him across it and through another door and into a passage, and there was the green-baized door that led to the kitchen quarters.

She grabbed the handle to open the door, but he stopped her, saying gently, "I know the way, my dear," and taking her hand, he lifted it to his mouth and pressed the palm against his lips. Then quite slowly, he opened the door, went through, and closed it after him.

Now she leant her back against it and, lifting her eyes to the ceiling, once again she asked of something beyond it how it was possible to love two men at the same time, and she wasn't including Dennison in her thoughts now.

❧ 4 ❧

SHE HAD WARNED REBECCA NOT TO MENTION DAVID'S VISIT
to her father, even knowing the while that this would be unlikely for Dennison rarely held any conversation with his
daughter even when he was sober, and feeling, too, that her
daughter had grown a little afraid of this distant man. Nevertheless, she warned her; however, she never expected that it
would be Dennison himself who would mention David's name
and through white fury.

It was more than three weeks since David arrived in England and he hadn't paid another visit to the house. Rebecca
was constantly asking after him and only yesterday she'd had
to reprimand her strongly and remind her that David was a
man who had his own life to live and was no longer a member
of the household. And her daughter had silenced her for a
moment when she said tearfully, "I like David, Mama. I love
him. And . . . and anyway, he's my cousin."

"Who . . . who told you that?"

"He did. And anyway, Mary explained it a long time ago.
His father was drowned in the river like William. His father
was my uncle, so he is my cousin, and . . . and I've always
known that Jennie was his mother."

The next question she could have asked her daughter was:
Did you know that Jennie wasn't married to your uncle and
so, therefore, legally he is no relation to you? He is what you

call illegitimate. Oh, that word, that beastly stigma. She had always thought it was unfair that a signature on a paper could scar so many lives. There were two children she remembered at the village school with her who bore the stigma and at times were taunted by others.

She wished from the bottom of her heart that David would return to Australia and without calling on them again.

She had noticed for days there was a strong atmosphere in the house: it was as if the staff knew something that she didn't know. She questioned Mary, saying, "Is anything afoot, Mary?" And Mary looked at her full in the face and said, "Not that I know of, yet I feel the same as you, ma'am. But I can't put my finger on anything. I feel that Robertson knows something, but what, he doesn't say, although I've quizzed him."

For the past week Dennison had been at home and he had been sober, but this was of necessity because there were only a few bottles of light wine left in the cellar. Yesterday he had come knocking on her bedroom door, and she had been surprised it was he who entered after she had called, "Come in."

"I must talk to you, Nancy Ann," he had said; and he seemed very much his old self. "Sit down." He had pointed to a chair near the window, and she had sat down. But he had remained standing, looking out over the balcony, and she could only see part of his profile. He had begun by saying, "I don't have to tell you things are in a bad way. You know I'm selling the farm and five hundred acres?"

She made no reply, and after a moment he went on, "Well, it went through today, but it's not going to make all that difference; the bank has swallowed up the lot. And I . . . I had better tell you that unless I can raise twenty thousand within the next few days, they'll . . . they'll foreclose." He swung round now and looked down on her and, his teeth grinding against each other, he said, "Did you hear what I said? They'll foreclose. More than that, they'll confiscate everything, every stick in the house. Do you understand?"

"Yes, I understand," she had said. "And now, I'll ask you a question, Dennison. Who are you blaming for this misfortune?"

She noticed his stomach and his chest swell before he ground out, "All right, all right. I've been mad, foolish, but I haven't been played straight with; there's been some dirty business. Myers is at the bottom of it. Yes, yes, my one-time mistress's husband. She said she would get even, and by God! she has, with the help of my one-time friend. I tell you, I've been cheated, drugged and cheated."

"Drugged?" Her face was screwed up and she repeated, "Drugged?"

"Yes, my dear, drugged. These things happen. Your drink is doped; you gamble stupidly, wildly, sure that you are going to make a fortune. It happened more than once. I should have known, twigged something, but I wouldn't believe it. I wouldn't have risked five thousand at a time, even ten thousand once, if I had been in my ordinary senses. Oh yes, you can look shocked, but these things happen. And now . . . oh my God!" He turned from her and put his hands to his head, grinding out the words, "I won't be able to stand it. I can't."

She looked at him, pity filling her as she watched him turn from the window and drop onto a chair and, resting his elbows on his knees, hold his head in his hands and say, "When the end comes, as it's bound to, you'll go and stay with your grandmama. She'll be pleased to have you, as will your friend Graham. He'll see you never starve."

She was on her feet, crying now in indignation, "How dare you!" And to this he raised a weary face, saying, "Oh, don't be silly, woman. I know how the man feels about you, even before we married. He was just too late stepping in, that's all. Had he had the courage to ask for you, your father would have welcomed him with open arms, whereas he loathed me from the day we first met. I represented the devil to him. Perhaps he was right." His voice sank on a weary note. "Anyway"—he now rose to his feet—"I've told you how things stand." And as he turned towards the door, she said quietly, "Dennison. I'm . . . I'm sorry. Believe me, I'm . . . I'm heart sorry. May I ask if you've sought help from any of your friends?"

He turned fully towards her now, his expression one of utter weariness as he said, "Yes, my dear, I've applied to my friends. Those who would have helped me, such as Pat and

George, are just managing to keep their own heads above water. Those of my so-called friends whose heads are well above the water have suddenly decided to take early holidays abroad.''

He now went to the door, but stopped there and looked down towards his hand gripping the knob and, quietly, he said, ''I'm sorry for my treatment of you over the past few years.''

''Dennison.''

He turned towards her.

''What . . . what will you do?''

''I don't know. I haven't got that far. I don't know how I'm going to take this, I really don't.''

''Dennison.'' She ran to him now and gripped his hand. ''There is one person who would help you. Go to Graham. He would . . . he would help you, I know he would.''

He looked at her sadly for a moment before he said, ''He has already offered a sum of ten thousand pounds. I thanked him, but refused, because it would just be like throwing money down a well, and, apart from taking advantage of a man whom I have never called friend, whom I've never even liked, I would have no hope of repaying him. The twenty thousand the bank needs is just the beginning. What would we live on? I have no money to pay the staff, nor the mountain of bills. I'll say this, Graham Mercer is a good man; I wish I'd had the sense to make friends with such as he years ago.''

She took her hand from his and watched him open the door and go out. She watched him walk along the landing on to the balcony. She saw him pause and look first one way then the other, before going down the stairs. She then went back into the bedroom and, sitting down on the couch, she buried her face in her hands, and, racked now with pity, she cried for him.

The farm had been sold through an agent. Dennison hadn't met the buyer, a man from abroad, by the name of Mather. Apparently he didn't want to farm the land, he wanted only the house but had been quite willing to take the five hundred acres which he was prepared to let off as agricultural land. Taylor and his wife were ready for retirement anyway. They had found a little place in Low Fell. Their sons, Billy and Frank, had found jobs on other farms and had taken the last of the stock to market before leaving three days ago.

The house was more than a farmhouse; it had once been the manor house before his present home had been built . . . his present home! He had said he didn't know how he was going to stand the break-up, and it was true. What could he do with his life? He had been trained for nothing but living like a gentleman.

The thought did enter his head that when the whole business was over he would take up Mercer's offer of ten thousand and perhaps he could start again somewhere. But then, his step quickening, he muttered aloud, "No, no. By God! no. Not from him," for it would be like accepting a fee for leaving his wife in his charge. He did not know how Nancy Ann felt about the man but he certainly knew how the man felt about her. He knew that Mercer desired her for the same reason as he had done all those years ago.

If only she had been the kind of wife who could have countenanced an affair on the side, even lightly, he knew he wouldn't have been in the position he was at this moment, for then he would have taken Rene again. Especially that time when she had openly offered herself to him in town and he had refused her, none too tactfully either. He knew he had been a fool, for, as Rene had pointed out, he was in any case dispensing his favours here and there, and so why not include her among them.

He could date the complete change in his luck from that meeting. She had been scorned and her rejection had likely become evident to Poulter Myers. The man had always hated him because his wife had made no secret of her feelings. So whether it had been openly planned or merely suggested, his downfall had been her aim. It had, however, been brought about by cheating, but in such a way that no one could lay a finger on them. He should have suspected something that night he had woken up in Freeman's rooms and found he owed him five thousand and Myers seven. They had all been very clever. They had let him win more than half of that back the next night. And so the pattern had gone on: one step forward and two steps backward.

He stopped on a rise and there, away down in the valley, lay the village. He could make out the chimneys and distinctly the spire of the small church, and bitterly he thought it was that House of God that had been his curse, not his gambling, his drinking, or his whoring. No, none of these, but because from out of the vicarage had come a little girl full of spirit and freshness and naive purity which had attracted him from the first time he laid eyes on her. And the attraction had grown into a desire, a craving that could not be assuaged except by having her. And he'd had her, and with what result? She had been his ruin. Knowingly or unknowingly, she had been his ruin.

He entered the farmyard. There was no bustle here today: the line of horse boxes had no bobbing heads sticking over the half doors; there was no sound of cattle from the byres; Minnie Taylor wasn't waddling her fat body towards him, her face one big smile; her husband wasn't there to doff his cap; there was no shepherd, no cowman; there were no stable hands. The yard was swept clean, the ivy-covered house looked lonely. There were no curtains fluttering from the window, but—his eyes narrowed—the kitchen door was open. He walked towards it; then, pushing it wide, he stepped into the stone-flagged kitchen with its only remaining piece of furniture, a trestle-table, and standing to the side of it was a tall, fair man.

They surveyed each other for a full minute while Dennison's heart leapt within his body. Here was his long lost brother, only taller and broader. The face was as he remembered it; yet, not quite. The eyes looking at him had not the soft quality of Tim's: these eyes were dark and brooding and sending towards him something that his own answered.

His voice was a growl as he said, "What do you want here? You're trespassing. Get out!"

"It is you who are trespassing, sir." The lips were drawn back from the teeth. For the moment David's face took on the ferocious look of a wild-cat; then the words were hissed through his teeth. "This is my property, as from yesterday.

Now, Mr. Harpcore, sir, I have pleasure in telling you to get out, off *my* property.''

My God! My God! No, not him! So he was the Mather that had bought the place. He recalled the name from dim memory: the servant girl's name had been Mather. He had paid nine thousand for it. Where had he got the money? Yes, yes, he remembered now rumours that he wouldn't listen to, conversation that broke off in the middle. The boy that had been brought up in his service had gone to Australia and had made his fortune. He had an uncle out there . . . yes, the uncle, that man who had confronted him, blackmailed him.

He appealed to something outside himself now, crying, *Oh, no, no, not this,* not this too. I can't stand this. And because he couldn't stand it he flung himself round and out of the door, across the yard and on to the path that led its twisting way back to the house. And he didn't stop until he was in sight of it, when he seemed to stagger towards a tree, against which he leant back, and gasping as if he had been running hard. His head was bowed and so deep did he feel his humiliation that he imagined it was touching the ground. . . .

When he reached the house Robertson, meeting him in the hall, thought for a moment that he was drunk, though knowing he couldn't be. And his master's sobriety was confirmed when he said, ''Tell your mistress I wish to see her in the library.''

A few moments later Nancy Ann entered the room, and immediately he rounded on her, crying, ''Did you know of this?''

Thinking, what now, she instinctively shook her head before she said, ''Know what? What are you talking about?''

''The farm.''

''The farm? No. Only that you said the matter was closed yesterday.''

''And who to? Who to?'' His voice was almost a scream now.

''I don't know who has bought it.''

''You mean to stand there and tell me you don't know?''

She stiffened and, her own voice also ringing now, she cried, ''Yes, I do. I don't know who has bought the farm.''

"Then it will be news to you that your protégé, your fair-haired boy is now the owner of it."

She put her hand up to her mouth and muttered through her fingers, "No, no."

"But yes, yes. Just one more humiliation for me to suffer. Do you know I would rather have burnt the place down."

She stood quietly now, her hands joined at her waist, staring at him, and then she said, "Would you? Would you have rather burnt the place down than your nephew have bought it?"

"Don't, woman. Don't aggravate me at this time, because I can't stand any more. He is no nephew of mine."

"He saved your son, or at least attempted to and risked his own life."

She watched his cheek bones push out against his mottled skin and, his words low now, and even appearing as a plea, he said again, "Don't woman, don't."

"I will. I will. Someone has to say it. You've let that boy be an obsession with you all your life, whereas he could have been a comfort to you."

The crash of his fist as it hit the sofa table and bounced oddments on to the floor caused her to jump back and clutch her throat. Then they were staring at each other across the space in silence.

She could stand no more. She turned and ran from the room and almost into the arms of Robertson who, halting her with his attentive touch on her arm, said, "Ma'am, there are two men"—he did not say gentlemen—"waiting in the hall. They . . . they wish to see the master." His voice was low, and there was meaning in his words which she did not comprehend at the moment, and she muttered, "Then tell him, tell him," before she rushed along the corridor and into the hall and passing two waiting men whose sombre appearance caused her to pause momentarily before running on upstairs and into her room.

Robertson delivered his message, held open the door for his master to pass him, then followed him into the hall. He stood to the side and watched one of the men hand his master a paper. He saw him scan it, then look at the men before turning his gaze towards the stairs; then, like a man in a daze, his glance swept the hall, and there was a pause while he wetted his lips, cleared his throat, before he said, "Show these gentlemen into . . . into the kitchen. Give them the assistance that they need."

"Yes, sir." Robertson stepped forward now and beckoned the men to follow him, leaving Dennison alone and standing quietly staring down at the floor. Slowly he walked across the hall and along the corridor again to the far end and into a room. After a while he emerged, took his hat and coat from the hall-stand and paused for a moment before a mirror, then went out.

The bums were in. The staff had been expecting them for days, but nevertheless it caused great consternation. Most of them had already arranged their future life and service. Robertson was to take over Mister David's new home. He had impressed upon the staff that the "Mister" was, from now on, compulsory for all of them. Cook was to take up her place in the smaller kitchen accompanied by Sarah Brown. Jane Renton was leaving to get married. But Annie Fuller, the second housemaid, was to be housemaid at the farm. Jimmy Tool the workhouse boy, now a young man and courting, was to be given the place as stable lad under Shane McLoughlin, and set up house in two of the rooms above the stables. Shane and his brother were to have the other two. It had all been worked out during the past three weeks. The remainder of the staff had applied for and had found positions elsewhere. This wasn't including Mary or Agnes, for it was understood that wherever the mistress went they would accompany her. And as they all knew, she was for the Manor, for . . . well, where else would she go?

As Mister David had said he had no intention of living in the farmhouse permanently for his business was in Australia, why then, they had asked each other, had he bought it? It was rumoured there had been numbers of people after it, real farmers, but he had outbid them. Was it to spite the master?

Aye, very likely, very likely. It was also rumoured that he had enough money to buy The House, too, if he liked. But that surely would have finished the master. It would be bad enough when he got to know who the new owner of the farm was, because they knew only too well he would never recognize him. Altogether a queer business, they said.

And that's what Shane McLoughlin said to David when he made a point of running across the grounds to the farm to tell him the latest news. Standing before David in the farmyard, he said, "I just thought I'd tell you. The end has come, the bums arrived a while ago. 'Tis a queer business that The House should end like this."

It was no surprise to David that the bums were in. He remained silent until Shane, looking hard at him said, "Could you do anything, Davey?" when he answered with a question, "What would you expect me to do?"

"Nothin.' If justice was to be observed, nothin', 'cos, God himself knows you've had a rotten deal right from the start through him. But . . . but it's her I'm thinkin' about, the mistress. God only knows what she's had to put up with since the child went. He's been like a maniac at times. Yet, I've got to say this word for him, as masters go you couldn't have found much better."

"As long as you kept your place, eh?"

"Aye, yes, well, I suppose so, as long as I kept me place, as long as we all kept our places. But that's in the scheme of things."

"Damn the scheme of things! And you know, inside you, you say the same."

"Perhaps. Aye, you may be right, but looking at you I ask meself, and I say this to your face, Davey, if you had been born into that house would you have acted any differently. It's the way things are. Money an' position set the standards, they pattern a man's life. Anyway, I thought I'd come and tell you. . . ."

"And ask me to go back there and offer to bail him out, is that the idea?"

"Aye, perhaps. Aye, somethin' of the sort."

"Well, we've met up already this morning, and for your information, Shane, I'll tell you that he ordered me out of the house. I was an intruder trespassing."

"No." The word was soft and low.

"Yes, yes. Anyway, there's one thing he and I share and in equal measure, and that's hate. I've always hated the sight of him, and it's never lessened; nor has it in his case, although I don't think he's set eyes on me for years, not since the encounter in the wood when I was a boy; or, for that matter, given me a thought. But he must have seen my father in me in that kitchen there"—he thumbed back over his shoulder—"for by God! wasn't he startled. That was some satisfaction anyway. No, Shane, I appreciate your motive, but to go back there and have my offer thrown in my face, as it would be, I couldn't attempt it."

"No, perhaps you're right. It was just a thought." Shane grinned. "It's the Irish in me. Me ma used to bring tears to me eyes tellin' me of the folks being turned out of their cabins by the agents of them English landlords." He stressed the words, then added soberly, "Now it's the landlord's turn an' I'm not cheering. . . . When are you proposin' to leave?"

"I've booked my passage for the nineteenth, that's eleven days' time. I hope you'll be all settled in by then."

"Aye. An' you can rely on me. I'll see things are kept shipshape: you'll find everythin' as you expect it even if you arrive on the hop." He smiled, then added, "I'll say it, Davey, your buyin' this place has been a godsend to us all, for we'd have been scattered to the four winds, an' most of us have worked together for years, an' you get used to people, like a family, so we're all grateful."

"How's your mother these days?"

"Oh, pretty fit considerin'. As long as she has her pipe and her porter she'll go on for many a long year. It's funny about families. You know, Davey, a nephew turned up from nowhere the other day. She had forgotten she had him. It was her youngest brother's son, and he had his son with him, a thirteen-year-old lad, and you know something, Davey?" Shane now poked his head forward. "Believe it or not, her nephew is an accountant. Did you hear that? An accountant connected with our family, and he's sendin' his son to a private school. We fell about laughin' after he'd gone. The McLoughlins are surely comin' up. An' you know what his name is, his surname? Flannagan. The McLoughlins an' the Flannagans. Talk about little Ireland."

David found himself laughing for the first time in days. He had always liked Shane. Shane had been his friend since he had first come into the yard. The others in the stables had just been men, but Shane had been different. He put out his hand to grip Shane's and, still laughing, said, "Long live the McLoughlins and the Flannagans."

"Amen to that. Amen to that, Davey." They nodded at each other. Then, seemingly embarrassed at his emotion. Shane rubbed his hands together as if chaffing corn and said, "Well, you'll be going straight back to Durham, I suppose."

"Not yet a while." I brought a hamper over with me, I've got a lunch in there. I'll walk around a bit . . . *around my land.*"

Shane said nothing, but after lowering his head and biting on his lip, he turned away muttering an unintelligible word of farewell.

And David did survey his land. All afternoon he walked through the fields, jumped drystone walls, passed through gates, all known ground to him, until he came to the river. And there, standing on the bank, he stared at the arch of the bridge, the water flowing calmly through it today. He should hate this river. It had taken his father; it had taken his cousin; and, in a way, it had taken his mother, for she had never recovered from the cold she had developed through plunging into the icy water on that fatal day. She had died of consumption, but she had never had consumption until after she had rushed into the river to save him. And it was a fact he had faced a long time ago: she had saved him, for he couldn't have held on much longer, when he too, with the child, would have swept to his death.

He turned and walked along the stretch of the river bank that was now his, until he came to where the brush had been cleared and where the white posts with wire attached denoted the limit of his property. He walked up by the side of this fence which now ran through a belt of trees beyond which the pasture land would start. It was pleasant walking for there was a wind blowing that tangled the branches and caused a singing in the tops of the trees.

He was about to emerge from the woodland and into the light of the open field when he glanced sideways to where, beyond the overgrown pathway, was a mass of brushwood that hid the boles of a number of trees. And he saw what he imagined at first to be a boot sticking out, an old boot.

He had moved forward two or three steps when he stood stock still, turned his head slowly and looked again in the direction of the boot. It wasn't an old boot, the light on it from this angle showed it to be a polished boot.

No, *no.* The words were deep but quiet in his head.

He didn't move. Again came the words, "No! no!" Loud now, yelling. Still he didn't move. Something was telling him to walk on and ignore the boot. Something else was saying, Go and look, it mightn't be. Yet, he knew it was. Even before he bent stiffly under the wire and crossed the path and parted the undergrowth, he knew what to expect.

The body was lying on its side. The face was bloody; the hand lying across the breast was bloody. The pistol was lying against his side. "Oh, my God! Oh, God Almighty!" As he stared down on to the shattered form, there swept over him a feeling of aloneness such as he had never experienced in his life before, and he had had plenty of experience of aloneness. But this was so intense, so devastating, for there at his feet lay his one and only relative in this world. He had hated him with a deep abiding hate; but he had been a live thing, something, in a way, part of himself, or he part of it. The same blood running in their veins; no class or legality had been able to wipe out that fact. Oh, God, why hadn't he gone and offered to help?

No, no. That would only have precipitated this just as likely his acquiring the ownership of the farm had done. He turned away and staggered now on to the path, and held his hand to his brow for a moment. Then he was running up the overgrown path, and not stopping until he reached the yard. And there he shouted, "Shane! Shane! Pollock!"

It was Shane who came from the stables, and David gripped him by the shoulders, crying, "Get a door! Fetch a door, he's . . . he's dead." He jerked his head to the side. "Shot. In the wood."

"Jesus, Mary and Joseph. No! No!"

"Yes. You'll need another hand. Fetch Robertson quick. . . ."

Before long the three servants were staring down on their

master while David stood to one side, now unable to look. Then when they went to place the door near the body it was Pollock who said, " 'Tis suicide. D'you think we should touch him? The police should be called."

Shane looked across at the young fellow in silence for a moment; then, turning to David, he said, "He's right. Pollock's right. I don't think we should touch anything." And to David, Shane's words seemed to imply: You found him and it was well known you didn't get on. Pollock's right, although he doesn't know how right.

Shane turned to the groom, saying, "Go on now, as fast as you can. You might find the constable in the village, he's roundabout there at this time. If not, ride on to Chester-le-Street. But put a move on."

After Pollock had left, Robertson said quietly, "Who's to break it to the mistress?" Then both he and Shane looked at David.

But David did not say anything, and Shane said, "Robertson and me will stay here, if you would, sir." Not Davey anymore, not Mr. David even, but sir.

Slowly David turned away and, his step dragging, he made for The House. . . .

He was standing before her and, his voice trembling, he muttered, "There's been an accident. He's in . . . in the wood. . . . No, it's no use going." He put out his hand towards her but didn't touch her, but when he saw the colour drain from her face and heard her whimper, "Oh, Dennison. Dennison," he pulled a chair forward and she sank into it and sat staring ahead for a moment; then she asked a question, seemingly of herself, when she said, "Why? Oh, why?"

It was almost two hours later when they brought the body back to The House. David was holding one end of the door on which they had laid it, and his hand was within inches of the mangled head. How strange, he thought, that it was only in death he had become close to his kinsman.

Nor, probably, was the strangeness of the situation lost upon those who waited in the hall.

❧ 5 ❧

"SUICIDE WHILE THE BALANCE OF HIS MIND WAS DIS-turbed." Such was the verdict. "The body had been found by Mr. David Mather who had only recently purchased part of the estate."

That was what the newspapers said. But the villagers and those in the county houses for miles around were now aware of who this Mr. Mather was, and the knowledge provoked many to think: Wasn't it a strange coincidence that almost the same day he takes on part of the estate the man whom legally he could have called uncle had taken his own life. And wasn't it more strange still that it should be this young man who had come into a fortune and who, in a way, had come back to flaunt it, should have found the body. Very strange. However, it had been verified as suicide, and that was that. And anyway, some of the wise ones said, what else could Harpcore have done? He wasn't a man who could have earned his own living. And what was more, he was too high-handed and proud to go begging. No, it was indeed the best thing that could have happened. But what about her, his wife?

The fact that Harpcore's suicide meant he would be buried in unconsecrated ground could not have deterred many from attending the burial, for people were there in their hordes: many had come in coaches and cabs, others had walked to the cemetery, the majority out of curiosity.

Nancy Ann had left The House and, with Rebecca and Mary, had taken up abode with her grandmother. There wasn't enough room to take Agnes, but Graham, in his constant kindness, had found a position for her in his overstaffed house, so that she could be near her sister until they could both make up their minds what they wanted to do: Rebecca now had no need of a nursemaid; nor had Nancy Ann of a housekeeper; but she was very definitely at the time in need of a companion and friend. And Mary was both to her. Also, she could in a way, handle Rebecca better than she herself could, as she'd had the early rearing of her.

Rebecca had been attending a private day school in Durham. But on being informed that she must now go to the village school, she had shown some pique, in fact, temper, which was surprising, for, generally, she had been a most obedient child. Mary put it down to what she called the recent narration, but Nancy Ann saw another source for the change in her daughter's character, and she could date the change from David's arrival. More than once she'd had to check her for the way she spoke to him and for making demands on him. Only yesterday she had asked him if he would take her back to Australia. And he had smiled as he answered her, saying, "Ask me that question in another five years' time." And at this she had flounced away.

Today was the last day of the sale in The House. Nancy Ann was sitting with her hands resting idly in the lap of her black gown. Jessica sat opposite to her. She was cracking her knuckles: she would put her right hand into a loose fist, push each finger on the left into the tunnel, then grip it and pull. The fingers did not crack every time as they once had done. She would break her bones, she used to say to amuse the boys and her when they were young. Later, she had discovered that her grandmama would often crack her knuckles when she was worried: and apparently she was worried now, for she said, "Do you think the money from the sale will cover all his debts?"

"No, not anywhere near, Grandmama. The House itself will have to be sold. The sale of that will take place after all the goods have gone."

"You say that David has stocked the farmhouse up with all the best pieces?"

"Yes, so Graham tells me."

"Well, I'm glad of that, although I don't think the farm is the kind of setting for French furniture, and there was a lot of that there, wasn't there?"

"Yes, Grandmama."

"They are dealing with the things outside today, I suppose?"

"Yes, Grandmama."

"And The House will come up after?"

"Yes, Grandmama." Oh she wished, she wished she would stop talking about it. Her head was going round and round. She felt ill. Since they had brought Dennison into The House and she had looked down on his shattered face, she had been haunted by the thought that the words he had levelled at her were true that nothing had gone right for him since he had married her and that, in a way, she was to blame for what had overtaken him.

She was feeling very tired. She had the great desire to lie down and sleep: if she could sleep long enough she would wake to find that at least the past five years were forgotten and that she could now start another life. But always the question would yell at her, Who with? Who with? In the small hours of this morning she had lain staring ahead in the comparatively small room upstairs and asking herself if she were on the verge of going mad. Her husband had just died a dreadful death; there was a mountain of business to be seen to, debts from every quarter to be cleared; and yet, she would keep asking herself, with whom would she begin her new life? Yes, she must be on the verge of going mad.

Her grandmama was saying, "I think I'll go and rest for a little while, dear," and so she got quickly to her feet in order to help her up, and when, her arm about her grandmama, they reached the sitting-room door, the old woman smiled at her wanly, saying, "I'm all right, dear. I'm all right. I can manage. I've been managing on my own for a long time now, you must remember. When I need help, there's always the girls."

It was as if she was being dismissed. She dropped her hand

from her grandmama's shoulder and watched her walk steadily across the small hall, then grip the bannister and slowly, one by one, pull herself up the stairs and then for some distance edge her way past the boxes containing their personal belongings now stacked against the landing wall.

There's always the girls. Her presence, and that of Rebecca and Mary, were going to disturb her grandmama. She had lived comparatively on her own for years now and she was happy that way. . . . Who shall I start a new life with?

Dear God! There it was again. She must get outside and walk, breathe deeply, try to flood her mind with sanity.

She took a light coat and a straw hat from the wardrobe in the hall, and she donned the coat and pulled on the hat as she hurried outside. She had the desire to run as she had done when a girl, but now it wasn't towards home or in joyful skipping along the river bank, but away, away from everything, everyone.

After walking some distance she wasn't surprised to find herself by the river and quite near the stone where she had first seen David sitting. She wasn't afraid of the river. It had taken her child; and for this she had herself accepted part of the blame; she should have been more watchful of him, knowing how high-spirited he was. No, she didn't blame the river, but she did blame God for allowing these things to happen. Her father had instilled into her that God was kind and merciful. Everything he did had a purpose behind it, even good came out of evil, you only had to wait long enough. Well, she had known quite a lot of evil of late, but where would the good come out of it? It all depended on whom she would begin her life with.

Oh, dear, dear God. She dropped down on to the stone and bowed her head deeply on to her chest. Please, she prayed now, stop me from thinking this way. Give me peace. Oh, please, give me peace. Oh, please, bring peace into my soul. I don't want to marry anyone. I don't. I don't. This twisted feeling of love inside me is not natural. I am ill. Make me better in my mind. Please, please, God, make me better in my mind. Oh, Papa, speak for me.

How long she sat on the stone she didn't know. An hour? Perhaps more. But when at last she got to her feet, she felt strangely calm. It was as if, in this instance at least, her prayer had been answered. She now turned and walked up through the tangled path, having to push the brambles back here and there, and she was nearing the end of it when she saw the figure hurrying towards her, and her heart jerked in her breast.

She stopped, and he stopped an arm's length from her, and quietly he said, ''Well, it's all done.''

''What? What did The House bring?'' Her voice sounded calm.

''It didn't go. Nobody would rise to the price. They were all out for bargains in every way. But the auctioneer saw that they got very few. You will do well out of the sale.''

''The creditors will.''

''Yes, yes, I suppose that's what I mean. I could have bought The House, you know. Yes, I could. But what would I do with it? Burn it down? Yes, I'd like to do that, burn it down. It's an unhappy house. Always has been, and not only in his time, from what I've gathered lately; the supposedly ideal marriage between his parents was a sham too. You're well out of it.''

She began to walk on, and he, suiting his step to hers, walked by her side, his hands behind his back. And, looking ahead, he said, ''Well, the farm is all ready for you.''

''What!'' She jerked her head towards him.

''The farmhouse. Most of your stuff is there and all the furniture that it would take, from the drawing-room and dining-room to kitchen ware.''

She stopped, and they faced each other again, and she said, ''Do you think I would go and live there? Is that why you've done this?''

''Yes, I think you will go and live there, and that's why I've done this.''

''Then''—she shook her head slowly—''you're suffering under a delusion. I couldn't possibly go and live in that house. You know that.''

''How do I know that?'' His face looked grim. ''What's to stop you going to live there? I'll be gone next week. I've outstayed my visit by a month just so that I could see you settled there.''

"Oh, David." Her voice was low now and sad. "You must have known, under the circumstances, I couldn't have accepted such an offer from you. I'm already in debt to so many people."

"But you don't want to be in debt to me? If you look at it that way, I'll sign the place over to you tomorrow."

She closed her eyes and put her hand tightly across them now, muttering, "Stop it! Stop it!"

Her hand was pulled roughly away from her face and his came close to hers and in a hoarse whisper he said, "A few weeks ago you said words to me, 'If you love me, do what I ask. Please go.' You said that, didn't you, because you knew I loved you? I've always loved you. Now I'm asking you something. Do you love me?"

She gave a shudder and pulled herself from his grasp and, stepping back from him, she stared at him, her mouth opening and shutting like a fish's before she could stammer, "I . . . I am eight years or more older than you. I . . . I've looked upon you as I might a s . . . son."

"Don't talk rot." He flashed his hand between them now, his little finger tweeking her nose in the process, causing her head to jerk back. "That was when you were a girl and I was a boy. I've thought of nobody but you for years. Do you know something? Women chase me. Yes, they chase me. Mothers with marriageable daughters hound me. Even the short time I've been in Durham I've had visitors, even a county lady or two. Can you believe that? Money talks; it can even cover bastardy. But every woman I look at, every girl I see, has your face, your manner, your voice, everything about you. But I know there is somebody else in the running. I've known that for a long time. He's a good man and I like him, but not for you. When I think of him having you I could hate him as much as I hated him that's gone. Do you love Mercer?"

She felt she was going to cry and was forbidding herself to do so. She wanted to sink to the ground. She wanted to rest. The tired feeling was on her again. She heard her voice saying limply, "I don't love anyone at the moment. No one. You . . . you forget, my husband has just died. . . ."

"Oh, don't be a hypocrite. What feelings you had for him died years ago, and Mercer stepped in. And he is sure to ask you to marry him, love or no love. What will you say? Tell me, tell me truthfully, what will you say?''

She opened her eyes wide as if to get him into focus. He looked beautiful. His hair was the colour of the sun. He was the most handsome man she had seen in years, or had ever seen, and he was young. Youth emanated from him. What was he? Twenty? Twenty-one? And she? Nearly twenty-nine. Soon she would be in her thirties and it would be a tired thirties, because oh, she was so tired, so tired of everything. But he, he would still be vibrating with youth. There would be no peace for her when near him; his very youth and energy would make demands on her that she wouldn't be able to meet. Whereas Graham, Graham with his tenderness, his consideration; Graham with his love that had been tried over the years; Graham had to have something for his loyalty, something for his kindness. And besides gratitude, she really did love him. Yes, she loved Graham.

Simply now, she answered, ''I shall say yes to him, David. He has earned my love and respect for years now. But I will say this to you. Yes, I do love you, but in a different way. And if you really love me you would not want to marry me, for marriage with you would bring me no peace. The gap in our ages is too wide; our outlooks are so different. And everything that has happened over the years has already created a gulf that neither of us can really step over.''

She watched his face tighten; she watched his whole body stiffen; and she pleaded now, ''Please, don't be bitter. And for all your thoughtfulness with regard to the farmhouse, I'll never forget your kindness. What . . . what will you do with it now?''

It was some time before he answered her. The tan of his face had paled, his eyes had darkened, they looked almost black; he wetted his lips a number of times before he said, ''What will I do with it?'' His voice rose higher. ''Leave it as it is. I'll come back every now and again. Who knows, I might even settle here in my old age. And, on one of my visits, should The House still be empty, I might buy it and wait for Guy Fawkes night and have one big splendid bonfire.''

She turned her head to the side and drew her lips tight

between her teeth before she murmured, "Oh, David," and he repeated scornfully, "Oh, David." But then he demanded, "And what would you say if, in five years' time when she's sixteen, I decide to marry your daughter? She'll be willing enough; she's had an affection for me since she was a tot. And you heard what she said yesterday, she wants to come back with me to Australia. So, my dear *old lady,* what would you say to that?"

"Goodbye, David." She half turned away, and he cried at her, "I mean it. I mean that, mind."

She took no heed but walked on; and then she found herself dragged round with his arms about her and his mouth on hers, and she was being kissed as even Dennison in the height of his passion had never kissed her. When it was over she staggered back from him, her mouth open, dragging in air to prevent herself from choking. Then, gripping the front of her skirt, she pulled it up and ran now as swiftly as when she was a young girl along the path and away from him. And she didn't stop until she reached the gate leading into Graham's estate. Once through it, she still ran until she was well within the shadow of the trees, and there she sank down by a broad bole and, leaning her head against it, she gave vent to a paroxysm of weeping.

And it was here, sometime later, that Graham came across her and, having gently lifted her up, he led her as gently back to the house, thinking that she had been overcome by all the turmoil and worry of the past days.

❧ 6 ❧

She'd had no word from David since he had returned to Australia, but the newspapers were prophesying a gold rush in the place where he lived, Kalgoorlie.

Life, she was finding, was not easy. The Dower House, as her grandmama said, housed so many people now that they were falling over each other. Rebecca, too, was proving more of a problem every day. She had taken into her head to pay uninvited visits to the farmhouse, and often Mary would have to go in search of her and would find her installed as if she owned the place. Apparently, too, she had got into the habit of giving orders to the staff, and when these weren't obeyed she would get a tantrum and say she would write and tell David.

This information Mary tactfully gave to Nancy Ann because, as she said, something had to be done and she wasn't in a position to take the matter into her own hands.

When Nancy Ann forbad Rebecca to go to the farmhouse on her own, the girl retorted, "David said I could. He said I had to keep an eye on it."

"David said nothing of the sort. You're lying."

And to this, Rebecca had come back, "He indicated as much, because he said we were going to live there. After Papa died he said we were going to live there."

Very likely he had. But what she said to her daughter was,

"Well, we're not living there and you're not to go unless accompanied by Mary or myself."

"But you don't go there," the girl had replied.

That was true; she didn't go there.

For weeks now she'd had the urge to get away, not only from this house, but from the confines of both estates, out in the open, as she put it. To this end, she had taken to walking to the village; she could do this now for the tradesmen's bills had been met, at least in most part. But even this outlet had been checked recently on a suggestion from Shane McLoughlin. Shane had actually made it his business to come to the house this day and to ask if he could speak to her. And he had begun, "I'm sure you'll pardon me, ma'am, but it's about your little walk to the village. There's . . . well, there's been one or two incidents lately, quite unpleasant, and I would be careful if I were you for the time bein'."

"What kind of incidents, Shane?" she had asked.

"Oh." He had seemed reluctant to explain the nature of the incidents but said, "Well, not pleasant things. And unless you have somebody with you, Mr. Mercer or one of the stable lads, well, I don't think it would be wise, not for the present anyway, to do any jauntin'."

She was puzzled. She had not heard of any incidents happening on the road between here and the village. And only last week she had been in the grocer's-cum-post office-cum-general stores, and Miss Waters the dressmaker was present and if there was any gossip going she was the one to spread it around: tragedies large and small were meat and drink to Miss Waters.

However, she had thanked Shane and said she would be careful.

But there came the day that Rebecca did not return from school at her appointed time. There were two roads to the school. One along the main coach road and through the village, and the other by a lane that branched off the coach road and ended at a field gate over which you had to climb because it had been padlocked for years, ever since some cattle had escaped through it and along the path and on to the coach road, and there caused havoc when meeting the horse-drawn post van head-on, resulting in a dead cow, an injured horse, a post van on its side in a ditch, the driver with a broken leg.

So on this early evening of a day that had been very hot and was still warm and soft, she did not bother to put a dust jacket over her grey spotted voile dress, with the black waist-band proclaiming she was still in mourning, but pulled on a light straw hat and made her way through the bottom of the garden, so avoiding coming within sight of the Manor House, and through a small wicket gate and onto the coach road. It was only a five minutes' walk to where the path that afforded the short cut branched off from the roadway, and she was within a few yards of it when she saw the landau approaching. But she took no notice—carriages were frequent sights on this road—but after she had turned into the side road and then heard the landau being driven from the main road into it, she did take notice.

What did a landau want on this narrow strip of road? It was a dead end, and the only place for it to turn would be near the gate, and it would have a hard job to do it there.

She stepped on to the grass sward at the side of the path and, as she did so, turned to look back, and experienced a feeling of fright like that which a child might at being faced with something ghoulish. And within seconds the fright turned into actual fear, for the landau had stopped, and there was a woman glaring at her; and still glaring, she thrust open the door of the landau and tottered down the step and towards her. One of the coachmen had alighted and was saying, "Careful, madam. Careful."

"I'll be careful, Hawkins, I'll be careful. Look at her, the white-livered bitch."

The woman's drunken breath was wafting over her now and she pushed her hands out to ward her off, saying, "Get out of my way. Let me pass."

"Oh, aye. I'll let you pass, my pious prig, after I've dealt with you. You finished him, didn't you? You killed him. If you had just let a bit of him go, he'd be alive today. But no, you had to have him all, you mealy-mouthed vicarage bitch, you. You once stripped me, didn't you? Well, now it's my turn. Yes, 'tis. Oh yes, 'tis . . . my turn!"

Before she knew what was happening the fat body had

hurled itself upon her and they were both borne to the ground. And now she was back in her young days, fighting with the McLoughlins but with a difference, for now she was trying to save her clothes from being torn from her back. Then she screamed as her hair seemed to leave her scalp.

There was a chorus of voices: the woman crying, "Hold her legs, Hawkins. Hold her legs!" and another voice yelling, "You do and I'll bash your face in."

A knee came in her stomach and for a moment everything went black.

When she came to herself it was to the sound of tearing and she knew there was air on her flesh. When a fist landed in her eye she cried aloud and groaned, and she heard herself pleading, "Please. Please." There was no resistance in her arms now. Then the weight of the knee on her stomach was lifted from her and a voice yelled, "Leave her be, you dirty drunken scab!"

And another voice cried, "Get up on the box unless you want to lose your job." And then the woman's voice, screaming, "Yes, do as Hawkins says, or you will lose your job."

"I've lost it, missis. You've sickened me belly for a long time now but this is the finish. I'd rather work for a whorehouse madam, than touch your bread again. You're a drunken slut, that's what you are." And the man spat in her direction.

"Hit him! Hit him, Hawkins!" the fat woman demanded and, swaying, clambered her way back to the landau.

But all Hawkins did was to put his hands on her fat buttocks and heave her up to her seat, then bang the door shut and mount the box and drive towards the gate.

Jim McLoughlin stood looking down at the almost bare body of the young vicarage lass, as he still thought of their Shane's mistress; her clothes were lying in ribbons around her. Quickly he gathered them up and placed them over her middle. And when a few minutes later, the landau passed them again he made a sign with his hand to his late mistress that caused her to turn in the seat and yell some obscenity back at him.

Returning to Nancy Ann, he raised her head, saying, "Are you all right, madam? Are you all right?" But receiving no reply, he stood up and looked around him. If she could have walked he could have helped her, but he had no hope of carrying her. He knew he must get help. But how could he leave her like this?

Bending down, he rearranged the torn clothes about her middle and legs. Then, taking off his short jacket, he covered her naked breasts and shoulders with it. Looking up, then down the roadway, he wondered what he should do. His first thought was to get his brother; but that would mean going to the farmhouse and twice the distance from the Manor.

With one last look down on the still figure that appeared now like a bundle of rags, he sprinted back up the side road and on to the coach road, and the half mile along it to the lodge gates of the Manor. The small side gate was open, and he ran through and, receiving no response to his battering on the lodge door, he continued his dash up the drive and into the yard, yelling as he did so. "I want help! Help!" This time and almost simultaneously, three men appeared, two from the stables and one from the house, and one of the men from the stables was his brother Mick.

Graham had been about to set out to pay his daily visit to the Dower House. But now he hurried to the man, calling, "What is it? What is it?"

"Miss . . . madam, she . . . she was attacked."

"Attacked? What do you mean attacked? Who?"

"Madam, Mrs. Harpcore, along the road, the fat one that I work for. She stopped the landau; been on the lookout for her for days. She stripped her. I've left her lying. . . . Come on!"

"My God!" Graham was running now, but Mick called after him, "Better bring a cover or somethin', sir, a shawl, a blanket."

At this, the other man dashed into a room next to the stables and came out carrying a couple of blankets. Then the four of them were running down the drive. . . .

Nancy Ann hadn't moved. Nothing mattered. She wasn't unconscious, but she knew that she was going into a deep sleep and that was good; she would get away, get away from everything.

She heard a voice saying, "Oh, my dear, my dear. Someone will pay for this. Oh, yes, they'll pay for this. That dirty creature, that madwoman.''

Then there were voices above her as if in discussion, and the sound of feet running away. And now there was that Irish voice, one of the McLoughlins. She would know that voice anywhere, and he was talking to Graham, saying, "I couldn't stand it. She's been out lookin' for her for weeks now. But I thought she would just have her say and that would be that, and it would satisfy her. She's never been sober for God knows how long; the cure last year was no cure. She'll end up in an asylum, that one."

"She'll end up in jail if I have anything to do with it."

She had never heard that tone in Graham's voice before. She wished they would stop talking, she just wanted to go to sleep.

And then, when they lifted her quite gently, the rocking of the carriage gave her her wish and she knew nothing for a long time after. . . . A countless time.

❧ 7 ❧

THEY HAD NOT CARRIED NANCY ANN TO THE DOWER HOUSE, for Graham had ordered her to be taken to the Manor. And there, she had lain for a week oblivious of where she was or what was going on.

Graham, determined in his way to bring the perpetrator of the outrage to justice, had informed the police. And this must have hastened the visit from Mr. Poulter Myers himself, apologizing profoundly and saying that his wife had been admitted to a clinic for a cure.

So rumours abounded again. Wasn't it strange, people said, that the ill luck of The House had seemed to follow her.

Mary and Rebecca, too, had taken up their abode in the Manor, and a new kind of life and routine had begun. Graham gave Rebecca a pony, much to her delight, and after a time she rode to school on it, and through it made friends with some of the children from whom she had kept aloof and they from her.

Mary was happy to be working in a big house once more. Admittedly it wasn't half as big as Rossburn, but it was more beautiful, more comfortable, and had an atmosphere of warmth about it.

It was a full four weeks before Nancy Ann showed signs of really being fully aware of her surroundings. And when the realisation came that she was being cared for in Graham's house, she did not protest, but continued to lie day after day on a chaise-longue at the window of the bedroom looking out on the gardens below, for it seemed that at last her mind was at peace. She could look back on the events of the past five years and feel no bitterness, no pain. The emotion she retained for Dennison was pity, and even when the recent past came up and her thoughts touched on David, they were calm. She saw his love as that of an impressionable young man for an older woman, and the feeling she had had for him as having been bred of his admiration for her, a form of vanity.

But that was all in the past now. Even the attack by that dreadful woman she saw as something that had to take place for the woman to expunge the hate she felt for her. And now there was only Graham, dear Graham, kind and loving Graham. If only she had married Graham in the first place. If only. If only. . . .

Three weeks later Graham accompanied her and Mary to Harrogate and saw her settled into a comfortable hotel, and on each of the following four weekends he visited them; then on the fifth weekend, when he had arrived to accompany her back home, she said to him, "I must return to the Dower House, Graham."

They were sitting on the couch in her private sitting-room, and quite firmly he answered, "You are not returning to the Dower House. There's not enough room for you all there, and what's more"—he smiled—"I must tell you, your grandmama is much happier to have the house to herself."

She was already aware of this, but she insisted quietly, "It . . . it wouldn't be right for me to stay on, I mean, to impose any longer."

"Don't talk nonsense, Nancy Ann." He turned to her now and, gripping her hands, repeated, "Don't talk nonsense. You are never going back to the Dower House. We are going to be married, aren't we? And I'm not going to apologize in a mealy-mouthed way by saying I am speaking too soon after your bereavement." He jerked himself nearer to her and held her hands tightly against his breast, and his deep brown eyes alight with the suppressed emotion of years, he said thickly, "You know I love you and have done so for years. At times it's been torment, seeing you so unhappy and being unable to do anything about it. But now I may, and I can. You . . . you do care for me a little, don't you?''

"Oh, Graham, Graham, yes, I care for you, very deeply." And she could say this in all truth.

When he put his arms about her and kissed her for the first time, she had a flashing memory of another kiss when the breath had been taken from her body, but it was only a flashing memory. And then she was responding to his embrace and in doing so she knew she was setting the seal on a life of peace and security, tenderness and caring. And what more could anyone wish for in this life?

Three months later she was married. The wedding was a quiet affair. Only personal friends and the staff attended. She was not married this time in the village church, but at Saint Saviour's in the next parish. Thirty people were at the reception. And when later, they all crowded round the coach that was to take them to the station, the last person she kissed and with deep affection was not Pat, nor her grandmama, but Mary, and she whispered, "Look after her, won't you?" And Mary, tears in her eyes, said, "Don't you worry, my dear. I'll see to her."

It was when all the guests had gone and Agnes and Mary were in the main bedroom tidying up that Agnes stopped and, looking out of the window, said, " 'Tis just as well. She'll be happy in a way. The other wouldn't have worked out."

"What did you say?"

Mary pushed a drawer in, straightened her back, then said again, "What did you say, our Agnes?"

Agnes turned from the window and answered, "With Davey. It wouldn't have worked out."

"What d'you mean, with Davey?"

"Oh, you know what I mean; don't play innocent, it's your Agnes you're lookin' at. You know for a fact there was something there, more than something. What d'you think he bought the farm for? You know very well he expected her to go and live there."

Mary sighed now and said, "You know more than is good for you. But I'm tellin' you, our Agnes"—she turned now and wagged her finger at her sister—"don't you breathe a word of what you're thinking outside this room."

"I'm not daft altogether."

"No, not altogether, just a bit."

They grinned at each other, then laughed. Then it was Mary who said, "But you're right, it would never have worked out. I was worried to death at one time wondering what he would get up to. Anyway, that's been nipped well and good in the bud. What she wants after what she's gone through is a peaceful life, not a mad romantic fling like he would have offered her."

"You're right. Oh, yes, you're right. But . . . but he has turned into a handsome fellow, hasn't he? My! just to look at him did something to your guts. An' wouldn't I have just loved a mad romantic fling with some like man."

"Our Agnes!"

At this Agnes turned from the window again and exclaimed in an equally loud voice, *"Our Mary!"* Then having the final word, she added, "What d'you think will happen when he comes back?"

"What can happen? Nothing. It's all signed and sealed. She's a married woman again."

❧ 8 ❧

NANCY ANN HAD BEEN MARRIED ABOUT EIGHTEEN MONTHS when word came that David had returned.

It had been a peaceful time, a happy time. Graham was a loving and tender husband. The feeling she'd had for him had deepened from day to day, and his love and care encased her. She felt secure and happy as she had never done in her life before. Even in those early days before she married her happiness had been a childish thing made up of externals. Now her happiness was deep inside her; it was a peaceful happiness, like floating on a calm sea. But a sea doesn't remain calm forever and now and again there had been a ripple caused by Rebecca.

Rebecca was jealous of the attention her mother paid to her new husband; in fact, she did not really like Graham, and this dislike was made evident in spurts of peevishness and temper. She had grown rapidly during the past two years; she was now twelve but could easily be taken for a girl of fourteen or more. She was mad on riding but objected to being accompanied by any of Graham's men, even by Mick who had taught her to ride. Whenever she could make her way unobserved from the house or yard, she went over to the farmhouse on foot or on horseback, for over the past six months there had been an added attraction there in Shane's nephew. Dennis Flannagan had become very attached to his uncle and spent most of his time with him during his holidays and odd weekends. He was a boy of fifteen with dark hair, deep brown eyes, a laughing mouth like his uncle's, and a sturdy athletic body. He, too, had a passion for riding.

In her childish way Rebecca had also taken a dislike to Shane and Robertson, because Shane had forbidden his nephew to accompany her into the farmhouse and Robertson had strongly endorsed this order. In fact, Robertson, at times, had told her that it was inconvenient for her to be in the house, as she got in the way of the maids.

On this particular day when she pushed the front door open and walked in, she was brought to a halt and an open-mouthed gape when she saw the man coming down the shallow staircase. It was David. Yet it wasn't David. This man looked larger, his skin was deeply tanned, and his hair looked almost white, so light it was. Then, when he reached the bottom of the stairs and said, "Hello, there," she answered, "Hello. Then . . . then you've come back?" She did not fly to him and throw her arms about him as she had been wont to do, and when he said, "Well, if this isn't me, I'm haunting the house," she asked, "When . . . when did you come?"

"Last night."

"Oh, how lovely to see you." Now she did spring towards him and throw her arms about him; but then immediately felt nonplussed when, his hand patting her head, he said, "Well now, well now, I thought I was being greeted by a young lady, not a little girl anymore."

Something in his voice made her loosen her hold on him, and she stepped back and gazed up into his face. And the thought that entered her mind was, He's different, different from the last time. And she was on the point of saying, What have you brought me? when she realized he had said she was no longer a child. And that was true; as her great-grandmama was always saying to her, she was at an age when she must mind her manners. And so she said, "How long are you here for this time?"

He moved from her across the small hall and towards the sitting-room as he said, "That depends. I have a little business to do."

Tentatively now, she followed him. There was something

strange about him. She felt slightly afraid of him, and that was silly. David was hers. He had always been hers. She hurried now to his side and said, "You know that Mama is married and we're living at the Manor House?"

He did not answer her until he reached the middle of the room and there, turning and looking down on her, he said, "Yes, I am aware that your mama is married and that you are living in the Manor House."

His voice was stiff, and then he smiled and his teeth looked very white in his tanned face as he said, "Marriages are in the air. I, too, am to be married shortly."

"What!"

"What! Young ladies don't say, What! You heard what I said: I, too, am to be married shortly."

"Married?"

"Yes, that's what I said, married."

She blinked at him; then in a small voice she said, "Is . . . is she from Australia?"

"No, no." He shook his head, still smiling, "She's an English lady."

An English lady. She did not say the words aloud. But the term made her feel very small, a little girl again.

There was a tap on the door and it opened and Robertson stood there, saying, "The cab has arrived, sir."

As David turned and said, "Thank you. I'll be there in a moment," it came to her that Robertson had been their servant, and this man standing in front of her giving orders had been a servant, although in an odd way he was a relation. For some strange reason she felt a desire to cry. Then she looked to where he was halting Robertson's departure by saying, "Henry, I'm expecting two ladies for dinner tonight: a Mrs. Dawson Maitland and her daughter. If I'm not back in time, make them comfortable. There will also be a Mr. Benedict; but he'll likely return with me. Ask cook to put on something good."

"I'll do that, sir. Yes, I'll do that."

"Well now—" He turned towards her, saying, "I must be off; I've a great deal of business to get through."

Her voice was merely a whisper as she said, "Are you going to live here?"

"Here?" He pointed his finger towards the floor, then said, "Well yes, partly I suppose, but I'll still have to spend some time in Kalgoorlie, although my fiancée doesn't care much for Kalgoorlie, what little she has seen of it." He now looked around the room, saying, "Yes, yes, we'll settle here for a time until I find a nice little estate, or a large one." He pursed his lips now. "It all depends on what takes my fancy. Well, now, I really must be off. Give my regards to your mother. I hope she is well."

"Yes, she is very well." Then she did not know what made her stress the last words for, looking up at him, her face straight, she added, *"Very well."*

"That is good to hear."

They were in the hall now and Robertson was helping him into his coat. Then they were in the yard and there was the cab with the cabbie standing holding the door open. She did not walk with him to the cab but stood in the middle of the yard. And as he was about to step into the vehicle, he turned and looked at her, and smiled. Then the door closed on him, the cabbie got on the box and drove away.

She stood where she was, feeling dazed. When she turned round towards the house the front door was closed, and she took it as a sort of symbol and she said to herself, "I'll never go in there again. Never. Never. Never."

She was running straight along the path towards the house that had once been her home, which now stood like a ghost house, empty, alone, deserted. She dashed into the yard, where the grass was growing up between the stone slabs, then through the archway, and through the overgrown gardens to the gate that led to home. And for the first time she thought of Mr. Mercer's house as home. And it was him she ran into at the top of the lawn as she sped from the trees. And when he caught her and looked down and into her streaming face, he said, "What is it, my dear? What is it?"

"Oh. Oh, Mr. Mercer." She always gave him his title. She now leant her head against him and he put his arms about her and said, "There, there. What has happened? Tell me."

"I . . . I want Mama. Where is she? Where is Mama?"

"I've just left her; she's in the conservatory. Go along, you'll likely find her still there."

She disengaged herself from him and nodded at him, then was running again.

Nancy Ann was watering plants when she found herself almost toppled over as Rebecca threw herself into her arms, causing the small watering can to drop to the ground.

"What is it? What is it, my dear? What's happened?"

"Oh, Mama. Mama."

"Come. Come." Nancy Ann led her to a white wrought iron seat at the end of the conservatory and, pressing her down, she said, "Tell me, what's upset you? Come along, now, stop that crying." And she stroked Rebecca's hair from her face the while thinking, It's that boy. They've had a tiff. She's likely found him riding with someone else. Dear, dear.

"He's back. He's come back . . . David."

Nancy Ann's body stiffened and became cold for a moment, but her voice sounded calm as she said, "Well, he was bound to come at some time, that's his home now."

"But . . . but he's changed, different. He . . . he's not nice, Mama."

"Not nice? What do you mean, not nice?"

The girl shook her head and she just stopped herself from saying something awful, which would have been, He was like Papa, Mama; instead, she said, "He looks different. He was nasty to me."

"Nasty? Now, now; explain yourself."

"Oh." Rebecca pressed her head against her mother's breast and muttered through her tears, "He was just nasty. He's going to be married, and they are coming to dinner tonight, a lady and her daughter. He gave the order to Robertson before he went off. He . . . he was going into Newcastle. I don't like him anymore. I don't. I don't. I don't."

Nancy Ann's hand became still on her daughter's hair. He was going to be married. Well, wasn't that the best thing? Yes, yes of course. But how would she react when he broke the news to her? Especially if he used the high-handed manner he had obviously taken with Rebecca. He had once said he would come back and marry Rebecca. Well, that was one thing she had to be thankful for. It had remained a secret dread in her that he would do just that. He was capable of it.

The door opened and Graham came in, saying, "What is the trouble?"

She pressed Rebecca from her and, her manner taking on a lightness, she said, "David is back, and apparently he is a much-changed individual, by what Rebecca tells me. And also, he's going to be married, she says."

"Oh. Oh." He pulled a long mouth, and gave her a sly smile as if he understood the situation. Then he looked to where Rebecca had turned herself towards the corner of the seat, her head resting on the end of it, and thinking to throw oil on to the troubled waters of a young passion, he said, "Well, he is an oldish man, isn't he, and it's about time he married. How old is he, my dear?"

Before Nancy Ann could force herself to answer in the same vein as her husband's playful mood, Rebecca swung round, crying, "He is not old. He is no older to me than you are to Mama."

"Yes, yes. Well, you're right there, my dear." His voice took on a soothing note. And now addressing Nancy Ann, he said, "I was thinking this morning about Harrogate again, and that now the school holiday had begun, I thought it would be nice if you two could go for a jaunt. It's such a refreshing place, Harrogate, and there's so much to do. Well, what about it?"

Nancy Ann grabbed eagerly at the suggestion, saying, "Oh, I should love that. And I think it's time Rebecca had some new clothes, more fashionable ones."

She turned to her daughter now, saying, "You're growing out of your present dresses at such a rate that . . . that you will soon be showing your knees." She laughed a forced laugh, which was cut off by her daughter jumping up from the seat and crying, "I don't want to go to Harrogate. I won't be able to ride."

"Of course you will. Of course you will."

"No, I won't, Mama. And now the holidays are here I want to ride. I want to ride every day. I don't want to go to Harrogate. I don't. I don't."

"Now stop that! And stop it immediately. Whether you like it or not, we are going to Harrogate. That's all that has to be said."

With that, Nancy Ann turned from her daughter, while giving Graham a silent signal to follow her, and she didn't speak until they were both in the privacy of the bedroom. And then, turning to him, she said, "We'll . . . we'll go tomorrow."

"As soon as that?"

"Oh, I'm sorry. It . . . it isn't that I want to leave you, or here, you know that."

She was within the circle of his arms when he replied quietly, "I know that, my dear, I know that. And I know the reason you are going, why you want to get her away. She's been much too fond of that gentleman for years. He was a nice enough boy when he was a boy, and as a youngster I liked him, but I can't say that I'm as fond of the man, at least, of the man I saw a couple of years ago. There was an arrogance about him that annoyed me, to say the least. And he was very fond of you, too, you know." He moved his head slowly up and down. "Rather possessive of you. I noticed that too. He acted as if you belonged to him. It was as if the blood tie was between you and him, and not Harpcore." Whenever he mentioned Dennison, he always referred to him as Harpcore. And he ended, "Somehow, it isn't as if his wealth has altered his character very much at all. As I see it, he felt he belonged to that house and acted likewise. Anyway"—he tossed his head now—"I'm due for a holiday too, aren't I? We'll all go to Harrogate." Then, his voice becoming sober, he added, "You know, it's only since you came into my life, really into my life, that I could think of leaving this place for more than a few days at a time, because it was the only life I had. But now, I have a wonderful, wonderful life, with a wonderful, wonderful, wonderful, wife."

When his lips fell on her, she returned his kiss, thinking, Yes, so have I, so have I. And I must cherish it. Yes, I must cherish it and appreciate it. But the quicker they got to Harrogate the better, for when they returned, *he* would be gone.

The visit to Harrogate turned out to be a success, particularly in Rebecca's case. She rode in the morning, grumbling at first because it was only for an hour; but accepted this when the afternoons turned out to be exciting with shopping, then tea at the Spa, or in a fashionable restaurant, and then on three evenings a week they attended either the theatre or a concert.

With regard to the shopping, Nancy Ann received a very generous dress allowance from Graham, and so she indulged her daughter, if not herself, in the dress departments. Graham had been with them for the first fortnight, but not relishing hotel life, he returned home, and for the next three weeks visited them at the weekend.

They were due to leave on the Saturday, and he arrived on the Friday night. After their first warm greeting Nancy Ann realized that he was disturbed. They were alone together when tentatively, she said, "Is something wrong, dear? Something worrying you?"

"Yes, you could say something is wrong and is worrying me," he answered her, "but only with regard to how it will affect you. It . . . it concerns the house."

"Rossburn, you mean?"

"Yes."

"What about it?"

"Well"—he took her hand and drew her down on to the window seat of the bedroom—"what I can gather from Brundle, who's gathered it from Mick who heard it from his brother Shane, Mather had bought the house some time ago. No wonder we couldn't understand its not being sold." There was a slight note of annoyance in his voice now as he went on, "Apparently, he was comparatively rich before the gold rush in this Kalgoorlie district, but now, as far as I can understand, he's a millionaire twice over, and he spends money like water. But it's always the way with the newly rich; they have no values."

He was indeed annoyed. Her voice had a soothing note in it as she said, "Well, perhaps, he intends to put it to some good use."

"Good use? My dear, he is having it pulled down."

"What!"

He nodded at her. "Just what I said, pulled down. I couldn't believe it. In fact, I went straightaway. Apparently his *lordship* had departed back to Australia sometime previously, together with his fiancée, I'm told. But he had engaged a contractor to level the whole place. I spoke to the man him-

self. The tiles were already off. It was a sorry sight. I felt
. . . well, really, my dear, I just don't know how I felt. If it
had been my own place I couldn't have felt worse at that
moment. The man himself said it was a da . . . shame, and
went on to list all the ways in which it could have been used,
some of which, of course, because the house is so near to us,
would have been unwelcome. Yet, I had to agree with him.
But no, it has to be levelled. He may sell, this is what the
man said to me, he may sell what he can, such as panelling,
doors, and the paintings from the drawing-room ceiling, if
he can get them down whole. There's one thing he was firmly
instructed he had to keep and place in the farm barn, likely
for shipment to Australia. And do you know what that is?''

She made a small motion with her head, while all the time
inside she was saying, Oh, David. Oh, David.

''A sloping beam from the far end of the roof, a truss, the
man called it. He said it's about twelve feet long. One end
rests on the wall and forms part of the eaves; the beam slopes
up to a height of about four feet at the apex of the room. The
man said it has carvings on it roughly hacked out here and
there and drawings in coloured crayons. It's something, he
said, one would see in a nursery, like the scribblings of a
child. But this is at the extreme end of a roof, not in the attics
proper.''

Oh, David. David.

''Can you understand it?''

Yes, yes, she could understand it. Oh, she could understand it all right. That corner had been his home for so long.
Very likely his harness had been attached to that beam. Oh,
she could understand it all right.

''You are upset. I knew you would be.''

''No, no. In a way, Graham, I can understand his action.''

''You can? Well, I certainly can't.'' He rose from the seat
and walked towards the middle of the room. ''It is sheer
wanton destruction. The exterior might have been stylized,
but it was a splendid house, beautifully built. And that drawing-room was magnificent. I think it's a sacrilege.''

''He . . . he suffered in that house, Graham.''

He turned on her almost roughly now and exclaimed loudly,
''Suffered? He was damn lucky under the circumstances to

be allowed to stay there. No matter what my opinion of Harp-core was, I admired him for taking on the responsibility of that boy.''

She too was on her feet. ''He took no responsibility, Gra-ham. You . . . you don't know anything about it and his life there. He . . . he was treated like an animal. It wasn't natu-ral; he hadn't any liberty at all. That beam he wants is the one he was tied to. He wouldn't have been treated so in an asylum.''

''Oh, my dear, my dear.'' He was holding her by the shoul-ders now, repeating, ''My dear, my dear, don't upset yourself so. I . . . I didn't look at it that way. Forgive me. Forgive me.''

She found she had to take in some deep breaths to stop the tears from starting, but as she stared at her husband's kindly and concerned countenance, she thought, They are all of a pattern underneath, these men who have been bred to think of themselves as landed gentry. Their opinions on most things might be diverse, but when it came to class and the division between the servant and the master, there they stood firmly together.

He was talking rapidly, soothingly now. ''I know you have always been concerned for the boy and I wasn't aware that he had been . . .'' he seemed to search for a word; he couldn't say humiliated as his mind suggested, but added, ''treated so roughly. Anyway, you have got to be prepared, my dear, to see merely a piece of land where once your home stood.''

A slight shudder passed through her. ''It was never my home, Graham,'' she said. ''It was as much my prison during the last five years I lived there as it had been David's from the day he was born. And . . . and don't worry''—she gently touched his cheek—''don't be so concerned for me, please. But I know one thing: he had to do this to try to expunge his feelings and the memories of his treatment, although I'm sure they will be with him until the day he dies. You know your-self, Graham, that those early years of environment remain with you always. I can't forget how happy my childhood days were in the vicarage. You, I am sure, have wonderful mem-ories of your early days too.''

She did not probe, nor ever had probed into the years preceding his being jilted; and so she went on, "You can see, at least I can, how those years under the roof must have affected that boy, and the man he is now cannot forget them."

"You were very fond of him, weren't you? I . . . I mean as a boy."

It was some seconds before she answered, "Yes, I was very fond of him." Then she forced herself to utter the next words to allay any suspicion that he might be harbouring in his mind. "He . . . he looked upon me, in a way, as his mother. More so, after I was the means of sending him to school. But there is"—she smiled—"one thing I must tell you, and that is, I can't wait to get home. In fact, I've been very impatient for the past week or more for your coming."

"Oh, my dear, dear Nancy Ann. How it does my heart good to hear you say that, because at times I wonder if you are happy."

"Oh, never doubt that I am, I am. Life now is like heaven . . . the vicarage transported."

At this they both laughed and clung to each other, and as he kissed her, she thought, And that is true. Then, as if she were indeed transported back to those days in the vicarage when she would ask herself funny questions, especially in church, she wondered now if angels in heaven were as happy as they were supposed to be.

❈ 9 ❈

After arriving home she had made up her mind not to go and view the destruction of The House, nor to enter the grounds again.

Life reassumed its normal pattern and sometimes she found herself slightly bored, because the household ran on such well-oiled wheels. They had visitors, but not a great many. Pat and George called in at least once a week and often stayed for a meal. But she and Graham rarely made a return visit. Graham did not take to visiting. He preferred their evenings by the fire when she did her embroidery or played the piano and he looked through his collection of stamps or read, or when he tried to instruct her in the intricacies of chess . . . there was no playing cards in this house.

Each day she walked through the grounds to the Dower House, where Jessica was still in amazingly good health, but the closeness between them seemed to have dwindled of late. Nancy Ann put this down to aging for her grandmama must now be nearing eighty, although she would never state her true age.

At times, Nancy Ann was made to wonder what she would have done without the companionship of Mary. And one morning, on her way back to the Manor House, she was startled when she thought that she might lose her, at least be forced to have only her divided attention.

It was an early October day. The air was brisk; there was a light wind blowing; it was a day for walking. So she left the main drive connecting the houses and cut down by a pathway that would take her through the wood and into the Manor gardens, and it was where it left the wood and entered the formal gardens that she saw the man standing by the tall hedge. For a moment she thought he was a gardener taking a breather to have a smoke of his pipe. But when the figure turned towards her, she saw that it was Shane McLoughlin, and there was surprise on her face as she walked towards him. And he, looking a shade embarrassed, greeted her with, "I'm sorry, ma'am. I hope I didn't disturb you. I mean . . ."

"No, no, not at all, Shane. Is . . . is anything the matter?"

He looked down at the ground for a moment, saying now, "Nothin' that you would call serious, ma'am, but . . . well, it's . . . it's Miss Hetherington."

She repeated the name to herself and with some consternation, which gathered force when he said, "I've . . . I've asked her to come into the open, but . . . but she won't, ma'am. She doesn't like to disturb things, and . . . and I'm not gettin' any younger. And neither is she, as I tell her."

No, she wasn't; Mary was over forty. And how old was Shane? He must be over thirty-five. Again the older woman and the younger man.

"I wanted to do the honourable thing, ma'am, an' come an' put it to you, but she wouldn't let me. I've never been underhand, as I hope you realize, ma'am. Straightforward, that's what I am, and I hate this hole-and-corner business. Of course, as I know an' she knows, no matter how I do up the rooms above the stables, they won't be anything like the quarters she's got here, because she's in such a well-set-up position. But we've got a life to live, as you yourself only too well know, ma'am, an' this business has been goin' on for the last three years and I'm gettin' tired of it. I was goin' to give her . . . well, a sort of ultimatum this mornin'. She knows that, and that's why she hasn't turned up."

She felt slightly sick. Oh, Mary, Mary. What would she do without her? But she wouldn't have to do without her altogether, for Shane was saying now, "I've told her, it would just be a sort of change of quarters; she could come back here every day. And then she's put up another obstacle, saying that her sister, your Mary, you know, ma'am, mightn't like it.''

Nancy Ann felt her face spreading: she wanted to burst out laughing; she wanted to take his hand and say, ''Yes, by all means, Shane, you and Agnes must marry. I'll see to it.'' What she said was, ''You're talking about Agnes?''

''Yes, yes, of course, ma'am. Oh.'' His face stretched and then he put his head back and laughed aloud, before saying, ''You thought it was your Mary? Oh, ma'am, I like Mary, she's a fine woman, but . . . but a bit long in the tooth. Not that she wouldn't make a fine wife for any man. No, no''— he shook his head—'' 'tis Agnes.''

''Don't you worry.'' She actually did put her hand out and pat his sleeve as she said, ''I'll make her see sense.''

''Oh, thank you, ma'am, thank you.'' Then pausing for a moment, he stared at her, and his voice was much lower now as he asked, ''How are you, ma'am?''

''Me, Shane? Oh, I'm . . . I'm very well, thank you. Very well.''

''You . . . you are bound to be a bit upset.'' He jerked his head in the direction of the house. '' 'Twas a mad thing to do. I said that to him, but there was no gainsaying him. But in a way, I could understand it, ma'am. Yes, I could understand it.'' He was looking straight into her face as he went on quietly, ''He's not a happy man, ma'am. He was never a happy child, I know that, but all his money hasn't compensated him as one would think it should. Now wouldn't you, wouldn't you now think so? 'Cos he's a millionaire twice over, they say. An' between you and me, ma'am, I can't see his marriage makin' him any happier.''

''No? What makes you say that, Shane?''

''Well, ma'am, to my mind she's not the right type, not for a man like him, because he's the double of the old master if . . . Oh, ma'am, I'm sorry.''

''It's all right, Shane. It's all right.'' She reassured him by patting the air between them and adding, ''I've thought the same.''

''Have you, ma'am? Well, 'tis truly there, although he won't touch drink or go near a playing-card. Oh—'' He shook his head and closed his eyes, saying, "I'm talkin' me head off as usual, but, as I said, I don't think his afancied young woman is his type, too dollified. Now if it was her mother. Oh, you could tell, ma'am"—he was nodding at her now— "who was the pusher there. From what I understand it was her who pushed them both to Australia to visit him. That was after they had met for the first time in a friend's house in France. Melbourne or someplace she made for, then had to travel all those miles to Kalgoorlie." Now he was grinning widely. "From scraps that I heard of the dinner talk that came out of the dining-room, the young lady didn't take to Kalgoorlie at all. But that's where he proposes to build a house, so he told me. He wanted to take me across there with him. He did, ma'am, he did. And who knows, I might have taken him at his word if it hadn't been for Agnes." His mood changed again, his voice dropped as he said, "I felt sorry for him, ma'am. God knows he wasn't very happy in The House, but he was a damn sight . . . excuse me, he was a lot happier than he is now."

He was looking into her face, so straight that her gaze dropped from his. And she said, "I'm sorry to hear that, Shane."

"I knew you'd be, ma'am, for money isn't everything."

"No, indeed, Shane, money isn't everything. Anyway"— she glanced at him again, smiling now—"I will go and tell Agnes that someone is waiting in the shrubbery and that she's got to stop this nonsense and name the day. And I can assure you, Shane"—she bent slightly towards him—"we'll see that she's well set up, that you are both well set up."

"Oh, thank you, thank you, ma'am. You know, I've said to me ma, time and time again, it was the best thing that ever happened to us when you knocked our Mick out. It was a kind of introduction to the family, and if it was possible for every one of us to be in your service, we'd feel honoured, ma'am, we would that. You'll be pleased to know an' all, ma'am, I'm sure, that Jim's in good service again."

Touched by the commendation, she answered, "Oh, yes, indeed I am. And I, too, have benefited from that introduction, Shane. In many ways you have been more than a servant. You have acted as a friend and for that I am grateful, and always shall be. Now I must go and tell Agnes what she must do . . . or else.''

They were both smiling as she moved away. But she was no sooner out of his sight than she paused for a moment and, her head drooping, she said to herself, ''He's not a happy man . . . Oh, David. David.'' She walked swiftly now, not daring to ask herself, Was she a happy woman?

❧ 10 ❧

THERE WAS MUCH TALK IN THE NEWSPAPERS ABOUT THE UN-
rest among certain sections of womenfolk, and not in the
working class, let it be said, but among ladies, who considered their so-called sisters were being victimized: those who
worked in the attics of millinery shops fourteen hours a day
and slept where they worked; those who worked in damp
cellars; and those who worked in the mills, many of them
children, part-timers as they were called, and all for a pittance.

The century was coming to a close. There were great things
afoot. It was even stated that before long every household
would have an indoor closet. Of course that was taking things
too far. How could it be possible, even the most moderate
ones said, for every house to have an indoor closet? It was
like saying that all houses would have this new lighting called
electricity, and that gas would be done away with; and even
more so, a telephone communication.

It was acknowledged everywhere that things were moving
forward for the better, much thanks due to the glorious Old
Lady up there in London.

But all the change, all the advancement, all the stirring
headlines in the newspapers of wars and victories . . . and
defeats caused no impression on those in the estate of the
Manor House, for the period of the last four years had brought

its own particular wars and defeats, particularly to the woman who was now the sole owner of the estate.

Nancy Ann could not believe that Graham had gone from her, nor that her daughter had gone from her, both dead to her, though in different ways. At times she felt there must be a curse on her, else why should her daughter have behaved as she had done, knowing that her stepfather was dying? Well, she may not have been sure that his death was imminent, but she had assuredly known that he was seriously ill.

Just a week after her sixteenth birthday Rebecca had come to her and said, "I'm not going back to school, Mama. I . . . I want to marry Dennis Flannagan."

She remembered gazing at her daughter open-mouthed, and that before she could make any reply Rebecca was saying, "You weren't much older when you married Father."

And when she had spoken she had said the wrong thing: "Oh, that may be so, but . . . but you're still at school. And anyway, I don't think Mr. Mercer would countenance any such entanglement," for Rebecca had screamed at her, "I don't care what Mr. Mercer says or doesn't say. He's nothing to me. I've . . . I've never liked him. And I'm going to marry Dennis no matter what he or anybody else says. I . . . I thought I was doing the right thing by telling you."

At this Nancy Ann had hissed at her daughter, "Don't you raise your voice to me like that! And remember, whether you like my husband or not, he's been a very good father to you for years now, and he is, at this moment, rather ill. So mind your manners. You're ungrateful, spoilt and ungrateful. And have you thought what life would be like married to this boy?"

"He's not a boy, he's twenty. And he has a position, or will have shortly. And his people have no objection."

"No, of course, they wouldn't, but I have."

"Why have you?"

"First of all, because you are much too young—the word is immature. In all ways you are immature. And secondly, I know nothing about the man except that I have seen him at odd times."

"Well, Mama, I can tell you, I have seen him more than at odd times, at every possible time. If you hadn't been so taken up with yourself and him''—she had jerked her head upwards indicating the bedroom—''then you might have noticed what I was doing. As for being immature, if it comes to the point, I'm an old woman compared to what you were like at my age, so I've been told, because Uncle Peter said you were a scatterbrain and a tomboy up till you were married.''

She knew that Peter would not have said this in a derogatory way, and lamely she said so: ''Your uncle was joking. Anyway, I am not concerned with what I was like at sixteen or seventeen, but what you're like now. And I'm telling you I won't countenance your marrying anyone at all for at least another year, if not longer. And what you can do, madam, is send that young man to me and I will talk to him and tell him exactly what I have said now. If he can prove himself able to keep you, and I can imagine it will be two or three years before he's out of his time, then we'll talk about your marrying. That is all I have to say on the subject.''

Later she wondered if she had said too much on the subject. She put it to Mary, saying, ''What am I going to do with her?'' And Mary shook her head as she said, '' 'Tis a pity the master's laid up. He could go and see this fellow. But I tell you what I can do, I'll tell our Agnes to have a word with Shane, and he might be able to talk sense into him.''

And so it was left at that. And six days passed, during which Graham became much worse. He had sickness and diarrhoea, and the doctor, at first, frightened her to death by suggesting it might be cholera. Yet there had been no cases of cholera reported for some long time now. Later he had diagnosed his condition as gastric enteritis. Then it seemed that overnight he developed pneumonia.

Nancy Ann had never felt fearful of his condition until, sitting to the side of the bed, wiping his brow with a cold cloth, he lifted up his hand and caught hers. And through gasping breath, he said, ''Thank you, my dear, for the happy years you have given me.''

''Oh, Graham, Graham. It's going to be all right. You're going to get well. It will pass.''

His only answer was gently to press her fingers to his cheek. Then, after a while, he said, ''Everything's in order.''

On this, she lifted her agonized gaze to Mary at the other side of the bed and the fear in her own eyes was reflected in Mary's. And Mary couldn't, at this moment, beckon her from the room to tell her something that was worrying her, in fact, more than worrying her, astounding her. For when Brundle had come to tell her that Miss Rebecca's pony had been brought back to the yard by the carter and that she had given him this letter to be delivered to the house—it was addressed to her mother—she had dashed upstairs to the girl's room, opened the wardrobe door and seen that quite a number of her clothes were missing, as also was the jewellery box from the dressing-table. She had rushed downstairs into the bedroom, but realized she could not, at the moment, upset her dear friend and mistress with the news that her daughter had run away.

Some time later, following the doctor's visit and the installation of a nurse, Nancy Ann was persuaded by Mary to take a short rest from the sickroom. She saw to it that she had a glass of port before she told her the news. And then, sitting opposite to her, she held her hands as she said, "Now what I'm going to tell you is going to come as a shock. But your main concern at the moment is with the master; you can do nothing about this. I took it upon myself earlier on to send for Mr. Peter. I saw him and told him what was afoot, and he went straight over to Shane, and the last I heard is that they've both gone to this young fellow's house."

"What are you saying, Mary?" she had said. And Mary answered, "Well, it's plain, isn't it, ma'am? She's gone off with this young fellow. And look"—she put her hand into her apron pocket—"here's a letter she sent with the carrier who brought her pony back some time ago."

With trembling fingers Nancy Ann had opened the letter. Characteristically it had no beginning, it just said:

By the time you get this, Mama, I shall be married. You would never have given your consent, and even if you had, you would have made us wait, and we couldn't. You needn't worry about me, I'll be all right. I love Dennis and he will look after me.

The brief note was signed, "Rebecca."

She remembered thinking, Those few terse lines for sixteen years of love, tenderness, and caring. She also remembered Mary's surprise when she said calmly, "I'm sorry Peter and Shane have had the trouble of going to his home. She is gone, Mary, and at this moment, I can say to you, it doesn't matter if I never see her again. Somehow, she's the last link in a bad chain. All I'm concerned with at the moment is that my husband survives."

She knew that Mary thought her attitude somewhat strange, for it wasn't generally in her nature to show indifference or hardness. And so she had said to her, "It isn't like me to say that, is it, Mary? But that is honestly how I feel at the moment. For the last few years I've known a certain peace, and now, if it's about to be snatched from me I don't know what I'll do."

Mary had risen and put her arms about her and held her head against her breast, saying, "He'll pull through. He's of a good constitution. Never give up. Come on now, try to eat something."

As she shook her head against the mention of food, she thought in an odd way that most people, out of kindness, advise you to eat when you are in trouble. It seemed a panacea for all ills.

She remembered also that as she returned upstairs to the bedroom, she had begun to pray as she had done years ago, making a bargain with God: telling Him that if He would spare her husband's life she would never again miss her daily prayers or a Sunday service, and she would thrust all unworthy thoughts out of her mind forever. She did not elaborate on the type of thoughts that she would no longer think.

God did not answer her prayers. Fourteen hours later Graham Mercer died. And, from his going there was opened in her a chasm of loneliness that outdid all the combined feelings of aloneness she had experienced before.

⊁ *11* ⊁

THEY WERE IN THE LITTLE SITTING-ROOM ABOVE THE STA-
bles. The two armchairs were close together opposite the
small blazing fire. Shane and Agnes had been married for
three years now and Agnes was heavy with her first child.
Their hands were joined across the arms of the chairs and
they were sitting in silence, staring into the flames.

It was Shane who broke the silence, saying, "Well, he's
got to come back sometime. It's three years now since he
showed his face, and then it was only for a couple of days.
He was here and gone again. He was supposed to come again
before he left England, but he didn't. As they said at the table
the night"—he jerked his head backwards indicating the
farmhouse—"if Henry hadn't come across that heading in
that newspaper last week, we would have all gone on surmis-
ing he was married. Well, we did when he was last here,
didn't we? Henry remembers the night asking him if the mistress would be coming back with him. That was when he
promised to look in again afore leaving the country. And he
remembers him looking at him hard and saying, 'No,
she won't be coming back with me.' As Henry said then, he
thought something wasn't right. But he didn't think that he
hadn't been married at all. Anyway, there it was, the headlines with his photo: Bachelor millionaire, shareholder in
shipping company, and he was once a youth in the North.

And so on. And if it's right what you think, and what Mary thinks, and what Cook thinks, and Henry thinks, and meself have known for a fact for this long time, something should be done about it. What d'you say?''

"I say like you, something should be done about it, but what?''

"You could write, write him a letter.''

"Me write him a letter!'' She heaved her swollen body further up in the chair. "Why not you? I mean, he doesn't know I'm here; he doesn't know you're married. Or let Henry write, it's his place.''

"Oh, you know what Henry is like with a pen, nearly as good as meself. . . . Hope this finds you as it leaves me at present. That's about as far as both of us can go. Now you have a good hand.''

"Not to write a letter, telling him . . . well, what you want me to tell him.''

"You can put it atween the lines.''

"Our Mary is the one that could do it, but she won't. 'Twould be no use me askin' her, 'cos she wouldn't know how the mistress would take it.''

"Well, perhaps not. But I bet she wouldn't put a foot out to stop you if she knew you were doin' it.''

"No, perhaps not. But I wouldn't know how to start.''

"I'll show you.''

He got up swiftly and went to the chiffonier that was standing in the corner of the room, pulled open one of the doors, lifted out a box. Then, placing it on the table, he lifted the lid, took out a bottle of ink, a steel-nibbed pen and some loose sheets of paper and a packet of envelopes, and looking towards her, he said, "There, imagine you're writin' to your mother, and givin' her all the news. Only head it differently.''

Slowly she pulled herself up while shaking her head and smiling at him. Then, seated at the table, she dipped the pen in the ink, bit on her lip, stared down on the paper, and began in a round childish hand:

Dear David,
    You will never guess who this is. I am writing from one of the rooms above the stables. I'm Agnes, and me and

Shane got married sometime back. And I thought I would like you to know that we are very happy and I am expecting a baby in six weeks' time. I wish it was later 'cos I would like it to have been born at Christmas. But there, these things happen don't they?

She paused and looked across at Shane, and when he said, "Read what you've done," she answered firmly, "No, you'll just wait. If you want me to do it, you'll just wait. 'Cos I've got to think."

We have been expecting to see you back this long while, 'cos many things have happened. You won't know that Miss Rebecca ran off and got married when she had just passed her sixteenth birthday. And of course it upset madam, because she was very worried at the time as Mr. Mercer was very ill and died shortly afterwards. Miss Rebecca, or Mrs. Flannagan, as she now is, 'cos she married Shane's nephew who he says he's not proud of and has stopped liking because of the awful thing he did running off with Miss Rebecca. And Miss Rebecca never came to Mr. Mercer's funeral, and she's only been here once since to see her mother. And from what our Mary says she wasn't a bit nice, quite cocky like. But then she was always a bit cocky. You will likely remember when she was a child. Things are much the same here from day to day, except our Mary is worried about the mistress, 'cos she's got so thin and never goes out. Lady Pat calls sometimes, but even she can't get her out. Mary's gonna try and get her to Harrogate for the winter.

Everything in the farmhouse is all right. It is kept lovely and clean. But they all say they would like to see you. We read in the papers lately that you have got a ship now. That must be very nice for you. We all remember you fondly and hope you are very well. We are all well here, even Mrs. Hazel. She never seems to ail anything and her a good age.

I am, yours respectfully,
Agnes.

When she read the letter over to Shane, he kept nodding his head, until he came to the part where she had said he owned a ship. And he stopped her here and said, "He's only part of a company. He doesn't own a ship."

"Well," she answered, "he can put it down to my ignorance. I could have written a better letter if I'd given meself time to think. But then I wouldn't likely have got it all in. Anyway, there it is." She pushed it across to him. "It goes, or it doesn't. It's up to you."

"Well, if it's up to me, it goes."

And the letter went.

October was a windy blustery month. November was wet. It was the first week in December when Nancy Ann said to Mary, "All right, all right, have it your way. I'll go to Harrogate . . . we'll go to Harrogate. Although what I'll do sitting in an hotel all day, I don't know."

"You won't sit in an hotel all day. You'll get out and about, like you can't here. You've got to walk or drive miles to get to the town here. There you're on the main thoroughfare."

"Yes, and don't I know it at night; it takes me ages to get used to the noise."

"Oh, you'll soon get used to the noise. And we'll go to the concerts and the theatre and there'll be Christmas festivities in the hotel. . . ."

"Mary. Mary. It is only a matter of months since I was made a widow."

"It is close on a year, ma'am. And you've lived like a hermit all the time. It can't go on. We . . . we are all worried about you. The flesh has dropped off you; just look at yourself. Anyway, there'll be nobody in Harrogate to criticise if they see you attending a concert, and you'll be in company."

Nancy Ann turned her head away, shaking it the while as she said, "Oh, Mary, Mary. I thought you knew me better than that. I don't want company. That's the last thing I want at this moment, is company."

"Excuse me for contradicting you, ma'am." Mary's voice was prim now, that of a servant. "It is company you want at this time. You keep up this attitude, ma'am, and you'll go into decline, like lots of ladies afore you. And I'm not the only one concerned about you. Lady Pat is very concerned, and so is Sir George, and others an' all, Mr. Peter and his wife. And then there's all the staff. Oh, yes, all your staff, ma'am, so I think it is only fair that you consider them. An' don't forget Lady Beatrice. She's forever writing, she's so concerned and only wishes she could be with you but has to look after that cousin of hers with her broken back. There's only one good thing about that, it's she who can do the bossing now.''

Nancy Ann looked at Mary and smiled wanly. What would she have done without this woman? Gone mad likely. Yes, gone mad. For there was a time after Graham's death when she felt so desolate that she thought she was losing her mind. During that time she couldn't bear company at all. Peter had come over two or three times a week bringing Eva with him. And Eva had held her hand and spoken words, as she thought, of comfort, but which had almost made her want to scream, when her thoughts would return to Rebecca and her screaming fits, causing her to realize how easy it would be to let go.

But now she realized, as Mary said, she must make an effort, and perhaps in making the effort this feeling of guilt that was with her constantly would fade. Because at times her feeling of desolation wasn't so much that she had lost Graham, though his loss was genuine, but that she hadn't loved him enough when he was alive. Oh, she had been loving, but that wasn't love. Of one thing she was certain, the emptiness within her would prevail until the day she died.

She'd had visits from the vicar who had talked to her of the love of God and told her that she must not worry because her husband, who was a very good man, was now in heaven. On each visit his theme was always the same, and the very last time he was there she had been prompted to say, ''But what of my other husband? Where is he? the man who was buried in unconsecrated ground. Would you say that he was in hell?'' His answer had been so garbled that at the end of the visit she was none the wiser for asking.

She had never been to church since the day they buried Graham. At times she accused herself of being childish in this matter, paying God out as it were for not answering her prayer. . . .

It had been snowing on and off for two days now and the roads in parts were impassable. And she smiled as she said to Mary, "Well, there's one thing, you won't be able to get me to Harrogate within the next day or so, I should think." And to this Mary answered lightly, "Oh, we'll get to the station somehow."

"Go and get your supper," she said, dismissing Mary with a light wave of her hand. As seemed fitting, when they were at home, Mary ate with the rest of the staff in the servants' quarters which, as in Rossburn, had its own hierarchy, but when in Harrogate they ate together.

She had finished her meal some time ago. She very rarely ate in the dining-room but had her main meals served in the small drawing-room where she was now sitting. It was a very comfortable room, beamed and half-panelled, with a large open stone fireplace, holding a basket of logs which gave off a fierce heat. She sat in the corner of the deep brown velvet couch, staring towards it.

The room was situated at the far end of the house and no sounds from the hall or kitchen quarters penetrated to it. Outside, too, was the deadening silence snow brings. The world . . . her world was quiet. There was no crackle, even from the logs, for they were all settled into a scarlet mush. She, too, was quiet inside; she was thinking over what Mary had said, and she was agreeing with her in her mind. The sojourn in Harrogate would be a move for the better, for she knew no matter how great the depth of loneliness was inside her she couldn't go on in this forced isolation much longer.

She wondered at times, if she'd had Rebecca for company would she have felt different. Perhaps her daughter's presence would have forced her before now to have made some effort. But she hadn't Rebecca; all she had of Rebecca was a feeling of sadness, tinged with bitterness. And sometimes these emotions were eclipsed by bewilderment that a daughter of hers could have acted in such a callous way. Yet, at such times she would remind herself that Rebecca wasn't her daughter only, she was Dennison's too.

Then there was James. She rarely heard from him now, but she gauged he was living with a woman, and reading between the lines of his last letter, she'd had children to him. And he couldn't have married her, for that would have made him a bigamist.

She felt no sense of shock knowing that her brother, son of a parson, was sinning grievously. What was sin anyway? Mostly the outcome of circumstances, at least in cases like James'. But Dennison's sins, were they the outcome of circumstances? Her mind became still, waiting, but there was no answer forthcoming to that question.

So sitting, her mind probing, she did not hear the commotion on the drive; she did not hear the talk and bustle in the hall; she heard nothing till Mary thrust open the door and hurried up the room, saying, "You . . . you have a visitor."

Nancy Ann pulled herself up into a sitting position on the couch, saying, "Lady Pat in this weather?"

"No, no." Mary's face was bright. "No, not Lady Pat. Someone . . . someone else."

Nancy Ann stared up at her quite bemused. Then she thought, It's Rebecca. I must . . . I must be loving towards her. Something has happened; perhaps she has come home. I must make her welcome.

The thought became choked in her mind as she pulled herself up from the couch and looked down the room to where a tall bronzed-skinned man was standing. He had a handkerchief to his face and was wiping the snow from his eyebrows. She saw the snow was still clinging to the laceholes of his high-topped boots. He was wearing a thick tweed jacket and she saw him unbutton the top two buttons and look at Mary as she hurried back down the room and passed him, nodding at him all the while. And then the door closed and he was moving towards her. When he stopped, she stared at him. This was David, yet not David. It was four years since they had met. Then he had been a handsome young man. He was still handsome, but . . . but in a different way. His skin was brown, his hair looked bleached and it was long, reaching almost to his shoulders, and the sides were trimmed down to his cheekbones. He looked bigger, broader, not fatter, but older, so much older. What was he, twenty-six? He could be thirty-six . . . forty.

"Hello."

She couldn't answer him. She swallowed deeply. Then as if she were greeting a guest, she pointed to the couch and with an effort said, "Won't . . . won't you sit down?"

435

"No, no." He shook his head. "I don't want to sit down. I've been sitting for hours, for days. It's a long way from Australia."

"Have you come straight from Australia?"

"Yes, as straight as one can travel when coming from that country."

He was being facetious. Why had he come?

He was saying now, "But you sit down. I disturbed you. Are you not well?"

She sat down slowly, and looked up at him as she answered, "I am well enough."

"You have got very thin."

She made herself answer lightly, "That is fashionable these days." Then she asked politely, "Is . . . is your wife with you?"

"Which one?"

Dear God! She drooped her head and closed her eyes. He was in one of these moods, was he? She remembered them only too well. He was fencing, but why? Why was he here? To torment her?

"That was silly of me. That's what you're thinking, isn't it? Just like him to be facetious, you're saying. I can read your thoughts still, you know." He was smiling down on her now. And then quite suddenly he dropped on to the couch within a bent arm's length from her. And his nearness brought sweat oozing out of every pore in her body. She felt faint and his voice seemed to come to her from a distance as he said, "Everyone asks me if I have my wife with me, and that is my stock answer, because up till now, unfortunately, I haven't had a wife."

His voice was clearer now.

"What!" she said. "You didn't marry?"

"No. I didn't marry."

"But everyone thought . . ."

"Yes, everyone thought and I let them think. I nearly did marry. Oh yes." His eyebrows moved upwards and his wide lips went into a pout. "But the young lady in question was horrified when she knew that I meant to spend part of my life, and expected her to spend it with me, in Kalgoorlie. Now her mother wouldn't have minded, she was a sensible woman and knew that money could buy most things, and she had trained her daughter to think the same, but her daughter couldn't see any of the things she wanted to buy in Kalgoorlie. Then there was another thing: the society was a little rough for her delicate mind. Her mother offered to take her place, but I declined as gracefully as possible. It cost me, but it was worth it in the end.''

She had turned her head away from him and was staring stiffly towards the fireplace when, his voice changing, he said, "I'm being objectionable. It's the only way I can cover my feelings at the moment. Look at me, Nancy Ann.''

She did not obey him, she couldn't, and when his hand came on hers, she shivered. And now he was speaking quietly, saying, "I didn't know you had lost your husband until quite recently. A kind friend sent me a letter. I wasn't in Kalgoorlie when it arrived. But as soon as I got back and read it I left immediately. I can't say I am sorry he died. I am no hypocrite, whatever else. I can only say that at this moment I'm so churned up inside I really don't know quite where I am. I cannot believe yet that I'm sitting here holding your hand, and that there is nothing in the wide world separating us any more. Look at me, Nancy Ann. Please look at me.''

She looked at him. Although her whole body was sweating her mouth was dry and her eyes were burning. She too couldn't believe that he was sitting there and there was nothing separating them anymore. No, no, she couldn't believe it. She was dreaming and she would wake up and turn her head into the pillow and cry for a life that could never be.

"If you love me, do as I ask.'' His voice came soft to her. "You once said that to me, remember? Now I say that to you, if you love me, Nancy Ann, look at me and at least say, David, I am glad to see you.''

The dryness was going out of her eyes, the moisture was filling them. She turned her head slowly towards him, her lids blinking and, her voice a mere croak, she said, "David, I am glad to see you.''

"Just glad?''

She gulped now before she could utter the words, "More than glad.''

When the tears welled from her eyes, his arms went about her and they both fell into the corner of the couch. And his mouth on hers now, he kissed her as he had done once before until the breath seemed to leave her body. But it didn't matter, nothing mattered, nothing would ever matter again; she was in his arms, at last, at last, at last. Now he was kissing her face, her hair, her neck, gasping out words, "We'll never be separated again, never, never, never. Do you hear, never, never." He laughed now and, his voice low, he said, "Can I sleep here tonight?" And her voice low and matching his mood, she replied, "No, sir, you may not sleep here tonight. You have a house of your own."

"Oh, my, yes." Still within the circle of his arms, he pulled her upwards and they leant against the back of the couch, their faces so close that they breathed each other's breath. And he said softly, "This time next week we shall be married."

As she went to pull away sharply from him, he held her tight, saying, "Now then, now then. What is it?"

"Oh, no, David, not so soon. I . . . well, it's only."

"It's only almost a year since he died, and I wouldn't care if it was two months. We are to be married next week by special licence. My secretary is making arrangements."

"Your what?" She screwed up her face.

"My secretary. Don't look so surprised. Wherever I go, business follows me, and I have to have a secretary. You'll like him. I call him Willie. He's an Australian and talks like a London Cockney. But he's very efficient, marvellous at making arrangements."

She made small movements with her head and he laughed now, saying, "Don't look so surprised; there's lots of things you'll have to get used to when we're travelling."

"Travel . . . ?"

"Yes, I said travelling. We'll spend our honeymoon in France. Yes." He now rubbed his nose against hers, so close was he that she couldn't make out his features, only the depth and dark light in his eyes. "I said, honeymoon, Nancy Ann." Gently now, his lips touched hers before his head moved away from her again and back into focus. "And we'll spend some time in Italy, any place where it's warm. Then it will be Australia, here we come. You must see Kalgoorlie. All the fervour, all the dirt, all the heroism, all the good, the bad, and the indifferent. The place has grown in the last few years since the rush, but I'll always remember it as I first saw it. You know, Nancy Ann, my love, I did not gain my education here, although you gave me the chance. No, it started when I got to Kalgoorlie, and for the first time I understood the word greed, and another word, stupidity. This was attached to supposedly normal men working like slaves; then when they made a find, little or much, losing it again through drink or gambling. If they had gambled when they were stone sober there might have been hope for them, but the sharks were too clever and too many. And men who, the previous night, would have had enough to set them up modestly for life, found themselves the next morning sober, but standing up with only the clothes on their back and one dollar in their pocket." His voice had turned serious now, the smile had left his face, as he ended, "Joe Barrow was, and still is, a good, what you would call, God-fearing churchman. He's as honest as the day's long. But I hadn't been over there a week when he took me the rounds through the dives and showed me what would happen if I let myself be led to drink, gambling . . . *or women.*"

Taking note of the quirk to his lips, she now asked, "Did you resist all temptation?"

The quirk widened. He looked to the side, then said, "Not all, madam, not all."

When her gaze suddenly turned from his, he brought her face almost roughly towards him again with the palm of his hand against her cheek and, his mood taking a lightning change, he said thickly, "Remember, Nancy Ann, you have been married twice."

There was a tight feeling in her chest. He was right of course, he was right. She had been married twice. But the thought of him with other women. Don't be stupid, woman, don't be stupid. The voice seemed to be shouting at her. He's a man and has been for a long time, and so attractive women must have swarmed about him. And remember how upset you were by the name of Parson's Prig. You were never priggish, so don't start now. Accept the miracle that has happened. As he said, you've been married twice and the fact must have been agony to him.

She smiled at him as she asked, within an assumed prim manner, "Are Australian ladies pretty?"

She saw him now bow his head and press his lips tightly together before he answered, "Oh, so pretty, madam, beautiful, voluptuous"—made a curving movement with his hand—"you have no idea." Then his voice breaking into a laugh, he said, "There was hardly an Australian among them, my dear. From every gutter in the world they came. No, I can honestly say that those ladies didn't attract me. But now"—he wagged his finger at her—"the French mademoiselles. Oh, la-la. And the Italians. Oh, very warm, the Italians." His fingers twirled. Then on a sound that was half a shout, he pulled her roughly towards him, saying, "Why are we playing this game? The past is past for both of us. There is only the future and I can see it stretching down the years. We have a lot of time to make up for, you and I, Nancy Ann."

He now turned his head away from her for a moment and looked upwards towards the ceiling, and then to the fireplace. "I could live here," he said; "I like this house, it would hold no ghosts for me, not like the other place. And I thought Peter might like the farmhouse. What do you say? From what I know of boarding schools there's no comfort for either master or pupil. That would be a good arrangement, wouldn't it?"

She stared at him in amazement, saying now, "You have it all planned out."

"Yes, yes, I've had a lot of time to think on the journey here. Yes, my dear, my beloved, I've got it all planned out. And this time it's going to work just as I planned."

Then again his mood changed and, his voice dropping so low she could scarcely hear the words, he muttered, "Hold me, dear. Hold me." And when she put her arms about him, he closed his eyes and said, "Tightly." And she held him tightly to her. Then, as if she was listening to the voices of the child she had first seen sitting on the stone by the river, he said, "Never let me go. Promise you'll never let me go. Promise you'll stay with me always, no matter what happens."

His head buried in her shoulder, the tears were streaming down her face and her voice too was a mutter as she answered, "I'll never let you go, my David. Never. Never. You'll always be mine, as you have been from the beginning."

Neither of them saw Mary open the door and hold it wide to allow Brundle to push in the trolley of food. But what greeted her gaze caused her to push the trolley backwards and pull the door softly closed. And she smiled at Brundle. "We'll have to wait a bit."

"But the broth'll be cold."

"I don't think they'll mind." Mary's smile widened. Then instinctively, they pushed their hands out towards each other's shoulders, and Mary said something that Brundle couldn't understand, for what she said was, "God bless our Agnes and Shane."